ask the posts of the house

A RAUPO BOOK

Published by the Penguin Group
Penguin Group (NZ), 67 Apollo Drive, Rosedale,
North Shore 0632, New Zealand (a division of Pearson New Zealand Ltd)
Penguin Group (USA) Inc., 375 Hudson Street,
New York, New York 10014, USA
Penguin Group (Canada), 90 Eglinton Avenue East, Suite 700, Toronto,
Ontario, M4P 2Y3, Canada (a division of Pearson Penguin Canada Inc.)
Penguin Books Ltd, 80 Strand, London, WC2R 0RL, England
Penguin Ireland, 25 St Stephen's Green,
Dublin 2, Ireland (a division of Penguin Books Ltd)
Penguin Group (Australia), 250 Camberwell Road, Camberwell,
Victoria 3124, Australia (a division of Pearson Australia Group Pty Ltd)
Penguin Books India Pvt Ltd, 11, Community Centre,
Panchsheel Park, New Delhi – 110 017, India
Penguin Books (South Africa) (Pty) Ltd, 24 Sturdee Avenue,
Rosebank, Johannesburg 2196, South Africa

Penguin Books Ltd, Registered Offices: 80 Strand, London, WC2R 0RL, England

Originally published by Reed Publishing (NZ) Ltd, 2007
First published by Penguin Group (NZ), 2008
1 3 5 7 9 10 8 6 4 2

Copyright © Witi Ihimaera, 2007

Editor: Gillian Tewsley
Design: Sarah Healey

Cover image: Poutokomanawa (interior support post figure),
from a whare near Taupo. Otago Museum D10.285. Photograph: Brian Brake.
Reproduced with permission from Otago Museum and the Estate of Brian Brake.
Cover illustration: Hone Te Ihi o Te Rangi Ngata
Typeset in Husqy

Printed in Australia by McPherson's Printing Group

ISBN: 978 0 14 301011 1

A catalogue record for this book is available
from the National Library of New Zealand.

www.penguin.co.nz

WITI IHIMAERA

ask the posts of the house

RAUPO

For Jane, Jessica and Olivia

also by witi ihimaera

contents

i've been thinking about you, sister

1

B rian rang yesterday to ask if I would send him a short story for an anthology he was planning to publish. The trouble was he wanted the kind of story I used to write thirty years ago.

'It should be easy for you,' he began. 'People love your comic stories about hockey games or sentimental ones about old ladies playing cards, not to mention the epic tales of girls who ride whales to save their iwi.'

'Brian,' I answered, 'I was just a young man when I wrote those stories and the world was a different place. I'm not that same person any more, not as innocent and my voice is not as lyrical. Nor is my work so essentialist any longer; it's more synthesised. And I'm a professor of English, into postcolonial discourse, Freire, Derrida and The Empire Writes Back.'

'I was afraid you'd say something like that,' Brian sighed, but he was not about to give up. 'Maybe you've got a story that you put in a bottom drawer years ago, something you wrote before you became, well, political? Something like the story you wrote about the wily Maori tohunga who puts a spell on a red-headed Irish woman? Readers just love that one! Can you take a look? And if you can't find a story, can you try to write one for me of the kind you wrote when you were younger? And keep politics out of it? Not that there's anything wrong with the stories you write now,' he added hastily, 'but they're, well, a bit more difficult for the gentle reader. You don't mind my saying that, do you?'

Irritated, I put the telephone down. I had worked so hard to become an indigenous writer of some critical distinction, somebody whom critics could admire for my polish and fearlessness in articulating the indigenous position. I had established myself as a writer who was not afraid to engage the complexities of race, identity and representation and examine the polarities that existed between majority and minority cultures. Despite this, while I now garnered hard-earned accolades from critics, the people who actually bought my books were always telling me that my earlier stories and novels were better. Some reviewers, when I started rewriting the earlier work, scolded me. Ah well, tutae happens.

Two days later, however, I began the following story, which happened to my mother in 1989. Being a fiction writer, I have altered some of the details and names of those involved in the story.

—

My mother was looking out the kitchen window of the house at Haig Street, Gisborne, when she saw her brother Rangiora sitting in the sunlight on the back lawn. She was baking scones for a kindergarten bring-and-buy and had just taken the last batch from the oven; she almost dropped them.

Mum was seventy at the time and although her impulse was to rush out the door and give Uncle Rangiora a hug, instead she first went to the bathroom to splash water on her face, run a comb through her hair and put some lipstick on. The bathroom window looked over the back lawn, so Mum was able to check that he was still there — he was. He was in his army uniform, wearing his khaki cap, and he didn't look a day older than when he had left for the war. She looked at her own reflection in the bathroom mirror. In comparison, with her grey hair and her dull skin, she looked so old. She was overwhelmed with self-pity and embarrassment.

Smoothing out her dress, Mum walked out the back door and towards Uncle Rangiora. As she approached, he stood up, took off his cap and smiled at her — it didn't seem to matter at all that he was still so young and she was so old.

'Hello, brother,' she said to him. 'Why have you come to see me?'

His eyes were twinkling as he gave a deep, grave bow. 'I've been thinking about you, sister,' he said. 'It's a long time since we had a waltz.'

He opened his arms in invitation and, with a laugh of pure joy, she stepped into them.

> When I grow too old to dream,
> I'll have you to remember,
> When I grow too old to dream,
> Your love will stay in my heart —

After the waltz, Uncle Rangiora bowed again and left my mother standing alone in the sunlight. As he did so, a brown bird flew past her, heading after him, and she watched it as it sped across the sky.

—

My father didn't know about Uncle Rangiora's visit until he returned from Waituhi; he had been shifting cattle from the hill paddock to the flat in preparation for the trucks that would come the next morning to take them to the saleyards. When he arrived home he found my mother speaking on the telephone. There was something different about her, something radiant.

When Mum hung up, Dad asked her, 'Who have you been talking to?'

'I've been making enquiries,' she answered. 'First of all I rang the Returned Servicemen's Association and then the army at Waiouru and the Maori Battalion Association in Wellington. I wanted to know when they were making their next visit to the Commonwealth war graves in Egypt and the Middle East.'

'What for?' Dad asked, puzzled. He could tell that Mum had a bee in her bonnet about something.

'I want to visit Rangiora's grave,' Mum answered. 'The Battalion aren't going until next year though, so it looks like you and I will have to make the trip by ourselves. I've just asked the travel agent to book our trip for us. He wants us to go into town to see him and to have our photos taken for our passports.'

My father was seventy-seven, and he was waiting to have a replacement hip operation. He didn't think Mum was serious but when she said, 'We're going and that's that,' he tried stonewalling. 'I better have my operation first,' he said.

Once Mum has made up her mind about something, however, nothing can stop her. She's always been strong-willed and even though she loves my dad there are moments when, if he gets in her way, he'd better watch out. 'In that case,' she said, 'Wikitoria can come with me,' referring to one of my sisters, 'and you can stay home.'

—

My mother wanted to go to Tunisia because Uncle Rangiora had been killed there on 26 March 1943, at Point 201, Tebaga Gap. He had been a member of C Company, part of the platoon led by Second Lieutenant Ngarimu as they tried to take the German-held position. Twenty-two Battalion soldiers, including Ngarimu and Uncle Rangiora, were killed that day.

Not only was Mum strong-willed but, when she made up her mind, she moved really fast. Once she'd had her discussion with Dad she rang Wikitoria and told her to meet her at the travel agent's the next morning. Satisfied that she was getting somewhere, she went to have a shower and prepare for bed. While she was in the shower, Dad rang me up in Wellington to try to get me to talk some sense into her.

'She's much too old to go travelling to the other side of the world,' Dad said. 'And how is Wikitoria going to get somebody to look after her fish and chip shop? Hoha, your mother, hoha.'

I knew there was no way of stopping Mum. Once she had the bit between her teeth she was off and away. Uncle Rangiora had been her favourite brother. He was just two years older than her and, while they were growing up, he looked out for her; he loved taking her to swim down at the local river and together they would dive for beautiful white river stones. Even when he was a young man and had girlfriends, he and Mum were still as close as ever. Whenever church dances were held at Tokomaru Bay, Uncle Rangiora always saved the last waltz for her. There was a photograph of Mum and Uncle Rangiora taken just before he went to war — Mum always had it on her dressing table. In the photo, Uncle Rangiora was a handsome, laughing, cavalier boy; my mother was a slip of a girl in a pretty white dress, holding him as if she never wanted to let him go.

When Uncle Rangiora was killed, Mum was inconsolable. However, life goes on and, after the war ended, she moved to Gisborne to stay with her sister, Mattie, and worked as a shedhand in various shearing gangs. Dad was a shearer — that's how they met. But she never forgot Uncle Rangiora, who had been buried in the Commonwealth war cemetery at Sfax, Tunisia. For as long as I can remember, every year without fail, Mum has walked in to *The Gisborne Herald* office and placed the same notice in the In Memoriam column:

To my brother, Private Rangiora Wharepapa, killed in action in Tunisia, 1943. Sadly missed, never forgotten. Your sister, Aroha.

Of course my sisters, brothers and I knew that Dad would never let Mum go to Tunisia without him. I was not surprised when Wikitoria telephoned to tell me, 'Well, as usual, there's no Judy without Punch.' Apparently, Dad had shown up at the travel agent's on his truck just when Wiki and Mum had almost completed the arrangements for the trip and were handing over a cheque for the deposit.

'You can go back to your fish and chip shop, Wikitoria,' Dad said to my sister. 'How will that husband of yours cope without you to boss him around?' He turned to the travel agent, a nice young boy named Donald. 'My name is Tom Mahana and I'm going to Tunisia with Mrs Mahana.'

Mum looked at Dad askance. 'With your bad hip you'll be a nuisance,' she told him. 'Look at you! You can't get around anywhere without a walking stick.'

'And look at *you*,' Dad retorted. 'You're an old woman, or have you forgotten? You've never been able to find your way around without my help, so how do you think you'll manage when you go overseas?'

'You'll slow me down,' Mum answered defensively. 'It's a long way to go with a lot of connections to catch. I don't want to miss the planes.'

'Your wife is right,' Donald said, pursing his lips. 'If you have hip trouble you'll have enormous difficulties.'

Dad was in no mood for an argument. Today was the cattle sales and he should have been there. 'We won't miss any planes,' he said. 'What do you think I am? I may have to use a walking stick but I'm not entirely hopeless.'

'And I'm not clever enough to get to Tunisia with Wikitoria, is that it?' Mum asked. She looked at Donald, who was really only the meat in the sandwich. 'You know,' she confided in him, 'when my husband asked me to marry him I didn't want to because he was so much older than me. But I thought, "Better to be an old man's darling than a young man's slave." I never realised, that when men get older it doesn't matter what their age is. They're all hopeless.'

Donald excused himself while Mum and Dad continued their argument, but eventually Dad got his way. After all, the money for the trip was coming from their joint account, so that was that.

—

Now I have to admit that the idea of the trip would have been much easier on the family's nerves if Mum and Dad had been flying on a, well, English-speaking airline. With an eye to economies, however, Mum had chosen to fly on Aerolineas Argentinas from Auckland to Buenos Aires to Barcelona to Paris, and thence to Tunisia by some airline that nobody had ever heard of.

'How are you going to communicate?' Wikitoria asked. 'How are you going to find your way around when you won't be able to read the signs?'

And, man oh man, the connections. When Mum sent me their itinerary I just about had a heart attack. 'How do you know whether those terminals have air bridges?' I said to her on the telephone. 'How's Dad going to get up and down all those stairs to and from the planes? And why does it look like the gates to your connecting flights are in other terminals? I'd better get our cousin Watene to fly from New York to Paris and go with you to Tunisia.'

'And spoil our great adventure?' she answered. 'Don't you dare! Anyhow, your father's already in training.'

I'd heard all about Mum's training from neighbours in Gisborne. 'Oh, your poor father,' they told me. 'Your mother has been getting him up at six in the morning for a run around the block. We hadn't realised she was so fit. She takes off like a rocket and your father hobbles after her, walking stick in hand. We can hear him complaining all the way about the new trainers she has bought for him. He says they're too big and he doesn't like the colour.' True, my father has always been proud of his small feet and, well, aren't all trainers white? 'Does your mother listen to him?' the neighbours asked. 'No, she just keeps on yelling at him, "If you can't keep up, you can stay at home." By the time they finish their run your dad is absolutely exhausted.'

Exhausted or not, Dad managed to pass Mum's fitness test. As the time for departure approached, they bought backpacks, got their passports and changed their money into pesos, francs and dinar. Mum gave Dad a haircut to save him the trouble of getting one while they were away. Three days before they were due to leave, she went up to Tolaga Bay where she and Uncle Rangiora had lived. There, she headed for the river where they had loved to swim.

What a nuisance. Mum had hoped to gather white stones from the riverbank but the best ones were at the bottom of the river, and the water was too deep to wade out to them. However, two Pakeha boys who were playing truant from school were jumping off branches into the water. She waved them over.

'Yes, lady?' they asked.

'See those white stones?' she said. 'I've come to get some.' She explained that she wanted to take them to Tunisia to put on Uncle Rangiora's grave.

The young boys nodded and were soon duckdiving to the bottom of the river. Mum could see them, gliding like dreams through the sparkling water. When the boys returned, gasping, to the surface, they brought the white river stones to the bank. They soon had a good pile but they sorted through them, throwing some away. 'They have to be perfect,' they said to Mum, 'You can't take any old stones, can you, lady?'

'No,' Mum smiled. 'Only the best.'

The boys dived again. They were enjoying themselves. While Mum waited for them she filled a small bottle with river water. Uncle Rangiora would like that — he probably missed the cool of the water there in the desert.

'Thank you, boys,' Mum said when the job had been done. She gave them a five-dollar note. 'Don't spend it all at once. I'm glad you played truant today.'

She left and gave them their river back.

—

At this point, my cousin Clarrie, her husband Chad and my Auntie Taina come into the picture. Somehow Clarrie found out about Mum and Dad going to Tunisia —probably from Wiki. Chad was American and, as it happened, they were planning with Auntie Taina to make one of their infrequent trips to catch up with his folks in Montana.

'Don't worry, cuz,' Clarrie said to me on the phone from Wanganui, 'we'll meet them in Auckland. We've changed our bookings and are now on the same flight as Auntie and Uncle as far as Buenos Aires. When we get there, we'll make sure they catch their connection to Barcelona.' There was a slight tone of disapproval in her voice that I was letting Mum and Dad wander around in a dangerous world where they could get mugged or murdered, the poor things.

'Thank you, Clarrie,' I answered, trying to sound suitably chastised.

—

The day came for Mum and Dad's departure. The terminal at Gisborne airport was crowded with my brothers and sisters, all trying to be brave. Mum sat stony-faced as they pleaded with her to change her mind; she was clutching her airline bag with its passport, money, river stones and bottle of river water, and turned a deaf ear to their words.

As for Dad, well, he was surrounded by his adoring grandchildren, all weeping and wailing and gnashing their teeth as if they would never see him again.

The departure call was given. 'Time to go,' Mum said. 'Come on, Dad.' She walked out to the plane without a backward glance. As for Dad, he was the last to board. He had to hobble really fast to get there before the door closed, his new white trainers flashing across the tarmac.

2

I took a break from writing the story.

See what I mean about its essentialist nature? I recalled a meeting I had with the great English–Caribbean writer V.S. Naipaul when he visited Wellington in the 1970s. The poor man had been taken out for 'a drive' and suffered an over-enthusiastic seven-hour odyssey to Palmerston North and back. That evening, I joined him at a local PEN dinner where Professor Beeby, a wonderful raconteur, prefaced every comment to him with phrases like, 'When I was in India . . .' or 'When I spoke to Nehru about the partition with Pakistan . . .' or 'When I spoke to Mrs Gandhi in Paris.' Attempting to pull me into the conversation, Professor Beeby said to Mr Naipaul, 'Of course we have a young Maori writer here whose work reminds me very much of your own first collection, *Miguel Street*.' Mr Naipaul's response was to give me a somewhat acidic look, sigh, and say, 'Oh, he'll have to do much better than that.'

I remembered with gloom how critics of my early work had pounced on its simplicity and pronounced that it was the literary equivalent of naïve paintings done by unsophisticated native artists: bold colours, representations of village life, but no subtlety — and where was the subtext? The critics seemed to be looking for somebody else; some Maori writer who was aware of literary theory, whose work they could fit into a more refined aesthetic and theoretical model — of cultural displacement, perhaps, directly concerned with the economic and political fabric of cultural existence, or with the racialised discourses of apartheid or colonialism — who would affirm the indigenous voice within the long-standing western European cultural anxieties to do with modernist texts. They wanted literature that operated on a more complex national, political, aesthetic, linguistic and cognitive level, contesting the language and discursive conventions that had historically been instruments ensuring that 'the Other' was kept subordinate.

Although I was Maori, I had the suspicion that ultimately the critics wanted that other writer to undo the discursive crime against Africa and to trace a genealogy through Foucault, Barthes and the later Blanchot to a reading — albeit from the South Pacific — of the upheavals in French literary culture precipitated by the anticolonial struggle in Algeria and by the events of May 1968.

Instead, they got me. That other writer must have got delayed when old lady Muse swung by in her Peugeot and mistakenly picked me up instead. Did she ever lose on the deal. She opened the door to sweet, stupid, lyrically voiced me, writing from the heart and not from the intellect, overabundant when I should have been minimalist, without any of those traits that critics wanted to see — particularly cynicism or pessimism.

You get what you get.

—

According to cousin Clarrie, the trip to Buenos Aires went very smoothly. She, Chad and Auntie Taina met Mum and Dad's flight in Auckland.

'Hello Uncle Tom,' Clarrie smiled at Dad. 'What flash white trainers you have. Auntie Aroha? Mum's just over there with the suitcases.' Mum was glad to have Auntie Taina's company; they had been close for all the years since they became sisters-in-law. They chatted on the bus to the international terminal about whanau, who had died, who had married, who had had children, their own hopeless kids and thank goodness for the compensation of lovely grandchildren. When the bus arrived, Dad was delighted to see that a group of strapping young rugby players were on the same flight. Just his chance to let them know how terrific he had been as a left winger.

Dad has always loved talking to strangers. He loves to tell them about his tribe, his big family of brothers and sisters, his girlfriends (when Mum isn't listening), his children, the farm, his exploits as a top shearer, how he almost became an All Black, how he could have been a world champion wrestler, and so on. Once he gets started he is difficult to stop — and on the flight he had a group of eager young boys who were trapped and couldn't escape. They were polite and kept nodding their heads at his stories — which only encouraged him.

Clarrie told me later, 'Don't be so critical of your father! He's just lovely! A real patriarch! Young boys love to hear your father telling about his life and giving them advice on what to do if the girl you like doesn't like you back — even if it's, well, somewhat old-fashioned and past its use-by date.'

'I know what you mean,' I said. 'The difference is, of course, that strangers have never heard Dad's stories before, whereas us kids have heard them again and again. And as for Dad's advice — well, if I listened to it, I would still be a virgin.'

But to strangers like the rugby boys, Dad's stories came out as fresh, lively, splendid epics of trials that had been faced and triumphs accomplished against all odds. This was why people loved our father: he was such a terrific storyteller and a real spellbinder. By the time the plane landed in Buenos Aires, Dad had made many friends and received several invitations to come and visit.

'Thank you,' Mum said. 'We'll think about it.' This was her usual reply whenever Dad received such invitations. It was much better than saying yes or no. People liked to think there was the possibility of a maybe.

—

My mother had strict instructions to call home at each leg of the journey so that the family could rest easy, knowing they had survived another day. Somewhat grumpily she telephoned from a hotel close to Buenos Aires airport.

'The eagles have landed,' Mum said, 'and, yes, your father is still hobbling along after me on his walking stick, so I haven't been able to give him the slip — pity.' I soon realised why she was grumpy when she gave me what-for. 'And I have a bone to pick with you, son! You have to get Clarrie, Chad and Taina off our case. They've made arrangements for your father and me to be met at the airport in Paris by one of Chad's old Vietnam veterans mates, who has plans to take us to dinner. But I've made bookings for us to see the Folies Bergère.'

I wasn't listening to her. I was more alarmed at what I could hear in the background: screams, yells, lots of laughter, motorbikes revving up . . . and then, over her words, were those gunshots? 'What the heck's all the commotion?' I asked.

'When I told Donald to book us into cheap accommodation,' Mum explained, 'I didn't expect he would put us somewhere we might get murdered in our beds. The taxi driver didn't even want to bring us here. But Clarrie and Chad have barricaded the door and rung the rugby boys we met on the plane. We are expecting the football cavalry to arrive any minute.'

Of course, that was the kind of news guaranteed to keep me awake all night worrying about my parents. But Clarrie rang me the next morning from the airport to tell me that they had just put Mum and Dad on the plane to Barcelona. Clarrie sounded tired and strained.

'What kind of hotel were you staying at?' I asked.

'Is that what it was?' Clarrie answered. 'You don't want to know, cuz. Do they have Mafia in South America? Whatever was going down, your poor mum and dad were in the middle of it. You owe me big time.'

However, my relief was shortlived when Mum failed to telephone in from Barcelona. And then I received a call from Charles de Gaulle International Airport in Paris, from Chad's friend, who introduced himself as Addison. 'Oh, hi ya,' he drawled. 'Say, I've been waiting for your folks at customs but we must have missed each other. Should I call the police?'

'No,' I sighed. 'I am sure they are okay.' Yeah, right. My mind was filled with visions of them being kidnapped by French thugs, robbed of their money and their bodies thrown into the River Seine.

Two hours later, Dad phoned. 'Your mother is getting all dressed up to take me out on the town,' he said.

'Why didn't you phone me from Barcelona?' I screamed. 'And why didn't you meet up with Addison at the airport?'

'Were we supposed to telephone you from Barcelona?' Dad answered. 'And who's Addison?'

Mum took the telephone from Dad. 'We gave him the slip,' she said. 'As soon as I saw a man dressed like Rambo holding up a sign with our names on it, I took Dad off in the opposite direction. Otherwise we'd never be able to get to you-know-where.'

'How did you find your hotel?' I asked. Dad only had a smattering of French, learnt when he was a schoolboy in the 1920s, and I couldn't imagine how that would enable them to negotiate the horrors of the Métro, not to mention being prey to every pickpocket, pimp and prostitute as they trundled their bags through the streets — and any thief after Dad's white trainers.

'Oh, you know your father,' Mum answered. 'Talks to anybody. On the plane he got into a conversation with three boys who were backpacking through Europe and he ended up playing cards with them. Poker, the naughty man. How many matchsticks did you win, dear? Anyhow, they offered to escort us to this place; at least this one has locks on the door. But we can't stop, son, otherwise we'll be late for the show. I'll phone you when we get back.'

Two months later, I received a postcard from the three boys:

DEAR MISTER MAHANA, MY FRIENDS AND I FELL IN LOVE WITH YOUR FATHER. BUT COULD YOU TELL US, DID HE AND YOUR MOTHER REACH THEIR DESTINATION AND THEN RETURN SAFELY TO NEW ZEALAND? WE ARE ANXIOUS TO KNOW. FELIX, MARTIN AND PLACIDO.

The three boys weren't the only ones to fall in love with Dad. When he and Mum arrived at the Folies Bergère, the maître d' was entranced by their formality and elegance. Dad was wearing his black suit. The jacket is a perfect fit, but it doesn't do to look too closely at his trousers, as he usually cuts the waistband to give some slack so that his stomach can fit in. Mum was wearing her blue sequinned dress and lovely cape of kiwi feathers. They were seated at a table right at the front. The programme they brought home after their trip has the scrawled signatures of Lolo, Dodo, Jou-jou, Frou-frou, Clou-clou, Margot and Valencienne, so obviously Dad was a hit with the girls, too. Apparently he was so thrilled by the show that he got up at the end and did a haka.

'I wish your father would just clap like ordinary people,' Mum said on the telephone when she checked in with me. 'But your father became . . . well . . . somewhat excited. You'd think he'd never seen bare breasts before.'

'Or bare anything,' I heard Dad grumble in the background, referring to my mother's legendary modesty.

'Enough of that,' Mum reproved him. 'Our big day tomorrow, Dad. No funny business tonight.' Then she remembered I was still on the phone. 'You still there, son? I better hang up now. Dad and I have to get up very early to catch the plane to Tunisia. Don't worry about us. Love you.'

My mother was not going to leave anything to chance, particularly seeing her beloved brother who, many years ago, always kept the last waltz for her.

> So kiss me again, and then let us part,
> And when I grow too old to dream
> Your kiss will stay in my heart —

The next morning Mum and Dad took a taxi, thank god, back to the airport to catch their flight to Tunisia. Mum had organised with Donald that they would stay in Sfax for two days. This would give her and Dad plenty of time to visit Uncle Rangiora's grave. They would check into their hotel, go out to the Sfax War Cemetery, spend some time with Uncle Rangiora in the cemetery and return to Sfax in the late afternoon. They would stay at the hotel that evening, possibly go back to the grave for a second visit the next day to say goodbye to Uncle Rangiora, and then catch the plane back to Paris.

The flight was smooth and uneventful. Dad was in an aisle seat and Mum was squeezed between him and an extremely well groomed gentleman sitting next to the window. The man wore a dark suit and a blue tie to match the blue handkerchief in his jacket pocket. But what Mum remembered most about him was that he had the shiniest shoes that she had ever seen. They were like mirrors.

I don't know who the man was, and Mum and Dad lost the card he gave them, but I can't write about him without giving him a name — so let us call him Monsieur Samaritan. Dad leaned across Mum and, as usual, began to speak to the man. Dad told him he was from New Zealand, and immediately Monsieur Samaritan's face lit up. 'Ah! Néo-zélandais! Go the All Blacks!' When Dad elaborated and said he and Mum were Maori, Monsieur Samaritan clapped his thighs and said, 'Ka mate, ka mate, ka ora, ka ora! Kia ora!'

Dad and Monsieur Samaritan shook hands, Dad exchanged seats with Mum, and very soon he and Monsieur Samaritan were talking as if they were old friends. Monsieur Samaritan told them that he was an official for the Tunisian government and had been on business in Paris, renegotiating landing rights for Air France in Tunisia; the negotiations had been somewhat exhausting and he was looking forward to getting home to his wife and children. He had never been to New Zealand, but he had met some New Zealand officials in his business — and he was a rugby fan.

'We're on our way to the Commonwealth graveyard at Sfax,' Dad said. He told him about Mum's river stones and bottle of river water, and Monsieur Samaritan was affected by Mum's simple gesture of love for her brother. He took his handkerchief out of his pocket and, dabbing at his eyes, waved to some other passengers across the aisle.

'C'est mon frère, le libérateur de la Tunisie —'

Well, that did it. Before too long, Dad was the centre of attention, and more cards and greetings were exchanged.

—

In this mood of general friendliness and bonhomie, Mum and Dad landed at Sfax. They farewelled their new friends, all native Tunisians, and exited the plane. Officials saluted Monsieur Samaritan at the gate, ready to take him through VIP customs to a government limousine that would whisk him into the city.

'Monsieur Tom,' Monsieur Samaritan said, clicking his shiny shoes together, 'I wish you a good visit to Sfax and a safe return to your homeland. Kia ora.'

Then he bowed to Mum — so you mustn't think that my father was the only one to impress strangers. Mum has her own quiet dignity and inner luminosity, and intrigues in her own way. She has never regarded herself as beautiful — her face is too angular and as a young woman she was built like a man with her wide shoulders and slim hips — but where other women lose their beauty as they grow older, Mum has come into hers. I'm not sure what gives Mum this look of having eternity in her, but I have seen it in other women who have lived life and, somehow, understood its ebb and flow.

Mum rummaged in her bag for some gifts to give to him, and pulled out a bone pendant and an All Blacks T-shirt. 'For your children,' she said. 'And if ever you come to New Zealand, Dad will put down a hangi for you.'

Now I have never been to Tunisia and I have no idea what the airline terminal in Sfax looks like. You will have to bear with me as I let my imagination take over.

I imagine Mum and Dad walking along the concourse — Dad just keeping up with Mum — and looking out the windows to a sky almost white with heat. I can hear the excitement in my mother's voice as she says to Dad, 'Come on, Tom, almost there!' The air conditioning in the airport would have cocooned them in coolness. The concourse would have been crowded with Arab nationals in the majority, and foreigners like Mum and Dad would elicit glances of curiosity. I can imagine Mum, as they approached the customs hall, getting impatient to be on her way to the Commonwealth graveyard and her rendezvous with her brother. And I can just see her hopeful face as they waited for the customs official to stamp their passports and let them go through.

The official frowned. 'Would you come this way, please?'

Mystified, Mum and Dad followed him. 'Is there anything wrong?' Mum asked. She was getting a terrible feeling about this.

The customs officer did not reply. His supervisor stepped up to look at the passports. 'Do you have baggage?' he asked.

'Yes,' Mum answered. They were escorted to the carousel to collect their suitcases and then taken to a small room where they were asked a number of questions and their bags were searched. The customs officer wanted to know about the river stones and the bottle of water, and he took a hammer to one of the stones to see if there was anything inside. A long consultation took place, and Mum and Dad were then advised of their predicament.

'I am very sorry to inform you,' the customs officer said, 'that you will not be able to enter Tunisia. You will be kept here in the airport and, when your flight leaves tomorrow, you will be put on it for return to Paris.'

At his words, my father looked at my mother. Tears were streaming down her face. Dad's love for Mum showed in his concern for her and, heart beating fast, he tried to intercede with the customs officer. 'Will you not give us just today so that my wife can go to pay her respects to her brother? Sir, we —'

He gasped for air. Then he gave a moan and would have crumpled to the floor had Mum not supported him.

'It's all right, Dad,' Mum consoled him. She looked at the customs officer. 'Do you have a chair for my husband?' she asked.

3

I took another break from the story. Once upon a time, I would not have questioned the directness or ingenuousness of my writing. But I know more postcolonial theory now, and not only do I write literature, I also teach postcolonial identity. Is any of this reflected in the story? No.

My problem was that I was, well, still indigenous. Unlike Derek Walcott, a poet of African, Dutch and West Indian descent, born in St Lucia and commuting between Boston and Trinidad, I was not a 'divided child who entered the house of literature as a houseboy' and who had become a paradigm of the polycultural order, making of English a polyglot literature. Nor, like Salman Rushdie, Booker Prize winner for his tumultuous, multiheaded myth of modern India, *Midnight's Children*, Kazuo Ishigura, Vikram Seth, Timothy Mo, Rohinton Mistry or Pico Iyer, was I a transcultural writer, the product not so much of colonial division as of the international culture that has grown up since the war, and addressing an audience as mixed up and eclectic and uprooted as themselves. Situated at a crossroads, they reflected on their hyphenated status in the new-world global village with a different kind of sophistication than mine as an indigenous writer.

And where was my sense of irony? To this day, my closest friends bemoan the fact that I don't have an ironic bone in my body. If I had, I might have been able to undercut the otherwise positive, sacralised and hopeful nature of my mythmaking. I would, instead, have highlighted the nihilistic despair of the victimised and oppressed and the need to continue to propose political and revolutionary solutions. Hybrid writers have often commented, as Edward Saïd did, that: 'The centre is full of tired scepticism, a kind of knowing irony. There's something very stale about it.' As for American literature, it had been sapped by such trends as minimalism. Bharati Mukherjee has written, 'The real energy of American fiction is coming from people who have lived 400 years within a generation. They've been through wars, orbited the world, had traumatic histories prior to coming, and they've got big, extraordinary stories to tell. In place of the generic account of divorce in Hampstead or Connecticut, the international writers offer magically new kinds of subject matter and electric ways of expressing it.'

Perhaps there is another way out. My postcolonial colleagues might honour me not for the more political novelising that has been the central poutokomanawa of my artistry — but, rather, for the activism that has been associated with it.

For instance, First Nations friends still talk about the time, over twenty-five years ago, when they came to see me at the Harborfront Festival, Toronto, where I was to read my work. They told me that no First Nations writer had ever been invited to read in Canada's most prestigious literary festival, and they asked me to represent them. I was so angry that when I came to read I instead let rip to the primarily white and unsuspecting audience, accusing them and Canada of racism of the worst kind: denial of the native existence and erasure of First Nations culture as a wilful exercise of Canadian genocide. By the time I finished, there was a stony silence. Greg Gatenby said to me as I walked off the stage, 'Well, that was interesting. I've never seen a writer committing suicide in public before.'

I am an example of one of those writers who could never resist the disastrous.

—

Ah well, to proceed.

To be frank, I do not know why my parents were detained at the airport at Sfax. I imagine that there was some irregularity with their passports. The most likely explanation is this:

'I am very sorry to tell you both,' the senior customs officer said, 'but you must have a visa to enter our country. Without it, I cannot permit you to visit.'

But I am only guessing at the reason. There may have been another: perhaps their passports looked too new and clean and therefore suspiciously false. They may have needed different entry documents. The names on their airline tickets might have been different from the names on their passports — Mum and Dad had both Maori and Pakeha surnames. Perhaps they had been mistaken for a couple of criminals on Interpol's list.

'Therefore,' the senior customs officer advised them, 'I will retain your passports and, as I have already told you, you will both be held in custody at the airport. When your plane leaves tomorrow for Paris you will be escorted onto it. At that time, your passports will be returned to you.'

After a while, however, the senior customs officer relented somewhat, and agreed to allow Mum and Dad to remain in the transit area where at least there were dutyfree shops, food outlets and comfortable seating. After all, how far would an old lady and an old man with a walking stick have got if they decided to make a run for it? And without passports?

Mum and Dad were just two old people, bewildered and unable to get to their destination. But my father regained his strength. 'Sir,' he tried once again, 'whatever the problem is, surely, as reasonable people, we can find a solution? My wife and I are here in your country for only a short time. What harm can we do?' He showed the customs officer photographs of Uncle Rangiora. 'All my wife wishes to do is visit her brother's grave, pay her respects, and then we will be on our way. Will you not permit us to do that?'

No matter how much Dad tried to explain the situation and to apologise for any error they may have inadvertently made, he just couldn't get through to the senior customs officer, who was adamant.

What made it worse was that the incident really hurt my parents' sense of pride and personal honour. 'You are treating us as if we are criminals,' Dad said in a temper. 'I may have received the occasional parking ticket but my wife and I have never been before a judge or committed any crimes. To be treated like this is deeply shaming.'

The customs officer would not be swayed. He retained their passports, showed them the transit lounge, deposited their bags beside them and advised them that under no circumstances were they to leave. Of course, as soon as he had gone, Mum burst into tears. She's generally a strong woman but her tears were from embarrassment and humiliation. 'And now look at us, Dad,' she wept, 'we've become a bag lady and a bag man.' She was also aching because to come all this way with her river stones and not be able to put them on her brother's grave was a terrible heartbreak for her.

They sat, talked, waited, and slept. Every now and then Dad wandered off to get Mum a sandwich and a cup of chocolate. Mum talked about Uncle Rangiora and how they would waltz together. 'He was such a good brother to me,' she told Dad. 'He always saved the last waltz for me. I remember well when we danced together for the last time. It was on the platform of the railway station in 1941, just before all the East Coast boys got on the train to Wellington. I was still a teenager. Rangiora was looking so handsome in his soldier's cap and uniform; I had on my best white dress so that he would always remember me while he was fighting in the war. Rangiora had a girlfriend, a lovely girl from Te Araroa, but just before he got the order to fall in, he turned to me and asked, "Would you like to waltz, sister?" He opened his arms, I stepped into them, we both went onto our toes, and we began —

> So kiss me again, and then let us part,
> And when we grow too old to dream,
> Your kiss will stay in my heart —

I mean no disrespect to my father, but Uncle Rangiora was the love of my mother's life. Dad knew it and we, her children, knew it. I suspect that when you lose someone you love when you are both young, the love for that person is heightened and romanticised in some way. The rest of us had to fit in and around that big love, realising that we had no chance of winning because, well, Mum knows our faults too well to let us get away with anything.

My parents continued to while away the day at the airport. They were distressed — but really, there was nothing that could be done about their situation. I imagine that some of the cafeteria workers, puzzled by Dad's constant visits for more hot chocolate and food, sympathised with their plight and offered words of comfort. When night came, I can imagine my parents sleeping sitting up, a crescent moon gliding overhead and shining on Dad's white trainers. I can see cleaners going by, hushing each other so as not to wake them. I know that Dad must have disengaged himself from Mum's arms a couple of times to go to the toilet, as his waterworks were not always reliable. But I know he would have hobbled back as fast as he could to make sure that Mum was not alone for too long. There have not been many nights when they have slept apart. No doubt Mum woke a couple of times to stare out into the dark velvet of the Tunisian sky, her face enigmatic and eternal.

The new day dawned. Mum went to wash her face, comb her hair and make herself respectable. When she came back, Dad did the same. She scolded him to put on a new white shirt and tie. 'That's better,' she said when he returned. 'Seven hours from now we'll be on the plane, Dad.' She tried to be light-hearted about it.

Mum's head nodded and she drifted into sleep. Then she felt someone shaking her awake. When she opened her eyes the first thing she saw was a pair of very shiny shoes. She would have recognised those shoes anywhere.

'Madam? Aroha? Did you enjoy your visit to Sfax?' It was Monsieur Samaritan, their companion on the plane from Paris.

Mum saw that Dad was still sleeping, his mouth wide open, and his trousers wide open too. She nudged him awake. Dad told Monsieur Samaritan what had happened. 'We have been in the airport all this time,' he said. 'Our passports were taken from us.'

Well, there's no other way to say it — Monsieur Samaritan went ballistic. 'Please come with me,' he said, tight-lipped. Mum and Dad had known he was a VIP but they had not realised that he was such a powerful government official. He stormed into the customs area and began to speak rapidly to every underling around, and then to the senior customs officer. I have no idea what he said but I can imagine that it was something like this:

'Don't you fools know that these two people have come all the way from New Zealand? Who was the imbecile who said they should not be allowed into our country? Do you realise that this lady's brother fought and died to enable our freedom? Why am I surrounded by such incompetent and stupid people? Do you think they are terrorists? Do they look like terrorists? Where are their passports? Give them back immediately!'

Monsieur Samaritan then looked at his watch. He mopped his brow and, calming down, bowed gravely to Mum and Dad. 'Please accept my apologies,' he said, 'but perhaps I can be of some service? Although you only have a short time left before your plane departs, it would be my great privilege to accompany you to the Commonwealth graves.'

He hastened them out of the terminal and into the heat to his car, and ordered the driver to put his foot down. 'Quick! Quick! As fast as you can!'

As I have said, I have never been to Tunisia, so I don't know what the roads are like from the airport to the Commonwealth war graves. My imagination conjures up heat and dust, roads crowded with traffic, the occasional camel, and the shimmering haze of a bright white day. Conscious of the restricted time, I can hear Monsieur Samaritan urging his driver to 'Go faster! Faster!', and the car, with its official pennant flying, speeding through a city of Arabic architecture, serrated walls and minarets.

At last, they arrived. But what was this? The gates were closed. Monsieur Samaritan commanded the driver to go and investigate.

'Alas, Monsieur Tom,' Monsieur Samaritan said, 'the cemetery is closed during the middle of the day.' Monsieur Samaritan instructed the driver to ring the bell at the gateway, and keep ringing until someone came. As luck would have it, a gatekeeper arrived and let them in.

'Thank you,' Mum said. She reached into her bag for one of her bone pendants to give the gatekeeper, but the car was already moving swiftly through the gateway.

—

I'm told that the cemetery at Sfax is huge — rows and rows of white crosses — and Mum and Dad's time was ticking by. Even Monsieur Samaritan saw the hopelessness of the task. 'How will your wife be able to find her brother,' he said to Dad, 'among all these dead?'

The gatekeeper had pointed them in the general direction of the Australian and New Zealand section. Suddenly Mum yelled 'Stop!' She opened the door of the car and took off. 'I'll find him,' she said. All that training, running around the block in Te Hapara, was about to pay off.

'Aroha,' Dad called, reaching for his walking stick. 'Wait for me —'

But she was already far away, sprinting like a sixteen-year-old through all those rows of white crosses. She stopped at a rise in the graveyard. When Dad and Monsieur Samaritan reached her, they saw more crosses. Which one was Rangiora's?

'It really is impossible,' Monsieur Samaritan said.

Mum was standing with the sun shining full upon her face. Perspiration beaded her forehead and neck. Dad saw her face crumple and went to offer her solace. 'Keep your hands off me,' she screamed, frustrated.

Then she saw a little brown bird. It fluttered above her, cocked an eye and turned away. With a cry, Mum took off after it, following the bird as it dipped and sashayed around the white crosses, up, over and down a small hillock. When Dad and Monsieur Samaritan reached the top of the hillock, they saw Mum in the distance, kneeling beside a small cross, weeping. By the time they caught up with her again, she was putting her river stones on Uncle Rangiora's grave. She had already poured her river water out of its bottle and it was seeping into the sand. There was a radiant look on her face, as if something important had been completed.

Dad and Monsieur Samaritan waited in silence. Then, 'I will go back to the car and wait for you,' Monsieur Samaritan said. 'Please take as much time as you wish, but we should be returning to the airport shortly.'

Dad nodded at him. He watched Mum as she finished laying her stones. She stood up, wiped her hands on her dress, smiled at Dad and put out her hands. 'I'm sorry I yelled at you. Will you dance a waltz with me, Dad?'

Gripping his walking stick in one hand and Mum in the other, Dad did his best.

When I grow too old to dream,
I'll have you to remember,
When I grow too old to dream,
Your love will stay in my heart —

Mum and Dad returned to the airport. Monsieur Samaritan escorted them through customs and saw them to their flight. 'I'm so sorry you didn't have more time with your brother,' he said to Mum.

'Sorry?' Mum answered. 'Please don't be. And thank you, Monsieur Samaritan.'

From Paris, my parents went on to New York. There's a photograph taken by a sidewalk photographer which captures the glow of Mum's happiness. She's with Dad, and he's balancing on his walking stick and wearing his white trainers. My cousin Watene took them to see *42nd Street* and *Cats*. Mum told Dad she didn't want to sleep for one minute, and dragged him up the Empire State Building and down to the ferry to see the Statue of Liberty.

Four days later, they boarded a bus for a tour across America all the way to the West Coast. Dad was looking forward to the trip and his eyes brightened when he saw all the other tourists boarding the bus. As I have mentioned before, he loves to talk to strangers about his family, his tribe, and his sporting exploits.

However, his face fell when he discovered that the other tourists on the bus were German-speaking and didn't understand English very well.

—

My parents survived the bus tour. They caught the plane from Los Angeles back to New Zealand, where they were welcomed with tears and much elation by a huge whanau that has never wanted them to go away overseas again — ever.

On their return home, Mum bought four huge scrapbooks and pasted every postcard, photograph and programme into it, including the souvenir programme from the Folies Bergère and the photograph taken in New York. Pride of place was reserved for a blow-up of a photograph of her and Dad standing at Uncle Rangiora's grave in the hot sun in Tunisia; with them is a gentleman dressed formally and wearing the shiniest shoes — Monsieur Samaritan. Dad had his hip operation, and put away his walking stick and his new white trainers.

If you go home to Te Hapara, you will see the map of Mum and Dad's travels on the wall in the living room.

—

Three months after the trip, Mum telephoned me in Wellington. She told me she was bothered about Rangiora being buried so far away from New Zealand. 'I want him to come back home,' she told me.

On her behalf I wrote to the Minister of Defence and the Minister of Maori Affairs. They both gave the same response: the Maori Battalion had made a collective agreement that all the boys who died on the battlefield should stay together in the country where they had fallen.

Dad is ninety-two this year. Mum is eighty-five. She still puts a memorial notice about Uncle Rangiora in *The Gisborne Herald* every year.

ask the posts of the house

1

I am flying backwards in business class from Bangkok. It's a strange feeling, but I'm getting accustomed to it. The seats convert into completely flat beds when one wants to go to sleep and for some reason (perhaps to fit as many sleeping passengers as possible into the cabin) they are in rows of six in a herringbone pattern, alternating one passenger facing forwards and one backwards. I'm reminded of boyhood days when my cousins and I slept top and toe in the same crowded community arrangement, sometimes four per bed — except that my fellow passengers aren't as attractive or congenial.

I've been on business in the UK, with a brief stopover in Thailand. I've never liked Bangkok, too hot and fetid. The first time I went through the city, over thirty years ago now, not even the overheated and fevered joys of Patpong could convince me to stay; I rang the airport and told them to get me out on the first available flight anywhere. Too many disgusting foreigners seeking sex with underage Thai girls and boys.

Why is it that business class always attracts such arrogant people? On this trip, for some reason, my bags hadn't been checked all the way from

Heathrow to New Zealand and I had to go through Thai customs to pick them up and then recheck myself and my luggage back through customs. Admittedly, therefore, I was already in a foul mood when a stupid pasty-faced overweight Englishman of the kind I thought was extinct in the tropics put a hand on me — I was watching from my window the last of the luggage being loaded into the underbelly of the plane — and told me I was sitting in his seat; nor did he apologise when I read his ticket back to him and pointed out that he was over by the door suitably next to the toilet. Then, a woman, somewhat overdressed with fake diamonds, insisted that I move my carry-on luggage from 'her' space in the compartment above 14G where she was sitting. I asked if I could see her ticket for the luggage compartment, upon which she complained to the purser; he explained to her that although seats are reserved, compartments are not. I enjoyed watching her park her faux leather overnight vanity, undoubtedly filled with cheap perfume, more fake diamonds and the distasteful array of powders and lotions that accompany women of her age and class, above 12D.

I should be accustomed to such ignorant behaviour. Brown faces like mine are no longer a rarity in business class, but it appears that some passengers persist in believing that the sun has not set on the Empire, and are incensed that I am not travelling in steerage where they consider I belong.

Yes, I am in a mood. The business negotiations with my English counterparts have gone very well indeed — I am board chairman of a New Zealand education publishing company which exports literacy materials internationally, and I have just fired one company and hired another to be our distributors in the UK — so my mood has nothing to do with the trip, which has been extremely successful: I like hiring and firing people as it gives me a great sense of power, something I've inherited from my warlike ancestors.

No, it's the business concerning Talia, Makareti's daughter, that is bothering me. Over the past three weeks, I have been able to forget all about it and conveniently put it — awful expression — 'on hold'. However, now that I am heading back to New Zealand, via a brief stopover in Australia, I realise that I am also heading toward the inevitability of sorting it out.

Already I am developing a headache just thinking about it. The champagne that the airline staff served as I settled into my seat has not been able to get rid of it. And now the lovely hostess — she must be Thai — has taken even that pleasure away from me by asking for my glass: the plane is ready for takeoff.

2

I should introduce myself: I am Isaac Tairawhiti Jnr. Although my father, Isaac Senior, died twelve years ago, people still call me Junior to distinguish me from him.

Come to think of it, flying backwards is an appropriate physical position to be in as I think about the whole messy business of Talia. After all, what do Maori people say? We walk backwards into the future is one saying; another is that we take our past with us into the future. Both sayings are meant to be positive.

How ironic to be able to invoke a Maori proverb! In this particular case, however, the past is a burden and I wouldn't mind being divested of it. But can I do that? No. Since I became a successful businessman, oh, some thirty years ago now, the burden was thrust upon me; my extended whanau elevated me to their head — not that that was entirely consensual but, listen, for a constantly cash-strapped family, it was either take me or go into bankruptcy. Over the years I've become like Don Corleone in *The Godfather* — an unlikely and surprising elevation, given my early childhood as the runt of the clan, weak, a cissy with a clubfoot who couldn't even fish for paua and who hated puha and pork bones. Members of the whanau who watched my rise in status, using my brains, while they worked away trying to wrest important lives with their brawn, have subsequently eaten a lot of crow in accepting my ascendancy. However, over the years they've got used to it and so have I, and whatever residual grievances they may harbour against me, they have forgiven me because of my capacity to help them whenever they are in need. Their financial problems are easily sorted out: Uncle Solomon wanting more injections of cash so he can purchase further worthless land to add to the family's portfolio; Cousin Bella with the house she always mortgages because she has a gambling problem and has become a permanent resident at the Auckland casino; Nephew Rawiri, inevitably in debt to some Black Power gang or other who are threatening to kill him for not paying for his drugs; Auntie Hariata, wanting some cash to pay for a daughter's wedding or a son's university education; Whaea Hera, still pursuing her dream of a carving school in the valley but not wanting to pay for it — where does she think the money will come from? Out of the air? All these family requests are easily solved by my quick signature to a cheque. But it's the other problems to do with blood, history, whakapapa, old squabbles and feuds, skeletons rattling in the whanau cupboard that won't go away — these are the ones I find messy, distasteful to deal with and difficult. This business of Talia, Makareti's daughter, is one of them.

Ah well, now that the plane is on its way, above the clouds, bound for Sydney and Auckland, I can give some attention to it.

—

Makareti is my daughter. She's in her mid thirties now, married to a nice Pakeha man, Glen, who works in insurance. Makareti's eldest child is Talia, the sweetest girl imaginable. My granddaughter is now nineteen and in her second year at the University of Auckland; she's doing very well. Glen is not her father; Makareti was an unmarried mother when Glen met her, fell in love with her and married her.

Makareti and Glen subsequently have had three very boisterous boys — Glen Junior, eleven, Rawiri, nine, and Simon, eight, but I call them, affectionately, Huey, Dewey and Louey, after characters in some ancient Walt Disney cartoon I watched when I was a boy. They're a rough and tumble lot, and every third weekend of the month they get delivered to me by Makareti so that they can take me out to Rainbow's End. 'Are you home, Dad?' she yells unnecessarily before they come screaming up the stairs. 'Time for you to be taken out for a run!' Anybody would think I was a dog that had to be let off the leash. But I like to humour Makareti and, to tell you true, I enjoy the outing. The boys run me ragged, of course, wanting to go on every ride including the rollercoaster — lately I have been using my clubfoot as an excuse not to squeeze on with them — but Dewey (alias Rawiri) was onto me when we went on the bumper car circuit and I was the best and most ferocious driver on the course. Surveying the wreckage he said, with an exaggerated sigh, 'Poor Papa, winning like that and him with his clubfoot and all, too.' I made sure to target him for bigger bumper car smashes, and afterwards I fed him lots of candyfloss and popcorn — he got his comeuppance when he became sick and threw up, the dear boy.

'Papa, you don't play fair,' he wailed. 'The first rule of survival,' I answered him. The sooner he realised, the better.

I love the boys, but of all Makareti's children, the one closest to my heart is Talia. It's not just the matter of the prettiness which she has had ever since she was a baby — perfect skin, sparkling eyes and a disarming smile — but throughout all these years I have watched with excitement the development of her enquiring mind and the special intelligence that has marked her out as singular among her sex. Who could not love a young woman who, while blossoming into the intelligence of adulthood, has also kept the loveliness of youth?

Okay, so the three boys I take to Rainbow's End; Talia I take to fine restaurants. A number of my friends who have seen us out together have told me we make an attractive couple. The restaurant visit is part of the bargain we came to when I agreed to put her through university rather than see her taking out a student loan or being at the mercy of generic Maori grants. I like the fact that she chooses the very best and that haute cuisine matters to her. I tend to arrive a few minutes before she does, as every gentleman should, and wait for her at the bar. Like her mother, Talia always makes the effort to be well groomed and she turns many a young head as she makes her entrance. On one occasion the handsome boy sitting at the bar beside me nudged me and remarked, 'Now that's what you call a babe.' He was rather shocked when Talia hugged me, took my arm quite unprompted and said, cheekily, 'Hi, honey, have you had a nice day at the office?' As we walked to our table I whispered to her, 'Talia, you are in danger of becoming too cute.'

If this sounds as if I am besotted with my granddaughter, I will not deny it. Nor will I deny that our dinner engagements are a highlight for me. During dinner I am able to play the stern grandfather and ask how she is getting on with her academic studies, and she is able to play the penitent granddaughter for only getting As instead of A+s in her essays. At the end of dinner I give her a cheque so that she can buy something special, and although this has become ritualised, her delight seems always to be unforced; the repetition has not numbed her and she does not take me for granted. As usual, I tell her to bring her boyfriend, Victor, with her to the next dinner but she has always declined — and I love her all the more that she respects our special time together.

Apart from which I have a special bond to Talia and to her mother Makareti through Makareti's mother, Georgina. When I was cradling Georgina's head in my lap, almost forty years ago, watching her coughing up blood, she said to me, 'Promise me, Isaac, that you will look after Makareti? Promise.'

'I promise,' I answered, watching her life ebbing away — and raging inside that this was happening, despairing at the unfairness of it all.

'Nor do I want anybody to know what happened to us,' Georgina said, digging her fingers into me fiercely. 'Nobody is to know the secret. Promise me.'

I promised again. I have kept both promises all these years. But a month ago Whaea Hera, my aging aunt, in some ugly fit of temper, let the secret out.

3

A dismal morning, and the plane has landed at Sydney airport. I have discovered something interesting: it doesn't really matter if you're flying backwards or forwards, the sensation is just the same — and just as boring.

Last night I couldn't cope with my anger at what Aunt Hera has done so, immediately after midnight dinner — a goodish, fresh, seasonal salad served with vinaigrette followed by a grilled medallion of beef with baby carrots and shallots, washed down with a smooth Australian shiraz from the Barossa Valley — I took a sleeping pill. Rather stupidly, I couldn't resist the small glass of Muscat dessert wine that the lovely Thai hostess so enticingly waved under my nose, and it's a wonder that I got any sleep at all. At least my induced slumber has given me respite from the difficulties ahead when I arrive home in Auckland.

'Papa Isaac,' Talia had wailed over the telephone to me when I was in the UK, 'please tell me it's not true. Please, Papa, please.'

All the blood drained from my face; white is an inappropriate colour for a Maori. I immediately telephoned Makareti. She was hysterical. 'Yes,' she sobbed, 'that whole horrible story, Talia knows it now. I denied it of course but she didn't believe me —'

'Who told her?' I asked. I could barely stand. A huge hole had opened from the past and something terrifying and ugly had been thrown out of it, a piece of rotten meat, steaming at my feet.

'Whaea Hera,' Makareti answered. 'But why should she do that? We never did anything to her, Dad.'

I rang Hera immediately. 'What did you tell Talia?' I was so angry that my forehead was popping with veins and I felt my eyeballs ready to explode.

'It was her own fault,' my aunt answered defensively. 'Putting on airs, pretending she's better than the rest of us. It was time she was taken down a peg or two. She's getting whakahihi. Somebody had to teach her a lesson.'

'You count yourself lucky, Hera, that I'm out of the country,' I said to her. 'But when I get back, I'm coming after you.'

I could scarcely control myself. If I had been in the same room as my aunt I would have broken every bone in her worthless body.

—

I look out the window of the plane. Outside it's raining, and the ground staff have put on wet weather gear; they unload the bags, load new cargo and refuel for our onward flight to Auckland. I try to remain calm — but my clubfoot is throbbing badly. I shall blame Aunt Hera for it.

It's because of my clubfoot that the Australian customs authorities have allowed me to stay on board. The other passengers have had to disembark, including Mr Pasty-Faced Overweight Englishman; perhaps Australia is his final destination, in which case, he and Australia thoroughly deserve each other. Of course Diamond Lil in 14G remonstrated at what she considered to be my privileged treatment; I rolled up my left trouser leg and took the sock off my foot — the sight of it would put anybody off their breakfast and, gasping for air, she quickly made her exit, clutching her paste diamonds to her pneumatic chest.

Having a clubfoot, *Talipes equinovarus*, is a congenital condition caused by intrauterine compression on the baby's foot. The joints, tendons and ligaments all conjoin to create the deformity: the ankle and foot are turned inward and downward, resembling a cloven horse's hoof — high-arched foot, drawn-up heel and toes pointed down. Is the condition as common these days as it was when I was a boy?

In my case, when I was born, I had a bilateral condition: both my feet were affected, one more severely than the other. My unsuspecting parents were shocked, especially my father, who was a highly regarded Maori sportsman in tennis, rugby and wrestling. As for my mother, Rewa, she blamed herself — and, hey, so did my Dad — but she loved me unconditionally and did her best. In the old days of Polynesia, she would probably have taken me to a high cliff overlooking the sea and thrown me into it. Instead, she took counsel from the doctors and I began a correction therapy known as the Ponseti Method.

Please do not flinch, but at six weeks I had an Achilles tendotomy, an incision in the tendon, on both my feet. They were then stretched, pushed, twisted, manipulated and reshaped into an overcorrected position, and periodically cast to maintain the position. Oh, why should I spare you the details? After all I've had to bear the pain and indignity all my life; you're getting off lightly. The casts were changed every two weeks. At three months a special type of splint called a Dennis Brown bar, otherwise known as a foot abduction brace, was attached to my feet. I wore it nearly fulltime for three months and then at night and during naps for the next three years. I understand the correction is extremely painful but my mother liked to tell me I was a brave baby and hardly ever cried when the splint had to be periodically realigned; if that was the case, perhaps my stoicism dates from babyhood.

I am told that Isaac Senior tried his best to bond with me when I was growing up, but the sight of his first male child stumping along on his ankles, crying 'Daddy, daddy daddee', did not endear me to him. Later, when I was in foot braces and could walk — courtesy of surgical tendon transfers to correct persistent muscle imbalances and to realign the joints of the feet — I soon realised that it was no use counting on Dad for sympathy. The look of disgust in his eyes made it plain that I had no part in his life's plans. I didn't blame him: to be blighted with a damaged child must have seemed grossly unfair. I would never be the sportsman son to kick a football around with and he would never be able to stand on the spectator line watching me as I scored a try.

The Ponseti Method worked on my right leg but not on my left which, as a consequence, is two inches shorter. The calf muscle is severely attenuated and I have a special shoe for that foot. One should be thankful for small mercies — and I am grateful that, unlike others with a clubfoot, I am able to walk, albeit with the aid of a cane but without that ludicrous lurching movement that afflicts my kind and that proved so amusing to my healthy cousins and the other children down at the marae. They liked to follow just behind me and imitate my walk. I am still haunted by their shrill cries of pleasure that they were so perfectly ambulatory, the way God expected all his creatures to be, whereas I was like some subhuman being, half man half animal, with a cloven foot.

—

My cousin Georgina, however, was not like the other cousins and friends of my childhood. Her father, Aaron, was my dad's oldest brother, and married to my lovely Auntie Agnes. He was also head of the extended whanau and when Georgina was born he went into a blue funk, raging against his Lord for not having given him the required son. That honour went to my father, Isaac, the second brother, when I was born, five months after Georgina. Although I was only the progeny of the second son, I was at least a boy; Georgina, being female, albeit unblemished, had to stand aside as I took the position of honour as the 'eldest' in our generation.

For some reason, my ascendancy didn't make Georgina vengeful; you might have thought she would bide her time and, like other villainous children throughout history, find the opportunity to snuff me out with a pillow or drown me in a wine vat . . . but I am becoming melodramatic. Georgina had no ambition for herself whatsoever. I think she was relieved that she would not have to fulfil any expectations. Instead, she took it upon herself to be my special friend. When we were infants, Georgina was a tomboy and strong enough to protect me from all those roistering, loud, bullying children, both male and female, in our whanau. At five years of age, she took to coming around to my house on her tricycle, leveraging me into the tray on the back, and taking me for long rides to the marae. If anybody ridiculed me in her presence, she gave them a bloodied nose. By the time we were eight, she was my companion when we walked to our native school, handing me my cane whenever I needed it and, if one of the other children stole it in fun, piggybacking me from schoolroom to playground.

I still harbour a startling memory of a game of baseball at school. Much to my chagrin, Georgina had picked me to play on her side — usually I would have been propped under a tree along with the other hopeless, handicapped or decrepit children like Big Fat Wallace or Four Eyes Sally. But no, Georgina insisted I was to play and that was that. When the umpire said, 'Batter up!' I hobbled to the plate, balanced on my cane, swung once, swung twice, and then in a fit of exasperation swung really high and hard — and my bat connected with the ball. 'Quick!' Georgina yelled. I jumped onto her back and she was away, running like crazy to first base — and we made it! From there, we stole a run to second base, but Georgina almost lost me as I started to slide off her shoulders. Although we managed to get to third base, Georgina was tiring. 'You've got to help me run home,' she panted. 'I can't carry you any more so we will just have to do it three-legged. If we tie your bad leg to my leg with my hair ribbon, and you lean on me, I can run for the both of us.'

My heart was thumping like mad. 'What if I fall down? In front of everybody?'

'You won't fall down,' Georgina said grumpily. She draped my arms around her neck and said, 'Hold on tight.' We were lucky that Hori Jones was the batter. When he hit the ball, it soared over the fence into Mrs Haddock's backyard. 'Come on, Isaac!' Georgina cried.

I will remember every bone-wrenching, juddering, excruciatingly painful step we took until the day I die. I can still hear my cousins and classmates yelling out to Georgina, 'Drop him! Run by yourself! Quick!' From the corner of my eye I saw Kepa Karaka retrieve the ball and throw it back towards the diamond. But most of all, I remember Georgina's face, intent, focused, dragging me along with her. 'Dive, cuz, dive!' she yelled.

I fell forward, falling home, falling with Georgina in a tangle onto the homeplate.

'Safe!'

And Georgina was laughing and laughing. 'You did it, Isaac! You did it!'

Not I did it or we did it.

You did it.

—

Ah, memories of small victories are sweet when you are a handicapped child. Remembering that baseball game has obviously put a beatific smile on my face, if the responsive smiles from passengers filing back onto the plane are anything to go by. Not so Madame Cubic Zirconia in 14G, however — she studiously avoids my gaze and settles down in a cloud of stale unwashed body odour that not even cheap perfume can mask. If only

I had one of Dewey's trick cushions, the one that emits a farting sound when you sit on it.

We are ready to resume our journey. The lovely Thai hostess has left the flight in Sydney and been replaced by a male attendant whose bright-eyed smiling manner will be the closest he will ever get to walking the Hollywood red carpet; perhaps if I offer to take his photograph he might let me keep my glass of champagne as we take off.

Sadly he does not oblige — there is no glass of champagne at all. As the plane rises across the morning sea, I take my mind off my irritation with him by trying to think higher thoughts and turning to loving memories of Georgina again.

By the time we were teenagers we were still very close — though as she entered puberty, Georgina traded in her tomboyishness for beauty and, therefore, the odd testosterone-driven boy would come between us and drive me insane with jealousy. My mother, Rewa, approved of the relationship, even when it became very close and suspiciously like love. 'Between cousins is all right,' she said.

By this time we were catching the bus to the high school in the city closest to our village — and, to be frank, I had begun to look forward to the daily escape it afforded me from my father, uncles and aunts and all my cousins down at the marae. After all, I was already so different from them, bookish and serious, and only the accident of birth connected us. Already an outsider by dint of my clubfoot, I saw no disadvantage in going to high school and further ostracising myself by choice.

Did I enjoy high school? Did I what. I compensated for my physical deficiencies by providing evidence of my intelligence. I grabbed at every scholastic and cultural experience available — getting good grades, entering into spelling competitions and speech contests, joining the stamp club and the chorus for the annual Gilbert and Sullivan dramatic production — I was a pegleg sailor in *The Pirates of Penzance* — and otherwise distinguishing myself with highly commendable academic triumphs which are the last bastion of the nerdy student in the Also Ran Competition of Life.

Georgina remained my heart's companion. Apart from coming into her beauty, she also became somewhat romantically inclined, and what she loved most about our relationship was when I secretly read to her from romantic novels. Having Georgina's bounteous gift of love was like having divinity conferred upon me. She loved R.D. Blackmore's *Lorna Doone*, which I read to her down by the wild river in the hills just behind the marae. She especially enjoyed the chapter when the young hero, John Ridd, comes to a black whirlpool and meets the young Lorna:

> When I came to myself again, my hands were full of young grass and mould, and a little girl was kneeling at my side rubbing tenderly with a dock-leaf and a handkerchief.
>
> 'Oh, I am so glad,' she whispered softly, as I opened my eyes and looked at her, 'now you will try to be better won't you?'
>
> I had never heard so sweet a sound as came from between her bright red lips, while there she knelt and gazed at me, nor seen anything so beautiful as the large dark eyes intent upon me, full of pity and wonder . . .

I would see Georgina's eyes glaze over at the thought of being in love with a handsome hero.

On another occasion, after having read *Of Human Bondage* by Somerset Maugham, she arranged that we should play truant from high school and go to see the film with Laurence Harvey and Kim Novak. The main character, you will recall, is named Philip Carey, and he has a clubfoot. He falls hopelessly in love with a slatternly barmaid, Mildred Rogers, with whom he embarks on a corrosive and doomed relationship. After the movie, on our way back on the bus to the village, Georgina insisted on drawing a closer parallel between myself and Philip Carey than really existed. We had a huge argument in which I told her that having a clubfoot could never be romanticised, and, give me a break, maybe Laurence Harvey could get away with it because he had the compensation of being incredibly handsome whereas I was not — at which stage Georgina, seeing herself as Mildred, burst out, 'But I wouldn't desert you, cousin, not ever.' Well, one thing led to another and before we knew it we were vowing that no matter who came between us — oh yes, we knew that eventually Georgina would find some handsome boy to marry — we would always love one another. Always. Forever and ever.

Sometimes, however, Georgina could be such an idiot. She took to calling my clubfoot 'Laurence' and would ask me, 'How is Laurence today?' And on one occasion — she must have been planning on saying it to me for weeks — she asked me, 'Did you know that Lord Byron had a clubfoot?' as if that would make me feel better. But why oh why did she then have to spoil it by adding that Josef Goebbels — the consonants rolled around in her mouth like gravel — also had a clubfoot and wore a metal leg brace for most of his life? Georgina had found his name on a list of people with clubfeet and had thought he was a German film star.

Remembering, I lift an imaginary champagne flute to my lips. 'This one's for you, my gorgeous, funny, exasperating Georgina. If I was to admit to loving anybody, it would be you, cousin. I loved you, I idolised you, I was loyal to you.'

Yes, indeed I was. Then Auntie Agnes, Georgina's mother, died of emphysema.

And I could do nothing to save Georgina.

4

It's usually a great thrill to arrive in New Zealand again, after such a long trip away, but my excitement has been undercut by this gloomy business involving Talia, my granddaughter.

Yes, my mood has not dissipated and, while the bright-eyed attendant has at least compensated for the lack of champagne at the beginning of the flight by courteously leaving the bottle with me as we have flown across the Tasman, I have been discourteous in not thanking him as I disembark. I have realised, yet again, how much I loathe flying. Perhaps it is time for me to hand over all the international travel to young Florian, whom I promoted this year to CEO of the company.

When it comes down to it, flying is flying. It's all about being belted into a moving steel tube in the sky, over which one has no control, piloted by a couple of young men — or women these days, Lord preserve us — to whom one would never loan one's BMW.

But at least the trip is over and Mrs Faux Diamonds and I have now parted ways. As I go through customs I watch her walking ahead, clutching her assortment of carry-on luggage, to the carousel to collect the Pierre Cardin matching suitcases she probably bought at some rip-off merchant's stall in Bangkok. Throughout the flight, whenever I got something from the overhead compartment, she watched me like a hawk to make sure I was not interfering with her valuables. If I was wanting to do that, I wouldn't pickpocket her false paste versions from Marks and Sparks. But, aha, I did manage to secrete a half-eaten banana and a biscuit into one of those plastic carry-on bags of hers. I wonder how much she will have to pay for a false declaration that she is not carrying any food items into New Zealand?

Ah well, onward and upward. I push my trolley of suitcases ahead of me and think that young Dewey would only roll his eyes, 'Yeah, typical of Papa, and him with his clubfoot and all,' as I smash my way through the other trolleys in the race for the exit. Among the people waiting on the New Zealand side of customs I see Sefulu, the young driver for my company, waiting to take me home. You can't miss Sefulu. He's a big, tall brute of a boy who used to be a sumo wrestler in Japan.

'Hello Mr Tairawhiti,' Sefulu smiles. 'Here, let me take your trolley. The car's just outside.'

The sun is bright and I blink to adjust my eyes to its light. Out come my sunglasses. Sefulu opens the door of the car for me and waits until I am settled. 'Okay, Mr Tairawhiti?' he asks, making sure both my feet and my cane are in the car before he starts it.

We speed along the motorway into the city. I call up Talia and, although usually I am irritated when her singsong answerphone clicks on, this time I am relieved not to have to talk to her personally.

'Talia? This is your grandfather speaking,' I respond. 'I'm sorry not to catch you but I just wanted to let you know that I am back from overseas. I know we have an important appointment tonight, and I will look forward to seeing you. Let's go to dinner afterwards? I'll make a reservation at Cibo's.'

Then I call my daughter, Makareti. As soon as she hears my voice, she bursts into tears. 'Oh, Dad, I'm so glad you're home. Talia has been absolutely terrified, screaming, crying, trying to get the truth out of me and the rest of the family.'

'But you've kept on denying what Whaea Hera told her, haven't you?' I ask quickly. 'Haven't you?'

'Yes,' Makareti sobs. 'It's such an ugly story, Dad, ugly.'

'I'll find out what Aunt Hera has told her,' I answer. 'As soon as I've dropped my bags at the house I'll go and see her. Once I know what she has done, that will make it easier for me when Talia comes to see me tonight.'

I disconnect the call. I see Sefulu looking anxiously at me. I wonder how much he knows about this business. I dial my office and talk to my PA, Anna. 'Cancel all my appointments today, Anna,' I tell her. Then I speak to

Florian and, although I should really take time to swing by and brief him on the contract that needs to be signed with our new UK distributors, I say to him, 'I'm leaving it to you, Florian. Go through the contract they've faxed us with our lawyers and, as long as it works to our advantage, sign it.' I am such a control freak that I would be surprised if Florian's jaw hasn't hit the floor. But, really, I have more important duties to attend to today.

Half an hour later, we reach my home in Herne Bay. I'm relieved that taggers have not sprayed graffiti on my concrete wall. The garden is blazing with colour; it was the right decision to tell my gardener to chuck out the dismal hollyhocks and replace them with dazzling tropical flora. The house itself is lovely — modern architecture, multilevel, lots of glass gleaming in the sun, with a terrace in front leading to large sliding front doors.

I well recall the first time I moved into this upper-class suburb. The Sultan of Oman had a house down by the sea. The place was stacked to the gills with judges, lawyers, bankers, corporate directors, highflying accountants and the like. When I bought my house and moved in, I had a Mercedes and dressed in white silk shirts and people thought I was Chinese. A few years later, I had decided to move to the North Shore but my friend, Teresa, a Maori married to a lawyer, got into her Rover and came around to see me immediately. 'You can't go,' she said. 'You and I are the only Maori living in the suburb. If you sell up the whole neighbourhood will turn either white or Asian.' I was greatly moved by her pleas and agreed to stay. Darling Teresa — a year later her husband divorced her, trading her in for a younger model, and when she moved back to Taranaki, I was left like some Polynesian potentate in solitary splendour.

Sefulu carries my suitcases to the house. His wife, Sofia, takes them at the door. I hire Sofia to clean for me, make the beds, do the washing and cook dinner. 'Talofa lava,' she calls cheerily. 'Welcome home. Did you had a nice trips?' Sofia has a problem with tenses and also the singular and plural.

For some reason, despite Sofia's greeting, I cannot get out of the car — some kind of psychic paralysis, I presume, concerning the job ahead.

'Mr Tairawhiti?' Sefulu asks, concerned, leaning in through the window.

My throat is dry. 'Would you mind waiting for me, Sefulu?' I ask him. 'I want you to take me to Manurewa.' That's where Aunt Hera lives with her gang of boys. 'I need your protection. It might be a difficult job. I hope you've been working out today.'

—

And now, I suppose, I should introduce you to my great, passionate, flawed clan. As I have already said, Uncle Aaron, Georgina's father, was the oldest, and head of the extended whanau. My father, Isaac Senior, was the second in the family. Following them came my uncles Joseph, David, Abraham and Solomon — though their names were disguised as Hohepa, Rawiri, Aperahama and Horomona — and if you're wondering about their biblical referentiality, it's because my grandparents belonged to a Pentecostal sect for which the Old Testament was a seminal text. Uncle Aaron and the brothers also had three sisters, Leah, Rebecca and Hera. All are dead now except Horomona, Rebecca and Hera.

Although I speak of them grudgingly, when I was growing up, my father and his brothers were all larger than life and superhuman. A kind of glamour attached to them, especially to Uncle Aaron with his matinée good looks. He was a Maori Errol Flynn, my generation's Tom Cruise, tall, muscular, with a disarming grin. The best way to describe him would be to say that he was easy in his skin. Such people take their own powers of persuasion — and the homage of others — for granted. They live in a world that serves them, and Uncle Aaron was accustomed to being served.

My uncles were smiling, physically imposing beings who strode through life with careless charm and abandon. They were also very sexual. Indeed, as young men they had been notoriously phallus-driven, creating the template by which my own weedy masculinity could only be measured in the negative. Uncle Aaron's amatory exploits, in particular, were legendary, and he was said to have shared women — usually, it was rumoured, after some festival sports tournament or cultural event when the rugby team was elated with their victory and any lone woman could be regarded as a natural prize to be taken on the altar of their joint lust. According to such tales, there was nothing wrong with sharing: to the victor the spoils. It was, after all, only some ancient version of droit de seigneur. As the leader of the pack, rather than being vilified for it, Uncle Aaron was indulged by his brothers and his doting sisters. Aunt Hera was forever proclaiming that it was never his fault; it was always the woman's. When he married Auntie Agnes the whole family breathed a sigh of relief; but when, during her first pregnancy, he had his first extramarital affair, my aunts and uncles — even Auntie Agnes — forgave him. Apparently, he was too much of a man for one woman and it was better to accept that this was his natural condition.

Yes, they were magnificent, my wonderful uncles and my father, those tragically flawed custodians of our lives. They kept the sky from falling. They lived in a state of grace. Although my father produced a cripple, I was the only runt and weakling among all the children that were produced from the fabulous genes that spilled so plentifully and carelessly from my uncles' loins.

My father and uncles were like the god brothers of Maori mythology. Around Uncle Aaron, a particular arrogant mythology developed. It was done so cleverly that in the end he expected to be able to get away with anything — and the whanau let him. He was like the god Tane incarnate, the god above all the other gods. Beside him, my father and other uncles were like Tumatauenga, god of war, Tangaroa, the sea god, Rongo, god of agriculture, Ruaumoko, god of earthquakes and Whiro, the death-dealing god.

All the gods were male, and it is told that the Lord Tane wished to create a race that was in his image: humankind. To do this, he needed to create a woman. Accordingly, he asked the Earth Mother, Papatuanuku, to help him. 'Haere atu koe ki a Kurawaka,' she told him. 'Go to Kurawaka, a sacred place at my sexual cleft and, from the red clay that you find there, make you a woman to mate with.' From this time, it is said, has been maintained the position for all males as high and sacred and that of women — after all, they are made of earthly material — as low and profane.

Tane went to Kurawaka and he did as Papatuanuku had told him to do. The woman he created was named Hineahuone, Woman made of Clay; and Papatuanuku was complicit in this act. Tane took her in his arms, pressed his nose to hers in the first hongi, shared his godly breath with her, and she passed from inanimate to animate being. She opened her eyes and sneezed, 'Tihei mauri ora!'

But when Tane came to mate with her, he wasn't sure which of her orifices should be the receptor of his male weapon. He tried her armpits, ears, nose, mouth and her anus — and this is why these places are associated with lubrication — before finding her vagina. One tribal variation tells that it wasn't only Tane but his other brothers, also, who tried to find the way to enter and have sex with her. Whenever I have heard Maori men retell this story, the narrative has always been associated with laughter and knowing humour. But could it not, also, be the first gang rape?

Hineahuone's role in the narrative was to become the mother of a beautiful daughter, Hinetitama, Girl of the Dawn. After she gave birth, having served her function, she disappeared from the story; I've often wondered what happened to her. Perhaps, like Eve, she went eastward of Eden into the Land of Nod.

—

But to get back to this business about Talia, Makareti's daughter, and what happened to my dear cousin Georgina.

At the time that Georgina's mother, Aunt Agnes, became hospitalised, I was fifteen and had become dux of my high school. On the recommendation of my headmaster, Mr Burns, I was awarded a fellowship to a prestigious Christchurch boarding college with an excellent upper school. When Mr Burns mentioned it to my father, he gave lip service to his sorrow that I would be leaving home; my mother's tears were more heartfelt.

The one desolating aspect was that I would have to say goodbye to Georgina. I arranged to meet her at the wild river in the hills behind the marae. She could sense my reluctance to leave her. 'But you must go,' she said when I expressed last-minute doubts about being so far away from family — and her. 'There's nothing for you here, Isaac. With Laurence holding you back, you will have to make your way through life with your brains.' I sighed, chalking up her reference to my clubfoot as yet another one of those exasperating comments that sprang so offensively but unintentionally to her lips. Life was changing for Georgina, too, and not for the better. 'Anyhow, Dad wants me to leave school,' she told me. 'With Mum in hospital somebody has to look after him and the boys.' Georgina was referring to her two younger brothers, Ramon and William. 'Dad says that it's a waste for a girl to be educated anyway.'

On my last day in the village, before leaving for Christchurch, I went to say goodbye to Georgina — and to Aunt Agnes, who had, in the interim, been released from hospital as they could do nothing further for her. Uncle Aaron met me at the door. 'Don't stay too long with your auntie, boy,' he said to me, 'you'll tire her out. And Georgina has work to do, so make your goodbyes quick.' Everything that Uncle Aaron said was like an order, but I never took any notice of him.

I paid my respects to Aunt Agnes and held her hand for a moment. She was hooked to a machine that gave her regular bursts of oxygen; it was awful hearing her gasp for air. In between one deep inhalation and the next she motioned me closer; I thought it was so that she could give me a kiss of farewell. Instead, she whispered in my ear: 'Your uncle is looking at her.' At the time, I didn't understand the import of what she was saying.

I pressed her hands in comfort. Georgina showed me to the door. Uncle Aaron was watching us carefully. 'Anybody would think you two were girlfriend and boyfriend,' he laughed.

Georgina shivered. 'Think of me, Isaac,' she said. 'Will you write? I'll write back, I promise.' We looked at each other in desperation and sadness. Childhood was over. Adulthood was ahead. Life was never going to be the same again for either of us.

That afternoon I took the train to Wellington. In the evening I went on the ferry to Christchurch. At Lyttelton Harbour, I was met by my housemaster, Mr Fox, and driven to the school, where I was enrolled in accountancy, mathematics, English and history. When Mr Fox enquired what sports I might like to take up, I surprised him by asking about the pugilistic art of boxing. On his part, noting the way I was nervously flicking my cane, he joked that I should take fencing instruction. I decided to take both.

I settled into boarding school and my lessons. I was surprised and pleased that my fellow students were of a Southern gentlemanly calibre and did not draw attention to my clubfoot. Instead I was treated as an equal and, in academic competition, soon proved to some of the Cantabrians' finest sons that I was a force to be reckoned with. In boxing, while my balance was an impediment, my reach compensated. And I soon valued my fencing instruction when, during a school visit into the city, some callow youths set upon one of my classmates; Georgina would have been proud of me had she seen me swashbuckling with my cane and driving them off.

I wrote every week to my mother, Rewa, and just as often to Georgina. My mother's replies were always warm and loving; of course, Georgina never wrote back, but I had not expected her to. Georgina was accustomed to being pursued and paid suit to; such people receive letters, yes, but the active role is that of the beholder, not the beholden.

However, my mother always gave me news of my heart's companion. 'Nursing her mother is taking up most of her time,' my mother wrote in one letter, 'and of course your Uncle Aaron and the boys need a lot of looking after. Your uncle doesn't realise how much work is required to keep a house and he expects Georgina to run it as smoothly as Agnes has done. The dinner has to be on the table when he comes home and he is a hard taskmaster.'

A month after I had arrived in Christchurch, Mum wrote to me that Aunt Agnes had died. Mr Fox gave me permission to telephone from the school office — in those days, telephoning from a boarding school, and receiving a telephone call, were possible only courtesy of one's head teacher or dormitory master, and only in cases of emergency. 'Should I come home for the tangi?' I asked Mum.

'No,' she replied, 'Agnes has already been buried. Your father and I decided that you were too far away and the trip back was too expensive — so that's why we didn't tell you at the time. Anyway, don't you have exams to think about? We made sure that you would be represented with a wreath in your name.'

I was a little disturbed that the choice had been taken away from me, and I asked that my mother give my special condolences to Georgina.

Mum promised she would and then, just as we were concluding our telephone conversation, said, 'Things are going to change now for Georgina. I pray for her. She is in God's hands.'

I didn't think anything of my mother's comment at the time, presuming that she was referring to the fact that now Georgina would have to assume all the chores, as the sole woman of my uncle's house. And forgive me, but I was busy and, frankly, enjoying my schooling — making fond friendships with future professors, judges and captains of industry that have proved their worth by being sustained throughout my youth into my mature adulthood. I didn't notice when my mother stopped giving me news of Georgina in her letters.

At the end of the year I sat the examination for university entrance and, having done that, prepared to go home to the whanau for the long summer holidays. I wish I could say that I was enthusiastic about the prospect, but I wasn't. An academic year had passed since I had come to Christchurch and I had received a number of invitations to spend the summer with new friends, particularly Anthony Walcott, whose parents had a large high-country estate inland from Timaru. But family is family and my mother was pining for me — and I was looking forward to seeing Georgina. I wrote to my mother, giving the date I would arrive, and then caught the train to Picton. That evening I crossed over the Cook Strait by ferry and, in Wellington, embarked on the long, tiring train trip to Gisborne.

The train arrived in the early evening and my mother was waiting on the platform; Isaac Senior had a tribal meeting to attend. Mum cried sentimental tears; in the past, they would have stained my shoulders, but now they left wet patches just below the breast pocket of my school blazer. 'Goodness,' she laughed, surprised, 'haven't you grown, son!' She patted my face, noting how lean I was looking, and poked and prodded, as mothers are prone to do, to discern my musculature. She looked forward to my father's reaction — which was not as forthcoming on my physical appearance, but concerned my elocution.

'Is that how they talk down in Christchurch?' Dad asked. 'Like an Englishman? Now that you're home we'll fix that.'

After dinner, I told my parents that I was going to see Georgina. They exchanged meaningful looks, and my mother suggested, 'Shouldn't you telephone first?'

I replied, 'No, I wrote to Georgina telling her I was arriving today. She will expect me to come around to see her. And if she doesn't, I'll be a surprise for her.' With that, I went to my room to collect her present — while in Christchurch I had found a poster of the Hollywood film, *Lorna Doone*, starring Barbara Hale and Richard Greene — and set off down the road to Uncle Aaron's house.

The twilight was falling and the hills were darkening with shadows. I imagined Georgina's face when she opened the door to me. How surprised would she be? Would she jump into my arms and smother me with hugs and kisses? But when I knocked on the door to her house, it was Uncle Aaron who answered. He took one puzzled look at me, realised who I was, and laughed out loud.

'Hello, boy!' he said. Then he turned and shouted down the hallway, 'Georgina, it's your old boyfriend.' He ushered me in. 'Come in, come in. We've just finished dinner.' He seemed to be enjoying some private joke.

When Aunt Agnes had been alive the house had always been full of noise. Ramon and William were often running around the sitting room, chasing after each other. Georgina was always busy helping her mother with the housework but, whenever I entered, would pull off her apron and, taking my hand, run with me out the door, 'Let's go to the river!'

Not any longer. The boys were sitting at the table, waiting and watching their father. When he appeared with me they asked him, 'May we go now, Dad?'

'Say hello to Isaac first,' Uncle Aaron told them.

'Hello, cousin,' they said. Then, taking another look at their father and their sister, Georgina, they left the room.

All this time, Georgina had been sitting, her face downcast, at the table in the place where her mother had once presided. I walked up to her and went to kiss her cheek.

'No, don't —' she said. She gave a frightened look at her father.

Uncle Aaron laughed again. 'What's wrong with you, Georgina? You've been looking forward to seeing your boyfriend. Give him a kiss.'

Have you ever seen a person with dead eyes? That's how Georgina's looked; behind them, nothing. She raised her face so that I could kiss her lips; they were cold, so cold. Quickly, she got up from her chair, collected some of the dishes and carried them to the kitchen.

Uncle Aaron began to laugh and laugh.

It was then that I knew what was happening.

—

'Your uncle is looking at her,' Aunt Agnes had whispered.

You may well ask how such an obscene thing as incest can happen. How can I explain it to you when, even now, the whole business still doesn't make sense to me? And you may well wonder about the confusion of a sixteen-year-old boy who is confronted with the realisation that such an act has occurred, an act which, it appeared, the adults had been unable to prevent or stop. Can you wonder, therefore, that it was from this time onward that I ceased believing in the capacity of adults to maintain the moral order?

When I returned home, the first words I spoke to my parents were, 'Please tell me it's not true. Please —'

'We tried to stop it,' Mum began. 'When rumours began to surface that Aaron was being intimate with Georgina, your father and I had a long discussion about what should be done. Even though Aaron is the oldest, your father did go over to him and tell him that what he was doing should end.'

I was so angry, I lashed out at Dad. 'Why did you have to wait for Mum to tell you what you should do? Any decent man would have known it was immoral. It's obscene. It's against all the laws of society.'

'Don't you use that tone of voice with me,' my father answered. 'And don't think I didn't do my best. Rewa was horrified, I was horrified, the whole family was horrified, all your uncles and aunties. Your Auntie Leah, she's the oldest girl of the family, she went right over there and tore a strip off him. She yelled at him and then she told Georgina to pack her bags and come with her.'

'But Georgina's still in there,' I moaned, shivering. 'She's still in there. With him —'

'She wouldn't leave her father,' Dad said.

'Because she's afraid of him,' I answered. 'I've seen her. Maybe she doesn't want to leave her brothers. Or maybe Uncle Aaron has threatened her in some way. She needed to be forced to go with Aunt Leah.'

'Well, she didn't want to leave her father,' Dad said, angrily. 'And now they've been together all this time, it's too late to do anything. There's nothing any of us can do.'

'Oh no?' I answered. 'We'll see about that.'

Over the following week I went to my other uncles and aunties.

What did my uncles say? 'How old are you, boy? This is none of your business. It's our business.'

And my aunties? By some strange process they had begun to rationalise the situation and accept it: make it right. But how could anybody find a way to justify what had happened? It beggared the imagination.

Aunt Leah explained it to me in this way: 'Just before your Auntie Agnes died, it was she who called Georgina in on her deathbed. It was she, her own mother, who told Georgina that she should go and lie with her father and give him comfort.'

I couldn't believe my ears. 'Auntie Agnes would never have done such a thing.' Aunt Leah was always making up stories and then making herself believe in them. And her two younger sisters were as gaga as she was.

'To lose a wife is a terrible thing,' Aunt Rebecca added. 'But when that wife paves the way for a man to gain another partner, it is a blessing.'

She signed to Aunt Rebecca, who got the Bible from the cabinet in the sitting room, wet her finger and began to page her way through it. 'The answers can always be found in the Holy Testament,' she began. 'Ah, here we are, Genesis, chapter 19, verse 30. You will recall, nephew, that Lot had just lost his wife. Against the Lord's instructions, she had looked back at the twin cities of Sodom and Gomorrah and had been turned into a pillar of salt. Poor Lot, his two daughters saw that he was disconsolate at the loss — and that he also needed an heir. This is what the Bible says:

> And Lot went up out of Zoar, and dwelt in the mountain, and his two daughters with him; for he feared to dwell in Zoar: and he dwelt in a cave. He and his two daughters. And the firstborn said unto the younger, 'Our father is old, and there is not a man in the earth to come in unto us; Come, let us make our father drink wine, and we will lie with him, that we may preserve the seed of our father . . .' Thus were both the daughters of Lot with child of their father. And the firstborn bore a son, and called his name Moab: the same is the father of the Moabites unto this day. And the younger, she also bore a son, and called his name Ben-ammi: the same is the father of the children of Ammon unto this day.

Aunt Rebecca closed her Bible and looked heavenward. 'In like wise, your cousin Georgina is like one of Lot's daughters. Her union has been sanctified by the example of the two daughters of Lot.'

My mind was reeling with the absolute nature of my aunts' Old Testament beliefs. Certainly, I had grown up within a literal Pentecostal world view — God had made the earth in seven days, the world was flat, man had been made in God's own image and, therefore, there was no such thing as evolution, and so forth — and, again, I had for the most part abided by family strictures relating to its patriarchal hierarchies. But I had never believed in them and, in this instance, Uncle Aaron's incest could not be condoned. I realised how dysfunctional my extended whanau was.

'My aunties, what I cannot understand is that you are all women and yet you have gone along with this disgusting charade. Auntie Leah, if Aunt Agnes was alive, she would call you out for being the liar that you are. Even as she was dying she said to me, "Your uncle is looking at her." Put that on your conscience and live with it, if you dare.'

My aunts looked at me, affronted. 'Whakahihi,' Aunt Rebecca said, the word curling through her mouth. 'Too big for your boots. Know your place, boy. You have no understanding of the pain a man goes through when he loses a wife. And to realise that his own daughter will provide him with solace is a blessing.'

Throughout the rest of the summer I tried to talk to Georgina: on the road as she was passing by, at church on Sundays or down on the marae whenever there was a tribal gathering. But word of my opposition to Uncle Aaron and what he was doing to my cousin had got round the whanau. I had always been considered an outsider so who knew what I might do: go to the police? The family banded together and unified around Uncle Aaron; instead of being supported, therefore, I found myself being cold-shouldered. I was astonished that this would occur but realised that the whanau was moving to protect one among itself — not the innocent one, either.

Oh, today, we see such conspiracies of silence and condonement so often, don't we? For instance, those darling twins whose extended family banded together so that the police would not find the murderer.

And so, whenever I tried to approach Georgina, either Uncle Hohepa or Uncle Aperahama would bar my way, saying, 'She doesn't want to speak to you, boy.' If I crossed the street to try to talk to her, one of my aunties, either Aunt Hera or Aunt Rebecca, would hustle her away and yell at me, 'You're only making things worse.' More painful was that Georgina herself, seeing me approaching, would turn and walk away of her own volition.

In desperation, one morning, I waited until Uncle Aaron had left the house and Georgina was alone with her two brothers. I didn't even bother to knock. I walked right in.

Ramon looked at me, scared. 'You're not supposed to be here,' he said. 'You better get out now.'

'I'm not leaving without Georgina,' I answered. I went down the hallway to her room. It was empty. I found her, instead, in the main bedroom sitting on the bed that had once been the marital bed of her parents.

'Hello, Isaac,' she smiled. 'Just like you, isn't it, to be like young John Ridd in *Lorna Doone* and try to rescue me —'

I sat down beside her. She leant in to me, putting her head on my shoulder. 'You remember?' I asked.

'Yes,' she nodded. 'Of course I remember.' She lightened her voice, as if she was a child and repeated her favourite lines. '"Oh, I am so glad . . . now you will try to be better, won't you?"'

I began to cry. I felt so helpless. 'Come with me,' I said.

'Where shall we go?' she asked. 'There's nowhere to run. Anyway, it's too late.'

'It's never too late,' I protested.

'For me it is,' she answered. 'I belong to my father. I've always belonged to him.'

'By what bizarre logic do you come to that conclusion?' I asked. 'What kind of brainwashing have they done to you?' I recognise the symptoms now: the victim begins to relate to the perpetrator and accepts the acts done against her. But no matter what I tried to tell my cousin — 'Get out of the house, come to Christchurch, come away, now, with me' — it was no use.

She shook her head, bewildered. 'I don't even understand half of what you're saying,' she said. 'All your big words, you're learning a lot at your high school, aren't you?' Pride and envy were in her voice. 'No, it's you who must go and never return. There's no place for you here. Not right now. The whole family's angry with you. I've come between you and your own father. And there's something else. I'm having a baby.'

Her words terrorised me. 'A baby?'

'I'll be a good mother,' Georgina said. 'I'm looking forward to having it. If it's a boy, I'll name him after you.'

Suddenly, we were interrupted by a noise at the door. I heard Uncle Aaron hitting Ramon and William and their cries of pain. Then Uncle Aaron spoke to somebody else: 'They must be in the bedroom.' And Uncle Aaron and my father came into the room. 'I'm here to take you home, son,' my father said. 'Nobody should ever come between a man and his wife.'

'His wife?' I asked incredulously. 'Georgina is not Uncle Aaron's wife. She's his daughter.'

Uncle Aaron's face stilled. I could tell he was angry — but Dad was there. He turned to Isaac Senior and laughed softly. 'Don't worry, brother, real men don't hit cripples.'

I got up from the bed. I think Uncle Aaron was surprised at how fast I could move. What's more, until that time, I don't think he had realised how much I had grown. I was eye to eye now, and he didn't tower over me. 'Real men might not hit cripples,' I said. 'They also don't commit incest with their daughters. As for cripples, we have no problem hitting sexual abusers.'

I slapped him. A good old backhander rather than a punch to the guts.

There's something about slapping a man, particularly when it's done by another man, that is more shocking than using fisticuffs. It sends a different kind of message: 'You are contemptible and, indeed, you are beneath contempt.' No wonder that, in the old days, slapping a man across the face with a glove was prelude to a duel with swords.

Of course Uncle Aaron slammed me. I went down and he put a foot to my throat. But as quick as I could I reached for my cane, aimed it at his stomach and pushed. With a cry of surprise he fell backward. I was up and parrying with him, flicking at his chest, mentally quartering him for the coup de grâce.

What interested me, however, was my father's reaction. 'Don't,' he said. He was enough of a sportsman to recognise that I was preparing to stab Uncle Aaron at his heart.

I put my cane down. I turned to Uncle Aaron. 'Congratulations,' I said. 'Real men do hit cripples after all. But be careful, Uncle. Young boys, even cripples, grow into strong men, and strong men like you grow into old men. When the balance is overturned and you are older and weaker, watch the shadows because I'll be there.' Even then, I used language, if foolishly, very cleverly.

As soon as we returned home, I told my father, 'I am ashamed of you, you are a weakling and you are a coward just like the rest of your brothers and sisters.'

'Apologise to your father,' my mother said.

My Uncle Aaron was indeed godlike. He was so adored and revered that when he took Georgina, his own daughter, 'to wife', nobody was prepared to stop him.

—

The weeks flew past. I received notification from my friend Anthony Walcott, who telephoned from Timaru, that we had both been successful in obtaining university entrance. 'Which university are you going to?' he asked, presuming that I would go on to further academic studies. I turned the question back on him and when he said that he was thinking of Canterbury I told him I would join him there. I raised it with Mum and Dad and they agreed to support me.

I caught the train and boat back to the South Island at the end of summer. My father said, 'Your Uncle Aaron and I have had a talk. Don't come back, son, not for a while anyhow.'

I looked him in the eye. 'Oh, I see,' I answered. 'So your brother comes before your son. Fine, Dad, so what's new. The family that sleeps together stays together, eh, Dad?'

When I arrived in Christchurch I couldn't rest. I telephoned the Christchurch police and made an anonymous report on Uncle Aaron. But police in those days were not as committed about tackling cases of domestic violence, rape or child molestation. My mother did tell me that the police had called on Uncle Aaron one day to make enquiries but they had decided not to press charges. I was flatting with Anthony and a couple of other boys, and in the middle of the night I was called to the phone. When I answered it, Uncle Aaron's voice came down the line, 'I know it was you, Isaac.'

I began my life as a university student. Aunt Hera was passing through Christchurch to go shearing down in Southland and dropped off a parcel from my mother; in it was a polo-necked jersey she had knitted to keep me warm that winter. It was she who told me, 'By the way, your Uncle Aaron and his wife have had a baby girl.' I shivered with anger at the way in which she said it. The fact of the incestuous relationship was being covered up. Georgina was in the process of being erased and, in her place, was a person who looked like her and talked like her but who was now 'Uncle Aaron's wife'.

This is the way it happens in incestuous relationships. Don't give credibility to any versions in which children are not mentioned. That's the convenient version to sanitise the messy reality. Today such births can be aborted, the best way to get rid of any possibility of some monstrous child. Of course that's what the literature leads us to expect — some twisted, deformed baby — which Makareti was not.

And so Makareti came howling into the world.

The night after Aunt Hera visited, I had a dream. I was back in the playground of my primary school and the umpire said, 'Batter up!' I hobbled to the plate, balanced on my cane, swung once, swung twice, and then in a fit of exasperation swung really high and hard — and my bat connected with the ball.

ask the posts of the house

'Quick!' Georgina yelled. But instead of me jumping on her back it was she who jumped onto mine. 'You've got to carry me, cuz,' she said.

My throat was dry. How could I do it? I began to stomp my way towards first base, but the closer I got the further away it was.

'Quickly, Isaac,' Georgina pleaded as she began to slide off my shoulders.

My heart was thumping like mad: 'Laurence, don't give up on me.' I remember every bone-wrenching, juddering, excruciatingly painful step.

'Please, cuz,' Georgina screamed again.

Oh, I tried. I tried so hard, but shadows were gathering all around us — and I stumbled and fell and, when I looked back, Georgina was lying on the ground.

When I awoke, my sheets were drenched with sweat. I grabbed and pulled them around me and gave a deep groan.

'I'm so sorry, Georgina,' I sobbed.

5

'Here we are then, Mr Tairawhiti,' Sofia says as she opens the door. 'Back home safes and sound.'

Like Sefulu, Sofia never calls me by my first name. Even so, she likes to get as up close and personal as possible. You can never keep a physical distance between yourself and Sofia; she doesn't believe in the sanctity of personal space and constantly invades it — as she does now, clucking her concern.

'You not been feeding yourself,' she scolds. 'You are looking too skinnys. But Sofia fix. Got nice chop sueys on the stove and good taro to make you happys.'

'No thank you, Sofia,' I say, trying to squeeze past her and, in the process, copping a whiff of her sweet-scented, coconut-oiled and greased body.

Sofia never likes to be turned down. 'I spend all days making you nice chop suey. You beddah try or Sofia will be very unhappys. And you know what happens when Sofia gets her unhappys.'

'I'm sorry, Sofia,' I say firmly. 'I have more important things on my mind.'

Bad choice of words. Sofia's eyes narrow as she pushes in front of me, carrying my suitcase up the stairs. As usual, whenever she is angry with me, I stop being Mr Tairawhiti and become somebody that she refers to in the third person. 'Somebodys is not being a very nice persons today,' she mutters loudly in my hearing. 'If somebodys keeps this up, Sofia will stop trying to make nice dates for somebodys with nice female ladies.'

Sofia is referring to the large number of Gauguin-tuan women cousins she has tried to fix up for me as blind dates. You know the kind: you see them every time you go supermarket shopping, exotic birds of paradise manning the checkout lanes at Foodtown. Calorifically challenged, the women all appear to have taken some hippopotamic oath; and my most recent date has been with the reigning Cleofatra of the Aisle, Miss Fatuisi Falofasofa.

She was virtuous, not far too easy. And in my unsuccessful wooing we did fall off a sofa.

'Sofia wait until somebodys is in a better mood,' she says as she puts the suitcase down in my bedroom.

'This is my better mood,' I answer.

Sofia leaves muttering her usual imprecations and vile threats. The unpacking can wait until later; meanwhile I take a shower. While I am dressing, the telephone in the bedroom rings: my dear granddaughter, Talia, returning my call. As soon as she hears my voice, 'Isaac Tairawhiti speaking,' she bursts into tears. The sound breaks my heart. 'Don't cry, darling,' I console her.

'Whaea Hera was so awful,' Talia cries. 'She told me so many horrible things about . . . about . . .'

'You mustn't believe what Hera told you,' I answer. 'I will tell you the truth when you arrive tonight and we have our little talk. Yes, at seven o'clock. Don't forget that afterwards we are going to Cibo's, so wear your best dress. I love you, darling.'

Once I have completed the call, I ring the restaurant and make a reservation. 'Your best table, by the window, as private as possible,' I say. Then I ring Aunt Hera and, when she answers the telephone in that smarmy voice of hers, I hang up on her.

Good, she is at home.

I put on a sports jacket, take up my cane and go down the stairs — but I can't escape Sofia. She stands by the door barring my way with a steaming spoonful of chop suey in her right hand. 'Somebodys beddah have a taste before they goes or else —'

I give up to the inevitable and let Sofia have her way. 'Mmmn,' I smile nodding my head and not swallowing. I hurry past her, shut the front door behind me and, when I am out of sight, spit the chop suey into the rosebushes where it will be of better use. It's not that I don't want the chop suey; it's just that in our battle of wills I prefer to win.

'Are we all set?' I ask Sefulu. 'Take me to Manurewa.'

He backs down the drive. Just as we turn into the street he draws my attention to Sofia, who has come onto the terrace and is looking at the roses and the strange brown threads that are hanging off them; she is putting two and two together.

'Somebodys will be for the high jump,' Sefulu says to me, playfully, 'when somebodys gets home later.'

—

Three years after I began university at Canterbury I graduated with a bachelor's degree in commerce. I had made some semblance of peace with my extended whanau and, from time to time, returned home to the valley for the occasional visit.

On one of those visits I bumped into Georgina at church. It was a sunny day and I was overjoyed to see my heart's companion. She was vivacious, with lustrous eyes and skin, and nothing about her gave any sense that she was a victim.

'Isaac! Isaac!' Georgina called. She ran towards me and almost bowled me to the ground when we hugged. 'Isaac, you must meet Makareti,' she said. 'Makareti? Haramai. Come and meet your uncle.'

A shy three-year-old child toddled over to me and, trustingly, put her arms up so I could hold her.

'Hello Makareti,' I said, as I breathed her in. I wasn't accustomed to children but tried my best to make a crook in my arm so that she could lie there while I spoke to her mother.

Georgina and I chatted on the church steps, and she was bright and happy. Across the way I saw Uncle Aaron, but not Ramon or William. 'They left home a few years ago,' Georgina said. 'They were arguing with Dad about me and so he threw them out.' She had blossomed into a young woman saddled with an increasingly aging husband. Not only that, but growing maturity had given her a stronger sense of independence; she was aware and knowing.

For instance, she saw me examining Makareti. Instead of being offended she smiled, 'No, she bears no mark of sin upon her — and to make sure I have no more children I've had my tubes tied. It's better that way. When Makareti was born I had her baptised immediately. The sin is her father's and mine, not hers.'

I was astonished that Georgina had come to this understanding. 'You've done well,' I said.

Uncle Aaron joined us. 'The old boyfriend is back home again,' he laughed. He put out his hand but I did not shake it. He made a gesture that he didn't care about my reaction and motioned to Georgina that it was time they left. Little Makareti skipped ahead in the sunlight.

I happened to glance at Uncle Aaron and the sunlight unmasked him.

Uncontrollably I began to shiver. My memory went back to Auntie Agnes when she had whispered in my ear:

'Your uncle is looking at her.'

I walked swiftly after Georgina and grabbed her arm. She laughed, surprised. 'Yes, Isaac?'

'Be careful,' I said. My mouth was dry with terror.

It wasn't over.

—

Shortly after that visit, my parents Isaac Senior and Rewa came down to Canterbury for my graduation. Afterwards I took them out to dinner with a few friends, including Anthony and a young girl, Felicity, whom I was dating. After dinner, my mother said, 'I like your girlfriend.' Then she added, 'When are you coming home?'

'Not for a while,' I answered. 'I've been offered a scholarship to York University in Toronto, Canada. I think I'll take it.'

I guess I was running away but, don't forget, by that time I was a young man, I had my own life ahead of me, and there was nothing I could do about my cousin Georgina and her situation. Something happens to the mind and memory, and I had anaesthetised myself from thinking about those parts of my life that couldn't be fixed. Why? Of course it was guilt. About not being able to help Georgina. Sure, every now and then I had fantastic ideas about returning to her house and, this time, picking her up in my arms and getting her out of there. But that only happens in sentimental films. Real life is not like that.

My mother was sad that I was travelling even further from home. 'You must come home before you go to Canada,' she said. 'Dad and I would like to give you a twenty-first birthday and the key to adulthood.'

Naturally I couldn't refuse. Part of me also wanted to poke my extended whanau in the eye and show them that, hey, I was doing very well, thank you very much, without their help — and that my clubfoot had not set me back. I invited Felicity, Anthony, my old housemaster Mr Fox and a number of my other university friends to the birthday. When it came, we decided to make an extended four-day weekend visit of it. We were a happy, boisterous group of companions on the long ferry- and train-trip back to the valley.

Mum and Dad were delighted to see us all. I had never realised how gracious a hostess my mother could be until I saw her in action with my friends. 'Please call me Auntie Rewa,' she told them. When I remarked to her how terrific I thought she was, she said, 'I've never had the chance to show you how much I loved you, son. So I'm doing it all at once while I have the chance because, when you go overseas, who knows when I will see you again.'

As for Isaac Senior, he enjoyed having young people in the house and taking them on excursions around the countryside, showing them the marae and the various historic sites of the tribe. 'Isaac Junior has never shown much interest in his Maori side,' Dad told them. As for my extended whanau, it was interesting to see their reaction to my friends, especially to Felicity and Anthony — Felicity's father was a member of parliament and somebody down at the marae clicked on Anthony's surname — Walcott — and realised his father had been a famous All Black. A strange thing happened: I began to go up in my whanau's estimation, primarily because of the divinity conferred upon me by my friends.

The only blot on the long weekend was the absence of Georgina in any of the family and friends get-togethers.

'Things are not going too well between Uncle Aaron and Georgina,' Mum explained. 'They are having a lot of arguments. Your uncle has been violent with Georgina. Just be careful, son, and don't make things worse. Georgina stays in the house; she's so devoted to her daughter and won't let her out of her sight. And sometimes Uncle Aaron won't let any of the family in. I don't understand it at all. When your father went over there to see Aaron and to tell him about your birthday party, he came to the door with a rifle and he told Dad to clear off. "Tell that crippled son of yours I don't want him to set foot on my property, either. I heard what he told Georgina, warning her against me." Why is Aaron angry with you, son? What's it about this time? He's keeping the rest of the family away. It's not a good sign when people do that. And he certainly doesn't want you anywhere near your cousin Georgina. Something's happening in that house. What is it?'

But Uncle Aaron could not stop Georgina from using the telephone. She rang me just before all the guests were due to go down to the marae for the birthday feast.

'I'm sorry, Isaac, that I won't be able to come to your birthday. I would like to, but if I do I have to come alone, and I can't leave Makareti with him. I rang to wish you all the best.'

In the background I could hear Uncle Aaron swearing and Makareti crying.

'Are you all right?' I asked Georgina.

'You were right to warn me,' she said.

—

The evening was lovely and warm, with just enough of a breeze to take off the heat of the day. The extended whanau had pitched in, helping to elevate the party to one of those family occasions that would long be remembered because the food was the best, the drink never ran out, and everybody boogied till dawn. The marae was strung with lightbulbs and the dining hall was festooned with balloons and streamers. When Mum and Dad and my friends walked through the door I was surprised to see the rest of the whanau arrayed in their evening finery preparing to give us a rousing welcome.

'Karangatia ra! Karangatia ra! Powhiritia ra, nga whanau o te motu!'

Auntie Rebecca and Auntie Hera kicked off their shoes and sang and danced as if their lives depended on it. Behind them, my uncles Hohepa and Aperahama led the men, stamping their feet and punching the air. Behind the group, Auntie Leah was presiding in the kitchen. Outside the window, I saw my two other uncles, Rawiri and Horomona, tending the hangi; sparks from the earth oven were sizzling in the air. Joining the welcoming group were cousins whom I remembered, like Bella, and aunts by marriage, like Hariata. Others I recalled as having followed after me when I was a boy, imitating my lurching walk and laughing at me. Many of them I didn't know at all.

Anthony turned to me. 'Wow,' he said, 'what a wonderful family.'

I am sorry to say that my cynicism had the best of me. 'Yes,' I nodded. 'We put on a good show.'

Was I wrong about my family? In all the years I was growing up in their bosom, was I the one who was dysfunctional and not them? Had I made the effort to know them, really get to know them?

I looked at my parents. Although my father had never said he loved me, Isaac Senior was standing up tall and as proud as a soldier. My mother has always been sentimental. There she was, gripping onto Dad's arm, looking at him as if to say, 'See? See how the whanau honours our son?'

The celebration proceeded. We sat down to the huge birthday feast. Tray after tray of food came out of the kitchen, and Auntie Leah wobbled regularly to my side in newly purchased high-heels to ask, 'Is the kai all right, nephew?' The mutton, chicken and fish were brought in from the earth oven and, unaccustomed as I was to Maori gesture, I managed a fair enough thumbs-up sign to Uncle Horomona. During the dinner the usual speeches were presented; the ones from Uncles Hohepa and Horomona were filled with heroic memories of myself that I couldn't remember — perhaps they had mistaken me for somebody else. Anthony told stories of riotous evenings when we had gone on the town, which proved that I was just as bad a bloke as everybody else in the dining room. Mr Fox rescued my reputation by praising Mum and Dad for having such a brilliant young son of whom great things were expected.

The highlight came when Dad presented me with a huge silver key with glittering ribbons tied to it. 'Son, you are now an adult,' he said. 'Open the doorway to adulthood and go through.'

All the while, I was watching him. In my mind I was pleading for him, 'Say it, say it, Dad, say that although I am a cripple you love me.' But he never did.

I made a suitable reply. I realised that occasions like birthdays were really opportunities to say not only 'We want to honour you' but also 'We want to tell you how sorry we are for any misdeeds between us. It's time to move on.' Birthdays were times of forgiveness as well as unity. I thanked Mum and Dad and the family for the occasion. I apologised for my long absences from everyone but assured them that I always knew where I belonged. I forgot all the skeletons in the family cupboard and, instead, dwelt on the good memories. My uncles and aunts sighed with relief at my diplomacy. For one night, at least, I was a good and obedient son of the whanau.

The tables were cleared. It was time for some serious dancing. Cousin Bella's boyfriend was a singer in a well-known band and had brought his players from the nearby city. The band dutifully played a waltz to begin with; I bravely made a few hesitant steps with my mother, enough to fulfil the requirement. Then Auntie Leah yelled out, 'Gee, you boys sure play slow!' and, next minute, it was all on. I led my mother back to the group of oldies clucking with disapproval in the corner, got a glass of champagne and went outside for a breath of fresh air. I looked across the starlit fields to a dark house among a copse of small trees. I lifted the glass.

'To us, Georgina,' I toasted.

—

It was just before dawn, a few hours after Mum and Dad, Felicity, Anthony, Mr Fox and I had managed to make our tipsy way home, that I was suddenly woken up by a sharp, loud sound. I was puzzled by it, listened for it again, and tried to get back to sleep. But the telephone rang and I saw the light switch on in the hallway as Dad answered it. He came to my bedroom. 'It's your cousin Georgina,' he said. 'She wants to talk to you. Something's happened at your Uncle Aaron's house. We better get over there.'

I went to the telephone. 'Is that you, Isaac?' Georgina asked. Her voice was small and sad. 'Will you come to the house to see me?'

My heart filled with dread. Dad was already backing the car out of the garage. I dressed quickly and joined him. We sped along the road and turned in at Uncle Aaron's driveway. As we were approaching the house, Auntie Leah appeared in the headlights; she lived next door to Uncle Aaron and, when she heard the same sharp report as I had, she had gone to investigate. She was in her dressing gown and she waved us down. When Dad opened the window of the car she ignored me and spoke to him.

'It's Georgina,' she said. 'I think she's shot our brother. She's got his rifle and won't let anyone in the house.'

Dad drove into the front yard. A few other people from the village had gathered. Among them was Uncle Horomona; he was trying to talk to Georgina through the front door.

'Go away,' she called. 'Don't anybody try to come in.'

I was out of the car in a flash. 'Georgina? It's me.'

'Isaac?' The door opened a little, and the muzzle of the rifle poked through.

'Let's rush her,' Uncle Horomona said.

'No,' I answered. 'She will talk to me. Don't anybody make a move until I come back out. Is that understood?'

I walked up to the door. Georgina opened it further, smiled, and said, 'Come in, cousin.' She had Makareti with her, trying to hush her. 'Will you take Makareti out? And then return to me?' She kissed Makareti. 'Stop crying now, darling. Go with Uncle Isaac.'

I took Makareti and gave her to Auntie Leah. 'Oh, thank God that the baby is unharmed,' she said.

When I went back into the house, Georgina was in the main bedroom sitting on the bed. She looked as if she hadn't slept for weeks; she had dark circles under her eyes and her face was filled with fatigue. Uncle Aaron was lying in the bed, still alive, his chest bloodied from a bullet wound. He was breathing hoarsely, his eyes wide with fear.

'Get help,' he whispered. 'Get help for me. I don't want to die.'

Georgina patted his hand. 'There, there, Dad.' Then she looked up at me. 'Will you stay with me, Isaac?' she asked. 'I have to wait until he has gone from this life. I've got no strength left to keep watching him. I'm so tired, cousin, and I want to sleep. I had to kill him; it's better this way. He's been interfering with Makareti, and he has to pay. It's what happens with men who have no boundaries. There's just one last thing to do, and that is stay awake long enough to make sure he is dead.'

We waited. Uncle Aaron tried to get out of bed; Georgina restrained him. He pleaded with her, sobbing for forgiveness, but she only nodded her head and settled him down again.

Outside I heard more cars arriving, car doors slamming, and raised voices. 'What's going on? What's happening?'

Very soon, Uncle Aaron stilled. I took his pulse. I nodded to Georgina, 'He's gone.'

Georgina closed his eyes and, with a strange tenderness, kissed both his cheeks. 'You are the only one I can trust,' Georgina said to me. 'I want your mother to bring up my baby. Nobody else. Auntie Rewa.'

She gave a deep sigh. Before I could stop her, she slammed the rifle butt between her feet, bent her chest over the barrel, reached down for the trigger and pressed it. The sound was shockingly loud in the room. The smell of cordite was acrid. I heard somebody cracking open the front door. Dad and Uncle Horomona burst into the room.

I caught Georgina as she fell. 'No, Georgina!' I cried. I was raging that this was happening, despairing at the unfairness of it all.

'Promise me you will look after Makareti,' she said.

'I promise,' I answered.

There was blood everywhere, and gouts of blood were coming out of Georgina's mouth every time she exhaled. 'Makareti is not to be told who her father was. Nobody is to know the secret. Promise me.'

She gave a huge gasp and her eyes started to flicker. 'Oh cousin, if I go to hell will you come and get me?'

The sun burst across the hills.

6

And now Sefulu and I leave the safety of Auckland. He turns the car off the motorway, and we are in another country.

South Auckland is the Maori and Pasifika part of the city. Sometimes Makareti loves to bring me and the boys here to the Otara Market before letting us loose at Rainbow's End. 'Time you had a walk on the wild side,' she likes to tease me. 'Get you out of Hernia Bay or Pon-snobby or Gay Lynn and among real live mean-as people. You know, Dad, your own colour? Anyway, they could do with some of your money down here! But don't flash it around too obviously will you, you fatcat you.'

Makareti forgets that I have visited quite a few dangerous neighbour-hoods in my time: black shantytowns in Johannesburg, Hispanic hotspots in Los Angeles, slums in Rio de Janeiro — and to prove that I'm not colourblind, I've even been in the middle of white supremacist riots in Hamburg. However, I must admit that there are parts of South Auckland which are on a par with the worst of any international metropolises: streets filled with crims, dealing P and other drugs on the corners, where every second house has a high fence, and gangs have pitbulls roaming the perimeter. The media is filled with stories of boys who seek their patch memberships by killing other young boys at bus stops, robbing some friendly local Indian shopkeeper or throwing rocks off overbridges at cars on the motorway. You take your life into your own hands when you visit South Auckland.

'It's the grey house, isn't it, Mr Tairawhiti?' Sefulu asks. He has turned into a cul de sac and is pointing to the third house in the crescent. I own the house: when Auntie Hera decided to leave the village and come to Auckland to stay with her daughter and that hopeless gang of crims her daughter supports — her tattooed freak of a husband, Bojangles, and two layabout brutish sons Ace and Rooter — they had no place to stay. I bought them the house as part of my — let's call it — layby deal to keep Auntie Hera in line on family matters. Well, she has just welshed on the deal and I might just kick her out on the street.

Sefulu pulls in at the kerb, trying to avoid the broken bottles from last weekend's kerbside party. The front of the house is littered with a broken-down car and miscellaneous junk. I sit there, having another of my headaches, wondering about Hera's viciousness. What did she say to Talia?

Nothing is ever ended. You think it is, but when you're not looking, it comes from out of nowhere. Although there have been so many fantastic achievements in the world — technological developments that attest to man's huge capacities of intelligence — has the world learnt anything about the human heart? The joys it can experience? The depths it can plunge to? I have seen so much of man's glorious achievements in the great cities of the world. But I have also seen so much of man's inhumanity to man in Asia, the Middle East and South America — child prostitution, slave trafficking, political killings — even in rotten little streets in middle America, let alone middle New Zealand. Something has gone wrong in the world. Lift up any brick to any front door for the key, but don't open the door and go in. There's something rotten in every house, even in this Godzone country of ours.

For all our magnificent achievements, are we better human beings? I think not.

'Time for the showdown,' I say to Sefulu. I take a deep breath, open the door of the car and step out. I see the front curtains open and Hera's face looking out of the window. I hear her yell to Ace and Rooter. Quickly, I give Sefulu his instructions: 'I want you to go to the front door. Hera will have her two boys blocking the way. But if I know her, she'll try to get out the back. You keep the boys occupied while I deal to her.'

Sefulu and I walk quickly to the front door. 'What the fuck do you want?' Rooter asks. Sefulu diverts their attention while I walk as fast as I can to the backyard. I am just in time. The door opens and Hera steps out, a lumbering antiquity, making for the garage, fumbling with the keys to her car.

'Going somewhere?' I ask her. I put out my cane and, with a yelp, she trips over it and falls on her driveway. I take my cane and give her a good, hard belt on her big black arse. 'I want to know every venomous word you spat at my granddaughter, you disgusting old bitch.' While I am not known for bad language there are times when it is the only means of communication that lowlifes can understand.

'Talia's not your granddaughter,' Hera whimpers, trying to scrabble away from me. She calls for her two sons and I hear them respond — but Sefulu is already dealing to them, keeping them under control.

'Wrong answer,' I say to Hera, and I give her another whack, this time across her kidneys; it feels good to lay into her. 'Is that what you told her? That I'm not her grandfather? What else did you say? What did you tell her about Uncle Aaron?'

Aunt Hera groans and, when I raise my cane again, she cries out, 'No!' She sits there, panting, having a weep to herself, but I am not swayed by her worthless tears. 'I told Talia that you weren't her grandfather, that you weren't Makareti's father and as for her whakapapa, it was shonky.' Aunt Hera is regaining her defiance. Another stroke of my cane, this time across her face, should keep her in submission.

'Did you tell her about Uncle Aaron —'

I wait with inward breath for her response.

'No.'

'— and the night Georgina killed him?'

'No. But she's heard the rumours all her life. And now she's a big girl, she can put two and two together all by herself. She doesn't need me or anybody else to join the dots for her. She knows, in her heart she knows.'

I lean against the house and watch as Hera gets up. 'You better pray that she doesn't know,' I say to her. 'Because if she does, I'm coming back.'

I leave her there and walk back to the car. Seeing me, Sefulu stops belting into Ace and Rooter. But Hera is not finished; she has one last lot of venom to spit out.

'That girl was always too whakahihi,' she yells. 'Always showing off how educated she is. She needed to be brought down a peg or two. Somebody had to tell her that she has tainted blood. She's not as good as the rest of us, and she never will be. She's lucky that the sin doesn't show in her but she better watch out — it will come out in her own kids, if she has any, sooner or later.'

Sefulu has to restrain me from going back and killing her.

'Hera, none of us will be safe until you are six feet under the ground. I hope that day comes soon. And when you die, nothing, not your Bible or your prayers, is going to save you. God knows what you've done. He saw you when you allowed your brother to commit incest with his daughter. You should have stopped it then. None of you did. And did you deal with the mess? No, I had to, and I am still dealing with it. May God have mercy on your soul.'

—

The mess — there was a lot of it following that day when Georgina shot and killed Uncle Aaron. Of course, our family, with its Pentecostal beliefs, vilified her. After all, she was the murderer and she had also killed herself. What possible place could she have before the throne of God? Was she brought onto the marae and farewelled in the appropriate manner? No. But Uncle Aaron was. I made sure to be at his funeral; I wanted to make sure he was in his coffin. I didn't leave until the lid was screwed down.

As for Georgina, she was buried just outside the family graveyard, but over the years, I have forcibly managed to get the fenceline altered. I delayed my trip to Canada to give evidence at the inquest. I told the judge about the incest. The family were angered that I would make it public.

The judge awarded custody of Makareti to my parents, Isaac Senior and Rewa. Although my mother had been shocked and saddened by the events that had overtaken the family, and worried about being able to look after a young child, she soon came to delight in the task. Makareti became Mum's baby cast upon the waters of the Nile and I started to call her Mrs Moses.

After the whole affair had quietened down I took Makareti to visit Georgina's grave. While we were sitting there, digging the earth so that

Makareti could plant her daisies and daffodils, I kept thinking about what to do about my promises to Georgina concerning Makareti's parentage and keeping everything secret.

The answer was simple. I spoke to Mum and Dad and they agreed. I then spoke to my extended whanau and, although there were some voices in dissent, particularly those of Auntie Leah and Auntie Hera, the consensus ruled.

I became Makareti's father. Although Mum and Dad brought her up, I adopted her. On the family whakapapa, Makareti's line shows that I am her dad and Georgina is her mother, and that my parents are her grandparents. I've managed to erase Uncle Aaron in the same way that he had tried to erase my cousin Georgina when he took her 'to wife'.

The whole business of the shooting and Georgina's suicide has been kept a secret by family pact. It has been easier to keep the secret as the old people die. But to make sure the secret is kept, I have been paying off those like Hera who still know of it. Not any longer; Hera is on her own.

As for me, I have never married. While I am attracted to women and have the occasional affair, I really am not the kind of man that women marry.

7

Later.

It is ten minutes to seven and I am back in my house, expecting Talia. I think of her grandmother, my cousin Georgina. There's a room two inches behind the eyes where all my memories are kept. For as long as I live, Georgina will always inhabit that room, safe from the world, safe from pain.

I've had to eat some of Sofia's chop suey and also send Sefulu to the doctor to get six stitches to the cut across his forehead from his fisticuffs with Ace and Rooter. I'll buy him and Sofia a big screen — that should put them both in Arnie Schwarzenegger movie heaven.

Showered and shaved, I am dressed in a sports coat and beige trousers. I've spoken to Makareti again and reassured her that my meeting with Talia will go well. Makareti has asked if I want to take Huey, Dewey and Louey to Rainbow's End this weekend. I remember a previous visit when an old man had come up to me and Makareti and complimented her on the family. Huey was puzzled. 'But we're just a normal family like everybody else, aren't we, Mum? Aren't we, Papa?'

—

Oh, there did come a time when Makareti was in her teens that somebody whispered to her, just like Hera has whispered to Talia — perhaps it was Hera that time also, she's always been so vindictive — that her family history was a lie. I can remember Makareti coming crying and wailing to me, just as Talia will be doing soon.

When it happened, I recalled the story of Hinetitama, Girl of the Dawn, whose mother had been made of clay. She grew up a very beautiful young woman and Tane, her father, desired her. He made her his wife and in the fullness of time, she bore a daughter.

But Hinetitama wanted to know the lineage, or whakapapa, so that she could tell her daughter. She knew who her mother was but she didn't know who her father was. When she asked Tane, he was evasive. In the end he said to her, 'Ask the posts of the house.'

The Maori meeting house is a world of its own. It has a head which you see when you approach from the outside and, when you enter, you are within the body of the house. You are literally within the stomach of the tribal ancestor who begat the tribe and with whom the tribe is associated. There are a number of carved posts which support the structure of the meeting house; the main ones are the poutokomanawa, the heart post, and the poutahuhu, the ridge post. In the old days, the pou, which also included wall posts, were said to be living, sacred, able to talk.

When Hinetitama entered the whare with her child she put her question to the posts of the house: 'Who is my father?' The first post answered, 'Tane the husband is also Tane the father.' Hinetitama would not believe the response so she asked the second post. Again the reply came back, 'Tane is both the father and the husband.' Still she wouldn't believe the answer. And so she asked every post of the house and when they all responded, 'Tane, Tane, Tane, Tane,' she realised the truth. This was the First Incest.

Hinetitama was the first of all the women of the world to take the blame upon herself; not the man but the woman. She was overwhelmed with shame. She was not worthy to stay in the overworld, the world of light. She therefore resolved to go to the underworld, Te Po, the world below. There, within the womb of Papa, the Earth Mother, she could find sanctuary and, possibly, redemption.

By means of a powerful karakia, Hinetitama therefore weakened Tane so that he would not follow her. Once he was incapacitated, she hastened to Rarohenga. At the entrance to the underworld she was confronted by the guard, Kuwatawata, who told her, 'Turn back, turn back before it is too late. All light and all pleasure lie behind you. The spirit world is before you. If you enter here you will never be able to return.'

But Hinetitama knew that she had to go onward. After all, her children, the children who were half godly and half earthly, would at some time have to suffer death. Her husband, Tane, could look after them in life; she chose to look after them in death.

When Tane arose from sleep and realised what she had done, he managed to reach her just before she turned to enter the underworld. Weeping, he said, 'Please don't go.'

Her words to him? They were of love and of sacrifice. 'Haere atu, Tane. Hapainga nga tamariki i te Ao. Go back, husband and father. Go back to the light and raise our children. And when they grow old and die, let me lovingly gather them in.'

Hinetitama achieved her transcendence. She became Hinenuitepo, which some have translated as 'The Goddess of Death'. I say to you, look to the literal translation of her name: just as the full name of Tane is Tanenuiarangi, Great Father of the Overworld, let us acknowledge Hinenuitepo's nurturing role. Malevolent Kali-like Goddess of Death? With eyes of paua, locks of hair — medusae of barracuda — and vaginal dentata? No. She is Great Mother of the Underworld. Hers is the redemptive role and it is through her that we achieve forgiveness.

—

Seven o'clock. I'm getting nervous.

I have opened the sliding doors and am looking across the front terrace. I want to be able to see Talia when she arrives. I plan to smile at her reassuringly and welcome her into my arms.

I am having a gin and tonic, but my hands are trembling and the ice is clinking like icebergs ready to sink the *Titanic*. I am not usually as anxious as this. Is that my Talia now? Stopping her car and stepping out of it?

If it is, I better wipe my eyes, otherwise she'll see that her stupid old grandfather has been crying — and that would not do my reputation as a stern old goat any good.

Shall I tell her the truth? Or shall I keep telling her the lie? Why should she take on the burden of something that was not her fault? Must the sins of the father continue to be visited on the heads of the children?

I stand to greet her. My clubfoot is aching badly. She looks up at me, her eyes glowing. 'Papa? Papa —'

Oh, how I love this child so. Makareti's daughter. Georgina's granddaughter. My mokopuna. My granddaughter.

And in the gentling night I tell her what I want her to hear.

in the year of prince harry

1

Here I am, lying in the dark, and I have absolutely no idea how I got here.

The last clear memory I have is of all my friends singing 'Happy birthday, Oliver'; the rest is a jumble of images of leaving the restaurant where the party was being held and heading for K Road. From that point onward it would be better not to scare the old ladies or horses.

Nor am I in my own bed. Mine is king-sized, with a hollow in the middle. The bed I currently find myself in is single, flat, and if I move a few centimetres I'll fall out of it. What's stopping me are the arms and legs of somebody holding me very tightly around my neck and ankles. Because here's the thing: whoever's bed this is, somebody else is in it.

Probably the owner.

Did I tell you that the bedroom — I presume that's where I am — is as black as pitch? Not even the luminous dial of a bedside clock or the comforting glow of a standby light from a CD player or television set. When I tried earlier to get up, I banged my head. I am in a *bunk*. And the other person beside me? From what I can make out he's young, smooth-skinned, has lots of luxuriant hair and all his teeth — the front ones feel as if they are capped — and, oops, he's buck naked.

Time to bail out.

I extricate myself from the tangle of the hunk in the bunk and fall a very long way to the floor. It's not a bunk after all; rather, the bed is an elevated platform in one of those modern Auckland apartment blocks put up by property developers who should be shot by a firing squad at dawn: two rooms if you're lucky, rented out to bachelor or bachelorette junior office executives, MBA students, or Asians in town to gamble at Sky City. Once I hit the floor I grope for my clothes: underpants, shirt, jeans, socks and boots. Out the door. Get my bearings. Yes, I am still in Auckland, thank God for that. Still dressing in the lift, I manage to tie my laces before I get to the lobby. When I exit into the dawn I flag down a taxi, 'Grey Lynn, thanks.'

'Nice night, mate?' the taxi driver asks.

'I'm not too sure,' I answer, and I wonder why he laughs. He's still chuckling when he drops me off at the big house close to Westmere that I share with Geoff, the owner, and Vladimir, a flautist from Prague. Geoff has the front half of the house and I can hear Ravel's *Bolero* playing through the walls. Vladimir has a room to one side of the hall and mine is on the other, sunnier, side of the house.

I put the key in the lock and it opens. Immediately, Horace comes ambling down the hall, dragging his lead with him. Oh no, he wants to be taken for his morning walk. 'Not now, Horace,' I say, 'I'm dying for a shower. Good boy, let's do it later.' But Horace begins to growl in a way that hints that he will brook no delay. He's a big old Alsatian, wouldn't hurt a fly, I've had him for years, but once his mind is made up nothing will change it. He butts me away from the door, down the steps and onto the pathway.

I accept the inevitable. 'You rotten, ungrateful, uncaring sod,' I say to him; there's no doubt who rules this house. As I am clipping on his lead, Victoria, my neighbour across the road, springs past on her usual marathon morning run.

Only later, when I have reached the place where Horace likes to lift his leg outside a furniture shop in Grey Lynn — the owners once caught him at it and berated me for the way the shop's paintwork was becoming discoloured — do I realise that in my haste to leave the apartment I have left my wristwatch behind.

2

People say that things always look better the morning after the night before, but my experience is that they look worse. What's more, the other people involved seem to know everything that happened, and are more than happy to hint at every gruesome detail.

'Nice party,' Geoff says when I finally rise from the hollow in my bed. 'You were really enjoying yourself.'

'What did I do?' I ask him. He is sitting out on the patio with the latest in the never-ending line of young women who come to learn the cello from him. He pats the young woman on her thigh and I realise that she has stayed overnight.

'You mean before or after you mooned everybody?' he answers. You can always tell when Geoff has got a girl with him. He plays Ravel's *Bolero*, a fastish version conducted by Charles Munch which takes fourteen minutes and fifty-seven seconds. The *Bolero* starts softly, the same tune repeating over and over; it's one of the most insinuating and erotic pieces of music ever composed. By the halfway mark the timpani drums are getting louder and louder and the music is becoming positively orgasmic. There's a key change around three minutes from the end when the music reaches the point of no return and '. . . all you can do,' according to Geoff, 'is charge on like a member of the light brigade'. While the brass is blaring and the timpani drums are thrumming, Geoff is thundering through the pass and up the valley, sabre drawn.

At that moment, Vladimir turns up. 'Oh good, we are wake up,' he says. 'We must not forget extra rehearsal this afternoon.'

'Bugger,' I answer. I had indeed forgotten that the orchestra is scheduled to play Tchaikovsky's Fourth Symphony in two weeks' time, hence the additional run-through so that we can all rise to some sense of competency in this fiendishly difficult work.

'But we don't want to be seen with Oliver today,' Vladimir continues, shaking a finger. 'You were werry naughty bad boy at party, Oliver, and do stupid things undressing Adrienne on top of table when people yell "Take it off! Take it off!" And why, when Celestine try to make you both stop you put birthday cake down Celestine's nice breasts? I have to take you away from restaurant in my car very quick. Celestine ring this morning early to make sure I have not been stupid silly boy like you. But I tell her I drop you off at Karangahape Road and come straight home to going to bed like innocent wirr-tuous wirr-gin.'

Vladimir, Geoff and I are all players in the city orchestra. Vladimir is having an affair with Celestine, the harpist, who doesn't mind the lugubrious and tortured nature of his Eastern European mentality; this has, however, angered Adrienne, who plays the viola — she gave Vladimir the heave-ho but now wants him back. Caught in the middle, Vladimir expects the worst to happen and, when it does, he will no doubt accept it with a stoic fatalism. For him, life is always werry, werry difficult.

Matters do not improve at the rehearsal. As I seat myself among the first violins, Adrienne asks me, 'What did you do with my bra?' and Celestine pokes me in the ribs and says, 'You owe me fifty dollars for my dry-cleaning.'

The maestro, Geraldo 'Ben Hur' De Montalk, decides to start the rehearsal by taking us through the third movement of the Tchaikovsky Fourth. Twenty minutes in, and it's clear that none of the players has recovered from the party. The maestro puts his baton down with a weary sigh. 'Ladies and gentlemen, please note that in the Scherzo, Tchaikovsky has given the instructions *pizzicato ostinato* and *allegretto*. Could we give Mr Tchaikovsky what he wanted and make it more light and lively?' He turns to me with a smile. 'Mr Goodenough, are you still with us? Synapses not firing very well this afternoon?'

I rest my bow and smile back at him. The players don't call him Ben Hur for nothing: sometimes, as today, he likes to think he's Charlton Heston driving us like a chariot around the Colosseum. If he doesn't watch out I'll *pizzi* all over his lovely sports *cato* and I won't have any *allegretto* about it, either.

Robert, the CEO of the orchestra, comes in just as we finish for the day. 'Ladies and gentlemen,' he begins, 'may I have your attention please? I know you need no reminding but, just in case, I hope you have all pencilled into your diaries your individual photo shoots next week.'

Sally, our lovely PR person, has had the bright idea that all members of the orchestra should pose with our instruments for a calendar that will help raise money for our cash-strapped organisation. I give Robert a suitable affirmative grunt but all I want to do right now is buy a new watch and then go back to the house and to bed; it's taken years of prodding, pressing, shoving and moulding to hollow the mattress out so that, like a happy hippo, I can slip, slide and wallow into it whenever I've had a bad day. As I am leaving the rehearsal room, Jack from the horns section slaps me on the shoulders. 'What a great party! But if I were you, I wouldn't go back to that restaurant again for a while. What a mess! I especially liked the way you mooned the proprietor from the car window as Vladimir sped you off to safety.'

Oh my God, maybe it was *true*.

3

Have you ever felt that life is picking on you?

You know, you can be blissfully lying around doing no harm to anybody and life insists on sending you a message from some higher power. Take your pick: Buddha, God, Allah, Kali, Jehovah, Papatuanuku, the Wirr-gin Mary, Father Christmas, the Tooth Fairy, the Force, Whoever.

That's what happens to me this morning, a few days after my party, when I am sunning myself on the patio, cottonwool in my ears against Geoff's infernal *Bolero*. All is otherwise happy with the world: Horace is cross-eyed with delirium, burying a bone in the rose garden, Vladimir is practising a tricky passage that comes up in the Tchaikovsky and I am watching the seagulls weaving lovely patterns across the inner harbour . . . when one chooses me out of all the millions of people in the world to void his breakfast onto: ready, aim, splatter, bullseye.

War is declared on all seabird species and their infernal faeces.

Swearing, I go inside to clean myself and, while I am in the bathroom, I hear the telephone ringing. Why doesn't Vladimir pick it up? It's still ringing when I come out and I notice that, like me, he has cottonwool in his ears. 'Hello?' I ask grumpily. 'May I help you?'

It's a voice I haven't heard for a few months. 'Is that you, Oliver?'

'Laurence,' I reply, with a smile of pleasure. 'How nice to hear from you.' Laurence is my ninety-one-year-old father-in-law. The poor man lost his wife Mereana six years ago. Hounded by his four daughters (my late wife Fleur was daughter number five until she died) — all of whom felt it was their duty as whanau to have Papa live in the room at the back — he ran away to hide among the Pakehas in an old people's home up at Orewa.

I've always had a great deal of affection for Laurence, an old Maori Battalion veteran — mainly because he took my side when I came out. After Fleur died and I went through the 'change', as Anahera, his eldest daughter, darkly put it, he took it all in his stride. 'Look, daughter,' he said to her in a fit of exasperation, 'better for Oliver to remain faithful to Fleur than to go out with another woman.' Anahera stared at him as if he was mad.

'So, Oliver,' Laurence coughs, 'are you doing anything important on the third weekend of July?'

I can hear from the tone of his voice that he is working himself up to some request. He probably wants me to go out skindiving at midnight and bring him a sack of illegal paua or kina for some boil-up at the home. Or drive up to Orewa to collect him and take him shopping for thermal underwear; he knows I won't walk into the changing room while he's doing a down trou, like his four daughters do, to see if the thermals fit. Or maybe he wants me to take him to the tangi of one of his old soldier mates . . . but how would he know one was going to die in July?

I look at the calendar. Four weeks from now. 'That weekend happens to be free,' I answer him, mystified.

'That's good,' Laurence says. 'I am getting married again to a nice lady I have met here in the home.'

'You old bugger,' I roar with laughter. 'Good on you.'

'I'm glad you are pleased for me,' Laurence answers. 'Esther's a good woman, much younger than me — eighty-six — but I think we can get over the age difference. She's a widow, hasn't been here long and, well, we've been keeping each other warm at nights. The trouble is I have to sneak over to her room because we're not allowed to cohabit. If we get married, we can stay together without all this sneaking around. It'll be cheaper, too.'

'Esther? That's a lovely name.'

'She's a Pakeha lady, though,' Laurence continues, 'so Anahera is not going to like it.'

I am well acquainted with Anahera's attitude from her reaction to my relationship with Fleur. When we got married, Anahera talked their other sisters Pearl, Whena and Kara into trying to convince Fleur not to do it; Pakeha were a no-no.

Then Laurence lays his bundle on me. 'I would like you to be my best man,' he says.

His offer takes my breath away, and I am truly touched. 'I'd be honoured,' I reply.

'Don't get too carried away,' Laurence cautions. 'The reason I am asking you is because all my brothers and mates of my age are dead. Apart from those sons of mine, Hemi and Joe-Joe, you're the only other male I know.'

'Laurence,' I joke, 'I'd quit while I was ahead if I was you.'

'One more thing,' Laurence asks, thinking he's on a roll. 'Could you tell Anahera?' In Maori, Anahera means Angel. Yeah, right.

'Sorry, Laurence,' I answer quickly. 'You're on your own there.'

—

The next day, on my way to lunch with Rawiri, Dylan and Eru, I am still stoked that my father-in-law has asked me to be his best man.

'Hi Dad,' Eru greets me when I park my car and walk across Ponsonby Road to his restaurant. 'How's it hanging? Amay-zing birthday last week. So what's it like being forty-nine? The big five-oh next year, right?' He's always been a tease, my youngest, constantly trying to wind me up; I refuse to rise to his bait and follow him to a table he's set up for us out front on the pavement. Traffic is zooming past rattling the cutlery, rocking the wine glasses and covering the food with a lovely petrol glaze.

'Are your brothers coming?' I ask.

Eru nods his head. 'Rawiri has just called from his cellphone that the traffic on spaghetti junction is diabolical but he's on his way. And didn't Dylan tell you? He's a prosecution witness in a drug bust, but he expects to be here for the mains. Now, Dad, I'm trying out a new wine that I think you'd like, a lovely pinot noir.' He calls one of his waiters to open it, sniffs the bouquet, and sighs with pleasure. 'Man, I love it already.'

My three grown-up sons and I meet for lunch every third Wednesday of the month. Our lives are all very busy but there are very few lunches that we have missed. Rawiri is twenty-five and an up-and-coming investment banker. He was supposed to be named Aubrey, which was my father's name, but Fleur wouldn't hear of it when she discovered it meant 'fairy king'. Dylan is twenty-three, and although he's younger than Rawiri, he's always been the leader of the bunch; his brothers have, by dint of his forceful personality, meekly fallen into line behind him. It's no surprise to any of us that he is a detective in the police force; when he was a nasty little boy, if his brothers were bad, instead of saying 'I'm going to tell Daddy' he would threaten to arrest them and put them in jail. Dylan always begrudged the fact that his was the only European name among his brothers and, one day, I found him busy at home constructing an alarming-looking contraption which he told me was going to be an electric chair — 'For you, Daddy,' he said darkly. As for Eru, he is Dylan's twin, the one who was hiding in the corner of Fleur's womb. Eru has always loved food and good wine. Feeding people is what makes him happy — and buying them presents, too. He's a bit of a Christmas psycho when the festive season comes along, always buying multiple prezzies for us. However, the gesture has to be reciprocated and woe betide any of us if we are one present short.

When the opportunity came for Eru to buy this restaurant he asked his brothers if they would like to stake him in it. Good oldest brother that he is, Rawiri did all the paper work and due diligence; and Dylan ensures that just about the entire police force of Auckland eats there. They are both signed on as Eru's silent partners.

Eru is looking at my hair in a strange way. 'What?' I say.

'There's something white in it,' Eru answers. 'Looks like bird shit. I'll wipe it away with a paper napkin.' Then he looks even closer.

'I'm not going bald, am I?' I ask, alarmed. After all, the late forties is the Season of Falling Hair.

'Let me see,' he says, shifting his chair behind me. My sons are all six-footers, a good four inches taller than I am, and Eru is able to look down on my scalp. I can feel his fingers carefully parting my hair. Then, 'Dad,' he continues, 'if I tell you the truth will you promise not to cut me out of your will?'

At that moment, Dylan arrives, parking his police car opposite where we are sitting. 'What's going on?' he asks. 'You two look like monkeys in a zoo. Have you got nits, Dad?'

Eru ignores his brother and continues with the task at hand. 'Dad is anxious that he is becoming follicly challenged,' he tells Dylan.

Dylan joins us at the table. 'You should have kept using Regaine, Dad. And don't you think it's time you stopped dyeing it? Brindle is a look that you only see on the backs of dogs.'

Then Rawiri turns up in his BMW. All my sons are handsome but Rawiri is something else. He has Fleur's olive skin, and a shock of blond curly hair and piercing blue eyes from my side of the family. It's a potent mixture. When he was younger, girls would follow him like soulful kittens, brushing against his legs and wanting to be picked up. Later, those kittens transmuted into sleek Persian cats of the rich Remuera kind, but Rawiri liked his common or garden variety moggies and married Shelley, a lovely unaffected young woman who liked to go jogging, swimming and mountain-climbing with him.

'Are we all picking on Dad?' he says, coming at the run. 'Oh, goody.'

Rawiri jumps onto my back and brings me to the footpath. Not to be outdone, his brothers pile onto me with a variety of judo holds, pinning me down. It's like old times when we would play rough and tumble with each other on my bed and, later, when they liked to show me what they had learnt at judo classes.

'Pax!' I yell.

Passers-by take my side. A little old lady smiles affectionately and wags a finger at the boys. 'Picking on an old man like that,' she clucks. 'Shame on you.'

The boys let me up and Eru comfortingly says, 'Actually, Dad, your baldness is not too bad and you could always get a number one.'

But Rawiri teases, 'Maybe you can get a hair transplant, Dad, or borrow some of mine if you get hair plugs done.'

And Dylan sighs, 'That won't work, Rawiri. There's only one hope for Dad and that's reincarnation.'

Eru takes pity on me. He hugs me around my neck and says to his brothers, 'Stop picking on my father.' He starts giving me a scalp massage, his fingers circling strong, and I suddenly remember something Fleur told me about how the head was sacred to her Maori people. Apparently, you never allow anybody to touch your head. But I would happily give up my sacredness to the trust of my sons. I lean back into Eru's fingers.

Over lunch I cautiously ask my sons, 'So, did you boys like my party?' I can always count on them to tell me the truth, devastating though it might be.

'It was great, Dad,' Dylan answers — and then the subject does an abrupt U-turn to his current police case. I breathe a sigh of relief: of course, I remember now, my sons had all bailed out around 2 am. Rawiri had said: 'Shelley's eyes are dropping out, Dad, and she's not been too well in the mornings, so we're going home.' Soon after, Dylan told me, 'I better shove off, Dad, I'm on the witness stand tomorrow. I'll take Eru as he's been working all night at the restaurant and he's asleep on his feet.'

Yay, so there is a God — one who had covered up my indiscretions and sent my sons home before I had done my down trou.

I tell them about their grandfather's impending wedding. Genuinely delighted for him, they chortle and snort, 'Go, Grandad!', and Rawiri immediately phones him. Very soon, all the boys are chatting away to Laurence and getting the goss about Esther. 'I hope you're practising safe sex,' they kid him.

Then Dylan just about falls off his chair. 'You really mean that, Grandad?' he asks, waving his brothers to listen in on the conversation. 'You want us to give you away? Hey guys, we're going to be fathers to the groom!'

Finally, just before we are all ready to leave, with Rawiri promising to drop by and pick up my cash books (he does my income tax) and Dylan checking out if I want to play touch rugby in a few weeks' time with his police mates, I remind them about their mother's birthday anniversary. Every year we go out to her graveyard to let her know she is still remembered.

I notice that Dylan, for some reason, is hesitant. Eru and Rawiri look at him, and Eru frowns. 'We'll pick you up, Dad,' he says.

Of all my boys, Eru was the one who allowed me to hold his hand when we walked together. When he was sixteen, and gloomily saw some of his schoolfriends pointing at him and chortling, he decided he should say something about it: 'Dad, don't you think we're getting too old to do this?' Although I recognised it was time to let go, I was crestfallen — and he saw it. The next time we went out, Eru sighed, rolled his eyes, shoved out his hand and said, 'Oh, take it then.'

4

Can you tell me something? Why is it that we get involved in stupid things?

The following week I turn up for the photo session for the calendar. Sally is flustered. 'Oh good,' she begins, 'you've brought your violin, tails and bow tie. Just put the clothes over there. For the first shot, you'll just need the violin.'

I look at her, puzzled. I'm wearing only a check shirt, jeans and crocs. Even so, I quite like the idea of the orchestra being seen in our day wear and getting down to the audience's level.

However, Sally's cheeks are going red. 'I forgot to tell everyone,' she continues, 'that the concept of the calendar is to show all the orchestra members undressed as well as dressed.'

'You mean,' I ask, 'you want us photographed naked, too?' I can't hide my surprise. Not only does Sally want us to get down, but she wants us to do *dirty* as well.

'You'll be a good sport, won't you?' Sally pleads. 'It's the done thing in the corporate world these days; the Inland Revenue Department appeared nude in their calendar last year and had a huge success. Some of the players, however, have not been able to grasp the concept.'

'I'll bet,' I answer.

'Surprisingly,' she goes on, 'the women have been more accepting than the men. Adrienne had no qualms and Celestine, when she saw Adrienne taking everything off in front of Vladimir, followed suit. What is going on between those two? But Vladimir was coy, and I can't understand Frank, for instance — he has a big cello that he can stand behind, and Alan has his timpani. I do appreciate George's problem, as he plays the piccolo. But Quentin has assured me that the photographs will be tasteful. We are definitely not going to show full frontal nudity and if, in the session, there's a hint of any offending appendages, male or female, they will be airbrushed out.' Sally is almost in tears and I am beginning to sympathise with her.

'I'll give it a go,' I tell her. After all, I've always been easy in my skin, and if I can moon when I'm drunk, I can certainly get my kit off when I'm sober.

She brightens up immediately. 'Oh, Quentin will be pleased.'

She hands me a bathrobe and I go and undress in the men's. Sally takes me through to the studio. The lights are blinding. Quentin and three minions mince up to me and shake my hand. 'Mr Goodenough? Thank you for allowing us to capture your portrait. You've brought your violin? Good. Would you like to stand here? Now, in your own good time, could you remove your bathrobe?'

I can tell that Quentin is having a boring day so I decide to spice it up, and give him his own personal show. '"Whenever I walked in the door," I sing to him, "I could tell you were a man of distinction, a real big spender."' Hey, I'm getting into this; put some dollars in my g-string, Quentin baby. '"Hey, big spender! Spend a little time with me!"' I shrug the bathrobe off my shoulders and it falls to the floor.

Ready for my close-up, Mr de Mille.

'Right,' Quentin says, pursing his lips and breathing deep. 'Let's get on with it, shall we?' He snaps me from all possible angles: above, below, left dressed, right dressed, easy over, sunny side up. . . Halfway through, his glasses fog up and I wipe them clear for him. 'Are we just about done?' I smile teasingly, batting my eyelashes. At the end of the session he asks me to sign a waiver of some kind.

When I return home, Horace is waiting to go and urinate against the furniture shop. As I lead him from the house, I see Victoria going on a run. 'Isn't it a lovely day?' she calls brightly. For some reason I am feeling cross with myself; I should have asked if I could see the photographs before any of them are published in the calendar. I beam a false smile across to Victoria; maybe she'll trip and fall into a pothole.

We're halfway to Grey Lynn when my mobile rings. Anahera is on the line and as soon as I hear her voice I wish I hadn't taken the call.

'I've heard that my fool of a father is getting married again and he's asked you to be his best man. Well, the whole whanau is dead against it so you are not to do it, do you hear, you bloody Pom?'

I should be used to Anahera's offensive and reductive remarks by now, but I'm not, and I can feel my blood beginning to boil. 'Why, Anahera,' I respond, 'how lovely to hear from you. Having a nice day?'

'You're not even a member of the family,' Anahera continues. 'How dare you agree to Dad's request! He's going gaga and you're not helping by indulging his every whim.'

When Anahera is in full flight nothing can stop her. 'Sorry, Anahera,' I say, 'I'm just coming to a big, black, lo-ong tunnel and you're breaking up. Bye-ee.'

Ever since Fleur took me up to Kaikohe to meet her family, Anahera, who's a district nurse, thought she had me sussed. She has a side interest in astrology and one of the first things she did was to read my astrological chart and pounce on my palm. Why she would ever privilege Pakeha astrology over Maori astrology was a great source of puzzlement to me, as she was both a radical and a racist.

Anahera looked at Fleur and said, 'Don't even think about it, Fleur, he's a Gemini, a bloody Pom, he has a big cross on his mound of Venus and no marriage line whatsoever.'

That was our first run-in. The second time was when Fleur decided that, cross or no cross, marriage line or no marriage line, Pom or not, she would marry me anyway. She liked to spit in the eye of Fate — or her sister — and Anahera hated the way that Fleur proved her predictions wrong. On the day we were married, I heard Anahera still trying to change my bride's mind as she came into the church — and that phrase, 'bloody Pom' again. By the reception I'd had enough. When I got up to thank Laurence and Mereana for hosting the wedding, I thought, 'To hell with it', and let Anahera have it between the eyes.

'Seeing as you lot like to trace your whakapapa,' I began, 'let me give you mine. I am Saxon-born from Brightlingsea, not far from Colchester in Essex. My ancestors go back to the original settlement of Colchester in the fifth century BC and they number among them Cunobelin, King of Camulodunum. Roman invaders occupied Colchester in 43 AD and it was my ancestor Boadicea who led a revolt against their rule. We Saxons fought against the Danish invaders, too, when they pillaged our coast during the Dark Ages. When Richard the First granted Colchester's town charter in 1190, my ancestor was one of his faithful warlords.'

I commandeered two drinks trays from passing waiters, the glasses crashing and breaking on the floor. Then I jumped onto the table and began to bang the trays together; I was pleased to see Anahera put her fingers in her ears. From my solar plexus I felt the rumbling growl of a good old Saxon pagan war cry and let it loose: 'Heilsa allur!'

The war cry was loud enough to scare the innards of the guests and bring the roof of the dining hall down. Then I shook my blond curls and stared at Anahera with my sky-bright blue eyes, amid cheers and whistles from the wedding guests. 'Okay, Anahera,' I thought, 'compare that with that ancestor of yours who only cut down a flimsy little flagpole at Kororareka, and suck on it.'

But what was her response? 'Boadicea? Yeah, I've heard of her.'

—

I hadn't expected to get married at all; I was in a relationship with some-body else when I was living in England. Indeed, I can still remember when Fleur and I were falling in love, lying in bed one bright morning with a new world looming perilously before us, and Fleur was compelled to probe my sexuality.

'I'm the first woman you've ever been with, aren't I?' she asked with barely concealed satisfaction. 'How did you ever escape the wicked wiles of some other wanton woman?' Then something must have clicked over in that amazing mind of hers, because she gave a mock sigh of horror. 'Oh no, you're gay, aren't you!'

I must have blushed or been silent for a second too long, and you know what women are like: once they get the scent of something suspicious they're hot on the trail and you're up a tree, snarling and spitting with nowhere to go. I had to admit that, yes, she was the first woman and, yes, before her there had been a boy in my life, Elijah, and a couple of others who hadn't been as significant.

Before I knew what was happening, Fleur had extracted a promise that there would be no secrets between us and then — it's always a huge mistake, believe me — we agreed to tell about the (significant) others who had been in our lives. Like a fool, I fell headfirst into it. Why? Well, Fleur was so offhand about my disclosure, as if it didn't matter to her, and she appeared to be genuinely objective about the question.

'You go first,' she said.

'I called him Eli for short,' I told Fleur, 'and you and Eli are the only people I have ever allowed to call me Ollie. Anybody else does so at their peril. Eli said if I was allowed to call him by his diminutive he should be able to do the same.'

We were sitting up in my big double bed, sipping some vile coffee and eating burnt toast which Fleur had made in my kitchen. 'I could always call you Vera,' Fleur giggled. 'Or Aloe Vera if you like. Were you as much in love with him as you are with me?'

'Fishing, are we?' I smiled, cuddling her close. 'I was twenty-three when I met him, and I was an only child with elderly parents; my arrival was a huge shock to Aubrey and Ruth's ordered lives. However, they did the best they could to raise me into a good Anglican adult and, when I developed an interest in classical music, they encouraged it. I studied the violin, was good at it, left Colchester and went down to London to attend the Guildhall. That's where I clapped eyes on Eli; he'd come over on a singing scholarship and, well, we just clicked. He was the first New Zealander I had ever met. But he wasn't a Maori like you.'

Clicked? That was putting it mildly. We couldn't keep our hands off each other. Or, at least, I couldn't keep my hands off him. But I wasn't about to tell Fleur all my secrets, not at the beginning, anyway. What do you think I am, stupid?

'Anyhow,' I continued, sipping away at the coffee and crunching at the burnt toast because I didn't want to hurt Fleur's feelings, 'I had just graduated top of my class in the violin and was offered a position with Glyndebourne when I saw an advertisement for a violinist for the New Zealand Symphony Orchestra. Because Eli was himself planning to return to his homeland I thought this might be a way of going back with him; I thought it was what he wanted. When I was offered the job he seemed really pleased for us both. He told me to go on ahead of him and as soon as he finished his studies he'd follow and we'd set up house in Wellington.'

'He never came back, did he?' Fleur said.

'No,' I answered. 'You can imagine how angry and isolated I felt. Here I was, in Wellington, New Zealand, at the other end of the bloody world and, four weeks later, I get a telephone call from Eli to say that he has met a Jamaican boy from West Ham. I mean, *West Ham*, for God's sake? Anyhow, I've always been a night owl and there was a jazz club that entertainers could go to after they had finished their own gigs for the night. After one of our symphonic concerts, I think the orchestra was playing Stravinsky's *Rite of Spring*, I decided to go and drown my sorrows in jazz — and met you.'

Yes, I met sweet, uncomplicated Fleur. A pocket Venus, dark skin, gorgeous hair, well stacked with a nicely balanced bottom, working in a law office in Porirua. She had come to the club with two of her girlfriends, out on the ran-tan and dangerously bored. I had brought my violin and, as happens in jazz clubs, I joined the bass player and drummer in playing an old Stéphane Grappelli standard:

> First you say you do and then you don't,
> Then you say you will and then you won't,
> I'm undecided now so what am I going to do —

According to Fleur, she and her mates divided our trio up and, 'I got the short end of the stick,' she said. She put out her stiletto heel just as I came off the stage and I fell over it and broke it. That wasn't in Fleur's master plan — actually, she was cross because the heels were her favourites. She insisted I take her home but she wouldn't take off the other stiletto so, there we were, walking down Cuba Street with her bobbing up and down like a yo-yo, one second up to my shoulder the next minute down to my waist, her angry voice fading in and out of my right ear. When she invited me in for one of her horribly made coffees I didn't take up her offer — 'I wondered about that,' she told me — but she decided I was worth persevering with and, besides, I owed her a new pair of stilettos. The next day I met her at a high fashion shoe shop and by the time she had tried on just about every model they had — Brazilian, Parisian, Russian, you name it — our fates were sealed. She liked the fact that I didn't flinch when she chose the most expensive pair in the shop and I liked the fact that she was an exhibitionist like me. Posing left and right, and bending provocatively over me to do up the straps, she sang, 'A kiss on the cheek may be quite continental but high heels are a girl's best friend.' A few days later, even though she was, well, the wrong sex, we fell into bed with each other. It was a mystery to me how it happened.

'So what do you think now?' Fleur asked me impishly, that long ago morning when we were having coffee and toast in bed. 'Are you still gay?'

Patiently I told her that it was a complex matter to do with practice, preference and identification. But I started to sound like a textbook and none of what I was saying was addressing what was happening to us. 'Until you came along,' I said finally, 'I never thought I could ever make love to a woman — but I have.'

'I'll give you five out of ten,' Fleur joked.

I looked at Fleur and laughed because a story had popped into my head. 'Have you heard of the well known stage actress, Coral Browne?' I asked her. 'She still tours the English provinces. I saw her on stage in Colchester just before I came out to New Zealand. Apparently she conceived a violent passion for one of the boys of the chorus and told the rest of the cast, "I'm going to sleep with that young man." Some of her fellow players told her, "Oh, that's impossible, he's gay." Miss Browne was never one to let something as inconsequential as that get in her way. "Nonsense," she answered. Then she bet the cast one pound that she would succeed. Later that evening, her fellow players saw her wining and dining said boy and, around midnight, heading with him to her hotel room. She gave a huge wink as she closed the door.'

'Are you trying to tell me something?' Fleur giggled.

I resumed my tale. 'Come the morning, all the cast were waiting with bated breath for Miss Browne and the boy's arrival at breakfast. The boy was not to be seen but Miss Browne made a magnificent entrance, swathed in black veils, descending the steps as if she had just attended a funeral. As she entered the breakfast room she drew herself up, gripped a chair and said, "I owe you all seven shillings and sixpence."'

Fleur exploded with laughter. 'But I'm expecting some improvement and, next time, you can lead.'

'Now it's your turn, you hussy,' I said. 'I want to know every misdemeanour, every boyfriend, every cowboy who has ridden roughshod through your life.' I think I was trying to turn her into a friend rather than a girlfriend; I didn't think we would last. But oh, she was so unfair.

'My past hasn't exactly been Rinso clean,' Fleur began. 'I'm not one to boast but, like Mae West, I used to be Snow White until I drifted.'

'Well then?' I had just blabbed my mouth off and all I get in exchange is *this?*

'Maybe when we get to know each other better,' she answered, 'I'll tell you all about *all* of my men. Meantime, as for us, I guess it will be either sink or swim.' She poked me in the ribs. 'And it better be swim.'

A few months later she took me up to see Laurence and Mereana and I asked for her hand in marriage. Anahera, Hemi, Joe-Joe, Pearl, Whena and Kara gave me the once over; Anahera gave me a look that said, 'Over my dead body.' She had me sussed, all right.

Somehow, after committing myself to Fleur, a new pattern for my life began to emerge out of the old pattern, and everything fell into place.

5

The evening of the concert arrives and the Auckland Town Hall is almost full for our very popular Tchaikovsky programme: the Symphony No. 4, and the Violin Concerto, op. 35 after the intermission.

Robert buttonholes the orchestra in our dressing rooms just before we go on, to make a mournful announcement. 'Thank you,' he begins, 'to all those of you who got into the spirit of things and had your photographs taken for our charity calendar. However, after considering the objections raised by some of you, management has reviewed the concept and taken it back to the drawing board.'

Sally sidles up to me. 'Quentin is so disappointed,' she tells me, 'especially since he's fallen in love with one of your shots.'

The sigh of relief is audible, and the orchestra trips gaily on stage to tune our instruments and await the arrival of Maestro De Montalk. However, as soon as he mounts the podium our relief turns to dismay. He stands there glaring at us and we realise we're in for a tumultuous night. The first downstroke of his baton almost unsettles his toupee — and we're off.

'Oh my Lord,' Adrienne hisses across to me. 'How does Ben Hur expect us to keep up this pace? And I've just had my hair done, too.' She beams a huge smile across to Vladimir, hoping that he has noticed.

The maestro is like a maniac in the first movement. It's marked *andante sostenato* and then *moderato con anima* but, following the strident opening theme, there's not much calmness and moderation in his approach. Forceful, massive and aggressive, his chariot is just managing to make it around the bends. Then, in the second movement, when respite is essential, what does Ben Hur do? He uses the whip. Is it an *andantino in modo di canzone,* calm and in the manner of a song? Not bloody likely. The brass section is trying to stay in rhythm and Alan is pounding so hard on his timpani it's a wonder the drums aren't in shreds.

'Here we go,' I whisper back to Adrienne when we get to the *scherzo* of the third movement. She is not amused: her hair has become electrified and she looks like a gorgon.

By this time, the maestro is looking very afraid because he can see the murder in our eyes as we neigh, snort and champ at the bit. He hasn't even given us a downbeat before we pull the reins from his hands, aha, and are off under our own hooves. Use the whip on us, eh? The woodwind and brass sections are explosive and hectic and in the string section our fingers are in flames as we bow, scrape, pick and pluck and *pizzicato* for all we're worth.

As for the Finale, no need to tell us that this is an *allegro con fuoco.* We've totally taken control, the wheels have come off the maestro's chariot and he is dragging along in our dust.

Of course the bloodthirsty crowd are roaring their tits off and giving us a standing ovation. The maestro dares to take a bow and then, seeing Adrienne leading the charge for his blood, flees for his dressing room.

After the performance, our sponsors have invited the orchestra to mix and mingle with first night guests for drinks and a buffet dinner; we're 'staff', of course, but we are also an appreciative audience for the speeches by the local member of parliament, Mrs Mayor, and the main sponsors. Protected by Robert, the maestro is pressing the flesh, making a dollar here, a dollar there, schmoozing the sirens of Parnell. Adrienne has restyled her hair and is getting quietly sozzled with Vladimir; off to one side, Celestine is smouldering with jealousy. Geoff is wooing the young Korean violinist who has been the soloist in the violin concerto. Throughout her performance he has been beaming at her, encouraging her to greater and greater heights of accomplishment, and she has responded with stunning virtuoso bow work that is positively orgasmic.

Later that night, back at the house, the *Bolero* starts up again. Vladimir and Celestine have had an argument and although he received a very blatant offer from Adrienne, he has decided it is wiser to retreat with a glass of wine to the terrace. 'We must something do about that terrible music,' he moans. 'Is so common, so werry bourgeois. No intellectual content, why Geoff like so much? Shostakovich much better.'

The one consolation is that at least the version of *Bolero* that Geoff plays is one of the shortest on the market.

And that gives me an idea. 'Oh, you wicked man, Mr Goodenough.'

6

'Rejoice in other's joys! To live is still possible!'

This is what Tchaikovsky wanted to express when he composed his Fourth Symphony. I recall his words the next month when I hear Eru beeping on his horn to let me know that he has arrived to take me out to the cemetery. I gather up the bouquet of red roses that I have bought to put on Fleur's grave. I can't believe that fourteen years have passed; Rawiri was only eleven and Dylan and Eru nine when they said goodbye to their mother.

'Hey, Dad,' Eru greets me. 'Lovely flowers, Mum will like those.'

I look in the back seat. Good boy that he is, he has brought the usual gas-filled balloons; they're bobbing about on the ceiling of the car as if they can't wait to be let loose.

We travel in to Queen Street to pick up Rawiri from his office. As he bounds down the stairs and into the back seat he tells me, 'Dylan can't make it today. There's been another homicide in South Auckland and he's been assigned to the investigation team.'

I see Rawiri exchange a quick glance with Eru, who frowns and says, 'Oh well, these things can't be helped, eh, Dad.' He is seeking an affirmation from me that I am taking this disappointment okay.

'We'll say hello to your mother for him,' I reply.

We head out across the harbour bridge northward on Highway 1. Just past Wellsford we take Highway 12 toward the Kauri Coast; we're planning to stop off at Orewa on our return trip to see Laurence in the old people's home. Through to Dargaville we speed. A quick pitstop for a cup of coffee and sandwiches, and then we are onward bound for the stunning white sand beaches at the head of the Hokianga harbour.

It's a long drive and, as usual, I tell Rawiri and Eru about their mother and me. I don't tell them everything, of course; like their mother, they have memories like elephants and as Confucius say: 'Person who open mouth too wide fall into it.'

'After we were married in 1980,' I begin, 'your mother and I got down to being a couple. I took her to England for our honeymoon and to meet my parents, your English grandparents. Aubrey was a retired professor of classics and Ruth was a music teacher; I inherited my appreciation of music from her. On his retirement, Aubrey converted my bedroom in our house in Brightlingsea into a library for his books and Anglo-Saxon manuscripts. This might seem a callous thing for him to have done but my parents were in the main unsentimental people and, anyway, I had been leaving home for quite some time before I actually left. Even so, I know my parents loved me, and they were delighted to meet your mother. They thought of her as an exotic Polynesian princess —'

Rawiri and Eru smile at each other. They have seen the photographs of our honeymoon; Fleur, having tea with the English in-laws, looking like a beautiful huia in her red dress and long greenstone earrings.

'I'll rephrase that,' I continue, 'a *bossy* exotic Polynesian princess who took over everything and everybody who came into her life; of all you boys, Dylan's the one most like her in that respect. "Fleur will be the making of you," Aubrey said to me, shaking my hand as if he couldn't believe it, and Ruth said, "I'm so glad you have found a companion, Oliver; your father and I won't last forever." We spent two weeks with them before embarking on a hilarious trip to the Continent. In Italy, Fleur kept getting her bum

in the year of prince harry

pinched by amorous Italian men, and she loved it. But nothing lasts forever and, after a quick return to say goodbye to my parents, we returned to New Zealand. Almost immediately on our arrival back in Wellington, your mother began to have morning sickness and discovered she was pregnant with you, Rawiri —'

'It must have been an immaculate conception,' Rawiri jokes to Eru.

'Boy, was she angry with me,' I continued. "Nobody gets pregnant on their honeymoon," she wailed. Then she rang your Aunt Anahera. "Guess what," she grumbled. "I thought I wasn't supposed to have children? Well, another one of your predictions is just about to hit the dust."

'In the middle of all this I had to take a flight back to England when my mother died. "Come to New Zealand with me," I said to Aubrey. But he shook his head, preferring to stay among his friends and colleagues and in the library of books and manuscripts that he had always loved. He did not linger long after my mother. I realised I could have been an orphan alone in the world had it not been for Fleur. Instead, I inherited her and her huge, rambunctious, quarrelling, passionate Maori family, which was a great shock to an innocent English boy —'

'Innocent?' Eru interjects. 'Come on, Dad!'

'— and then, when Fleur gave me a family, well that was an altogether greater shock.'

She insisted that I be with her in the delivery room when Rawiri was born, because she wanted me to 'share my pain, you bloody Pom'. It was the only time she used that invective and I forgave her under the circumstances. However, when she saw Rawiri for the first time, she burst into tears, 'Oh, look at our son, Oliver! Oh look.'

I turn to Rawiri. 'You were such a fair blondie little boy that nobody would believe you were Fleur's. But *you* knew. Put you in a room full of Grace Kellys and who would you run to? The darkest woman in the bunch.'

'It must have been the milkman,' Rawiri says in his usual droll manner.

'Well,' I continue, 'your mother had been planning to go back to work but when you were a year old, Rawiri, she started to get sick again in the mornings. We went in to have a scan done, and all we could see was one baby boy swimming in her womb. Then, all of a sudden, the doctor said, "What's this?" He pointed to a small hand holding onto Dylan's left leg. "There's another little chappie in there!"'

'I was trying to get in front of him,' Eru says.

'But Mum didn't want twins, eh Dad,' Rawiri interrupts. 'She told the doctor, "No, no, no, send one of them back."'

My two sons fall about laughing. Dylan and Eru's birth, however, had been no laughing matter. All tangled up in each other's arms, their entrance into the world was a messy and frightening business. I was white-faced with dismay watching Fleur grunting and hissing, her eyes popping out of their sockets, and perspiration pouring off her face. 'Come out, come out you little bastards,' she yelled as first Dylan swam out, and soon after, Eru, wailing like crazy because Dylan had kicked him back into second place. Afterwards, when she was blissfully sleeping, I stroked her hair and, when she woke up, I said to her, 'No more babies, Fleur, I can't go through this again.' She tried to smile. 'Just when I'm getting the hang of this?' she asked. I was stern. 'No, Fleur, no more children.'

—

'We're almost there, Dad,' Eru says.

I nod and watch as we drive through the small seaside settlement of Omapere. The highway offers stunning vistas of sand dunes, small harbours and inlets and the sea beyond.

We had a good innings, Fleur and I. She had the chance to see Rawiri grow into a courteous boy loved by the neighbourhood, little old ladies and young goggle-eyed girls. She had all the fun of watching Dylan and Eru grow into terrible twins, scrapping all the time. Eru was the soft one who always needed 'Bunny', a pink stuffed rabbit, to go to bed with. Dylan was the one who played cops and robbers — and woe betide if you were a robber because you were either put in jail or, worse, in his electric chair. One day, Dylan made the mistake of putting Bunny in jail. Eru was inconsolable and Dylan soon learnt his lesson about his sensitive brother and immediately released Bunny on home detention. Much later, when they were teenagers, and I was throwing things out, Dylan restrained me when I reached for Bunny; by then he had no arms, one leg and had been dribbled and sicked on for years. 'That's Bunny, Dad,' Dylan said, 'and you mustn't chuck him out.' For all I know, Eru still has that stuffed pink rabbit somewhere in his grown-up bedroom.

Fleur was my wife, my lover, my best friend, and I was faithful to her throughout our marriage. That's not to say there weren't stresses and strains. At one point, she saw that I was spending too much time with another member of the orchestra, Harry, and that it could get serious. I arrived home late one night after spending the evening at the pub with him. Our kiss in the street before I came through the door was not entirely innocent. Fleur had seen it and she shook the blazes out of me, shouting at me, 'Swim, Oliver, damn you, I'm not going to drown alone with our boys, *swim.*'

Then Fleur discovered she had cervical cancer just after I had moved our family up to Auckland to take up a position as First Violinist with the Auckland Philharmonia; she'd cocked her snook at Fate by getting married and having children, and now she was paying for it. Instead of crying, she went into a rage. 'I'm so pissed off,' she yelled, roaming through the house I had bought for us in Ponsonby with the money from my parents' will. The boys were in shock at their mother's hysteria and tried to clamber into her lap, 'What's wrong, Mummy, what's wrong?' but she kept on throwing them off like little pups before they could get a good hold. Still in a rage, she rang up Anahera, 'Well, you bitch, at least you got one thing right; you said I would die before I was forty and it looks like you're going to get your way.' We obtained a specialist, Dr Robinson, who tried every treatment that was available and finally told us the cancer was invasive.

It was so difficult to see Fleur in such pain — and the boys were bewildered about what was happening to their mother. They were all good sons and tried to offer her support in the simplest ways: making cups of tea, helping with the housework, always trying to be good. When she lost all her hair, what did they do? Dylan cut his brothers' hair off and then gave himself the worst mohawk you ever saw. Then Dr Robinson confirmed that Fleur's cancer was terminal.

'Time for *you* to swim, Fleur,' I said to her, on the eve of Dylan and Eru's ninth birthday. She was making their favourite pudding, Frogs in the Pond, out of green jelly; just before it sets, you put chocolate frogs into the jelly. But Fleur had waited too long and the jelly had already hardened. 'What kind of mother am I?' she sobbed. 'I can't even make a simple pudding any more.' But she had recovered by the next day. She had hacked away at the surface and then put some frogs heads-up in it and other frogs heads-down. 'They're just splashing out of the water or into it,' she explained to doubtful-looking Dylan and Eru.

While Fleur hated accepting the inevitability of death, it was clear that the returns from her life were diminishing. Oh, she tried a few flailing strokes for me and for her boys but, in the end, the day came when Dr Robinson advised that Fleur be taken to a hospice where she could be cared for and where we could visit her when she was at her best. One afternoon when I went, she was sitting up in bed, writing letters.

'Who are these to?' I asked her.

It was early 1992 and she was addressing envelopes to the boys: 'Not to be opened until my birthday in 1993', 'Not to be opened until my birthday in 1994', 'Not to be opened until my birthday in 1995', and so on. 'I'm not going to leave my boys alone in the world without their knowing every year that they have been loved by their mother,' she said, 'I just won't, Oliver, do you hear? Every year, on my birthday, bring them to say happy birthday to me and give them my letters.'

Then, one day, Dr Robinson told me, 'It's time, Mr Goodenough. Best for you and the boys to say your goodbyes.'

The boys came to talk with their mother. They had brought make-up with them and, while they chatted about school, they made her up. They plastered her face with cream, put some lippy on her, painted black brows where her eyebrows had once been, attached the longest false eyelashes you ever saw and hung her greenstone pendants in her earlobes. Then they painted her fingernails and toenails different colours; all that was missing was her red dress. 'Mummy's all pretty now,' Dylan said with satisfaction, as they showed Fleur what she looked like.

'Wow,' Fleur tried to smile, 'how much is that doggy in the window! If I was feeling better we could have all gone on a date to McDonald's.' Then she kissed them and said, 'Mummy's tired now and wants to go to sleep.'

Holding her hands as she slipped away I remembered a friend who, throughout his life, always followed this piece of advice: 'Whenever you go into a relationship you must always begin by saying yes to it. Not "Yes but" or "Yes maybe" but "Yes, yes, YES." Don't start editing it before you begin, or hedging it around with provisos or conditions. Go with your heart wide open.' The consequence was he went from one bad relationship to the next, trying vainly to make all those sow's purses into silk ears.

Thank God, though, Fleur was like he was. She had a great capacity for love. She always said *Yes* to life.

She had said *Yes* to me. It was so unfair.

The next day she was gone.

—

Halfway past Omapere on the road to Opononi, Eru turns off the main road and drives up a non-sealed road to a small tribal graveyard overlooking the sparkling sea. Because I have brought my violin, Rawiri says, 'I'll carry the roses, Dad.' Eru wraps the balloon strings around his hand so they won't fly off. We walk up the hillside to the graveyard, and Eru puts his other hand in mine as we go through the gateway.

Amid the gravestones and crosses Fleur's headstone stands out. Engraved just under her name is a pair of wicked-looking high heels.

Standing in front of the gravestone I address Fleur in the manner of her own people:

'Here we are again, Fleur, two of your boys and I, come to keep our promise to see you on your birthday. I'm sorry, sweetheart, but Dylan is not with us today. However, these flowers, red roses — you always said you only wanted red roses on your birthday — are from all of us.'

Rawiri and Eru and I are standing in front of Fleur's grave, the sun hot and the clouds turning overhead. When I first came to the Hokianga with Fleur I was surprised how bright and shimmering the sea was, glowing, luminescent, not like the sea off the coast of Essex at all.

I give Rawiri and Eru their letters from Fleur: 'Not to be opened until 2007'. I've never, in all these years, read what Fleur has written to her boys, though when Eru was twelve and needed cuddling, he showed me his:

'Dear Eru, you're a big boy now, aren't you! Thank you for coming to say happy birthday to me today. Here's a B I I I G hug coming at you, ready or not! Love, your mother, Fleur.'

The boys go off down the hill to read their letters. I take out my violin and place the bow across the strings.

Of all the songs I played on my violin, Fleur and her family loved the old Spanish-style songs the most. On holidays when Fleur and I would bring the boys back to their marae, here in the Hokianga, there was always a whanau concert. While the stars were wheeling across the sky, I would join Fleur's brothers — Hemi picking on his Spanish guitar and Joe-Joe squeezing the accordion he'd learnt to play while in prison — and we would start with 'Ramona' and go on through 'Estrellita', 'Core Ingrato', 'Spanish Harlem' and her favourite, 'Vaya con Dios'.

My first teacher, Mrs Grace, told me that there was a voice in the violin. I guess it was her way of trying to get me to place the bow right in the middle of the strings so that the notes would be full and rich. As I am playing I try to find that centre, that voice:

> Now the hacienda's dark, the town is sleeping;
> Now the time has come to part, the time for weeping.
> Vaya con Dios, my darling, may God be with you my love —

The notes rise, swell, take wing and there is not the slightest need to modulate them. And there it comes, the voice of the violin singing its heart out, the melody unfurling, unforced and lyrical, through the air.

'Fleur, look at your sons! You would be very proud of them. All of their best qualities of generosity, passion, humour, sexiness, honesty and sentimentality come from you. Thank you for giving me a life and a family that I never expected to have. Without you I would have had nothing.'

I lay my violin down. Out to sea a dolphin leaps from the sparkling water, dazzling diamonds falling from its sleek skin.

—

Rawiri and Eru come back, stuffing their letters in their pockets. They take out marker pens and write messages to Fleur across their balloons. It was Eru, when he was thirteen, who suggested doing either this or else attaching letters to the tails of the balloons. 'You always have to have balloons on a birthday,' he said indignantly. That year he had written a long letter to his mother and the balloon was so weighed down that it scraped and bumped down the hillside before finally being lifted by sea breezes into the sky.

Together, Rawiri, Eru and I scrawl our messages to Fleur. Rawiri's is HAPPY BIRTHDAY MUM. Eru's is I MISS YOU MUM. Mine is just a big heart with our names in the middle: OLIVER GOODENOUGH LOVES FLEUR WHAREPAPA.

'What should we do with Dylan's balloon?' Eru asks.

'We'll keep it for next year,' I answer.

We count, 'One, two, three!' and let the balloons go. Slowly they twirl and swirl as if reluctant to take flight.

'It's not the same without Dylan,' Eru says.

Suddenly we hear a siren and a car horn blaring repeatedly. Far off there is a plume of dust and a police car, headlights blazing, roaring up the unsealed road.

'He's decided to come!' Eru says, and is off yahooing loudly to meet his twin brother.

Decided to come?

When Dylan arrives he slams on the brakes and the dust swirls over the green landscape like angels. He looks really upset, as if he has been crying all the way here. He gets out of the car and leans against it, wiping his face with his sleeve. I can hear Eru saying to him, 'It's okay, Dylan, you're not late.' But Dylan is pointing at the balloons we have already released, speeding heavenward.

'What's wrong with your brother?' I ask Rawiri, mystified. 'I thought he wasn't coming.'

Dylan comes raging up the hillside. 'Why didn't you wait, Dad?' he yells at me. He charges through the gateway and along the rows of gravestones. 'Is that my balloon? Give it to me, you bastard.' He grabs his balloon from my hands and writes across its bright yellow surface with the marker pen LUVU4EVER.

With a cry he lets the balloon free. Swept by a wilful wind, the balloon rockets up through the air, chasing after the others.

Rawiri and Eru gather around Dylan. 'Go, go, go!' they yell at the balloon.

Very soon, the balloon appears to have caught up with the others. 'There you are, brother,' Eru says as all the balloons disappear into the blue.

I go to put my arms around Dylan's shoulders but he is still upset. 'Don't touch me,' he yells. 'Just give me my letter.' His eyes are streaming with tears. He goes off to one side to read it.

We leave him alone. Then, after a while, Eru goes to sit beside him. Rawiri goes down next. When I join them, Rawiri looks up at me. 'I'll ride back with Dylan, Dad.'

'God, I'll have so much explaining to do to my superior officer when I get the car back to Auckland,' he says.

'I'm glad you came, son,' I tell him.

His face crumples again. 'I can't do this for much longer though, Dad, I just can't.'

On the way back, we stop at the old people's home in Orewa to see Laurence. Eru and Rawiri rush in for a quick embrace with their grandfather.

'You're the man,' Eru says, slapping him on the back.

'And you like the ladies, don't you, Grandad?' Rawiri continues. 'We must get our love of pretty women from your side of the family.'

Laurence laughs at his grandsons. He is dressed casually in golf trousers and open-necked shirt, and beside him is his girlfriend, Esther, a lively old lady who looks as if she's just come back from having her red hair tinted and permed and her pretty face made up at the local beauty salon.

'This is my fiancée,' Laurence introduces her. 'Show them the ring I got you, lovey.'

'Wow,' Eru says, 'what a rock. It must have cost you your pension for the whole year.'

Dylan gives Eru a look that says, 'Stop horsing around.' He tells his grandad that he has to dash back to Auckland and that Rawiri is going with him. 'But Dad and Eru will stay on for a while,' he adds. Just to give the other residents of the old people's home a thrill, Dylan floors the accelerator and shows off some fancy pursuit manoeuvres around the front lawn; he hits the siren as they leave.

Meanwhile, Eru and I enjoy Esther's tea and cake. A number of the other women residents of the home come by to say hello. 'Is this one of your handsome grandsons, Laurence?' they ask as they chuck Eru under his resigned chin and pinch his cheeks.

Esther introduces us to her matron of honour, Bettina, who's ninety-five, and her bridesmaids Susan and Wendy, who are in their seventies. 'I wanted my daughter Gloria to be one of the bridesmaids, too,' Esther says, 'but like Laurence's daughter, Anahera, she and my son Herbert are not too happy about the wedding either.'

Later, Laurence comes out to the car to bid us goodbye. 'So what are you going to do about Anahera?' I ask him.

'I told her to stay home,' he answers. 'If she's not happy for me I don't want her around like the bad fairy come to spoil the party.'

7

Another day, another dollar.

I roll up and look over the rim of the hollow in my bed at the clock: 6.30 am, up and at 'em. I yawn, scratch, burp and fart and, with that extra propulsion, make my way to the bathroom. There I look into the mirror and perform my usual facial callisthenics, poke my tongue out, inspect the rims of my eyes, observe the clumps of hair growing out of my ears and nostrils and wonder about the lines and creases that seem to be multiplying across my face. Then, just as I am angling the mirror to see how many more grey hairs I have, I notice it: The Bald Patch. It looks like an empty parking lot in the middle of my hair. Maybe Rawiri will let me borrow some of his curls and I can paste and park them in the vacant space. Perhaps the medical profession has come up with a solution short of castration. Ah, misery, what a way to start the morning.

Ablutions done, I perform the other required duty of the morning — taking Horace for a walk — and I see my neighbour, Victoria, hobbling along on crutches.

'What happened to you?' I laugh.

'I tripped on the pavement three weeks ago,' she answers ruefully, 'just after I said hello to you, in fact, when you were taking Horace for a walk. But I'm on the mend.'

Oops. 'You'd think the council would come and fix all the potholes,' I cover quickly. 'It's a bloody disgrace. Sue them.' I rationalise that I hadn't put a hex on her. All of us are at the mercy of the Higher Power. As Horace pulls me after him I make sure I don't step on a crack.

—

At ten, an orchestra rehearsal is in progress.

Robert has managed to get us a contract playing the soundtrack for a new animated movie being made in New Zealand called, I kid you not, 'Lord of the Wings'. It's about a young Maori girl who changes into a bird and goes back in time to save forest birds from an invasion of seabirds. Transparently about Maori and Pakeha relationships, it sounds right up Anahera's tree; the music is all brass, bombast and stirring strings for aerial sequences. As the maestro conducts I look at his toupee and think that he might give me some advice about how to get a hair transplant. Like the knucklehead I am, I bail him up after the rehearsal.

'I have not had a hair transplant,' he glares at me, offended.

'I know that,' I explain, 'but because you have a toupee I thought you might —'

'I do *not* wear a rug,' he articulates firmly. 'Pull and see.'

Well, I am not to blame for what happens. After all, he asked for it. I pull — and it comes off.

'But I was told it wouldn't,' he moans. 'As for you, Mr Goodenough, be kind enough to keep my toupee to yourself.'

As I am leaving the rehearsal rooms, Sally comes rushing up to me. 'Oliver, I have just seen the photograph that Quentin has chosen, and it is just awesome. Are you coming along to the opening? Quentin told me he's sent you an invitation.'

'Oh, thanks,' I answer. Chosen? For what? And what opening? But my taxi is waiting to take me home and I don't pursue her puzzling remarks any further.

In the taxi, my mobile rings. It's Laurence, and he tells me that the arrangements for his wedding are progressing well. He's hired a suit for the day and Esther is wearing a floral dress and hat. 'Will you let Eru know,' he asks, 'how grateful I am he's offered to cater the wedding breakfast? Oh yes, I have got the wedding ring and will give it to you on the day. The ceremony will be simple, and then we'll go to the dining room for a good feed and some champagne. And that's really nice of Rawiri and Dylan to dub in for a limousine to take me and Esther to a hotel later for the night. Rawiri tells me it's a real passion pit. Waterbed, spa and television in the bedroom . . . what's the world coming to?'

'Have you heard from Anahera?' I ask.

'No,' he answers. 'But Hemi and Joe-Joe have now decided to come. They tell me Anahera is still persuading my other daughters against me. No news is good news.'

I'm not so sure.

—

In the afternoon, Dylan calls from the street. I grab my sports kit and run out to his car. I'm having a quick game of touch rugby with him and his police mates.

'Are you all set, Dad?' Dylan asks as he opens the door for me. The car is stacked to the gills with some of his burly mates: Iosefa, Chuck, Rajiv and Mohammed are evidence that today's police force is a multicultural lot. The boys let me squeeze in and we are soon zooming off to Western Springs Park.

There, we get down to the game. It's good, sweaty and energetic and I can feel my body responding. Nothing like a burst of sport to get the endorphins buzzing and bopping, and I like the occasional slam dunk of body contact and sense of being part of a team.

Although Dylan's mates are all much younger than me they don't seem to mind having his dad around. Actually, I don't mind being around *them*. Sometimes I wonder, was I ever that young? I admire their strength and seemingly inexhaustible reserves of energy as we play. Mind you, they think that I run them off *their* feet. 'Great game, Mr Goodenough,' they compliment me during our encounter. Huh! They should see me later when I am nursing my bruises, aches and pains and trying to walk without hobbling.

I watch Dylan as he comes up on the sideline. We like to compete against each other, and automatically take opposing sides. 'Don't let your dad get the best of you!' Iosefa yells at him. American Chuck is on my side, however, and responds, 'Get him, Pop!' I give him an offended glance: *Pop*? Dylan barges past, putting a ding in my aging bodywork as he goes, releasing the ball to Rajiv.

After the game we head for the showers; I am still being kidded for letting Dylan get that try. They splash, shimmy and jive under the showers, with dangly bits that show they are beneficiaries of all the growth hormones in fortified breakfast cereal. I shower freely with them and I don't think it even dawns on them that there's a gay man in their midst; I am simply Dylan's dad.

Dylan takes me home but, as usual, he just happens to drive past some newly renovated townhouses and apartments that are for sale. Since the boys all moved out of the family house in Ponsonby, and I sold it, Dylan has been trying to get me settled into something smaller. 'Do you want to take a look, Dad?' he asks hopefully as he stops outside a townhouse in Point Chev.

'I like staying with Geoff and Vladimir in Grey Lynn,' I answer, and I won't be budged.

Cross, Dylan calls the realtors he has made appointments with to tell them his father is being obstinate, and he'll call them again when I'm more amenable.

And that will be never. But I have to pay for my intransigence as Dylan keeps chipping away at me, 'Please let me buy you a place of your own, Dad, it's embarrassing to have a forty-nine-year-old father who is still, well, *flatting*. It's like you've never grown up and left home.'

We reach the house. 'Dylan,' I say, 'you don't have to keep on looking out for me. I'm really fine, honest.'

He frowns. He hates it when he doesn't get his way. Lucky for me that New Zealand doesn't have capital punishment, otherwise I would be for it. Just before he leaves he looks at me. His face is haunted. 'I'm sorry, Dad,' he begins, 'about the other day when you all went up to Mum's and I wasn't with you. Sometimes it's hard for me to keep things together. I just lost the plot.'

Then he zooms off and I am left wondering again, What is happening to you, son? What's this all about? Because what Dylan said isn't true; he's always been the strong one. At Fleur's tangi only Dylan kept his sanity, shepherding me and his brothers between the mourning rituals and the needs of our bodies: 'You must eat, Dad, and keep up your strength.' The three days of mourning expressed by Fleur's whanau was almost unbearable; in particular, I had never realised the depths of Anahera's love for her sister. I hugged the boys close to me as Fleur was being committed to the earth, thinking that this must have been the way it was in my own ancient Saxon culture — the ritual wailing and expressions of loss — the tribal outpouring as if a mortal wound had been inflicted on the collective psyche.

Following the tangi, numb with shock, the boys and I returned home to Auckland, and the reality really hit us. Fleur wasn't *there*, and she was never going to be *there* ever again, she wouldn't be coming back. For weeks Rawiri and Eru came to the big king-sized bed that I had once shared with their mother to huddle close to me. I welcomed them in and I am ashamed to say that, instead of comforting them, I sobbed with them. Again, Dylan was the only one who kept outside our indulgent need to wallow in our sadness. 'Mummy wouldn't want us to cry,' he would say as he pulled Rawiri and Eru out of their inconsolable grief. 'No, Rawiri, no Eru, you have to come back to your own beds. Now.' Night after night, this would happen; Rawiri and Eru would come to sleep with me and, night after night, Dylan would pull them out of my arms and back to their rooms again. 'Daddy, you're not helping,' he would yell at me. 'Mummy's gone now. You have to take control.'

Friends rallied around but it was nine-year-old Dylan who kept the household going. While I stayed in bed in the mornings, still grieving over Fleur, he was out in the kitchen making breakfast and spreading peanut butter on bread for lunch sandwiches. On those nights when I just wasn't up to making dinner he glared at me, 'Give me some money, Daddy, so that I can go to the supermarket and buy a cooked chicken or something for dinner.' He would order his brothers to peel the potatoes, put peas in a pot to boil, and set the table — and if it wasn't ready by the time he got back, *watch out*. In the weekends, he gave *me* my instructions about Rawiri's football timetable and Eru's swimming lessons.

After a month, things did get better. All the family routines began to re-establish themselves and, of course, I had to go back to work; fortunately, orchestra rehearsals and our performance timetable meant that I could manage the boys on most mornings. Even so, I still found the going tough and I made a foolish mistake: I called Anahera and asked her to take the boys off my hands for a while. She readily agreed but, when she turned up at the door, Dylan was terrified. 'Don't you want us any more, Daddy? Haven't I been doing enough?'

When he said that, what did I do? Had one of my self-pitying crying jags. I stood there, ineffectual, and watched Anahera drive with them away from the house.

—

With Fleur dead and the boys gone, I was alone again. I was thirty-five, and a widower. Celibacy and I had never been good companions, and although I tried desperately to pull myself together, I found myself seeking the affirming solace of skin on skin. I had lost my bed's companion and it was inevitable, I suppose, that my sexuality would assert itself. I slipped into a gay affair, my first since my marriage to Fleur. Like that hollow in my mattress, it was simply waiting for me to slide back into it.

It happened so simply. I couldn't sleep. It was three in the morning. I decided to go to a bar. There, I met Seth, a male nurse, who had just come off the night shift at Auckland Hospital. He was part Maori, my age, nice looking; we got to talking. After a couple of drinks he asked if I was gay.

I didn't say I was; I didn't say I wasn't. He took me home with him. Two weeks later we were still seeing each other.

Anahera found out about Seth. I don't know how — maybe it was because she was in the nursing profession herself, or maybe she knew Seth's rellies; everybody is related in Maori culture and the tomtom drums carry gossip mighty fast. When I went up to see the boys on a visit, armed with her knowledge, she went for my jugular.

'I've been hearing stories about you and another man,' she said. I blanched and she played on my embarrassment and sense of weakness. 'Fleur's not even in the ground two months and this is the way you treat her memory. Before you two were married she mentioned something about your habits. I tried to talk her out of marrying you, but she went ahead with it. Well, so you've gone over to the other side again, have you? It might be better for the boys to stay with me on a permanent basis.'

I wasn't thinking straight. I told her I would think about it. But she kept repeating that it would be best for all concerned. 'Without the boys,' she said with ill-disguised contempt, 'you'll be able to live the way you wish.' I said I'd let her know. Dylan must have been listening at the door. When I was leaving he came raging at me, his lips curled back in a snarl:

'You can't leave us here, we belong with you. Swim, Daddy, you have to *swim*.'

Dylan, I was the one who lost the plot.

8

Oh my *God,* there are some mornings when you just want to hide your face in a pillow and fast forward a hundred years.

No such luck. When I open my eyes Vladimir is sitting on my bed. He has a cup of black coffee in his hands and a mournful expression on his face. 'We are wake up?' he asks.

'Hello, Vlad,' I say carefully, wondering what has brought about his visit. 'Is that coffee for me?'

He shakes his head, 'No, this coffee mine.' He sits on the bed, appraising me in his lugubrious Eastern European fashion. Perhaps he wants to talk to me about the way Celestine and Adrienne are fighting over him. Then in the background I hear the telephone ringing; in fact the telephone has been ringing through my sleep like lots of fire engines with sirens on, rushing to put out a fire.

Geoff answers the call, speaks briefly, and then appears at the doorway of my bedroom shaking with mirth. 'You're a very popular man today,' he laughs. 'A journalist from the *Herald* has rung twice to talk to you. Have you told Oliver yet, Vladimir?'

'Told me *what?*' I ask.

Vladimir takes a deep sip of his coffee. 'We are werry embarrass,' he begins. 'Last night, go to werry interesting art exhibition. Sally ask Robert, Adrienne and I to go but Celestine take me. And what horrible thing do we see?' Vladimir shakes his head mournfully. 'Oliver been again werry stupid naughty boy. Is bad enough pouring wine down Celestine lovely breasts or hanging horrible arse out window taxi, but this werry dumb stupid even for Oliver.'

I turn to Geoff. 'What's Vlad talking about?'

'Your photo, matey,' Geoff laughs again. 'Life size. Huge gold frame. Full frontal. It's in the display window of an art gallery in Newmarket. And there's already a red "Sold" sign on it. Oh, you must have been a beautiful baby.'

Panicking, I leap out of bed and telephone our lovely Sally. 'I've just heard the news.'

'Isn't it wonderful?' she answers. 'Quentin is over the moon. He's never had such media interest before in any of his exhibitions. Nor has he sold an artwork so quickly. Television One is sending Wendy Petrie with a camera crew to interview him about your photograph. Are you available to talk to her as well?'

'But why didn't you tell me?' I moan.

'I thought you knew,' Sally answers, puzzled. 'Didn't you sign a piece of paper agreeing that Quentin could display it?'

'And who's bought it?!' I scream.

'Apparently some private collector in South Auckland. I understand he's a very serious collector of the nude male form.'

Oh no. My privates being perved at by some poxy person from Papakura, Papatoetoe or Pukekohe and his pals, misery.

And what will my sons say when they find out? But maybe they won't get to know about it.

Yeah, fat chance, Oliver.

On my way to our usual monthly lunch I ask the taxi to divert to Newmarket so that I can go past the gallery and take a look at the photograph. A crowd has gathered but I can see enough to confirm the gold frame and that it's *me* all right, wearing nothing but a cheeky grin, without the comfort of a leg crossed conveniently to censor my crotch, all very full and very frontal.

And it's clear that Rawiri and Eru know all about it. When I arrive at Eru's restaurant they are sitting with Rawiri's wife Shelley, and they're wearing huge sunglasses. 'Hello, Oliver,' Shelley greets me, 'you look positively overdressed today.'

I look at Rawiri and Eru. 'Gosh it's sunny in here,' I say sarcastically.

'We're incognito,' they say, not looking at me, 'and you're sitting over *there*.' They point to a table way in the darkest part of the room. 'Quite frankly, you are an embarrassment. Just wait until Dylan finds out.'

I blanch. 'You're not going to tell him, are you?' The look they give me says it all.

'Get real, Dad,' Rawiri snorts. 'Dylan's always found any of us out sooner or later, and he's a detective now, remember?'

'A *real* good cop,' Shelley adds. She kisses me sympathetically on the cheek and then picks up her bag. 'Well, see you later, hon,' she says to Rawiri.

'You're not going?' I ask her. With Shelley around, Dylan might not put me in plastic handcuffs and lock me up.

'I've got some serious shopping to do,' she explains.

'A new outfit for the wedding?' I ask.

Shelley glances at Rawiri. 'Something like that,' she says. Then, suddenly, we hear the squeal of brakes just outside the restaurant. 'Oops,' Shelley continues, 'that sounds like the vice squad. I'm outta here. Oliver, if I was you I would plead the Fifth Amendment and, if you need to be bailed out, Rawiri has some spare cash. Bye-ee.'

'I'll come with you,' I say to Shelley.

But it's too late. 'I need a drink,' Dylan says when he joins us. 'I've just had a horrible shock. I was driving over here and I was going past an art gallery and I thought I saw a painting of Dad in the nuddy.'

Rawiri and Eru look over their sunglasses at him. 'No, brother, it wasn't a painting.'

'Oh, thank God for that,' Dylan answers.

'It was a photograph,' Rawiri continues, 'and, sorry, brother, but it *was* your father. Airbrushed, of course, so that his bald spot doesn't show —'

'— and the dick isn't Dad's,' Eru adds meanly. 'It's either been digitally enhanced or else Dad's been suckered in by spam and is subscribing to enlargement pills.'

'But the photograph is still, recognisably, *your* father,' Rawiri smiles brightly.

Dylan has gone as white as a sheet.

I've noticed that whenever I've done something wrong the boys are always fobbing me off as the others' dad. 'You boys are being prudish,' I say. Then, as Dylan starts to growl and come at me, 'You two boys better save me.' But they join Dylan, and what else can I do but race for the toilet and lock myself in?

'Come out and face us like a man, you coward,' they yell through the door. And when I do, they jump on me, and Eru yells gleefully, 'All in boys! Let's scrag the old bugger!' Then he realises what he has said and adds, 'Oops, sorry Dad,' and we all fall about laughing, just like we have done all our lives.

Even so, they still get a few good playful punches in and end up all straddling me and pinning me to the floor.

'Say you're sorry, Dad,' Rawiri says. He puts me in a judo armlock.

'Sorry.' But I've got my fingers crossed, ha ha.

Dylan is on to my tricks. 'Really sorry?' he asks as he takes one of my legs and twists it into an impossible position. Ouch, that hurts.

'Okay, okay,' I answer. 'Why are you all so anal about this?'

We all laugh, and soft-hearted Eru comes to the rescue. 'Okay, boys, stop hurting my father. Looks like we'll have to forgive him for the hundredth time.'

—

But Eru's comment about forgiveness reminds me again of that time, after Fleur died, when I abandoned them to Anahera and I suddenly woke up. I asked myself, 'What am I *doing*?'

Yes, I did at least start to swim.

I went to collect them. It wasn't as easy as all that, of course. Rawiri and Eru ran into my arms as if I had been away for a thousand years. Dylan, however, stood back, watching me, glaring, fists clenched and bottom lip stuck way out. 'Why did you abandon us, Dad?' he asked, hurt. 'We've been waiting and waiting every day for you to come to get us.'

'Okay, Dylan,' I said. 'I'm sorry, son, I'm really sorry. But I'll never let you boys go again.' I tried to hug him.

'Don't touch me,' he yelled.

I tried to explain. 'Daddy was hurting, too,' I said. 'I've done wrong, but it's all over now. I promise you Dylan, I'll make it up to you.'

I brought the boys back to Auckland and I hired a young married Chinese couple, Hing Lee and Mei Lee, to come every second morning to give them breakfast, keep the house clean and have dinner ready on their return from school. As a special treat, Hing Lee and Mei Lee would also take the boys out to yum cha on Saturday mornings, and sometimes took them flying kites with the children of other Chinese friends. They were loving but also firm, and scolded the boys when they stepped over the line. Hing Lee introduced them to judo, which they all took to at once. They joined the local judo club and couldn't wait to pounce on me from behind the door whenever I got home from rehearsals, to try out their latest holds on me. 'All in, boys, all in!' Dylan would yell.

We all loved a good custard-pie fight, too, whenever we wanted to let off steam. It was Dylan's idea to go down to the local pie shop and buy every custard pie they had; we would undress down to our shorts and then let fly. 'Bombs away,' Dylan would yell as he and his brothers splattered me with custard. They loved nothing more than to gang up on me.

One night, when we had cleaned up the house after one of the fights and were sitting down to dinner, I complimented Hing Lee and Mei Lee on the beautiful Chinese meal. Dylan leant over to me and whispered in my ear, 'Dad, their names are really Henry and Mary.'

Hing Lee leant behind his chair and brought out one last custard pie and let me have it.

—

Order restored, the boys and I enjoy our lunch. But they are still picking on me, talking about my other past misdemeanours as a gay father and, especially, my partners.

'Can you remember Seth?' Rawiri asks his brothers. 'He was the first of our other fathers, wasn't he?'

'I liked him a lot,' Eru answers. 'Of course I was too young to know what him and Dad were *doing*, all that coming and going through the window when he got off duty and came to see Dad in the middle of the night. But then when Seth began to stay over —'

'I thought him and Dad were just having a pyjama party,' Rawiri laughs. 'It was only after Dylan gave us the facts of life that I realised something else disgusting was going on.'

'Too much information, brother!' Eru wails, punching Dylan in the chest.

'Well, somebody had to tell you,' Dylan answers grumpily. 'And I couldn't trust Dad to tell you properly, could I!'

By that stage Dylan was a know-it-all ten-year-old who thought it was time his brothers knew about sex. I was practising my violin when I heard the sound of fighting in Dylan's bedroom. When I went up to stop it, I found Rawiri looking over a sex manual with a great deal of interest and Dylan wrestling Eru to the ground. 'What on earth is going on?' I asked. Rawiri waved the book in my face brightly, 'Dylan is telling us about boys and girls,' he said. Eru then yelled at me, 'But he also told us about boys and boys and it just isn't true, is it, Daddy?'

I gulped; it was now or never. 'Actually, Eru, there's been something that I have been meaning to tell you,' I began. I watched as, wide-eyed and pale, he clutched Bunny close to his chest.

However, there was a bright side. When I told Seth we'd been outed he smiled and said, 'Yay, no more windows; I'll be able to come through the front door now.' Seth kept on coming through that door for two years; but he wanted to live with me and I couldn't take that step.

'Who was after Seth?' Eru asks Rawiri with a mischievous gleam. He's reaching for more salad to go with his fish; butter wouldn't melt in his mouth.

'Conrad was our next dad,' Rawiri glares, 'and you know it, Eru.'

Conrad was a ballet teacher and came into our lives when Rawiri was fourteen and the twins were twelve. He was a bit of a mistake but he had never had a family and I came with one that was readymade: stir in a little water and, voilà, three cute little boys and a cute dad to go with them. By that point, the boys were ready for an update on what they already knew about homosexuality: Rawiri was morose and told me he hated me; Dylan just frowned but didn't pass judgement; and Eru wouldn't hold my hand for weeks. What made it worse, however, was that they suspected Conrad was trying to meddle with their own incipient sexuality. They were attending a single-sex boys' school and found that the exclusive company of males, day and night, was not for them, thank you very much.

'Oh, those ballet lessons and those tights,' Dylan moaned. Conrad had decided that the boys should be introduced to ballet classes so that they would have an artistic as well as aggressive outlet. 'The only reason why we went was so we could meet some girls.'

Conrad only lasted a year before my boys clearly gave me notice that he would not do. 'Do you remember the end-of-year concert, Dad?' Rawiri asks me.

Do I what. Conrad's graduation concert was high on the social calendar for all his pupils. One of the dances, to Ponchielli's *Dance of the Hours*, involved eleven girls dressed as flowers in a lovely corps de ballet in which they inscribed beautiful patterns like a chain of daffodils. However, just before the curtain went up, one of the girls twisted her leg and couldn't go on. Conrad looked imperiously at Dylan and said, 'Dylan, *you* will be the eleventh daffodil.'

Wrong choice. Now, if Conrad had pointed at Eru, he might have been able to get away with it, but Dylan? Although Dylan was pinned into a tutu, given a wig and a wand, it was clear that rebellion was in the air. As soon as he appeared on stage he reconstructed the entire scenario. Off came the tutu, off came the wig — and out of the bottom drawer from hell came the most demented male dancer you ever saw. Worse, using the wand as some phallic extension, he chased after the daffodils, plucked all their petals off, and destroyed forever Conrad's perfect daffodil chain.

'Then there was Jake,' Dylan continues. 'You know, during Dad's political phase when he went public.'

Rawiri shudders. 'I was in the fifth form by then and we were getting hell from some of the other guys at school, especially when Dad started to work with the Aids Foundation.'

'That was very important work, boys,' I tell them, 'and people were dying of Aids. You should be proud of me.'

'We were, Dad,' Eru says. 'It's just that you were so vocal about it! Your picture started to appear in the newspapers —'

'You were wearing a handlebar moustache,' Rawiri adds, 'trying to clone yourself as the Marlboro Man —'

'— and you were also a member of other activist and gay groups. Didn't you meet Jake at the Gay Fathers Association, Dad, or was it when you were a member of the Gay Swimming Team?'

'No, that was Keith,' Dylan says. 'He was great! He helped me improve my swimming and I won the school butterfly the last year I was at school. Where's Keith now, Dad?'

'Then there was Mark,' Rawiri continues. 'He came during Dad's gay dance party phase when Dad became a gay icon.' He begins to shudder again. 'Man oh man, this is bringing back some terrible memories. Fill my glass, quick.'

My sons are talking about the time Mark and I first became involved in the Hero Parade. I joined a group of guys who were planning to make a float in the style of the Rio Carnival and met Mark there.

'I had just finished my masters,' Rawiri says, 'Dylan had graduated from Police College and Eru, you were on a polytech culinary course. We went down to Queen Street to watch the parade and this humungous float comes down the street with all these queens on it and in the middle is —'

'Is it a bird?' Eru laughs. 'Is it a plane? No, it's our exhibitionist Super-Gay Daddy, dancing his tiny tits off and wearing nothing but lots of glitter, a diamante jockstrap and long feathers. And what is he singing?'

Eru stands up and strikes a pose. Rawiri and Dylan join him as they start to sashay around the restaurant singing a Barry Manilow song. And who's going to tell them to sit down? Heck, they own the place.

> Her name was Lola, she was a showgirl
> With yellow feathers in her hair
> and a dress cut down to there!
> She would merengue and do the cha-cha —

'You boys are exaggerating,' I wince as they sway and jiggle, mince and wiggle and start a conga line through the restaurant.

The morning after the parade there I was, splashed all over the front page of the *Herald*. Not to mention what happened that same night. High on the fun of being on the float Mark and I had joined a carousing group of friends going from one club to the next. Around three in the morning, we turned up at the same club my boys were at. They were drinking at a bar with their girlfriends — Rawiri was dating Shelley — and I walked up to them and said, 'You boys should be at home.'

As soon as the words left my sweet stupid mouth I knew I was for the high jump. When I got home a few hours later, they were waiting up for me. Dylan as usual was the spokesman. 'Dad,' he began, 'what you did tonight was totally out of line. How do you think it looked to our girlfriends to have our father turn up at the same bar with his boyfriend du jour? Not only that, but you bore a faint resemblance to Big Bird on speed, shedding glitter and your feathers falling off all over the place. And who was the guy with you? He was really young-looking. You should be ashamed of yourself. Lucky for you I was off duty otherwise I would have asked him for evidence of his age.'

I tried to look meek and contrite, but Dylan had seen that before. 'From now on,' he continued sternly, 'if we are at the same bar, we don't know each other. You don't say hello to us, we won't say hello to you. Got it?'

I got it loud and clear. But Dylan wanted revenge; he bided his time, and one night, he struck. I went clubbing with some of the guys from the Gay Games and Dylan turned up in police uniform. He cuffed me! In the middle of the dance floor! 'Dylan,' I protested, 'this is ridiculous, you've had your fun.' And what did he say? 'Resisting arrest, are we?' He took me out of the club, put me in a paddywagon and I spent the night in jail while he lectured me on a parent's responsibility. 'Now go home,' he said, 'and try to be a good father.'

> At the Copa, Copacabana
> The hottest spot north of Havana —

The conga is making its way back to our table, and I think of Mark and the way he danced into my life.

Of all my men, I really fell for Mark. This will sound somewhat blasphemous, I know, but he was the closest I ever got to Fleur: larger than life, what you saw was what you got, and he had the same sense of exhibitionism and fun. The trouble was that on an emotional level we were just so volatile with each other: arguing one moment, loving the next. And I had split loyalties between Mark and my sons. There were times when I had to make a choice, and I always tried to put the boys first. Sometimes, when it might have been better to holiday with Mark alone, we took the boys with us and ended up not spending any time together at all. In circumstances like that, you can never win: Mark felt left out, and I'm sure there were times when the boys thought they were, too.

Mark and I kept up a rollercoaster relationship for two years, broke it off, but then tried to get back together. I suggested we go to Tahiti on a second honeymoon. But we ended up arguing again about the lovers we'd been seeing in between; the usual story of whether or not we should have an open or closed relationship. This was in 1997; I remember it vividly because halfway through our holiday we were at dinner and all of a sudden the manager came out and announced something to all the diners. Neither Mark nor I could understand French so I asked a man seated at a nearby table what was happening. He answered, 'La princesse Diana est morte.'

After that holiday we split forever, and Mark went to Australia: better that than the long descent out of passion and love. Better that than the onset of terminal boredom, waning of beauty, the lies, the simulation of love, the dissembling.

> Music and passion were always in fashion
> At the Copa . . . they fell in love!

The conga line concludes, and the patrons all clap my three clever sons, who bow from the waist and resume their seats. I am hoping that they will change the subject but they are still having their fun with me.

'Who were our other dads?' Eru asks the others.

'That's all there was,' I tell them. I am looking at the menu, trying to decide between crème brûlée and summer sweets.

'Oh, we're talking about the in-between dads now,' Eru says, batting his eyelashes. 'Like the American counter tenor, the Polynesian entertainer, the Italian stallion, the British professor —'

'Now he would have been a nice mother,' Rawiri says, not unkindly. I hadn't realised that Rob had an alter ego, Roberta, who liked to wear a dress on Sundays and cook a roast.

'You boys are making me sound like a slut,' I say grumpily.

'You have to admit you were busy, Dad,' Dylan says.

'Well, count yourselves lucky that I've been without a significant other for almost a year now,' I answer. As for sex, which is an entirely different matter, that too has been easy come, easy go, a matter of hits and misses. A lot of misses.

'And peace cometh to the valley,' Rawiri sighs.

'Until this photograph,' Dylan says darkly. 'Oh, Dad,' he continues, putting his forehead against mine. 'What am I going to do with you?'

—

I decide to walk from Eru's restaurant into Queen Street.

But my mind is still on Mark. In 2002, when I was on holiday with my latest boyfriend, Gordon, in Turtle Cove, Australia, I came across Mark again, staying at the same resort. I felt like I was in the middle of the sandwich, trying to be courteous to Mark while at the same time attentive to Gordon. Halfway into the holiday, the resort manager asked me, 'Which person are you here with, Mr Goodenough?' In the end it all turned to custard. Mark departed early, leaving a lovely note wishing me all the best. Gordon also left, telling me that seeing Mark and me together had made him realise how he still loved Chris, his former partner.

Ah well, you win some, you lose some; but, as I go along K Road, I think with affection and gratitude about the way life has treated me, and, in particular, the generosity of my sons in dealing with an errant and wayward dad. We had our moments, sure, and I can remember blazing rows with Dylan about my being gay. Rawiri disappeared from my life for a huge chunk of time; he went overseas, ostensibly for a year, but within six months he was back. 'I was homesick,' he told us. Dylan held himself together by focusing on what was important; making sure we stayed a family. Many times we'd all had to trust to the binding love that we had for each other to be able to find some accommodation. In the end, it was the sense of our family bond that enabled us to get over ourselves. Even today, whenever I have done something for which I have no excuse to offer, I still say, 'Oliver Goodenough, life's too short, get *over* yourself.'

Whistling, I go through the door of my favourite music shop. One of the group of hunky counter staff smiles and winks at me and I smile and wink back. I don't know him from Adam but he must recognise me from other times I've come in to buy CDs.

However, as I am going towards the classical section, he makes a sign that he will join me there. Mystified, I give him the thumbs up.

Oh-kayee. So here I am looking through the orchestral section: Ravel, *Bolero*: and, ger-reat, they have quite a few versions. Geoff's copy goes for fourteen minutes but, aha, here's one by Claudio Abbado that clocks in at fifteen minutes and two seconds; another by Simon Rattle at sixteen minutes and fifteen seconds; but, this will do it — a version by James Levine that goes for over seventeen minutes! Geoff, this one's for *you*.

I become aware that somebody is breathing down my neck. When I turn to look, the guy from the counter has joined me and is grinning at me in a very familiar way. 'I've been wondering,' he says in a smoky voice, 'when you were going to come by and pay me a visit.'

The penny drops. I didn't think I knew him — but now I remember. He's young, smooth-skinned and has lots of luxuriant hair. When I met him the last time I didn't notice his stunning tattooed Polynesian spiral. It begins at his neck, disappears into the collar of his T-shirt, and appears again on his right bicep.

'You must be missing this,' he says.

He pulls out my wristwatch.

9

I have tried to get through my life gracefully. Sometimes, however, that is not possible, and then I am so grateful for repentance.

Not that I need to repent, as nothing happens between me and Vincent. I know you probably think I am an animal, but all we do after he comes off his shift is go home to my place and have a cup of coffee. Afterwards, he comes with me and Horace on our usual daily walk and ingratiates himself forever with Horace by throwing him a stick for him to fetch at Westmere Park.

Sometimes, this is the way it happens. You sleep together first, and *then* you shake hands and start to get to know each other. 'I knew who you were as soon as you turned up at the club,' Vincent tells me as he throws the stick yet again for Horace. 'Man, you were out of it and becoming positively dangerous to traffic so I hauled you back to my apartment. I hope you got home in one piece in the morning.'

'And did we . . . ?' I ask.

'You don't remember?' he teases. He has a coy look on his face and I like the way he grins: lopsided, flirtatious, kidding me along.

By the time we get back to the house we are really getting to like each other. Vincent sees the photograph that I keep in the living room of myself with Rawiri, Dylan and Eru. 'Who are these guys?' he asks.

Might as well out with it. 'They're my sons.'

'Whoa,' Vincent answers, looking at me as if for the first time ever. 'How old did you say you were?'

'I'm in my forties.'

'Low end or high end?' He is staring closely at my face as if I do botox or use polyfillers or other miracle marvels on the market.

'How old are *you?*' I counter.

'I'm thirty-seven.' Twelve years age difference: permissible, just.

I throw him a curved ball just to see how he will handle it. 'Would you like to meet my sons?'

Vincent knows it's a test. 'Will this be before or after you take me on a first date,' he says boldly, 'to Salt, my favourite restaurant?'

'Oh I can do better than that,' I answer, thinking that I might surprise him by taking him to Eru's restaurant. 'But I'd be worried about my sons if I was you. They bite.'

Vincent is onto me. 'I'm not worried,' he smiles with his lopsided grin. 'I've had my shots.'

We shake hands. Then hug. As he leaves, he gives me my wristwatch.

—

After another orchestra rehearsal, I get home before Geoff.

Vladimir, stressed out from a blazing row with Celestine who has ordered him not to speak to Adrienne, brightens up when he sees me. I substitute Geoff's usual recording of *Bolero* with mine — the one that's at least three minutes longer. 'Oliver being werry naughty boy,' he says delightedly, wagging his finger.

I shower and go to bed. Horace manages to push the bedroom door open and comes plodding in, snuffling and wanting attention. I decide to give him a treat and pat at my bed, indicating that he can come and get a cuddle. After a couple of tries he manages to jump up and immediately slathers me with his grateful slobber. I give him a long rubdown and he groans with pleasure. Then I look into his aged red-rimmed eyes. I've had him since he was a pup.

Oh Horace, don't go just yet.

Vladimir pokes his head around the door gleefully. 'Is here, Geoff,' he says, 'with pretty new girl.' And my boys think *I* am busy, huh.

Vladimir and I listen as Geoff and his girl go into his bedroom. Very soon the *Bolero* starts up. We can hear him groaning and moaning in time with the music. But what's this? The music carries on, and on, and on, serenely past his climax. Payback time. 'Oh this *werry* good trick,' Vladimir tells me as we hear Geoff swearing and yelling about the way his staying power has betrayed him.

He discovers the new CD.

'Lock the door, quick,' Vladimir yells. He's as much of a coward as I am and, anyway, Geoff is bigger than both of us.

'I know it was you, Goodenough,' Geoff yells, pounding on the door. 'I'll get you for this.'

—

Next morning, I open the door slowly. Good, the coast is clear. Geoff has already left the house. I walk down the drive, yawning, to get the newspaper.

'Hello, Oliver,' Victoria calls. Her leg is out of plaster and she has resumed her usual morning run. 'Nice photo,' she winks.

I'm splashed all over the front page of the *Herald* in glorious colour with a figleaf decorously attached you-know-where. The headline is: IS THIS ART OR PORN? The accompanying caption reads:

> Outraged citizens are demanding the removal of a life-sized full-length nude photograph from the front window of the Bircher Gallery in Newmarket. 'It's absolutely disgusting that a naked man can be shown in public like this,' said nearby resident Mrs Maisie Collins, 'and I am calling on all decent citizens to boycott the gallery.' Well known photographer Quentin Fraser has defended the photograph on artistic grounds. 'I have already received an enquiry from the Museum of Modern Art in New York about the photograph and am currently negotiating with the owner to include it in an exhibition of nudes they are showing later this year.'

New York? Oh no. I read on.

Mr Fraser told the *Herald* he based the pose of the model on a well known sculpture by international artist Barbara Hepworth. 'If it's good enough for Ms Hepworth, it is good enough for me. I do not know what all the fuss is about.' Reliable sources advise that the model is well known gay icon and first violinist of the Auckland Philharmonia, Mr Oliver Goodenough, who previously appeared on the front page of the *Herald* in 1997 in similar undress at the Hero Party. He has not been available for comment.

A small inset of my previous front-page appearance appears with the article. Ah well, shovel it on, Lord.

10

And now it's Laurence's wedding day.

The sun is shining, the birds are singing, and the old people's home is abuzz with excitement. Laurence and Esther have invited the manager, staff and all the residents. The ceremony will take place at midday on the front lawn overlooking the sea, and the wedding breakfast will follow at 12.30, to fit in with the usual lunch arrangements. The elderly can get very cross if lunch isn't on the table at the appointed time, whether there's a wedding or not.

As I park my car and get my dinner suit out of the back, I see that my sons have everything under control. Dylan is in the carpark polishing the limousine for the getaway to the hotel after the wedding breakfast.

'Eru wants me to put a boy doll and girl doll on the bonnet,' Dylan says, 'but it might be a bit over the top. What do you think?'

Lord knows where Eru found them, but the boy doll is black with fuzzy wuzzy hair and the girl doll is a Barbie. 'Oh, why not,' I tell Dylan. 'Your grandfather doesn't get married every day.'

I wander around to the front lawn. Esther's grown-up son Herbert has done an amazing job. Herbert and his sister Gloria have come around to the inevitability of their mother's wedding and pitched in behind it. He is a jolly good sort; he's the office manager for Mitre 10, and has commandeered every white folding chair from the local shop plus some white shade umbrellas. He's also managed to find a long red canvas carpet and a white pergola, which is where the vows will be exchanged.

Meantime, Rawiri is hooking up the portable organ, running the cables into the resthome, and Shelley is giving instructions to young boys — I presume they are Esther's grandchildren — who will be acting as ushers. Some young girls are pinning little posies onto the chairs that line the red carpet.

'It's looking great,' I tell Herbert when I join him and the vicar, Reverend Johnson, beneath the pergola.

Herbert's a real softie. He's in tears. 'Anything for Mummy,' he says. 'But Gloria's still crying about it. She's taken to the gin and may be two sheets to the wind.'

As for the vicar, he seems to be taking this all in his stride. When I mention that he's looking very relaxed, he says, 'Oh, we're accustomed to weddings at the resthome. This is our fourth this year.'

Fourth? The lesson is clear. If you want to keep dear old granny out of the clutches of some ninety-year-old pensioner who's after her money or body or both, do not send dear granny to an old people's home.

Reverend Johnson looks at his watch. 'Is that the time already?' He claps his hands. 'Everybody? Time to get changed! Set your watches please at thirty minutes and counting!'

We all scatter. I take a quick look in the dining room. Eru, good boy that he is, has brought his restaurant kitchen team to do the cooking, and more of Esther's grandchildren are helping to set the tables. The menu is simple: ham, lamb, pork, chicken, lots of different salads, potatoes, peas and, for dessert, fruit salad and icecream. Eru is serving champagne for the toasts and then a lovely sauvignon blanc or merlot. 'Okay, Dad,' he waves cheerily. 'I'm hitting the shower now and I'll see you out on the lawn soon.'

I make my way to Laurence's room. 'How are you, Laurence?' I ask.

He is already dressed in tuxedo and white shirt. His shoes are spit-polished. His hair is brushed tight against his scalp and gleams with Brylcreem. He's already pinned his Maori Battalion medals to his tux but is still fiddling with his bow tie. 'Mereana used to do this for me,' he grumbles. 'I could never get the hang of the silly thing. No practical use to anybody whatsoever.'

I smile at him. 'Here, let me do that for you.'

Gosh, for a ninety-one-year-old man, my father-in-law is still a handsome dog. I make a wish to whoever's listening that I look that good when I get to be his age.

Time to get ready myself.

I am just slipping on my black jacket when Rawiri, Dylan and Eru knock on the door. 'Are you ready, Dad?' they ask. 'Have you got the ring?' My sons are looking handsome.

When we join Laurence, he insists on saying a prayer before we set off. He's one of the old-time Maori men, always saying a prayer before embarking on anything important. 'Right-o,' he says. 'Mustn't keep the preacher waiting.' With a spring in his step he leads the way out of his room, along the corridor, down the stairs and onto the front lawn.

The organist is playing the love theme from the movie *Titanic,* and the whole world seems to be waiting for us. I watch Laurence being greeted by his fellow friends from the home — and his genuine surprise that a couple of his Maori Battalion mates are there: 'E hika, I thought everybody else was dead!' — and I can't help getting a lump in my throat.

Eru asks me, concerned, 'Are you all right, Dad?'

'I've just been remembering your mother,' I tell him. 'She was so stunning on the day she and I got married.'

He takes my hand. 'I'm really glad,' he says, 'that you are thinking of her.'

We take our places in front of Reverend Johnson. 'Just in time,' he smiles at Laurence, 'Esther's on her way right now.'

The organist plays *Here Comes the Bride,* and we are on. Everybody stands. Some take longer than others but, after a lot of creaking knees and cracking joints, most are, well, in a kind of upright position.

Bettina, matron of honour, starts up her mobility scooter. With a roar and a puff of smoke she has ignition and comes putt-putt-putting along the red carpet; when she reaches the front she has a bit of trouble manoeuvring but, finally, with a little help from Dylan, she is stationed next to me. We give each other a smile of encouragement. 'Isn't this exciting?' she asks.

Next to come are Esther's three bridesmaids: Susan and Wendy from the home, and Esther's daughter Gloria. Susan is on two walking sticks, Wendy arrives pushing what looks like a Foodtown trolley, and Gloria has had two gins too many: she weaves from side to side, almost falls, but finally makes it to her berth beside Eru.

There's a sigh from the audience, 'Aaaahhh', and in comes Esther, on the arm of her proud son Herbert. She's looking beautiful in a powder blue dress of lace and a tiny hat with a veil and Ascot feathers. In her hands she holds a posy of summer flowers. Herbert delivers her to Laurence's side, looks at his sister Gloria and they collapse weeping into each other's arms. Sympathetic, Esther takes time out to pat them both. 'There, there, children, Mummy's only getting married.' Then she resumes her place beside Laurence, 'Goodness me, who would want to have children?' and smiles up at him.

'You are beautiful,' Laurence breathes. 'He tino ataahua koe.'

The organist stops playing. Reverend Johnson steps forward, smiling at us all. 'Please sit,' he tells the audience, and then winces at the sound of the cracking chairs as, with huge sighs of relief, the old people rest their weary bones. He begins his address, 'Ladies, gentlemen, friends, families of Laurence and Esther, we are gathered here today to witness —'

At this point I suddenly notice that the wind has changed direction, blowing from the west. Is it my imagination, or is that a huge cloud obliterating the sun, and are those Flying Monkeys coming our way? And is that the Wicked Witch of the West, flying in on her broomstick?

And Rawiri nudges me. 'Auntie Anahera has arrived.'

—

Well, Anahera and the rest of the whanau have gatecrashed the wedding after all. They have come in a huge caravan of cars, minibuses and taxis.

The bad news is that Anahera is still as angry as ever. She has dressed to the nines, looks very dramatic in black and a big picture hat and sunglasses, and — what's the use of being angry if nobody else knows it? — she stomps to the front, tells a poor unsuspecting Pakeha couple to 'Move, you're sitting on the family side,' striking a personal blow for the Treaty of Waitangi. Once ensconced, she calls to her sisters, 'Come on, girls, what are standing back there for?' Pearl, Whena and Kara meekly come at their sister's beck and squeeze in beside her; Hemi and Joe-Joe disappear to the very back.

Reverend Johnson is your usual inoffensive Anglican minister, and not accustomed to such drama. For the rest of the service he becomes increasingly fidgety. Have Laurence's people come to take their kaumatua hostage back to their tribal lands? Everybody is very nervous when the minister comes to the part: 'If there is anyone among those gathered here who is against this union, speak now or forever hold your peace.'

Now, I have never seen or heard of anyone intervening at this point except in novels or films. You know the kind of scene: young handsome boy on horseback, crying out the name of the beautiful girl who's getting married, sweeping all opposition to one side, grabbing her up onto his horse and riding off with her into the sunset.

This is not quite like that. But Anahera *does* get up, and everybody gives a collective gasp of horror. Laurence looks steadfastly forward without turning to listen to her, and Anahera addresses her comments to his back. However, instead of shouting, she speaks forcefully and quietly to him. I don't understand what she is saying because she speaks in Maori. Apparently she is crying — because Dylan tells me so. He understands Maori and he translates for me.

'Auntie Anahera is reminding Grandad about Grandma Mereana,' Dylan says. 'She is asking him to reconsider this marriage for the sake of her memory.'

The whole world stops as Laurence thinks over Anahera's words. Then he turns and embraces his daughters, one after another, and whispers in their ears. Weeping, they nod and sit down. Laurence resumes his place beside Esther.

'Do you wish to continue, Mr Wharepapa?' the vicar asks.

Laurence nods. 'Te mate ki te mate,' he says, 'te ora ki te ora. The dead to the dead, the living to the living. Yes, we carry on.'

Eru looks across at me and rolls his eyes to heaven, phew, and after a suspenseful moment, Anahera begins to melt before our eyes.

'All right, Dad,' she says. 'I am not happy about this but I will not stand in your way any longer.'

Of course it isn't over yet.

There's a flurry of activity as the whanau, now that Anahera has given her assent, pitch in behind Eru's cooks to accommodate the extra numbers. They furiously dig a hangi pit among the roses, set up extra trestle tables in the dining room, and embellish every dish with the usual Maori tidbits: crayfish, oysters, kina, raw fish, kumara and kamokamo.

But Anahera is still smouldering about Laurence's wedding, really hurting; I can understand that and I don't blame her. She had tried hard to stop the wedding, right up until the last moment before her father said 'Yes' to Esther; again, I know that her opposition came out of a deep and abiding love for her father and the memory of her mother.

Throughout the wedding breakfast I watch her brooding, pushing away the plates of sumptuous food as they are put before her. I see her fold her arms, refusing to be pulled into the bonhomie and affection that are clearly shown in the speeches in honour of her father and Esther. Rawiri gives a hilarious account of growing up with Grandad and proposes a toast to Sally and Wendy, the beautiful bridesmaids. Bettina responds with an equally funny set of reminiscences of how Laurence and Esther met at the home; 'I had my eye on him,' Bettina says grumpily, 'and was hoping that when we got older we could have races on our scooters.' Bettina proposes a toast to the gorgeous groomsmen, and everybody whistles.

Then it's my turn to talk about Laurence and Esther and the holy state of matrimony. I've spent quite some time writing my speech, and I've rehearsed it again and again with Eru. He has edited out all the appalling bits, including my joke about how I saw the stork flying this way so I shot it. What is left is not as funny but I know it is appropriate, has grace, and dignifies the proceedings. Indeed, as I talk I can see moist eyes among the audience, who are feeling mellow and sentimental.

All, that is, except Anahera.

I might have expected that she would stand up again just before I made the toast to the bride and groom. I already knew that she blamed me for Laurence's decision to marry again. What I didn't expect is her attack on me.

'You're a fine one to talk about the holy state of matrimony. You were living a sinful life before you married my sister and you live it now that she is gone. You should never have married Fleur. You should never have become a father.'

I am totally dismayed. All I can think of is: must my right to be married and a dad be so publicly challenged in this way — and not only in front of my father-in-law and his whanau, but also my sons?

Then I feel my Anglo-Saxon blood really *burning*. Still trying to take my boys from me, are you, Anahera? Just like that time when I left them up North with you and you went to get a court order to have them removed into your custody. What was your charge? That I was gay. But the judge threw that out. So what did you do? You asked my boys if they had ever seen me and Seth in bed together. Or if Seth or I had ever molested any of them. And when *that* didn't work, you told them lies about me. How I didn't want them around. That I'd given them away. You were so convincing. 'Why,' you asked Dylan, 'do you think your father gave you to me? If he'd wanted you he would have run after you when I took you away from Auckland, and hauled you out of the car. But he never did.' It was only when Laurence and Mereana told me what you were doing, Anahera, that I took action. Your own mother said to me, 'Oliver, you are the father. These are your kids. Come and get them. Now.' I drove like a maniac up to the Hokianga and I banged on your door and when you opened it I said, 'Where are my boys, you bitch? Give them back to me.'

—

The dining hall is completely silent. I go to respond to Anahera's bitter comments. But just as I begin to defend myself, Dylan lays a hand on my shoulder.

'No, Dad,' he says. 'Let me do it on behalf of myself and my brothers.' He gets up and in a quiet, reasonable voice begins to talk to his aunt. 'Hello Auntie,' he begins. 'First of all, let me acknowledge how grateful my brothers and I were to you when you took us in after Mum died. Yes, you are right, Rawiri, Eru and I often wondered why, for almost two months, Dad never came up to collect us and you are right, he should never have let us go in the first place.'

I lower my head, ashamed. *I made a mistake, Dylan. I am so sorry, please forgive me.*

'But the fact is, Auntie,' Dylan continues, breathing deep, 'in the end, Dad did come for us. He did come up and he did take us back to Auckland where we belonged, with him.' Dylan has to use his sleeve to wipe his eyes. 'Oh shit,' he says desperately, 'I'm not very good at this.'

Rawiri and Eru urge him on. 'You can do it, brother.' He's always been the leader, Dylan, the twin who beat Eru to be born into the world.

'As for your saying, Auntie, that Dad should never have married Mum or had us,' he resumes, 'maybe you're right. But the thing is that he did and we are here so the horses have bolted and it's too late to close the gate. And I am assuming you are basing your comments on the fact that Dad is gay. Well, there were times when my brothers and I used to wonder, why us? Eh, Rawiri, eh, Eru —'

Rawiri and Eru nod in agreement.

'There were times when we were so angry with Dad for being a gay man. Why couldn't we have had a father who was like the other fathers in the neighbourhood? And yes, why was Mum stupid enough to have him? Well, she was in love with him, he was in love with her, and they wanted children, they wanted *us*. Dad wanted *us*. And Auntie, when Mum was dying, do you know what Mum's last words to us were? "Your father will be lost without me. You boys look after him."'

Ah, so that's what has been wrong with you, Dylan, my son. You've faithfully kept your promise to your mother.

'All these years, Auntie, my brothers and I have done just that. It hasn't been easy, either. We've had to scrap our way through school and university over him, defending his honour and ours. When his photograph was on the front page of the paper on a float during the Hero Parade we had a huge argument in the university caf with some guys who were laughing at Dad; they wouldn't apologise, one thing led to another, and we ended up in a fight with them — Dad doesn't know this, but the vice-chancellor almost threw us out of university. Every person who has ever been in our lives has had to accept our dad before they get to first base with us. Can you remember, Shelley? The first question Rawiri asked you before he brought you home was, "By the way, my father is gay, do you have a problem with that?"'

Tears are brimming in my eyes. Of course I've suspected that the boys have sometimes had such a tough time. Perhaps I should walk out of their lives forever. Yes.

'Auntie, our father has been a good dad,' Dylan continues, revving up to the finish. 'And you know what? Every year, on Mum's birthday anniversary, he's taken us to see her and given us letters from her — except that her letters really stopped around six years ago, but the stupid bugger has kept on writing them for her, and he doesn't think we know about it. And he has insisted on our meeting every month at lunch even though there've been times when we don't want to come. Furthermore, he keeps on embarrassing us, like with this latest nudie stunt of his. But he's kept us together and he's the only dad we've got and we'll take on the whole world for him if we have to. Auntie, while Grandad was exchanging his marriage vows, he said something interesting, "The dead to the dead, the living to the living." You agreed to let him get on with his life, Auntie. Will you let us get on with ours?'

Anahera is like a reed swaying in the wind. Although she is still bitter, in the end she gives a nod, small, but a nod.

'As for the rest of you,' Dylan continues, defiant. 'I need to ask you all a question: Our dad is gay, do you have a problem with that?'

One venerable old gentleman asks, 'What's the lad been saying?'

'He's been telling us his father is gay.'

'Eh? What?'

'His father, Laurence's son-in-law is GAY.'

'He was the one who brought the crays? Oh, well done.'

Even so, Anahera tries to have the last word. 'I hear what you say, nephew,' she begins, 'but even so, that doesn't change the fact that gay people are not appropriate as parents and —'

But Laurence has had enough. He stands up and waves his walking stick around. 'Kati,' he says. 'Stop. Anahera, you and your sisters are spoiling my wedding. This is my day, not yours. You should be ashamed of yourselves. At least Esther's side, while they are not happy either, had the decency to sort out their feelings with us before our marriage.'

Then he turns to me and waves his walking stick again.

'You done good,' he says. 'You made Fleur happy and you brought up your boys and they are happy. What more could a father-in-law want than for the man in his daughter's life to be good to his daughter and to bless him with fine grandsons? You done good.'

He takes a breath and his eyes glitter.

'And now, could we all get on with it? Me and Esther are tuckered out already and there's still a few hours before you lot leave us and we can go to bed.'

11

Another lunch with Rawiri, Dylan and Eru.

I should have known something was up when Dylan came to collect me. He arrives with Iosefa, Chuck, Rajiv and Mohammed, and another carload of his police pals is following us.

'Are you all coming to lunch too?' I ask Iosefa. The boys are all dressed in old rugby shirts and shorts, which is strange attire to wear to a smart Ponsonby Road restaurant.

'We're your escort,' Iosefa answers, squeezing me in the middle of the back seat of Dylan's car, 'aren't we, boys?'

When we arrive at the restaurant and I see the notice — PRIVATE FUNCTION — displayed on the door and windows, I should have really twigged then that something was going on. Latecomers like Robert, Sally, Adrienne, Vladimir and Geoff are scooting in before me.

'Oh, this will be fun,' Geoff says to me, showing his teeth. He has never forgiven me for swapping his *Bolero*. For a moment, like all the other blokes over forty, he thought he might have to go onto Viagra.

Strange, but they have all come in mufti as well: old sweatshirts, and Adrienne, who is always vain about her hair, is wearing a scarf. 'You asked for this,' she mutters. 'That was my best bra.'

But it isn't until I walk through the front door and Rawiri snaps it shut, 'Gotcha!' and Eru runs to the toilet and locks it, that I realise that something really is up. Especially when I see all the people who are there: Maestro De Montalk wearing running shorts (not a good look), Dr Robinson in trackpants, Shelley of course, Quentin . . . and is that Hing Lee and Mei Lee? Yes, it is!

Oh God, other faces are looming out of my past. 'Hi, Seth,' I greet him; he grins back and gives me a high five. Keith, the swimmer, he's also here, but he's way out of condition with a pot gut balancing his huge shoulders. 'Rawiri sent me an invitation,' he says, 'and I had to come. You're looking good — so far.'

The rest of the group echo Keith's laughter, especially a man I haven't seen in years: Mark. He grips my hands and whispers to me, 'We should get together and have a talk after all this.' The old emotion swamps us both but I am wondering what does he mean: *After all this?*

It looks like everybody who has ever been in my life is here: members of the orchestra, Dylan's police rugby mates, friends from the gay community and, coming forward now, Anahera, Hemi, Joe-Joe, and Laurence and Esther. 'We're not part of this,' Laurence laughs. 'We just came to watch.'

I look at my boys in puzzlement. *Watch?* 'Is this a surprise birthday party?' I ask them. 'But it's not the big five-oh quite yet.'

'Does it look like a surprise birthday party?' Rawiri asks evilly. All the furniture in the restaurant has been cleared out. Huge sheets of plastic line the windows and on the floor is a large piece of canvas.

'Okay,' Dylan sighs, 'let's put the old man out of his misery.' He walks to the middle of the empty floor. 'Hi Dad,' he says brightly, 'I am master of ceremonies for the afternoon.' He turns to the guests. 'Thank you, everyone, for accepting the invitation that my brothers and I sent to you, and thank you also for coming in the appropriate dress. We have had almost one hundred percent RSVPs, which just goes to show how popular — or unpopular — our dad is.'

By now, I am getting a funny feeling about this and wondering if there's another exit.

'Going somewhere?' Vladimir asks. 'Oh, this will be werry good bloody fun.'

I'm not so sure. I watch as Eru's staff wheel in steel racks. Custard pies are stacked one on top of the other. Somebody has been busy cooking up a storm. 'You'll love some of the flavours, Dad,' Eru says. 'Lemon, strawberry, meringue-coated, your favorite, banana, yummy.'

I suddenly get the picture. Oh no, a custard pie fight; we haven't had one of those in years. But this one is like the King Kong of all custard fights. And I'm the target.

I make a run for it.

'Grab him, boys,' Dylan yells.

Before I know it I am imprisoned by Dylan, Rawiri, Eru, and some of Dylan's rugby mates.

'You all know the rules,' Dylan yells to everyone. 'Bombs away.'

Next moment there is an almighty rush for the racks. Custard pies come flying in my direction.

'This is for the *Bolero*,' Geoff says.

'This is for pulling off my toupee,' the Maestro yells.

'And this is for being werry bad boy,' Vladimir says, 'and pouring wine down Celestine's nice breasts.'

But Celestine is put out. 'Hey, Vlad, I can throw my own pie, thank you.' She's in the middle of throwing one at him when one splatters *her*.

'Oops,' Adrienne purrs, 'sorry. Slipped.'

I take the opportunity to grab a custard pie and aim it at Dylan, the dirty little rotter. He ducks and, unfortunately, Anahera is standing just behind him. 'I honestly didn't mean it,' I say to her as she advances on the steel trays and picks one up. 'Truly, cross my heart.'

'Oh yes you did,' Anahera answers, 'you . . . you bloody Pom.'

Keith gets a good one in and I recognise in it all the arguments and quarrels we had.

Then Mark taps him on the shoulder and says, 'Excuse me, I think it's my turn now.' He advances on me with two pies, one in each hand.

'I'm warning you, Mark,' I say to him, 'don't you even think about it.'

He does, and goes ahead with his aim. 'I've been wanting to do this for a very long time, you bastard,' he laughs.

Custard pies are flying everywhere. Women are squealing with laughter, chasing after each other. The rugby guys are having a great time, sighting on their mates and socking it to them. And who brought Horace? There he is, barking in the middle of it all.

Laughing, I manage to wrestle the key to the bathroom off Eru and run towards it, trying to unlock it.

'Don't let him get away!' Dylan calls. I can hear him in hot pursuit. The damned key won't go in.

A hail of pies comes flying in my direction and I go down. Dylan yells to his brothers, 'All in boys, all in! Let's scrag the old bugger!'

Next moment, Shelley is also there, but Rawiri says to her, 'Darling, be careful of the baby.'

The baby?

I wipe the custard off my face and stare at my sons. 'Gawd, please don't tell me I'm going to be a grandad.'

—

Life is a cabaret old chum, come to the cabaret.

With great wonder, I start to wipe the custard off my face.

Hey, a grandson. I can take him on adventures. Maybe we can go back to England for a visit and I can tell him about his Anglo-Saxon ancestors and teach him our pagan war cry: *Heilsa allur!* And —

'It's going to be a girl, Dad,' Rawiri says. 'We're going to call her Fleur after Mum.'

A girl?

Mmmn, this custard has a really nice flavour.

Okay, Oliver, you can do this. A baby girl, oh my, a *girl*. Wasn't Boadicea a girl? And girls can learn war cries too, right? And I'll be able to tell her about her gorgeous grandmother, buy her stilettos or Brazilians and take her swimming with stingrays in Tahiti or climbing the Himalayas or going to the Galapagos and —

Oh, the wonderful comedy of life. Sometimes you just have to laugh. I look at my three sons, Rawiri, Dylan the Brave, and Eru. I think to myself that it was they who taught me to swim. Without them I would have sunk to the bottom of the ocean. Even so, I know that they would have come to rescue me, I just know it.

With pies flying all over the place, and the screams and yells of the pie fight around me, I realise that it isn't true that you have all the time in the world; you don't. But while you have it, make sure you fill it with love.

All I've ever done is love life, tried to be a good husband, father, partner and friend. I must have done *something* right in my life after all.

Life has loved me back.

ihipi

the young prince

As soon as the young prince crossed the border into Ihipi, the entire landscape changed. One moment he had been traversing the steep cliff track to the top of the ridge, his tunic wrapped around his waist because of the hot sun and his hair tied up into a topknot because of the sweat. The next moment he had reached the pou whenua, the carved boundary marker of Ihipi. He stepped past it and entered through the cleft in the rocks and, immediately, a blast of wind wrapped him in bitter coldness.

The young prince shivered, unwrapped his tunic and put it on. He looked back the way he had come. The landscape he had left was golden with sun, stretching away to a far, azure sea. The slope that he had climbed was dazzling with lush green mosses and pinpricked with white alpine flowers. The sky was clear, blue and without blemish. On the Ihipi side, however, the sky was shredded with dark clouds, curtaining the sun. Whatever light penetrated bathed the landscape in a spectral winter glow.

Breathing deep, the young prince turned away from the land of light and descended into Ihipi, the land shrouded in darkness. The track plummeted through jagged rocks, and soon the young prince found himself in a grotesque forest shrouded in mist. The trunks of the trees were gnarled and misshapen and the branches were strangled with saprophytic vines. The young prince sensed that something was wrong in the forest. The moss softened the sound of his footfall, yes, but it was more than that: the forest was silent. There were no birds.

The young prince was relieved when the track took him out of the forest and onto the plains of Ihipi. Hulking in the distance, he could see the fabled citadel, Areraria, Ihipi's central fortress, situated on a spur rising from the plains. The spectral light was fading and rain began to fall, stinging his skin. Wishing to arrive at Areraria before nightfall, the young prince began to jog across the plains, along the banks of a black river. He came across a gap in the susurrating reeds, dived into the water, and swam to the other side.

The rain was falling heavily now. Resting, the young prince recalled the stories he had been told about Ihipi. Once, an entire tribe numbering over twenty thousand had lived here. Where he was standing was one of the many villages or hamlets of Ihipi; others had been scattered across the plains. Each village had been the centre of prosperous cultivations, kumara and taro gardens — but these no longer existed. The sleeping-houses of the village were now skeletal structures, the elevated storehouses had collapsed and the food storage pits had caved in. The fires in the small sunken fireplaces, takuahi lined with four stones, had long ago ceased to be lit. By the banks of the river were the derelict remains of fish traps and eel weirs. A spring, once virgin, was filled with brackish undrinkable water.

Ihipi was a wasteland, a place where nothing grew.

The young prince hastened onward through the slashing rain towards Areraria. He came to the first defensive earthworks, four miles in length, encircling the fortress. His heart was thudding as he climbed through the maze of stockaded terraces, linchets, massive ramparts, fosses, vallums, cross stockades and scarps.

Areraria was a pa whawhai, a fighting pa. Its engineers had taken advantage of every contour of the ground to raise defensive bulwarks on any available knoll, flanking angle and elevated projection; the defensive works enclosed separate fighting spaces that were able to be locked off one from the other.

'All I ever heard about the size of Areraria is true,' the young prince said to himself, still not believing it. Even the rumours did not do justice to the dimensions of the fortress; its immensity beggared description. Indeed, Areraria had been able to accommodate all the tribe whenever Ihipi was under attack. And during the Great Battle, this was where the people had retreated: to the famed citadel, this kohanga or nest.

The Great Battle had taken place before the young prince was born. Where were they now, the people of Ihipi? Either exiled or dead: human middens embedded within the earthworks of the very pa that had once been their glory.

The young prince reached the small bridge leading to the main gateway and overhanging watchtowers. On either side of the gateway the main walls pierced the sky; remnants of ladders and ropes could still be seen against the walls. The ground sloped down vertically from the defensive works on all sides. A huge ditch like a moat, filled with swampy water, provided added protection. Areraria floated within the moat like an armoured artificial islet.

'Karanga mai, karanga mai, karanga mai,' the young prince called to the fortifications in ritual challenge. 'Welcome me, welcome me, welcome me.'

But there was no answering call from the puwhara, the watchtowers, no challenge from any sentry stationed in the trenches or on the ramparts. His own voice faded away across the deserted landscape.

Taking out his patu, the young prince began his whakatau, his approach. He stepped quickly across the bridge and through the gateway, chanting and gesticulating as he went: 'Whakatau mai au, eke panuku, eke Tangaroa e.' He saw that the entrance passage had been cleverly blinded and protected with lateral defences, so he crossed over: 'Whakawhiti au, whano, whano e.' As he moved beyond the gateway he took note of the outer elevated screens, the serrated fighting stages, bastions, redoubts and defensive passages.

He penetrated further into the decaying labyrinthine structure with its series of inner stockades. 'Is anybody here?' he called again and again. Finally he reached his destination: the great courtyard in front of an elaborately carved wharenui at the centre of the citadel. He thought he saw shadows, and that at last the pa's defenders were nigh. 'Haramai te toki, haumi e, hui e, taiki e.'

Alert, quivering his patu, the young prince saw that his opponents were not warriors at all. He had reached the sacred precinct. Standing in front of the royal meeting house was a cluster of twenty pou — carved posts, supernaturally shaped — within which resided the many mauri, the talismanic life representations of the gods. But even they had fled.

Stopping, the young prince lowered his fighting weapon. 'Ka tika, it is true then. Areraria is deserted.'

Not quite. Beyond the door of the meeting house the young prince could see the flickering of a fire. There was life after all in this dead land.

The young prince saw a shape coming through the dark doorway of the wharenui. The next moment, an old man stepped out into the grey light.

Raising his patu, the young prince held it at the ready. But something about the way the koroua was dressed and the way he moved made him hesitate. The old man was completely covered in a black feather cloak, and he wore a white mask of bleached flax with holes for his eyes and mouth. As he made his way towards a pile of wood at the side of the meeting house, he stumbled.

The koroua was blind.

With compassion the young prince sheathed his patu.

The old man looked up quickly, his mask swivelling towards the skimming sound of the patu as it slid sharply back into its sheath. 'Ko wai tera?' he asked. 'Who is there?'

the blind man

In the world of the blind, although sight may have gone, the other senses compensate for the loss. Like the night bat, therefore, the koroua could hear the slightest rustle of a rat in the flax, or smell a lizard as it shed its skin. His fingertips could touch the air and know when something was moving through it.

With his hands he sculpted the shape of the stranger he knew was standing on the marae. 'Who are you?'

The stranger's voice, when it came, was masculine. Young. It hinted at strength but also at humanity. It lacked malice. When he heard it, the old man knew he was not destined to die by its owner's hand. Not yet.

'He waewae tapu,' the young stranger answered. 'I am a foreigner to the land of Ihipi and the court of Areraria.'

The old man wheezed with laughter: 'Haha te whenua, haha te tangata, Ihipi is deserted of people and there is no court in Areraria.' He grew suspicious. 'He aha to pirangi? What are you doing here? What do you want? If you seek plunder, there is nothing here.'

'What do I want?' the young stranger echoed. 'My curiosity about Ihipi and what happened here has drawn me to Areraria. In particular, the great love story of Ihi, the queen of this land, for the warrior Ohiri is one of the most famous korero throughout our world. Whoever hears the story cannot remain unaffected by its magnificence and its tragic dimension.'

The old man nodded. 'Ka tika,' he answered. 'You cannot ask about Areraria without asking about the arikinui Ihi and her husband Ohiri. But is your interest that of a historian or do you have some more personal compulsion?'

'I seek only the truth. The arikinui's story is now so accreted with legend that one can no longer discern what is the fantasy and what is the reality. As for the rest, yes, I do have a personal interest. My whakapapa, my genealogy, joins me to her —'

'To the queen?' the old man asked quickly.

'Ae,' the young stranger nodded. 'When the kingdom fell, I was one of the many morehu, the survivors. I was taken, as a child, into the land on Ihipi's western border. I have many questions about my papakainga, my homeland, and I have come in the hope that I might find some remnant of the original tangata whenua still keeping ahi ka. I am pleased to have found you, koroua. So first, welcome me back to the wa kainga. I come in peace. Let us talk, and perhaps in our conversations, I might discover the answers that elude me. In particular: Why did this great kingdom fall? Were you an eyewitness to Ihipi's fortunes, and to the love of Ihi for Ohiri?'

'All right,' the old man nodded, weighing the words of the young stranger. 'If you want to talk, let us korero. I grow weary of my own company and conversation with a stranger will be a pleasing diversion. Kei te tu ake ahau ki te powhiri. Come and share my world of darkness if you dare, and I will tell you the truth. I pray that you have the courage to listen to it.'

So saying, the old man began a chant to the young stranger which was both a welcome and a warning. 'Piki mai ra, kake mai ra, homai te waiora ki ahau. Climb towards me, ascend, bring with you the waters of life.' The words were ritualistic, gnomic, talismanic. 'Troubled has been your sleep, young stranger, and so the tides of time have brought you here to find your destiny. It could be death, it could be life, face it if you dare, even though the tides might take you to Te Reinga.'

The young stranger accepted the challenge. 'Call me on, old man.'

'In that case,' the koroua answered, 'homai ki te hariru.'

The young stranger stepped onto the marae. He shook the old man's hand. 'Remove your mask, koroua,' he asked, 'so that we can hongi, press noses.'

'No, I cannot show you my face,' the old man said. Before the young stranger knew what was happening, the koroua swept a foot under his legs and fell with him to the ground. 'What do you really want?' He held a shard of obsidian at the young stranger's throat. But even as he spoke he felt the shadow of the young stranger's patu at his head.

The voice of the young stranger was unafraid. 'Be careful with your weapon, koroua. Strike if you wish but, in the same instant, my patu will lift your cranium.' The patu glowed, highlighting a seam of black which curved like a shadow patu within the greenstone.

The old man rolled off the young stranger. 'I wanted to take your measure,' he said. 'I can tell that you are a warrior, as once I was also. Help me up.' The young stranger did so and the old man gripped him tightly.

'More tricks, koroua?'

'No,' the old man answered. His fingertips were moving lightly like spiders across the young stranger's face. 'You are indeed youthful, and handsome, too,' he said, and there was envy in his voice. 'Once I was young and handsome like you. My skin, also, was tight across the face and enhanced my cheekbones. And, like you, my nose was aquiline and my lips did not show any of the fleshiness that suggests unseemly appetites. I could kill you just to get into your youthful skin.'

The koroua suddenly pushed his fingers into the young stranger's mouth, probing to count his teeth. 'How old are you?'

'I am nineteen years,' the young stranger answered.

'And not yet with moko?' the old man asked, enjoying this game.

'My father still lives. Not until he dies will I consent to the tattooist's chisel. Until then, my face will be unfinished.'

The koroua nodded approvingly. 'Forgive an old man his eccentric ways. Haramai, it is cold standing out here. Help me take some wood for the fire and come inside.'

The young stranger grabbed an armload of wood and followed the old man, stepping across the threshold. At that moment, the daylight winked out. A gust of wind swirled, and rain drummed loudly like dreams.

One moment light, the next moment darkness.

'None too soon,' the old man said. 'Any later, and you would have had to wait until morning for the welcoming ceremony.' People never welcomed strangers after dark. Only spirits, ghosts or malevolent beings were abroad at night, and to welcome any visitors after sunset was to invite the possibility of doom or death.

He beckoned the young stranger towards the fire. The flames flickered throughout the interior. The carvings were glorious, hieratic friezes depicting life at the royal court of Areraria. The vignettes seemed to come to life, dancing, fighting, playing, through the burning flames.

'E noho.' The old man motioned that the young stranger should sit. He reached for a plate of kumara, yams and other root vegetables and offered the food to his guest. The young stranger had brought some dried shark meat and a calabash of water, which he shared with the old man.

It was the wai, cleansing and clear, that opened the koroua's memory. 'Tatou te korero ki whakarongo i a koe, ka tika. Now let me tell you about Ihi and her fabled love for Ohiri.' And the old man began to korero about the kingdom of Ihipi before the Time of Madness.

—

'Every story about Ihipi must begin with Ihi, the queen of this land. She was so magnificent it is no wonder she has become the stuff of legends. People who met her when she became queen were swayed by her beauty, but others who had known her longer said of her, "If you think our arikinui is dazzling now, you should have seen her as a young woman." Then, she was flawless. The perfect sheen of her skin was unmatched. Her eyes were wide, the irises flecked as if with the iridescent colours of the paua shell; many a man, looking into Ihi's eyes, was immediately enslaved with love for her. Her nose was small, her lips generous and her hair like the dark blue-black feathers of the tui. Whenever she walked in sunlight, her hair shimmered blue, black or lustrous green as pounamu. She was tall, shapely, truly a descendant of the gods come to live among the common folk.'

The young stranger heard the desire in the old man's voice. He himself felt a quickening in his blood at the description of the godlike Ihi, the woman accustomed to getting what she wanted.

'Legendary also,' the old man continued, 'was the land of Ihipi. I nga ra o mua, Ihipi was a land always in an indomitable summer, not as it is now, enshrouded in mists and cloud. As a young girl, Ihi lived in happiness here. The only blemish occurred when her father died. As sole claimant to the kingdom, she inherited the crown. However, immediately her inheritance was challenged both from within and from without. Her male cousin, Whiti, refused to accept a matriarchy, and raised a rebellion in the east. Ihi quelled it with great force, granted Whiti clemency and ordered him into exile. But on the way out of Ihipi, his travelling ope was set upon by unknown bandits, who murdered him.'

'Some people say,' the young stranger interrupted, 'that Ihi had secretly ordered the assassination.'

The old man chuckled. 'Such stories about Ihi! We will never know. Even as a young queen Ihi had the political intelligence to match her incredible beauty, and her motivations may well have included murder for political purposes. But the greatest challenges to her ascension to power came from three chiefs whose lands bordered on hers.'

'The one-eyed Heti, Rewhita and Huhia,' the young stranger whispered, recalling the legends. 'People say that Heti was the most dangerous of the triad. Was it true that he lusted after Ihi, and that Ihi laughed in his face when he presented his suit?'

'Beauty of face and form,' the old man said, smiling, 'is not always reflected by beauty of temperament. Ihi could be cruel and heartless and lacking in diplomacy. In particular, she possessed a vein of arrogance, an assumption that the world and all that existed in it was there only for her pleasure.' The old man shifted into a more comfortable position. 'Never forget, young warrior, that in the hierarchy of our world, Ihi was arikinui. Her decisions were not necessarily motivated by tribal consensus, but by what she personally wished. There's no doubt that Heti's offer of marriage was an affront to her. Accordingly, she played a cruel trick on him. She found a one-eyed woman in Ihipi and said to Heti, "Let beauty go to beauty, and a one-eyed man go to a one-eyed woman. Here is your one-eyed bride." It was a costly joke. From that moment, Heti vowed that he would have his vengeance and he began to plot against her. But before he could declare war, Ihi had already moved to take the upper hand. She was a strategist and she knew that, by herself, she could not hold Ihipi against the combined armies of Heti and the other warrior kings of the borderlands. "I need a husband to rule by my side," she decided. "I need a warrior whose physical power, name and strength, conjoined with my mana and wairua, will strike fear into the hearts of my enemies. Is there such a man?"'

'And there was,' the young stranger nodded. 'Ohiri, the great wanderer. I have heard many tales of why Ihi selected him. Which is the true one?'

The old man chuckled. 'Again, legend surrounds Ohiri — but isn't that always the way with people who bestride the world and who are larger than life? What is of more importance is that Ihi was intrigued by him —'

—

Just as Ihi was beautiful, Ohiri was reputed to be among the most handsome of men; therefore, a suitable match. Just as she, from girlhood, had been trained in the arts of leadership, so too had Ohiri, from boyhood, been schooled in military skills; he was said to possess the strength of twelve men, and he had been employed by many chiefs as a mercenary in their intertribal battles. Famed as a lover, could he be equal to Ihi in the art of lovemaking? Would he make a suitable consort? There was only one way to find out.

Ihi heard that Ohiri was appearing at a cultural and sports tournament in a coastal kainga two days' travel from Ihipi. 'I will go and observe, and if Ohiri's strength and skills are as people say they are, perhaps we may talk of betrothal.'

She travelled by ceremonial double-hulled waka to the tournament. Although she arrived on the evening before the games, not once did she make an appearance among the gathering of iwi. She stayed on the waka, a shimmering enigmatic figure only barely perceptible within her curtained quarters.

And what did she see of Ohiri when the tournament began? A tall warrior who despatched all his opponents in individual combat with patu and taiaha, the hand club and fighting spear. A man who, in wrestling matches, could not be held down, even when ranged against four or five others. In the marathon, Ohiri was the frontrunner from start to finish. In the haka, nobody could match him. In diving and swimming, although Ohiri was not of a coastal iwi, he swam longer distances and dived deeper than anyone else; when he rose from the sea, aware that Ihi was watching, he had covered his body with octopi and the most succulent shellfish. 'Take these to the foreign queen,' he laughed, pulling the octopi and paua one by one from his body, exposing the long eel of his manhood.

And, on his part, what did Ohiri see? He saw a woman who challenged him. His playful seduction of Ihi in the offering of octopi and paua was rebuffed when Ihi returned the seafood with the message that it was too salty. Ohiri was irritated. He was accustomed to women throwing themselves at him; to be rejected offended him. He knew Ihi had come to the tournament to look him over. Accordingly, he mocked her, saying, 'Who does she think she is? I am not some stud to be chosen by any woman. I do my own choosing, and have no interest in her beauty, no matter how legendary. Besides, some people say that beneath her gown she has a lizard's tail.'

All the same his interest was piqued. At the end of the tournament, when he was being acclaimed as the greatest warrior of all, he looked in her direction. 'All right, my queen,' he muttered to himself, 'come and ask me to be your husband and give me the satisfaction of turning you down.'

'I have seen Ohiri,' she said, 'and everything that has been said about him is true. But I will not descend to making any offer to him. Nor am I prepared to be a feminine sacrifice on the altar of his victory.' She ordered the immediate departure of the ceremonial waka.

Astonished, Ohiri and the many iwi at the tournament heard Ihi's paddlers calling, 'Timata! Hoki atu matou ki te wa kainga, ki te whenua o to matou arikinui! Hoe, hoe, hoia ra! Let us go! Let us return to our homeland, to the lands of our queen! Paddle onward, paddle!'

Ohiri made his decision. He leapt into the sea and began to swim after the waka. Ihi's captain was already unfurling the sails. Ohiri doubled his stroke and caught a trailing rope. As the sails belled full he was whipped along in the canoe's wake. Pulling himself hand over hand, he clambered on board.

Ihi was waiting for him in her quarters. 'We welcome the noble Ohiri,' she said, her head bowed, 'most excellent among all warriors.' He approached her and lifted her face so that he could look into her eyes. By the time the waka reached Ihipi, Ohiri had become her husband. On arrival, she presented him to the court and to her iwi. The marriage celebrations lasted many days. Within the sacred precinct marked out by the pou, Ihi and Ohiri affirmed their vows.

'We bless this union,' the mauri sang, 'and for as long as you both honour us with your worship, we will honour you.' The mauri danced and shimmered, creating rainbows of light by day and overarching aurora by night.

Ihi's stratagem worked. Seeing Ohiri by her side, Heti and the other warrior kings let rest all dreams of immediate conquest. Heti, however, did not give up his thoughts of revenge; he only postponed them.

—

'Is it true,' the young stranger asked the old man, 'that Ihi was ten years older than Ohiri — almost thirty? How could Ihi, a mature woman, manage to seduce such a young gladiator to be her consort?'

The old man nodded. 'Some people say that it was her tohunga, Horuhi — Ihi's chief minister and reputed to be the most powerful shaman who had ever lived — who aided her. If Ihi wished it, Horuhi could stop the sun in its daily traverse of the sky. Compared with that feat, enabling Ihi to seduce a young man with spells and charms would have been a simple matter. I can assure you however, young stranger, that Ihi required no such sorcery. She had a remarkable force of will and persuasion — against which Ohiri was powerless. He ceased his wandering once he became Ihi's husband, and settled down in Ihipi. But there was one wish Horuhi could not grant his queen: a son from her union with Ohiri. Instead, Ihi and Ohiri had four daughters.'

'Tell me about them,' the young stranger asked. 'Were they as lovely and as innocent as the legends tell?'

The old man sighed heavily, and the young stranger heard him weeping beneath his flax mask.

Why would the old man not take it off?

'Young stranger, your question is a painful one. Hera was the firstborn, a laughing child who was adored wherever she went because she made people laugh. Maraea and Rawinia came soon after, both tomboyish and always wanting to be off playing with the young boys of Ihipi. But the one who was most loved by the people was the youngest, Ata, named after the dawn. Unlike the others, Ata was always hiding behind her sisters' skirts, always timid and needing to be protected. The princesses all became delightful young women and the people of Ihi continued to adore them.

'But what was the attitude of their mother to them? This may seem strange to you; Ihi was accustomed to being the only sun shining in the sky. Not only that, but the love of her husband had become an obsession for her. She did not welcome rivals for his love, even from her daughters. Besotted with Ohiri, her daughters came second in her life.'

'Second?' the young stranger asked.

'This might seem an unnatural maternity,' the old man tried to explain, 'but, after all, I say again that Ihi was an arikinui and the usual rules of human relationships did not apply to her. However, the four daughters were doted on by their father ,who loved them unconditionally. And while they honoured their mother, they loved their father. They would approach Ihi as anyone would approach an arikinui, heads bowed in recognition of her great mana. But whenever their father was near, they would run to him with cries of joy, and leap into his arms. Lucky indeed were they as the daughters of Ihi, otherwise they may well have been exiled from Ihipi. As it was, being half of Ohiri's blood made them tolerable in her eyes. Ihi studied them, and was glad when they showed adolescent blemishes. She was especially pleased that the prettiest of them all, the youngest, Ata, was not as vivacious as Ihi herself.'

'You sound bitter, old man,' the young stranger interrupted. 'This is not what I have heard about Queen Ihi. The legends tell only of the great love and devotion of the people of Ihipi for their arikinui. Similarly, they relate that the children loved their mother deeply. Otherwise, how could her daughters have loyally obeyed their mother after the Great Battle of Areraria?'

'They did what they did for their father.' The old man's voice rose in anger. 'It was not for their mother. Ohiri remained forever grateful that Ihi, when she took him to husband, gave him a life, a purpose, a country to rule and, more than anything else, a family to love. His daughters, especially Ata, became the most precious objects in all the world to Ohiri. That didn't mean he loved the arikinui less — but did she understand that? No —'

The old man began to weep. 'What kind of mother would be jealous of her own daughters? Oh, Hera, Maraea, Rawinia. Ki a koe, Ata, kua haere koe ki te Po —'

The young stranger put out a sympathetic hand. The old man recoiled from it. 'Why have you come to stir my memories? Leave me in peace. Haere atu.'

Understanding that he would have to wait until the next day to hear the rest of the story, the young stranger took his leave for the evening. 'Good night, koroua,' he said. He chose a place on the visitor's side of the meeting house and pulled his garments around him and the sleeping-mats on top of him.

The old man grinned as he heard the young stranger unsheath his greenstone patu and place it close to hand. 'Yes,' the old man thought, 'protect yourself, young stranger. Who knows? Danger may come from inside as well as from outside. No man is safe in Ihipi.'

The light from the flickering fire illuminated the patu as if something was burning inside it.

the attack of the furies

The young prince awoke with a start to a grey dawn. There was something heavy upon his chest and face. For a moment he panicked, thinking the blind man was trying to smother him in his sleep. He leapt up, his heart thudding. With relief he realised that the heaviness was the weight of the sleeping-mats; the blind man was still asleep, wheezing, snuffling, holding his breath, choking.

The young prince stretched, yawned, and threw aside the mats. He took a drink from his calabash of water. The fire had burnt down during the night so he built it up again, blowing on the embers and bringing them quickly to flame. As the fire danced high, it illuminated the walls of the meeting house with its medley of friezes and carvings. Drawn to the friezes, the young prince studied them. They were historical accounts, in brightly painted colours, of Ihipi: bucolic scenes of agricultural prosperity; the floating of twenty sacred pou from Hawaiki-nui across the sea to Ihipi; workers mining the greenstone from the mountains; the hauling of the sacred posts up the escarpment to Ihipi; farmers hunting forest birds and cultivating the fields; builders erecting the fabled pallisaded citadel that was Areraria; and the ceremonies by which the mauri of the gods were invoked to reside within the sacred precinct. The vignettes showed Ihi's father praising the mauri at the completion of the pa whawhai.

How different from Areraria as it existed now.

At that moment there was a sighing sound outside the door. The young prince turned, just in time to glimpse three white shapes leaving something at the doorstep and gliding away.

'Ko wai koutou?' he called. 'Who goes there?'

He stepped forward to see who the visitors were, and he was suddenly struck with a world of whiteness. He saw that it was snowing, the flakes swirling and dancing down like wraiths. He lifted his face gratefully to the moisture and sucked the snow into his mouth.

Whoever had come to the doorway had left a steaming bowl of broth.

Behind him, the young prince heard the blind man waking up. 'Are there others living in Areraria?' the young prince asked.

'They are only three old women,' the blind man answered grumpily. 'Hoha ratou, but they have their uses. They come every morning to leave kai for my breakfast. Kaore he kai o te kainga nei. Otherwise there is no food here.'

The young prince stirred the broth. 'What is in it?'

'Better not to ask,' the blind man said. 'Probably sparse puwha or other herbs they have found growing fitfully in some corner. Or some kiore they managed to catch as it scuttled, looking for food. The rats now rule Ihipi, thousands of them, they are the rangatira here. Sometimes the women bring a blind eel from the moat.' The blind man sniffed hopefully at the broth. 'Not today, aue, so just close your eyes, pretend it's fish or muttonbird, and eat.'

The young prince heard shrill cries. The three white shapes, surprised at his appearance at the doorway, had returned. They were challenging him, taunting him. 'Come out, stranger. Leave our koroua alone.'

The young prince picked up his patu, wrapped his tunic around him and said, 'I shall speak with them.'

'Suit yourself,' the blind man answered, tipping his mask halfway back on his face to sip at the broth. 'They are only mad women, mad like me.'

The young prince caught a glimpse of the blind man's face beneath the mask. A trick of light made it appear as smooth as a young girl's.

—

The three old women floated above the snow. Entirely white of face, hair and body, they were almost invisible; only their red-lined eyes and mouths indicated their presence. As soon as they saw they had enticed the young prince outside, they flew at him like vampires, hissing and snarling. 'Who are you? Why are you here?' In their hands they held fighting staffs. 'Kill him, sisters,' they screamed, feinting, trying to get through his defences, 'before he kills us!' With aerobatic skill, the three old women circled, swooped and went on the offensive.

The young prince drew his greenstone patu. He thought he had the upper hand but it soon became clear that the three old women had been well trained in military combat. They worked as a formidable team. Fighting for his life, the young prince slashed the air, defending himself. 'Kia tupato, sisters,' one of the old women cried. 'He has a patu! Get under his guard! Haramai te toki, hui e, haumi e, taiki e!'

The triad swept aerially around the young prince, disappearing in and out of the falling snow, their long white cloaks swirling deceptive figurations of confusion. In desperation, he leapt high and by luck felt the flick of a cloak as it flowed past. He pulled hard at the cloak and sliced the arm of its owner with his patu. With a cry, one of the old women fell to the ground.

'Sisters, I am down!' she wailed. Her blood beaded the snow like rubies.

In a flurry of fear and anger, the other two rained blows on the young prince and, when he retreated, grabbed their wounded companion and pulled her to safety. Using the falling snow as camouflage, they wrapped it around themselves and disappeared into it.

The fight was over as quickly as it had begun. The oppressive silence returned.

the story of the great battle of areraria

The old man heard the young stranger returning to the wharenui. 'So they escaped you, did they?' he asked mockingly. 'Never mind, they'll be back.'

'Where do they live?' the young stranger asked. His adrenalin was still racing as he sat by the fire.

'Over by the west wall,' the old man answered. 'There are caves there and that is where they have their lair.' He sighed again and patted his puku. 'I didn't think you'd be coming back, so I ate all the broth.' Then he gave a small laugh. 'Just kidding, young stranger.' He motioned to a flax bowl. 'But be careful, I may have poisoned it.'

'If you have put some fatal herb in the food,' the young stranger answered, 'there'll still be enough time to kill you before I die.'

'You think so?' the old man asked. 'What if I have stirred in some powder that instantly paralyses you? What sport I could have with you! While you are still living I could cut slices of meat off you, sizzle them over the fire and eat them. It is a long time since I had the exquisite taste of human flesh.'

'I'll take my chances,' the young stranger said. He lifted the bowl and sipped deep. His mind was whirling. Who was the old man? With his knowledge of herbs and his obvious survival skills, was he Horuhi, the shaman? And were the three old women his priestesses, feeding him, doing his bidding and keeping him alive?

'Still alive then?' the old man mocked.

Short of temper, the young stranger responded, 'Why don't you take your mask off, koroua?'

The old man laughed, peals of laughter spilling out. They shook the world with dread. 'If I did that, you would be turned to stone,' he said.

—

'Now where was I in our story?' the old man asked.

'You were telling me about Ihi, Ohiri, and their four daughters,' the young stranger answered. He put a new log on the fire.

'Ah yes,' the old man resumed. 'Following the ascension of Ihi and Ohiri, and with Horuhi as chief minister, there were twenty years of peace in Ihipi. Ruled by this benevolent triumvirate, the people prospered and Ihipi became the richest land in all the known world. In the north the kumara, taro and other plantations were expanded to supply an ever increasing export market. In the luxuriant western forests, careful conservation practices ensured a ready supply of rare and exotic bird life; the huia and other precious feathers which Ihipi traded were highly prized. To the west, in the mountain escarpment where all the rivers had their origins, Ihipi had fabled greenstone mines: the pounamu was of such clarity, colour and strength that some tribes would have no other for their adornment or weapons of war — the edge of any patu made from Ihipi's greenstone could never be blunted, and the glow of a pounamu breastpiece made even an ordinary woman beautiful.'

'All this I have heard about,' the young stranger nodded. He glanced again at the painted friezes along the walls. 'Was the court of Areraria as splendid as people say it was?'

'Oh yes, young stranger. The kainga became celebrated for its festivals, tournaments and great feasts, attracting visitors from throughout the world.

And the diadem in the crown of Areraria was the royal family: Ihi, Ohiri, and their four princess daughters. It was they who gave the great wonder that was Areraria its very special joy and lustre. However, then —'

'Don't hesitate, koroua,' the young stranger said.

'Just before the occasion of the youngest princess Ata's sixteenth birthday, intelligence reached us that Ihi's old nemesis, Heti, still smarting from her slight against him those many years ago, had decided it was time to move on Ihipi. Vigorous and ambitious, he resurrected his alliance with Rewhita and Huhia. "Look how rich Ihipi has become, brother warlords! The matriarchy is now a prize worthy of our attention. Let us take it and divide it among ourselves." The chieftains began a series of minor skirmishes, calculated to test whether Ohiri, in particular, had grown soft and vulnerable in his husbandhood. The skirmishes involved raids across the border into Ihipi, testing the country's defences and its will to respond.'

'Why didn't Ohiri move to counterattack?' the young stranger asked.

'Ihi persuaded Ohiri to believe in their invulnerability,' the old man answered. 'She wasn't the first leader to miscalculate the intentions of her enemies, nor will she be the last. Secure in her own superiority, she had always considered the borderland warlords as being of little account. When Ohiri wanted to take his warriors to confront them, she said, "The border chieftains would not dare to take arms against me. After all, am I not the arikinui, and therefore protected by the gods? Does not the greatest warrior of all time, you, my Lord Ohiri, sit beside me? And as my left hand, do I not have Horuhi, my chief minister and shaman, to ensure Areraria's victory and my enemies' defeat by supernatural means?"'

In agitation, the old man stood up. 'Her assumptions were arrogant, young stranger. Yes, the gods were on her side, but they would remain so only if she honoured them, placed them at the highest level, flattered them, gave them tribute and placated them.'

'It was rumoured,' the young stranger said, 'that before Ihi married Ohiri, Horuhi had been her lover. Is that true?'

The old man roared with laughter. 'Horuhi? Never! Horuhi had been Ihi's father's trusted elder, priest, guide and mentor, but never Ihi's lover. It was only to be expected that he would maintain those roles when Ihi herself assumed power; he was loyal to her. No, the only man Ihi ever loved was Ohiri. Ever since that first night, when he had clambered aboard the royal waka, she was obsessed with him. "Let me get inside your skin," she would say whenever they took each other. "Let me meld with you, my husband. Let me in, let me in," she would scream at her climax. One day, she chilled his heart by saying, "If I had to, I would kill for you — even my own children."'

A sudden blast of air bellowed the fire and it showered with sparks that drifted like burning souls through the interior.

'Where were we?' the old man asked, recovering. 'Ah yes, the moves by Heti, Rewhita and Huhia on Ihipi. One day, news came that the armies of the warlords were massing on all Ihipi's borders. The skirmishes escalated into more serious encounters. Heti initiated regular attacks against the convoys taking pounamu down from the fabled greenstone mines to Ihipi's port on the coast.

'When this occurred, Ohiri could not fail to realise how big and dangerous the threat from Heti, Rewhita and Huhia had become. Invasion was now imminent. As was customary in such situations, the people of Ihipi began to retreat to Areraria; soon the citadel was overflowing with refugees. Quickly, Ohiri ordered troops to delay the approach of the enemy armies. He told Ihi, "Wife, we need to create a diversion. I will take a group of our strongest warriors against Huhia's stronghold. If the three borderland lords see that one of their pa is under attack from my pre-emptive strike, they might turn from Areraria and come running to the defence."

'But it was too late. The fires of the approaching army could be seen from the ramparts, dotting the plains. Very soon, the enemy army had entirely encircled Areraria. In desperation, Ohiri pleaded with Ihi: "There is another option. Let us hold peace talks and see if we can reach some accommodation."

'Ohiri's proposal angered Ihi. "I will not bargain with thieves and robbers," she said. "Nobody has been able to take Areraria in the past. The fortress is impregnable. If the border warlords want a long siege, so be it." An impish smile danced on her lips. "But since they have come this far, let us invite them to Ata's birthday celebrations."'

Ihi's bravado took the young stranger's breath away.

'Ihi was always a law unto herself,' the old man said. 'And so the invitation was sent to Heti's encampment —'

—

'It's a trick,' Rewhita said when Heti shared the birthday invitation with him and Huhia. 'The queen plans to murder us, just as she assassinated her cousin Whiti on his way into exile from Ihipi.'

'Ohiri would not allow it,' Heti answered, 'He is a warrior, a man of honour, living by the warrior's code, and he will ensure our safe passage to his daughter's ra whanau.' By the time evening descended, Heti had persuaded his fellow chiefs to accept the invitation. Ohiri sent warrior escorts, and the chiefs followed them to the birthday celebration.

The warlords ascended into the pa whawhai. On reaching the small bridge leading to the central citadel, they saw that Areraria was ablaze with lights. 'It is true, then,' Huhia remarked. 'Of all the daughters of Ihi and Ohiri, the people surely love Ata the most.' As they made their way through the gateway, they were showered with petals from the overtowering ramparts, as if they were distinguished guests.

'The people of Ihipi act as if there is no army surrounding them,' Rewhita said in wonder. 'Nor do they appear concerned about the battle with us.'

'Let Ihi the queen sit pretty,' Heti answered. 'If she wishes to assume that she has control, let her assume it.'

The three chieftains reached the sacred precinct with its rows of spiritual pou — and that was when they truly began to doubt their wisdom in making war on Ihipi. The mauri were in residence, sending dazzling figurations of light through the darkness. 'How can we bring down the citadel,' Rewhita asked Heti, 'protected as it is by such supernatural guardians?'

The warlords passed through and, to great pageantry, karanga and waiata, were welcomed into the royal meeting house.

'Haere mai ra nga manuhiri tuarangi ki waenganui i a tatou, haere mai.'

In the radiance of Ihi's blinding beauty, they were welcomed as honoured guests. 'I bid you enter, warrior chieftains,' Ihi greeted them, 'and I give you the freedom of Areraria.' But her words were teasing and contemptuous.

The feasting began. In between the singing and dancing, whanau group after whanau group presented their birthday gifts to the youngest princess. 'Truly,' Huhia said. 'Ata is like a flower in the springtime, and all the birds of earth come to sip at her nectar.'

The evening deepened. Around midnight, Horuhi stood to give the birthday karakia. Everybody in the wharenui clapped and sang to honour Ata:

'Kotiro, Ata e, taku ripene pai! O makawe hoki nga ngaru o te tai! Ko te parehuia he tohu rangatira e! Ko Ata ataahua e, no Ihipi e! Young princess, you are like a beautiful gift! You are like the brightest foam on the sea! You are truly a princess, you, lovely Ata, of Ihipi!'

The celebration ended and the poroporoaki, leave-taking, began. Just as the borderland warlords were about to leave the royal meeting house, Ihi called to them, 'E nga rangatira, titiro koutou ki au. Chieftains, look upon me. Am I such a terrible enemy?'

Heti bowed before her in acknowledgement. 'Of all those who will fight against us tomorrow, we are relieved that you, noble lady, will not be among them. Warriors who come up against you would be swayed by your beauty, delay their spear strike, and you would come under their guard with your patu.'

The guests at the celebration murmured their approval of Heti's elliptical compliment.

'What say you, Rewhita?' Ohiri asked.

'It is not only your consort's beauty that is her weapon,' Rewhita began. 'It is also her intelligence and stamina. Where does she obtain it? Do you, Horuhi, get it for her from the gods? What contract have you signed with them on her behalf? We three chieftains do well to heed your warnings that when we begin our battle tomorrow we may well be fighting the gods themselves.'

Ihi took a step forward and her wrathful gaze was direct and clear. 'So you still intend to fight? In that case, take counsel among yourselves. My army has been made invincible by Horuhi's powerful karakia. All I have to do is command my shaman to kill any person who takes up arms against me, and that person will fall down lifeless. And if I change my mind and ask Horuhi to raise that warrior from the dead, he will bring that warrior to life again. Horuhi has the power of life and death, enemy chiefs. For you will be reserved the most painful deaths of all.'

Rewhita and Huhia blanched. Heti remained unmoved. 'Gracious lady, I can see why your people would follow you to battle. When you stand before your army with your husband and children, it is no wonder that all the people of Ihipi, not only the warriors but also women and children, take up arms on your behalf. Not for you the proverb, "He puta taua ki te tane, he whanau tamariki ki te wahine; the battlefield for man, childbirth for woman." Nevertheless, supremely confident as you are, you are not invincible and I do not bow down before you. I tell you that Areraria can be easily defeated.'

The crowd stirred at Heti's words. 'Defeated?' Ihi laughed. 'Have you not seen the strength of the fortress? You have no hope of taking it. And did you not see that Areraria is further protected by the mauri?'

'Our battle will be ferocious but it will be short. We need kill only one person among all of you and Areraria will fall.'

At his words, Ihi's eyes dilated. 'Think twice before you dare to kill me, warrior lord,' she said. 'You will be struck dead even before you raise your weapon.'

Heti smiled, turned to Ata and bowed to her. 'I bid you good evening, princess,' he said. He turned to Ihi, Ohiri and Horuhi, 'Pray to your gods tonight, as we will to ours. Let us see whom the gods will favour.'

—

'The Great Battle of Areraria began,' the old man continued. 'Ohiri posted extra palace guards around Ihi, just in case an assassin made his way into the royal compound. Of course, the battle was not short and, in fact, Ihi had been correct about Areraria's impregnability: Heti, Rewhita and Huhia had to lay siege to our citadel for over thirty days. Young stranger, you have seen the defensive ramparts, stockades, walls and moat of our pa whawhai; they were massive and, when guarded by the best warriors, no army could make headway. Day after day, all the attacks mounted by the warlords were repulsed. Meanwhile, inside the fortifications, Areraria boasted plentiful food stores and water supplies. Clearly, the kainga would have been able to withstand all the onslaughts of the enemy army for many more months. Eventually, realising Areraria's invincibility and the pressing matters of their own homelands, the borderland chieftains would have had to acknowledge Areraria's impregnability, perform a haka acknowledging Ihi's victory and retreat across our plains.'

'Then how did this great citadel fall?' the young stranger asked.

'We were foolish strategists,' the old man said. 'Confident in our own strength, we miscalculated our enemy's. We thought that every day the siege held was another day we had defeated the warlords. But Heti's game plan was different. He was happy to play a waiting game — and why? He knew Ihi, and how vainglorious she was; one day, without realising it, she would make an error of judgement. Heti also knew that, as our complacency increased — our assumption that the borderland chieftains would tire of the siege and depart — we would become careless.'

'Careless?' the young stranger asked.

The old man nodded. 'Just one mistake, that's all the warlords were waiting for. It's not that they won the Battle of Areraria at all; rather, that we lost it. When we finally made an error, it was costly to us.

'Ihi was so self-absorbed that, one day, she omitted to make sacrifice to the mauri. Watching from his encampment, Ohiri noticed that, for the first time during the siege, that there was no morning plume of smoke from Areraria's sacrificial fires. "The gods won't like that," he muttered. A few days later, when Ihi did indeed resume her propitiation to the mauri, her people instead raised her above the gods and made the sacrifice to *her*. This happened again the following day. When it was reported to the warlords, Heti's elation knew no bounds.

'By the fortieth day of the Great Battle of Areraria, he was confident enough to announce to his fellow chiefs:

'"Today is the day when Areraria will fall."'

—

The auguries were ominous.

On the fortieth day, the mist closed around Areraria. Horuhi was beside himself with fear. With great alarm he had noticed that, as the siege progressed, the people of Ihipi had begun to credit Ihi, not the gods, with their success, saying 'Look how clever our arikinui is, and how strong.' And Ihi herself, albeit unintentionally, had set herself up for the people to worship, saying, 'If the people see me at the head of our army, they will follow me even unto Rarohenga, the Underworld.'

Horuhi's fears were confirmed when he went to consult the pou. There he witnessed the departure of the mauri, the talismanic life forces from within the posts. 'When Ihi and Ohiri gave their marriage vows, we promised to honour them as long as they honoured us. Your foolish queen has placed herself above us. In that case, let her pay the price.'

Dazzling figures of light, the mauri lifted and spun away from Areraria, flying north, south, east and west, and were gone like sprinkled dust into the mist. Heti, tracing their soaring, sparkling departure, called his troops to readiness. 'We march within the hour on Areraria.'

That fateful morning, fearing to tell Ihi of her transgression, Horuhi instead confided to Ohiri: 'We have grown too proud. The gods are always capricious, and today they are angry. They have withdrawn their protection. Our warriors no longer have the cloak of invincibility. It may be temporary or it may be permanent. Whatever happens while the gods are away, happens. We are on our own. Today they favour neither one side nor the other.'

'Don't be afraid, tohunga,' Ohiri answered. 'We will hold the fortress until the mauri return.' He made the order for the sentries to be extra vigilant as they patrolled the terraces. Through the mist they called:

'Kia hiwa ra, kia hiwa ra! Kia hiwa ra tenei tuku! Kia hiwa ra tera tuku! Kei whakapurua koe ki te toto! Be watchful, be wakeful! Be alert on this terrace, be alert on that terrace! If you are not alert, the enemy will wound you and draw blood!'

As the earth warmed, the mist shredded. The sun rose, a bloodied orb like a decapitated head, ghostly crimson. From beyond the walls of Areraria came the chanting of the enemy in the haka: 'Ka mate, ka mate! Ka ora, ka ora! Ka mate, ka mate! Ka ora, ka ora!' Ohiri prepared himself. He dressed in his warrior apparel and wrapped the thong of his greenstone patu tight around his wrist. The patu was of a curious design, having a shadow companion — a ghost patu — within it.

With a sense of foreboding, Horuhi noted that the wind had changed direction and was now blowing from the sea, over the escarpment, across Ihipi and into Areraria.

Heti noted the wind change, too. 'Make fires,' he commanded. 'Build them against the fortifications where they will catch and burn. Let us smoke the people of Areraria out of the pa whawhai.' The fires were lit and were soon a raging inferno.

In response, Ohiri called to the people, 'Ka reareaia a tama tuki tona hiwa ra! Stand in your places! Stand!' He took his place at the head of the defenders.

The flames were fanned high by the inblowing winds. The smoke billowed thickly over the pa and, under its cover, Heti ordered his borderland chieftains to the assault. The enemy troops rushed upward through the maze of stockaded terraces. At the first level within the cross stockades they were met by Ohiri and the strongest warriors of north Ihipi. The enemy push was too great, and the warriors were outnumbered. The defenders at the second level of scarps rushed forward to reinforce the stockades. 'Kia kutia!' Ohiri cried. 'Au! Au! Whiti! Whiti e! Close your ranks, au, au, and cross over! Quickly!'

The battle swayed back and forth. The blood lust was awakened in all warriors, attackers and defenders alike. Verily, ka tuwhera te tawaha o te riri, kaore e titiro ki te Ao Marama. When the gates of war are open, no man takes notice of the world of light. Once the battle lust is on him, he is unconscious of anything but the fight in which he is engaged.

Watching Ohiri from the ramparts, Ihi was a glowing figurehead. 'A ra ra, ka panapana!' At the high sound of her voice, further reinforcements of men, women and children rushed out of the inner city to join the battle on the perimeters. Patu sliced skin, clashing against bone. Taiaha jabbed sinew, skewering body. Everywhere, warriors were engaged in hand-to-hand combat. 'Ka tohe tatou, ka tohe tatou! We will persist!' Ohiri yelled.

However, the defenders of Areraria were again being pushed back. 'Retreat into the citadel,' Ohiri commanded.

'Why do the gods not intervene?' Ihi cried in fury.

In the mêlée, Ohiri caught a glimpse of Heti. 'If I kill Heti,' he thought, 'his men may lose heart and flee from their attack.' But no matter how hard Ohiri fought his way towards the warlords, the press of defenders repelled him. Indeed, there were many among Heti's troops who threw themselves at Ohiri, for Heti had placed a bounty on him. 'Tell all the men,' Heti said to Huhia and Rewhita, 'that I want Ohiri's head. Whoever overcomes him, that warrior will instantly be made a general.' Immediately, there was another surge of the enemy, pushing Ohiri and the defenders back towards the main gateway of the pa.

'Raise the bridge,' Ohiri ordered. He ran up to the watchtowers overhanging the bridge. There he joined Ihi, his four daughters and Horuhi, watching the attack. For the first time Ohiri caught a glimpse of his wife's surprise as she saw the way the battle was going.

'Why is this happening?' she demanded. 'Why, noble husband, have you not won the day? And why do my warriors lie dead and not rise to fight again?'

Ignoring this reprimand, Ohiri turned to Horuhi. 'Te tai ra, te tai ra, e pari ana te tai ki whea? The tide, the tide, which way does it flow?'

'The gods still stand aside, watching,' Horuhi answered, casting his divinations. 'They do not intervene.'

Now Ihi began to sway like a reed. 'The gods have deserted us?' Arrogant though she was, she realised her fault. She kissed Ohiri tenderly. 'Not even you, husband, could prevail without their favour. I must go back to the sacred precinct to prostrate myself and ask their forgiveness.'

'It is too late,' Horuhi said. 'The tides are still swirling. They can go either way.' Hearing this, Ata screamed in fear.

Heti had ordered his warriors to bring ladders and ropes so they could scale the walls of the citadel. Already enemy troops were wading across the moat and ascending through the billowing smoke and flames. Along the ramparts, defenders and enemy were locked in ferocious combat. Everywhere was dismemberment, disembowelling, decapitation and death.

The enemy troops broke through the defences and surged into Areraria.

Ohiri looked to the billowing sky. 'Oh gods, I pre-empt your consideration but I pray that you will be with me as I return to the field of battle.' He leapt from the ramparts into the black water.

'Father, no!' Ata cried.

Other defenders joined Ohiri as, jabbing with his taiaha, he tried to open up a space. But he had acted precipitately. Watching, the gods were offended and remained silent. In triumph, Heti surrounded Ohiri with a phalanx of men.

'Ohiri,' Heti said. 'There was a time when your wife gave a one-eyed woman to me, saying, "Let beauty go to beauty, and a one-eyed man go to a one-eyed woman!" I will give to you the same treatment as she gave me. Let Ohiri, the warrior with the strength of twelve men, meet in combat with twelve men.'

With that, the legends say that Ohiri entered into the greatest gladiatorial encounter the world had ever witnessed. Fighting with his greenstone club, he despatched three warriors before the fourth sliced the hamstring of his left leg. Even so, he persisted, killing two more warriors, before his right arm was sliced to the bone. All who watched from the ramparts were weeping as Ohiri continued to fight, and when he despatched another warrior to the next world, there was a roar of elation. But it was only a matter of time before he was finally disarmed. That is when Heti approached him, holding aloft his patu.

'Ohiri,' Heti said. 'Your time has come.'

A blow to his head, and Ohiri fell.

The old man gave a deep moan.

'Just before I lost consciousness, I heard a voice screaming. I think it was Ata, calling, "E a, turakina! He is down!"'

The young stranger stepped back. 'You? Lost consciousness?'

'I heard the voice of my wife, the queen: "He falls, he falls, the greenstone pendant of my life falls and shatters!" After that, blackness overwhelmed me and I remembered nothing until —'

The old man could not go on. Sparks from the fire swirled around him. For a moment there was silence in the firelit whare. Then:

'Who are you, old man?' The young stranger's heart was beating fast. Even so, there was a tenderness in his question. The silence deepened.

'I am Ohiri.'

With a hiss, the young stranger raised his patu, ready to strike. But something stayed his hand. The patu quivered in indecision, the shadow weapon within struggling with the weapon without. The young stranger lowered the patu. He asked a second question:

'The three old women, are they your daughters?' Again, tenderness inflected his question.

'Yes, they are Hera, Maraea and Rawinia.'

The young stranger's voice was halting, unsure, almost afraid to ask the third question. 'There was a fourth daughter —'

With a cry, Ohiri leapt toward the voice of the young stranger. 'Ko wai koe? No hea koe? Who are you? Why do you want to know? He aha tou pirangi? What do you want from me?' He crumpled to the floor. He pulled his black cloak around him. The flames from the fire flickered across his mask.

The young stranger raised Ohiri's head and tried to look in through the sockets of the mask. No eyes returned his gaze, only the blackest blackness.

'Ask my daughters about their youngest sister,' Ohiri said. 'They will tell you everything.'

in the lair of the furies

That afternoon the weather worsened. The snow turned to sleet, slamming against the walls of Areraria.

'You're not going out, are you?' the koroua, Ohiri, asked when he heard the young prince preparing to leave the whare. 'E noho, stay. Why don't you wait until tomorrow? The women will be back with food in the morning. Talk to them then.'

'There may be no tomorrow,' the young prince said, undeterred.

'Suit yourself,' Ohiri answered. 'Makariri ki waho,' he shivered.

The young prince set off, bending against the sleet, through the decaying necropolis. The sleet stung his face as he stepped past the sacred precinct and made for the gateway. For a moment, he rested under the serrated fighting stages. Then, taking a breath, he sprinted up a stairway to the top of the front stockade and followed the ramparts, heading for the western wall of Areraria. His whakatau took him through defensive bulwarks and up another external stairway to the watchtower at the corner where the west wall intersected the south wall.

Beyond the citadel, on the south side, the countryside was completely blotted out by the snowstorm. However, when the young prince stepped around the corner and onto the west wall, magically, the wind and sleet ceased. 'The old women live in the lee of the city,' he thought to himself. He looked up at the sky and saw that the stormy weather was rolling over the top of Areraria, inscribing icy koru patterns in the gloom.

Then, suddenly, the young prince saw the three kuia. He was relieved that they were all accounted for; when he had used his patu in his earlier fight with one of them, he had intended only to wing her, not kill her.

The old women were climbing slowly down the wall, holding on with their hands and feet. When they reached the moat below them, one of them cracked the ice and held a wriggling rat just above it. He saw that they were fishing, using the rat as bait.

Almost at once there was a rush of water and a huge, black blind eel leapt out of the hole for the rat. 'Arara!' the old kuia exclaimed. The blind eel swallowed the rat and half the kuia's arm. Laughing, she took out a blade of obsidian and slit the eel in half. The upper part of the blind eel was still attached to her arm. Triumphantly she peeled it from her arm and put it, wriggling, into her flax kit. At this point, one of the other women sniffed the air. Her head swivelled toward the watchtower where the young prince was watching. 'Sisters!' she cried. 'Our enemy is at hand.'

The young prince was astonished at how quickly the three old women moved. Snarling and spitting, their white cloaks flowing behind them like wings, they scaled the wall on all fours. As they came, they pulled loose rocks from the wall and hurled them at him. When they reached the top, they flew at the young prince like harpies. 'This time you will not escape us,' they spat, their blood-red eyes blazing.

Again the young prince was fighting for his life, weaving from side to side as the three sisters engaged him in combat. Retreating, he began to climb the defensive western bulwarks, jumping from one elevated fighting stage to the next.

'You can't escape,' the old kuia called as they sprang after him. They moved to encircle him, one flying ahead to outflank him on his right and the other two to cut him off on the left. Cornered, the young prince stood on a very flimsy defensive platform. The old women landed on the same platform, which creaked and swayed. 'Rush him, sisters!' one called. The platform collapsed and, in a shower of timber and snow, the young prince and the three kuia fell into the caves beneath Areraria.

The young prince was dazed by the fall. When he came to, he saw that he was in their lair.

Two of the old women took wing immediately, advancing on the young prince for the kill. He rolled to one side and when their third sister joined in the attack he put up an arm in surrender. 'E tu,' he said. 'Your father told me where to find you. I come in peace. I know who you are.'

The three old women stopped in their tracks and looked at each other, puzzled. 'He knows who we are? But who is he?'

Then one of them spied the young prince's greenstone patu. She gave a cry of surprise and started purring. 'Where did you get this? It doesn't belong to you. It's ours. You stole it, didn't you! It belongs to our father! He had it when he was killed . . . but that was twenty years ago. How did you get it?'

A second kuia recited a strange riddle:

> When will Areraria live again?
> When the dead child comes in thundering rain

Born in a dead womb, born in pain
And the dead man dies again.

The three women stared intently at the young prince. They sniffed him
and poked him in the chest, babbling away in overlapping voices. 'Kia
ora, nice of you to drop in. Where's your invitation? Do you always go
around clipping the wings of innocent old women? Couldn't you tell we
were harmless, only trying to protect our koroua? You big bully, shame on
you.' The first woman stepped quickly before him. She looked up at him,
her eyes moistening. The other two joined her and one of them started to
tangi in recognition.

'Are you the one we have been waiting for?' the three kuia asked, their
eyes shining with gladness.

———

Wind, rain and sleet outside. Inside, the young prince was being fussed
over by the three old women. Hera skinned the eel and roasted it over a
fire. Maraea and Rawinia plied him with drink. At their urging, the young
prince removed his clothes so they could be dried out. The fire limned his
body with glowing beauty.

'It's a long time since I saw a handsome boy,' Maraea sighed dreamily.

'You never ever saw a handsome boy,' Hera replied grumpily, trying
to push her out of the way and edge closer to the young prince. 'All your
boyfriends were leftovers from our suitors, weren't they, Rawinia?'

'At least I had boyfriends,' Maraea scoffed. 'Not like you two. Still
virgins, sisters?'

The young prince laughed. 'I'll bet you all ran rings around the men
when you were younger,' he said.

Maraea cocked her head. 'Yes, I was kept busy.'

The other two kuia roared at her salaciousness. 'You must forgive our
sister,' Hera said. 'She was always the boastful one. Always away with some
warrior or other . . . if they were unlucky.'

'Ah well,' Rawinia began, 'perhaps we'd better get on with the story.
After all,' she nodded at the young prince, 'that's what you've come for, isn't
it? You begin, Hera, you're the oldest. You tell him about the coming of the
Time of Darkness.'

The fire crackled. The three sisters shivered. Their eyes took on a haunted look.

'When our father fell,' Hera said, 'we all thought that Heti had struck him a mortal blow. Immediately, our warriors doubled their efforts and, although they were without the support of the mauri, they were able to wrest victory from the jaws of defeat. The citadel held, and the warlords were compelled to retreat. Oh, it was bittersweet to hear Heti cry, "Fall back! Fall back!", and to see his armies being beaten back to our perimeters and standing off Areraria.'

'Then we heard,' Rawinia continued, 'that our father was still alive! He had been taken to Heti's encampment. I hate to think what sport they had with him, and the pain he must have endured. Throughout the day we could hear them celebrating. Although they had not captured the city they had taken its greatest warrior, and they taunted us with their haka of triumph.'

'You would have thought our mother would have been distraught at our father's capture,' Maraea intervened. 'Instead, a strange quiet settled over her; she was already thinking of ways to get him back. She could have had Horuhi killed for not advising her of the departure of the mauri. Instead, she asked him, "Have I become such a monster that even you, my faithful mentor, could not tell me when I erred?" In the waning light, we watched her kneeling in the sacred precinct, entreating the mauri to return to Areraria. When the posts remained silent and without illumination, her intensity became frightening. She called for Horuhi. "Send a messenger to the camp of the three borderland warlords," she instructed. "Tell them I will be willing to discuss a treaty."'

—

Ihi dressed carefully for her meeting with the warlord chieftains. She was not above using her beauty and sexuality to secure her objectives. When evening came she was charismatic, transcendent, already seated with Horuhi in the royal meeting house, greeting the warlords. She was not just a woman or a queen. She was also a phenomenon, fantastic, both tellurian and divine. Even so, she was prepared to give up Ihipi for the sake of her husband.

From afar, Ihi saw the three chieftains arriving, stepping through the sacred precinct. The arikinui hoped Heti might have brought Ohiri with them. Instead, their escorts were carrying four carved wooden caskets of curious size and design.

'Welcome, lords,' Horuhi greeted them, 'chieftains of your own kingdoms. Haere mai koutou ki konei.'

Heti, Rewhita and Huhia bowed and returned the welcome. 'It is again our pleasure to be in the royal court of Areraria,' they said. When they looked up they averted their eyes from Horuhi, lest he discover their secret.

What was in the boxes?

Ihi leaned forward. 'Let us get down to business,' she began. 'It will do none of us any good to continue with our war. It will be costly for you. I assure you Areraria is the finest pa whawhai in all the land; you have already tried to take it once and, although you briefly breached our walls, you failed — my people are determined never to let you in again. Warlords, certainly fight on, if you wish, but I ask you to consider the consequences. Many on your side will die. And while you might have possession of the lands of Ihipi, what profit is there if you do not have the people to work it for you?'

'Will you surrender Areraria to us?' Huhia asked bluntly.

'Give up Areraria?' Ihi smiled. 'Warlord, it is you who should surrender to me!' Her words were honeyed, smooth, forgiving. 'My people are farmers, foresters and miners. Your people are fishermen. Your people would not be good at the work we do. We have been doing this all our lives. It is our taonga.'

'The Queen speaks truly,' Heti said to Huhia. Persuaded by her goodwill, he wondered why anybody would believe that this beautiful woman was their enemy. Immediately, Ihi turned to him, seductive. 'You understand my reasoning, noble lord? Good. Let Ihipi enter into an alliance with all of you. We will commit to growing crops for your benefit. We are the ones with the knowledge; you do not have it. Here is a taste of what you could expect from the treaty.'

Ihi signed to Horuhi. 'Bring forward gifts for our partners,' she commanded. 'The brightest feather cloaks, mats and jade, lords; and the slaves that bring them are also part of the tribute.' Truly, the procession that followed was spectacular. The slaves had been oiled and, in the torchlight, the greenstone jewellery, ivory breastpieces and huia-feather cloaks blazed with splendour.

Heti inclined his head and opened his arms. 'And for this, all you wish is an alliance?' he mocked.

'That,' Ihi answered, 'and the return of my husband Ohiri.'

'I can agree to that,' Heti smiled.

Ihi suppressed a cry of relief and triumph. Who needed the gods? Horuhi, however, was made more wary. Sick at heart, he watched as Heti motioned for one of the four boxes to be brought forward.

'You give us gifts,' Heti said. 'Here is mine to you, arikinui.' He opened one of the boxes. 'As you have just requested, I give you back your husband.'

In the box was Ohiri's head.

—

Reliving the horror of that moment, the three kuia lifted from the floor of the cave. Holding each other, they began to wheel and circle in the air.

'Taka ka taka, taka ka taka,' they grieved, 'ka taka ki te motoi! E kapo ki te whetu! E kapo ki te marama! E kapo ki te ata o taku raukura e!' Ululations overlapping, their plaintive cries resounded through the caves. 'Ripiripia! Tihaehaea! Ripiripia! Tihaehaea! E a turakina!' Swirling, weaving, singing, chanting, the kuia circled. 'Paranikia te upoko te ngangarana kai tangata e! Aue! Aue! Taukiri e.'

Every time they passed over the fire it blossomed, leapt and roared, and cinders sizzled through the darkness.

'Our mother flinched, swayed, recovered,' Hera sobbed. 'Her eyes widened, their irises wan with the light. When she spoke, her voice was filled with loss. "Aa, kua pouarutia nga iwi o te motu nei. Indeed, the tribes of Ihipi are widowed." Do you remember, Maraea?'

The three sisters ceased their funeral carousel and began to float back to earth.

'Yes, I remember,' Maraea answered. 'I remember everything. I only wish I could forget Heti's voice as he addressed our mother. "Great queen," he said, "you are in no position to bargain with us. Without the mauri to protect it, Areraria will be ours. Even so, I have enjoyed watching you play your amusing games. I warned you, when I came to your daughter's birthday, that I needed to kill only one person and your kingdom would fall. You mistakenly thought I was referring to you, but I knew that at some point you would lose the favour of your gods and be no threat to us."'

—

Ihi's eyes blazed wide with anger at Heti's presumption.

'Great Queen,' Heti mocked. 'Ohiri was executed. He died bravely and without pain. Better for us that he is dead, because alive, even with Ihipi in bondage to us, he could raise another army. His head lies in the box before you. His body has been dismembered and lies, in three parts, in the other boxes.'

'Why have you done this terrible thing?' Horuhi asked.

'You ask me this, great shaman? You, the highest practitioner of the occult arts in all the land? You are the reason why! At your queen's bidding you would commit any act, any heresy. At her command you would raise her lord from the dead so that he could live again. This way, that will never be a possibility.'

Heti turned to Ihi. 'I see you do not even bother to shed taniwha tears. Well do I remember how you mocked me with your one-eyed woman. This is my revenge. You will never see Ohiri again.'

Ihi stepped forward and struck him savagely on the cheek. 'You dare to belittle the love I have for my husband? Because of what you've done, any thought of alliance between us is gone. Areraria will continue with the war and I assure you that it will be a fight to the death.'

Heti restrained his anger. 'Be grateful, arikinui, that I am generous to you. I will give you and your daughters a brief time to grieve over Ohiri. Then four of my warrior squads will take one box each to our own lands, away from your reach. E noho ra, arikinui.'

—

'We were given one hour with our father,' Hera cried. 'Sixty precious minutes. Oh, we loved our father, didn't we, sisters? We mourned his body. We placed our cheeks next to his. But, young prince,' she continued, 'not once did our mother weep.'

'Not one tear?' the young prince asked.

'Not a single one,' Maraea answered. 'While we grieved, she simply sat there, staring into the air. Her face was remote, withdrawn, enigmatic. When finally the boxes containing his remains were taken away, not even then did she weep. And then she began to call on the elements to empower her.'

—

'Come winds, come storms, come cyclones, come lightning,' the queen called, 'transform me, give me metamorphosis.' Her invocation was so powerful that the ground shook. The night sky broke apart and the stars fell through it. Then, 'Oh cease your wailing, daughters.' She turned to Horuhi. 'Find a way, tohunga, find a way that I might bring my husband back.'

'It is impossible,' Horuhi answered. 'He is already dead and his body split into pieces.'

'I will not accept your answer,' Ihi said. She saw from the corner of her eyes a faint smudge of light in the sacred precinct. At last, the mauri had returned. The posts scintillated and glowed in the night. 'Ask!' she commanded. 'Find a way.'

Filled with dread, Horuhi approached the pou. Had they forgiven the people of Areraria or were they still angry? He knelt before them, made obeisance, and consulted the mauri therein. 'Great ones, return your favour to Ihipi, and hear the request of she who serves you, Ihi, arikinui of Areraria.'

The mauri within the posts swirled and sparkled. 'Has she learnt her lesson, priest?'

'Yes,' Horuhi nodded, 'grievously so, as Ohiri was killed while you were absent from us. Although he travels to the world of the dead, she begs for forgiveness and asks if his journey may be stopped and he may be returned to her.'

The mauri swirled, coalesced, split, circled and shimmered from pou to pou. Their unearthly colours, white hot, clashed and struck each other, as if in unholy argument. Horuhi knew his own death was nigh. But ribbons of red and blue began to infiltrate the mauri, diminishing their evident anger.

'Although you and your queen test our patience,' the voices of the mauri began, 'we have accepted our responsibility in Ohiri's death and have voted to support your queen's request.' The voices overlapped one another like dissonant music. 'Tell her she must go to Kurawaka. There, at the mons veneris of Papatuanuku, the Lord Tane made woman. From Papatuanuku's sexual cleft the arikinui must collect the dew of Papatuanuku. She must bring the dew back to you, great shaman, and of it you will create the

Water of Life. Prepare a womb, fill it with the Water of Life, and place Ohiri in it.'

Horuhi listened with dread as the mauri went on. 'You are correct that Ohiri already travels to Te Reinga. Insolent priest, why did you not advise us that he does not travel whole of body?' A jagged bolt of white lightning came from the central pou and struck at Horuhi's heart.

'Forgive me, great ones,' Horuhi pleaded.

'Time is of the essence. The four princesses who love their lord also have their role. Each must make haste to find the pieces of their father. This must be done within the day, as Ohiri has been dead too long already and his body is beginning to turn, becoming corrupted, and soon will bloat with gases, liquefy and rot. Once the daughters have their father, they must bring him back to you. He must be submerged fully in the Water of Life. When that is done, await the karakia we will give you to enable him to rise again.'

The mauri stilled, became silent, and dissolved into the posts. Horuhi hastened to tell Ihi their korero. Her eyes dilated and she was already reaching for her travelling cape.

'I go with the royal guards immediately to Kurawaka,' Ihi said. She turned to her daughters and kissed them all. 'The enemy squads taking your father's remains are only one day ahead. Each of you, take eight warriors and go after them.' Ihi's voice rose with authority. 'Intercept them before they reach the borders of Ihipi. Kill them if you must. Bring your father back.'

—

'What happened then?' the young prince asked.

'We cannot tell you,' the three old women screamed, harsh, fearful. 'Oh, leave Areraria, beautiful one, and do not look into the Time of Darkness.'

Again the three kuia took flight, their white cloaks flowing, bewailing their memories. 'Taka ka taka ! Taka ka taka! He falls! He falls! The greenstone ear pendant falls! We snatch at the stars, we snatch at the moon, we snatch at the shadow of our lost feather plumes!' Around and around they flew, weaving patterns of distress. 'We search, we seek, where have you gone? Aue, you have been taken into death, eaten by the man-eating monster.'

Down they fell, their red-rimmed eyes filled with despair, to whimper and shelter in the young prince's arms.

the ghosts of the beautiful queen and the fourth princess

The light was fading quickly as the young prince made his way back through the gaunt citadel to the royal whare. The storm had increased sixfold, the sleet and wind stabbing like knives through his skin.

'I must hasten,' the young prince said to himself, 'before the day winks out. When night comes, nobody is safe.'

The sleet squalled and flurried, lashing Areraria with supernatural force. The young prince reached the gateway and stumbled through the sacred precinct. Light crackled on the sacred posts, making of them a spectral coronet. Heart pounding, he hurled himself through the door of the meeting house and slammed it behind him. He closed his eyes with relief for a moment, and therefore did not see that two aria, ghosts, had slipped in behind him and, making their way along the walls, found places to rest and to wait.

The meeting house was filled with a spectral glow. 'Kei whea koe, koroua?' the young prince called. 'Where are you, old man?' He hurried to the fire to warm himself and found Ohiri there, already asleep. The young prince tiptoed over to him. For a moment he watched the rise and fall of his chest, and heard the air soughing through his aged lungs.

What was Ohiri hiding behind his mask?

Tempted, the young prince reached for the mask to remove it.

'No,' a voice said. 'Kaore. Don't do that.' The voice was musical and beautiful.

The young prince was startled. He looked around. 'Who is there?' he asked. He could see nothing, only the gleam of the night sky, seeping through the meeting house and filling it with shafts of shadow and light. He reached again for Ohiri's mask.

'Young prince, no,' the voice said again.

This time, when the young prince looked, he saw two carved figures at the far end of the meeting house. Whoever had carved them had done so with great aroha and skill. The figures were women, mother and daughter. The mother was looking straight ahead, her eyes wide and fearless. On her chin was the royal moko and her forehead was traced with the diadem of mana. Her attitude was challenging, as if there was nothing in heaven or earth that she feared. Her daughter was carved in profile; the carving was softer, shaped and curved with vulnerability. Nevertheless, there was great love expressed between the women, the one holding the other, protective. However, something must have been in error in the carver's art. A veil had been placed over the younger figure so that her head was obscured; from beneath the veil came the sound of weeping.

The aria, the ghosts of Queen Ihi and her youngest daughter, Ata, stepped out of the two carved figures and floated toward the young prince and the sleeping koroua.

The young prince gave a cry of fear. The aria of the queen put a finger to her lips. 'Shhh, otherwise you will wake the koroua. You're not afraid, are you?'

'No,' the young prince answered, once he realised who she was. 'Not now.'

'Kei te pai,' Ihi answered. 'After all, you know who I am, don't you?'

The young prince nodded. He yearned to reach out and embrace his queen. 'It's just that you are even more beautiful than people told me.' Tears sprang to his eyes. She was so radiant; he felt blessed.

Ihi smiled. 'There should be no tears between us, young prince, only gladness. And look how you've grown! So handsome, just like your father. He would be proud of you.'

Together the young prince, Ihi and Ata looked at the sleeping Ohiri. 'He still speaks harshly of me, doesn't he?' the aria of the queen mourned. 'Yet everything I did was for love of him. Of all my emotions, my aroha for my husband was my only flaw — and it was fatal. For him I gave everything, even my daughter.'

'No, mother,' the aria of the youngest princess interjected. 'You are not to blame for an act of love that I made freely for both of you.'

'But my lord's rejection of me still hurts, daughter,' Ihi said. 'Even in dreams, when I try to slip into his skin, my protean lord pushes me away.' She turned to look at the young prince, a teasing smile on her lips. 'I was accustomed to enslaving my lovers to my own desires. Men and women alike were attracted to me, and did my bidding. I always took the active position. I was not afraid to use sex as a weapon or a stratagem to obtain submission. But Ohiri overpowered me. He was the ruthless one. It was he who ransacked me for all my treasures. I was defeated by him. I was the one who was enslaved. He will never forgive me for what I did. Never —'

Jagged lightning struck again. 'Why is the koroua so against you?' the young prince asked. He turned to Ata. 'And what is it that your sisters are so afraid to tell me?' The aria of Ata whimpered and, beneath her veil, fingered her neck and the red line that entirely circled it.

'Whakarongo,' the queen said. 'Listen, and judge for yourself. All I was, was a wife who loved her husband. And as a wife, I wanted to do everything to save him. Is this not what wives do? Thus, as soon as I received Horuhi's instructions, I and my beloved daughters set out on our various missions. The immediate task was to get through the enemy lines undetected. Do you know the caves beneath Areraria? They are the remnants of an underground riverbed; the river once flowed from the mountains where the greenstone mines are. They comprise a track, a secret route from Areraria. I ordered my daughters to go quickly. Together with my royal guards and their eight-man squads, we made our way beneath the walls of the citadel and the army encamped around its perimeter. My darling Ata was lagging behind — she has always been the slowcoach — but by the time we climbed to the surface, she and her warriors had caught up. From our vantage point, I could see that it was morning and Heti had resumed the Great Battle of Areraria. I prayed that Horuhi would hold the pa whawhai until our return. Once the enemy saw that Ohiri had been resurrected, I felt confident that they would take flight. Meantime, I had instructed that effigies be made of us all — eidolons of Ohiri, myself and my daughters — and displayed on the walls of the city. I wanted the enemy and my own people to believe that we were still within. I kissed Hera, Rawinia, Maraea and Ata farewell. "I go to Kurawaka at speed," I told them. "Before the night comes, all of us must be back in Areraria, having fulfilled our tasks. You, Hera, will make for the western pass. Maraea and Rawinia, head for the southern and eastern passes in the mountains. Ata, you take your warriors north to the river track. The passes and the river track are the only ways out of Ihipi and you will surely come across the four enemy squads as they carry your father out of our lands. Do not fail me, daughters. Your father loved us all. Now we must show our love for him."'

The aria of the queen nudged Ata playfully. 'Of course, my youngest daughter was worried that she would not be able to fulfil my command.'

Ata spoke for the second time. 'I asked my mother, "What if I fail?"' Her voice was sweet and plaintive. 'Even as a small child I was the slowest, losing my way, always so hopeless. My father and my sisters were constantly rescuing me.'

Ihi pressed Ata close to her. '"None of you will fail," I said to Ata. "Kua reri matou? Are we ready? Timata! Let us begin." With that, I turned and was already on the run to Kurawaka. When I reached the top of the escarpment, where there is a pou whenua, I looked back. My daughters had already commenced their own journeys. Only the barest shiver in the treetops indicated Hera, Rawinia and Maraea's progress as they ran with their warriors beneath. Of course, Ata was always noisy in the bush and I could follow her route by the birds which, as she pushed northward, rose above the trees and circled in the air. Satisfied that they were making good headway, I pressed on toward Kurawaka, eight hours away. I decided to head for the ocean and, boarding the royal waka, go by the southern tides beyond the twin mountains. From there I could strike inland and thereby reduce the travelling time. With that plan in mind, I ordered my fastest runner to go ahead and alert the captain of the waka that I was coming, so that when we arrived we could immediately set sail. By mid morning, exhausted from our run, the royal guards and I reached the waka. My captain cast off, caught excellent winds, and we were winging swiftly southward.'

'At that point,' Ata continued, 'Hera was fast approaching the western pass. Lo and behold, they crossed just behind the first of the enemy squads carrying one of the boxes. Picking up the trail, they were soon engaged in hand-to-hand combat. Three of her eight warriors were killed in the fight, but by the end of it they had secured the box. They began the trek back to the underground entrance to Areraria.'

'The waka made land at the twin mountains just after midday,' Queen Ihi resumed. 'From there to Kurawaka took just under an hour. However, when we arrived the hot sun had dried up all the moisture from the earth. How I railed against Ra, the Sun God! My royal guards and I lost valuable time looking for the precious dew — Horuhi had told me only a small amount was required — and I prayed to Papatuanuku, "Earth Mother, succour me." The goddess heard my karakia and sent a shimmer of wind through the curling ferns which formed the mat of her pubic hair. Within a dark fold of her labia, we found a moist place that the sun had not been able to reach. There I obtained two teardrops of the Water of Life. Our mission fulfilled, I urged my men to return to the waka. But I knew that the voyage back to Ihipi would be against the winds and the tides. My sailors had to paddle all the way and, when some fainted from the exhaustion, my royal guards substituted for them. Even I, Queen of Ihipi, took the paddle. By the time we reached the place where we had departed, four paddlers had died from the exertion. Those paddlers now have a place of pride in Rarohenga.'

'Rawinia and Maraea had also completed their task,' the aria of Ata said. 'Rawinia had reached the southern track and found no trace of any enemy squad. She quickly deduced that two of the squads must be travelling together. She ordered her warriors to make for the eastern pass, where she joined Maraea. They came across the squads, resting after noon kai. The enemy were not expecting any attack. Why should they? When Rawinia and Maraea fell upon them, they were quickly defeated.' Ata gave a wan smile. 'My sisters have always had more brains than I. They made the enemy squads carry their two boxes back to the underground caverns and, when they arrived, killed them. As for me, I was still heading for the river track —'

Suddenly, Ata began to weep. The sound was piteous. 'Don't weep, daughter,' the aria of Queen Ihi comforted. But Ata could not restrain her sadness, and even the young prince felt tears spring to his eyes at her distress.

'My mother was right,' she continued after a while. 'I always make a noise. The enemy squad I was pursuing saw the birds suddenly lifting from the trees and knew I was coming. They laid a trap for me and my warriors.' Ata sobbed even more loudly, the veil drifting strangely, as if there was nothing beneath it. 'Oh mother, I am so sorry —'

'I knew nothing of this,' Queen Ihi said. 'I had already joined up with Rawinia and Maraea and we quickly made our way back to Areraria. There, Hera was waiting for us with Horuhi. He had created the womb into which my consort would be consigned; it was filled with the purest water. "Homai ki au te Wai Ora," Horuhi ordered. I gave him the dew of Papatuanuku and he added it to the womb. From it the Water of Life began to evolve, red as blood and just as viscous. My daughters and I opened the three boxes. Inside were the three parts of the body of Ohiri. My daughters were weeping as we bound their father's body together with flax cords. Lovingly, we placed Ohiri into the womb. All that was missing was his head. But I had faith in my youngest daughter, Ata. I knew she would do all she could to bring the fourth box back to me.' The queen paused. 'Little did I know that the gods had another journey for me to take, to test my resolve and my desire to raise Ohiri from the dead.'

The young prince made a grave bow. 'All Maoridom knows of your great haerenga, valiant Queen. When I was a young boy growing up in exile, the first story I ever heard was of your second, magnificent journey.'

The arikinui gave an ironic smile. 'While we were waiting for Ata to return, Horuhi told me, "Even when she arrives, it will be too late, arikinui. Although we may be able to revive his body, I have consulted the mauri, and they tell me that your lord's soul has already passed through the gateway to the Underworld. Once a soul has passed the gatekeeper, Te Kuwatawata, it cannot return." Young prince, there was no hesitation in my reply to Horuhi:

"Then I myself will go to get him."'

—

And the people say that the great Queen Ihi embarked on a second, epic journey. Tired of body though she was, she was again on the run out of Areraria — and this time her travels took her beyond the bounds of the natural world into the world beyond imagining.

Moving quickly, she travelled to Te Reinga, at the northernmost location of Te Ika a Maui. Legend tells us that Ra, the Sun God, came to her aid; admiring her fearless spirit he rewarded her by sending a chariot made of fire. Once she was aboard, he pulled her across the sky like a flaming meteor. When Ihi dismounted at the place where the pohutukawa bloomed, she dived into the circling sea and, finding the centre of the terrifying whirlpool of souls, approached the looming gateway between the Overworld and the Underworld.

This is how the legend begins, this legend of the great love of Ihi, Queen of Areraria, for her husband Ohiri. When she came to the gateway, with utter fearlessness she moved through the clamouring dead to bargain with the gatekeeper, Te Kuwatawata.

'Let me pass,' she said.

Blinded by her beauty, he warned her, 'If you come through, you will not be able to return. Keep your loveliness for the light, oh Queen; the Underworld is the domain of the spirit world.'

'If you let me pass and return again,' Ihi said, 'I will make a bargain with you. You have no woman and your life must be lonely. When my time comes to die, I will be your partner for all eternity.' Ihi had no intention of keeping to her bargain. Somehow she would find a way of overturning it. Meantime, there was her husband to save.

Te Kuwatawata was quick to agree. 'As you wish, so it will be, for you are comely, my queen.' He stepped aside.

And Ihi journeyed into the Underworld.

Now, the people say that there are as many kingdoms in the Underworld as there are in the Overworld, places of phantasmagoric splendour that are like reflections of our own. The legend tells that Ihi travelled from one kingdom to the next. She travelled through worlds without end. And she slipped through the fabric of time from one level of the Underworld to the next and ever backwards into the past.

The further she ventured, the more she encountered other cultures and other civilisations. New worlds sprang up before her, worlds unknown, whose beings were not human; supernatural, supranatural, they were evidence of the great fertility of Creation.

As she went, Ihi called, 'Ohiri! Taku tane! Kei whea koe?'

She came to a great confluence where all the kingdoms joined, on a cliff. There, so the legend tells us, Ihi found herself in a magnificent Hall of the Gods. It was as tall as the sky, wide as the universe, deep as the ocean, and rows and rows of deities bordered the great River of Life and Death that flows from the beginning of Time to Time's end.

Ihi moved swiftly along the river, crying out, 'Homai koutou taku tane! Give me my husband, O Gods! Homai ia ki ahau.'

The people say that the gods had never witnessed such a thing. They were amused by this foolish, mortal queen whom they could kill in an instant. Even so, they acknowledged her daring and that she did not bow her head to them. They gave her leave to go forward to the cliff.

Ihi looked into the Gathering Place of Souls — and dived. She fell through space and time, through utter blackness. Her determination shone like the uraeus as she sought the umbilical of Ohiri's soul. Already disconnected, it floated with others, but Ihi caught his distinctive smell and, reaching out her hands, managed to catch the one that was Ohiri's before it disappeared forever. Pulling herself along its length, she came to him.

'Ohiri, haere mai,' she said. 'Me te kaioha te roimata, he puna wai kai aku roimata. Like driving rain are my tears, a spring bubbling from my eyes. Husband, come with me.'

It was as if those millions of years that Ihi searched for Ohiri were one day. She brought Ohiri back to the gateway and took him out of that place into the sunshine of her own world.

'Remember your bargain,' Te Kuwatawata said. 'When you return at death, you will belong not to him but to me.'

The people say that Ihi and Ohiri travelled back from Te Reinga together. They approached the Overworld, where Ihi could hear the tides beating. They clambered up through the sea, back into the world of the living. He was coming back! Returning. It was night, then dawn, and then, with his return, it was day.

And Queen Ihi came back with the soul of Ohiri to Areraria. She arrived at the caverns beneath the citadel to see that her youngest daughter, Ata, had arrived.

Ata's face was streaming with tears. Her hands were empty.

'Mother,' Ata said, 'forgive me.'

This is what the legend tells us.

This is what the people say.

the young prince

Suddenly the young prince heard loud thunder, like an ominous drum roll. A few moments later lightning bolts cracked through the clouds roiling above Areraria. By the light could be seen strange shapes, unnatural apparitions, all contained within a whirling cyclone.

The tribunal of the dead was coming.

—

'I offered my own head,' the aria of the dead princess said.

The tribunal of the dead dropped down from the cyclone, swirling down in circles onto the roof of the royal meeting house and the snow all around.

'What else could I do?' Ata continued. 'My mother was in such despair. I told her that my warriors and I had been ambushed and defeated; I wanted to kill myself for having failed my mother and my lord. My mother asked Horuhi whether there was still time to go after the enemy squad that had evaded me. He said no. Finally, my mother broke down, and I never heard such pain, "Aue, kei noho au i te Ao taka maero e! Haere maiangi ai, anewa raumati ai! Alas, I am destined therefore to be but an aimless wanderer in this life, weak and faint as with summer's heat. My lord is forever gone." That is when I said to her, "Mother, take my head in exchange for my father's. I love you both."'

At her words, the tribunal of the dead began to pound on the roof, walls and door: *Let us in, let us in.*

Why had they come? This is why: tonight, the great queen would be called to judgement. This was her crime:

'I accepted my daughter's offer,' Queen Ihi said.

—

The tribunal of the dead were drumming on the roof of the royal meeting house in a storm of rage and anger. The sound was so deafening that the young prince put his hands against his ears. More fists began to beat against the walls and door.

The aria of Queen Ihi raised her face to the unseen court. 'I offer no excuse,' she called, defiant. 'I am not the first nor am I the last in the ancient world to sacrifice a child. Horuhi begged me not to do it; he is not to pay for my act and should be given clemency. I made the sacrifice clean and swift. Before Ata even knew it, I had slipped my dagger into her heart and while she was falling, slit her throat —'

And Ihi gave her daughter's head to Horuhi and said to him, 'Homai te Wai Ora ki a ia, taku rangatira. Complete the ceremony. Raise my husband fully from the Water of Life.'

Horuhi did so. He fixed Ata's head upon the shoulders of Ohiri's body and, using the karakia the gods had given him, turned to the task of resurrecting Ohiri and ensuring the connection with his soul.

'I te Po, Po, ka awatea, papaki tu ana te tai ki Te Reinga, ki te Po, ka Ao, ka Awatea. Let my karakia go through the veil of death, let it go into the spirit world, let it go to the great night where our rangatira has already journeyed. Let my karakia go to the Underworld. Let it overrule the decision of death and allow the return of life to the dead man. Let the dead man live again. Ka Ao, ka Ao, ka Awatea! Hui e! Haumi e! Taiki e.'

With a gasp, Ohiri revived. He rose from the Water of Life renewed, glorious. The water streamed from him. He stood up. Ihi welcomed him. She held him tightly: 'Let me in, let me in.' He turned to Hera, Rawinia and Maraea and was puzzled when they backed away from him.

'Where is your sister?' he asked. 'He aha te mate? What is wrong?'

And Ohiri touched his face. His fingers recoiled. He touched his face again. He turned to Ihi.

'What have you done, wife?'

'I loved you,' she said. 'I wanted you back.'

He called for a bowl of water. He filled it with water. He looked into it at his reflection.

'She wanted to do this for you,' Ihi, Queen of Areraria, said.

—

The aria of Queen Ihi and Ata disappeared.

All around was the sound of the tribunal of the dead, drumming, drumming, drumming. The blind man, Ohiri, consort to Ihi, arikinui of Areraria, awoke with a start. He saw the young prince looming above him, his face stinging with tears and, thinking that his time to be killed had come, leapt up with a cry and rushed to the door.

'No,' the young prince called. He was afraid that the tribunal of the dead would take Ohiri before he completed his task. But when Ohiri opened the door, the tribunal suddenly dispersed like wraiths. The storm abated and soft snow began to fall. And Ohiri knelt within the sacred precinct.

'These sacred posts saw the deed,' he told the young prince. 'The mauri grieved that Ihi had transgressed their boundaries by taking one life for another. They departed, leaving behind a riddle:

'When will Areraria live again?
When the dead child comes in thundering rain

Born in a dead womb, born in pain
And the dead man dies again.'

He pulled aside his mask so that the young prince could see his face. 'He wahine, he whenua, ka ngaro ai te tangata,' he began. 'For women or for land, man dies. These are the two principal causes of warfare. For my wife I would have done anything, but no father would want his own daughter to sacrifice her life for his. All I could think of was how beautiful Ata had been in life. Now she had been murdered, and by my wife's own hand.'

Still unlined, the face of Ata stared back at the young prince. Where the eyes had once been were two dark sockets.

'I killed Ihi,' Ohiri went on. 'I strangled her. As I was doing so, I caught sight of my face again in the bowl of water. I could not bear the horror of it. I took a blade of obsidian and hacked out both my eyes. I wanted to make sure that there would be no further accidental reflection of myself in the water, or in any shining pounamu or obsidian surface. I commanded Horuhi not to raise my wife from her well deserved death. He told me of the bargain she had made with Te Kuwatawata; Ihi would never be able to return to the world of the living. Satisfied, I went onto the ramparts of Areraria, carrying the headless body of my beloved youngest daughter in my arms, and allowed the three borderland chiefs to look upon my face and her body.'

The borderland kings could not comprehend what had happened. 'What evil is this?' Heti asked. 'What heresy?' As much as he and his warrior lords had wanted to conquer Ihipi, they now became uneasy and disturbed. Heti was alarmed that they had contributed to the evil and could also be punished by the gods for it. 'We shall place a rahui on Areraria,' he announced to his brother warlords. They nodded in assent.

'Ka tika,' Heti decided.

'He turned to address me,' said Ohiri. '"We will cease our fight with you, great Lord, and leave your land immediately. Evil resides here now. Where evil is, goodness cannot grow. We leave you to live with your pain for ever and ever."'

'I pleaded with them to kill me, to give me peace. They refused. So did my daughters and my people. Why did I not kill myself? I tried, so many times I tried, but the Water of Life prevented it. All I have been left with is a riddle that makes no sense. Aue, I am doomed to live with my guilt forever — it was I who razed the land of Ihipi. In my madness it was also I who brought about the Time of Darkness. I refused to let the people grow crops. Ehara, nga mate haramai ki konei ki runga o te whenua. From that moment onward, Areraria became accursed. Eventually, a plague came upon the land. Most of those who stayed, died, littering Ihipi with their bones and skulls. They became the feast for the black carrion birds. Disheartened, the remainder left Ihipi and became exiled in the lands of our neighbours. Kei whea nga manu? Even the birds left, including the very carrion birds that had fed on the sinews of Ihipi's dead.

'Ever since, there has been eternal winter.'

he who was born of the dead

'But the story is not over,' the young prince said. 'For he who was born of the dead has come, my lord.'

'You?' Ohiri asked.

The young prince nodded. He saw that the three old women had joined him. He called to them, 'Tuahine, haere mai, sisters, the time has come.' They embraced him, weeping.

The young prince told Ohiri who he was. 'You were not to know,' he began, 'that your queen was six months pregnant when you killed her. Although Horuhi, your shaman, could not bring her back to life, he kept her body alive in the same Water of Life that had sustained you. He delivered her body, when it had come to term, of a son.'

'You are my son?' Ohiri's bloodied eyes looked up at the young prince. A single tear fell. 'Then give me my release —'

The young prince drew the patu across the old king's neck. The edge of the greenstone was razor sharp. It sliced deep and, with a gasp of gratitude, the old king grabbed the upper arms of the young prince and drew him close in a loving embrace.

Weeping, the young prince made ritual farewell to his father. 'Haere atu ra, e te rangatira, ki te paepae o Matariki, o Rehua, haere atu ra. Farewell, great chief, to the threshold of the Pleiades, to Antares, farewell. Go beyond, go to the ancestors who have gone to the night, the dark night, the dense night, the bottomless night. The rough cloak of death is upon you, old man, go.'

'Thank you, son,' the old king said as he gave up his life and began his journey back to the gathering place of his ancestors. The blood spilled from his neck and, like glowing red stones, stained the snow before seeping through and into the earth below. The three old daughters of Ohiri took their father from the young prince's arms and began to keen over him. 'Aue te koroua e, aue —'

There was a shimmering in the air, and the aria of Queen Ihi and her daughter, Ata, reappeared before the young prince. 'Was he still angry with me when he died?' the Queen asked.

'Yes, mother,' the young prince answered.

The aria of the Queen bowed her head, mourning. 'Te au ko te moe; to kona ake ana ki runga, e ra, na te mamae era ka huri ronake. You would think that in death I would find peace. But even there sleep does not come, for my thoughts are endlessly of my country and my lord, and what I did to him. It was hubris that brought about Areraria's downfall; it was vainglory that led to my own demise. I have paid the price; I loved my country but I loved Ohiri even more in life, and I still love him in death — but now I belong to Te Kuwatawata. Your father need have no further thought of me, for there is no way I can break my bargain with the gatekeeper and, believe me, I have tried often.' Ihi lifted her face to the light, imperious, valiant. 'Do not pity me. I loved Ohiri, and what I did was for love of him.' She gave a quick look northward. 'I can already see him approaching Te Reinga. How glorious he is! When he reaches the gateway Te Kuwatawata has allowed me a moment to speak to him. Then I will let him pass through to where Ata is waiting for him. She will lovingly keep him company in the Underworld and minister to him until her sisters join her. Come, Ata, quickly, and attend upon your father.'

A shimmer, and the aria of the two women disappeared.

—

Breathing deep, the young prince called into the air.

'Whakataka te hau ki te uru! Whakataka te hau ki te tonga! Kia makinakina ki uta! Kia mataratara ki tai! Come, the winds of the west! Gather here, winds from the south! Warm the land! Make calm and still the tides —'

The snow stopped falling. The clouds which had covered Ihipi for twenty years rolled apart. Dawn came and the sun's rays, long absent from the land, pierced the earth. A soft breeze began to blow across the azure sea, spilling up the escarpment and over, to be received into the bowl of Ihipi.

The young prince continued his invocation, his voice growing stronger and stronger with joy and hope.

'E hiakina te atakura! He tio! He huka! He hauhunga! Tihei mauriora! Tuturu whamaua ki a tina! Haumi e! Hui e! Taiki e! Let the calm be widespread now! Let the ocean glisten as greenstone! Bring the sparkle of sunlight again to ever dance across the pathway to Ihipi! Bind together! Gather together! Let it be done!'

There was a scintillation in the air above Areraria. The mauri returned and the pou, the carved posts in the sacred precinct in front of the meeting house, began to stir, glow and become luminescent.

From the very place where Ohiri's blood had spilled, the snow melted away to show green shoots piercing through the earth's skin.

Throughout Ihipi came a great sigh. The snow's recession was rapid. The ice cracked open on the surface of the riverbeds. From the deep wells of the earth, fresh spring water began to flow upwards, washing away all the soil's rot, cleansing the land. The forests, once barren of foliage, blossomed with leaves. Across the landscape, mosses and flowers sparkled and perfumed the warming air.

From far away, the forest birds began to call to each other in excitement at the sight of the sunlight over Ihipi, and to wing their way back. The men and women, long exiled, seeing the birds flying towards a shining kingdom, knew that the Time of Darkness was over.

'Hoki mai tatou ki te wa kainga,' they called to each other. 'Let us return to our home.'

Taking up their belongings they began to trek over the ranges to Ihipi to farewell the old king Ohiri and install the young prince.

Spring came to the dead land.

dead of night

written with Howard Carmichael and David Wiltshire

10

The table is set for six. The host, Captain Walter Craig, has invited the guests for pre-dinner drinks at 7.30. Time, of course, has long lost all real meaning, but on board ship a 24-hour day is still observed; it continues to locate, structure and define, calculate the days and measure the distances.

The ship is called the *Endeavour*. It is named after the vessel which set sail for Tahiti under Captain James Cook in 1769 to observe the transit of Venus across the sun. Cook also had secret instructions from the British Admiralty to search for the great southern continent, which some eighteenth-century scientists claimed must balance the great land masses of the northern hemisphere; instead, he discovered New Zealand.

The purser is standing beside the table. He steps to one side so that Captain Craig is able to approve the setting. For this, the last dinner of the voyage, the purser has laid out the finest silver and, in the middle, a display of beautiful crystallised white orchids; the wine glasses are antique Waterford. Written in ornate script on place cards are the names of the guests:

Mrs Joan Cortland
Professor Van Straaten
Doctor Eliot Foley
Monsignor Maxwell Frère
Miss Sally O'Hara

Mrs Cortland will sit on the Captain's left. She will enjoy that, as it will give her a de facto role as hostess. Then, clockwise, the purser has seated Professor Van Straaten, Dr Foley and Monsignor Frère; he has carefully ensured that the Professor is not seated next to the Monsignor. Miss O'Hara is seated on the Captain's right.

'As usual, perfection,' Captain Craig says to the purser, noting that he has the ladies on either side of him.

'Thank you, sir.' The purser gives a slight nod. He is amused to see the Captain rearrange one of the dessert forks.

'What's on the menu this evening?' Captain Craig asks.

'The chef is offering a choice of entrée: twice-roasted quail or a Balinese warm salad of lime, coconut, beans, spinach and shallots. The mains tonight are either seven-spice duck done with Singapore flavours, or steamed fish à la polynésienne and served with aubergines in lacquered purple coats.'

'And dessert?'

'Dessert will be lychee jelly with green tea pannacotta, or Pacific fruits, including mango, guava and banana, accompanied by lime ice cream.'

'What about wine?'

'May I suggest the Tohu 2004 Gisborne Reserve Chardonnay? It displays stonefruit characteristics and has a light touch of oak which will complement the Asian–Pacific theme of the menu.'

'We have Tohu 2004 in our ship's cellar? Professor Van Straaten will be impressed.' The Professor, in addition to being a Nobel prize-winning physicist, is a connoisseur of fine wines. 'Are our guests awake?'

'Yes, sir,' the purser replies. 'Monsignor Frère complained of queasiness from the last, somewhat rough passage, and Dr Foley joked that he has still to regain his sealegs, but all guests are dressing for dinner. Mrs Cortland has advised she will make a late entrance.'

Mrs Cortland has both the beautiful woman's flair for making the most of the moment and the expectation that it is a woman's prerogative to be the last to be seated.

9

As usual, Monsignor Frère is first to arrive. Resplendent in his ecclesiastical robes, he shows no sign of illness. 'I find, Captain Craig,' he says as they shake hands, 'that prayer aids recovery much quicker than an aspirin.' He notices the dinner music and winces. 'We are beginning with Miss O'Hara's choice, are we? Ah well, the young and their tastes!'

At that moment Miss O'Hara herself arrives, gallantly escorted by Dr Foley. This evening she has dressed in a unisex retropunk style: a clash of vivid greens and purples over basic black that was fashionable at the turn of the millennium. As soon as she hears the music she begins to bop and gyrate.

'Hi, Captain,' she calls. 'Do you know this music? It's from an album by Sonic Youth. Aren't they fantastic?'

Miss O'Hara is the only one of the passengers whose wellbeing and comfort had worried Captain Craig — after all, she was an actress in popular cinema, and much younger than everyone else — but from the outset she has been a joy and a surprise. Both she and Mrs Cortland have proved ideal antidotes to the lugubrious academic male company.

'Seldom has an underground band been so archetypically NYC in their music,' Miss O'Hara explains to the Monsignor. 'Don't you think they're sublime?'

Mesmerising instrumental passages, hazy indie ballads, devastating blasts of noise and free-form textural riffs build to a climax. It's all so New York City: dirty, sprawling, complex, harsh, self-obsessed, art-damaged, beautiful and cool as hell.

'Yes,' Monsignor Frère answers. 'Sublime.'

Next to join the dinner party is Professor Van Straaten, still fussing and apologising over his appearance. He has mislaid his dark suit and, instead, presents himself in tails.

'What, no top hat?' Monsignor Frère jests.

Miss O'Hara and Dr Foley exchange glances: it is more likely that the Professor has been put out by the Monsignor's sartorial elegance at previous dinners and has dressed formally to provide fair competition.

True to form, Mrs Cortland arrives last, just in time to button the Professor's wing collar and help him with his bow tie. 'You need a wife,' she says.

'Are you offering?' he asks.

Mrs Cortland appraises him with an ironic smile. 'You dear man,' she says noncommittally. Through her marriage to nanotech magnate and condensed-matter physicist Peter Cortland, she became one of the richest people in the world. Now a widow, and still beautiful, she has been accustomed to offers of marriage, though primarily from other billionaires more interested in a corporate merger. She turns to Miss O'Hara. 'I am so glad we don't clash.' She is wearing an evening dress of shimmering blue which contrasts stunningly with her red hair. The two women look like mother and daughter.

—

A waiter arrives with flutes of Laurent-Perrier on a shining silver platter, and Captain Craig orders the radiation shields across the windows lowered.

'Hemi, let's look at the view,' he says.

The shields slide down to reveal the *Endeavour*'s beautiful light-wings, like sails billowing. But it is not wind that is propelling this vessel. The sails are catching subatomic particles generated by the ultra-energetic jets spat out of black holes, particularly supermassive Kerr black holes, in the centres of active galaxies.

The ship is an Artificial Intelligence of the latest design. It wears its name proudly. In the days of eighteenth-century sail, Captain Cook sailed its namesake from Plymouth, knowing that there were a certain number of days to the Bay of Biscay. From there, the distance would have been calculated by sextant and compass, and the numbers of days of westerly sail that it would take to round Cape Horn. Again, distance would have been calculated to the South Pacific and time measured by days of sail.

Although 400 years separate Cook's voyage and Captain Craig's, nothing has really changed. Computer may have replaced compass, and distance and time may be defined in light-years and parsecs, but bearings are still taken and distance measured by setting the destination: from Earth via Matariki to the Magellanic Clouds, 50 kiloparsecs at the far edge of Earth's galactic disc; then across the Milky Way, 130 kiloparsecs to the Great Square of Pegasus and the Palomar 13 global cluster buried beneath it. From there the ship has jumped 670 kiloparsecs to the Magellanic stream and the Andromeda Spiral Galaxy.

Whenever Captain Craig wishes to convey instructions to *Endeavour*, he does so through Hemi, its avatar. The Captain has a communication implant in his brain and, courtesy of nanotechnological advances, needs only to issue his orders from wherever he is standing for the Hypertime Engineering Matrix Intelligence to reply.

'Thank you, Hemi,' the Captain says now. 'Please maintain current speed and smoothness during dinner.'

'Yes, Captain,' Hemi answers. 'May I say that the ladies are looking especially lovely this evening?'

Captain Craig channels the avatar's voice into the ship's sound system so that all the guests can hear Hemi's compliment.

'You flatterer,' Mrs Cortland responds.

'Enjoy your dinner,' Hemi says.

Captain Craig and his guests resume looking at the view. The *Endeavour* is travelling so fast that it leaves a phosphorescent trail through the space–time continuum. The view is corrected by the ship's computers for relativistic distortions. A slideshow of the passing galaxy clusters flashes up in a never-ending kaleidoscope of forms.

'I wouldn't be surprised to see dolphins,' Mrs Cortland laughs. 'Moments of beauty, like this, make me proud that ships are called "she". Hemi won't mind, will he?' Then, uncharacteristically, she shivers. 'We're almost there, aren't we?'

'Yes,' Captain Craig answers.

—

'Ah!' Monsignor Frère clasps his hands together, pleased.

As his choice of dinner music, he has selected Johann Sebastian Bach's cantata, 'Ich habe genug'. When the great baritone Hans Hotter begins to sing the aria, he closes his eyes with pleasure.

'Now there's sublimity,' he says to Miss O'Hara. 'Bach wrote this cantata in 1727 for the Feast of the Blessed Virgin Mary. Hotter recorded it in 1950 and his interpretation attains utter perfection. Listen to the peculiarly profound utterance, the warmth and sincerity and the hushed, awestruck *mezza voce* above the solo oboe and murmuring strings.'

'The good Monsignor is already transported to heaven,' Professor Van Straaten whispers in a voice which, unfortunately, carries.

Quickly, the Captain turns to all. 'Ladies and gentlemen,' he says, 'shall we go in to dinner? Mrs Cortland, may I escort you to your place?'

> It is enough! My consolation is only that
> My Saviour, Jesus, may be mine,
> So shall I escape from all the sorrow
> That enslaves me in this life

8

The Asian–Pacific thematic of the dinner is a total success. Professor Van Straaten has gone into raptures about the 2004 Tohu Reserve.

'I'm not the only one to be transported to heaven,' Monsignor Frère mutters to Dr Foley. But he, also, is enjoying the quality of the wine. The subtle flavours reach his tastebuds and delicately rinse away the last of the chemical life-support fluids that sustained him, and the others, in deep sleep. 'How long have we been in suspended animation this time?'

'Better not to know,' Dr Foley advises him. 'Could your mind accept it?'

Endeavour possesses a photon epsilon matter-antimatter drive which uses the Penrose process to mine the rotational energy of the Kerr black holes, the energy caught by the ship's light-wings. Boosted by this extraordinary power source, the ship is able to travel arbitrarily close to the speed of light.

The Monsignor, however, will not be diverted. 'Tell me,' he insists.

'We are now cruising at 99.99999999999999999996 percent of the speed of light,' Dr Foley answers. 'Therefore, if one uses human reckoning, by relativistic time dilation one hour by ship time is 126 million light-years.'

Monsignor Frère blanches. Prior to embarking on this voyage, he was the principal cosmologist at the Vatican Observatory. Despite some understanding of Dr Foley's information, the magnitude of the mathematics still staggers him. 'We've travelled that amount of time, every hour on ship, regardless of whether or not I am asleep?'

Dr Foley nods. 'More or less. Every time we've stopped for sightseeing, the slow-downs have been a really complicated series of manoeuvres; the time dilation becomes much, much less. Without those sleeps, before and after the stopovers, you and I would have been history long ago, so to speak. But they add millions of years to the time that Hemi has experienced.'

And the elapsed universal cosmic time since they left Earth? By now it would be several hundred billion years. Even Dr Foley's mind has gone into arrest as he contemplates this fact.

Miss O'Hara presses Dr Foley's arm and brings him back to the present. Professor Van Straaten is holding forth on the art of wine tasting and requires everyone's attention. He asks the wine waiter to bring him a medium-sized wine glass with a rim that is narrower than its base. 'This is the best shape to hold the wine's aroma,' he explains. He instructs the waiter to fill it to just below the widest part of the glass and tilts it slightly against a white background to look at the true colour of the wine. 'It should be clear and bright and never cloudy.'

Everyone watches, amused at the theatricality of the Professor's presentation. He sniffs the wine and swirls it gently in the glass to maximise its interaction with the air. 'One must think about the differences, if any, before and after swirling,' he continues, taking a couple more long, controlled sniffs. 'One must ask oneself, "What is my first impression? Is the wine dominated by fruit smells or something else? Is it easy to identify or is it a mixture of things that make it more complex?" Wine should never smell vinegary or mouldy, although earthy can be okay.' Next, he tastes the wine by taking a small mouthful, moving it across his mouth and breathing a little air across it to intensify the flavours. He nods his approval and gestures to the waiter to fill the glasses of the others. 'Pay attention not just to the initial taste,' he says, 'but the flavours that linger after you have swallowed — the *finish*.' He raises his glass in a toast. 'To truth,' he begins, 'and beauty,' he ends, saluting Mrs Cortland and Miss O'Hara.

—

To while away the time between one near-to-light-speed boost and the next, Captain Craig and his passengers have taken to playing a game during dinner. It was Mrs Cortland's idea, and they first played it when *Endeavour* reached the perimeter of the Local Group, 1000 kiloparsecs out. From there they had made a quick jump to the Triangulum/M33 and onward through the multifaceted spectacle of the Virgo and Coma clusters. Dancing along the black holes in the centres of the galaxies of the Great Wall, and gaining vast energies at each encounter, the ship had shot off towards the Hubble Ultra Deep Field that marked the outer perimeter of the known universe. Once expansion of space was allowed for, it was a journey of 51 billion light-years.

The game requires that each guest tell the others what they think has been the most transforming event in the history of science and, in particular, cosmological science.

'I think it's your turn to begin, Eliot,' Mrs Cortland prompts. 'As a prizewinning historian, your offerings have always been fascinating, and I am sure you have left the best to last.'

'In fact,' Dr Foley replies, 'I have an overture to begin with. Hemi, maestro, please!'

Dr Foley has a singular sense of humour. The first bars of Richard Strauss's tone poem, 'Thus Spake Zarathustra', featured in the opening moments of Stanley Kubrick's *2001: A Space Odyssey*, roll grandiloquently through Hemi's sound system. Everybody starts to laugh. They laugh even louder when Dr Foley turns to Miss O'Hara and says, 'The next part is for you, darling,' and the Strauss is replaced with 'Good Vibrations' by the Beach Boys.

'Oh, Eliot!' Miss O'Hara blushes. Although Dr Foley is ten years older than she, he is the youngest of the men on board; and they have fallen in love. In the last deep sleep they shared the same crystal life-support unit, Sleeping Beauty and Prince Charming in suspended animation in each other's arms.

'My older colleagues will indulge me in my choice of music,' Dr Foley begins, 'but sublimity, I would submit to you, Monsignor Frère, comes in many forms. "Good Vibrations" was one of the great achievements of popular music, so complexly constructed that even classical music critics considered it a masterpiece. It's the Rosetta stone of American mid twentieth-century music, and subsequently became part of the world's collective unconscious.'

Monsignor Frère nods grudgingly. 'Even in my tribal village in Nigeria when I was a boy, we sang the lyrics: "Good good good good vibrations —"'

'There!' Miss O'Hara laughs excitedly. 'Eliot's point exactly.' As for Mrs Cortland, the thought of the dear Monsignor, who is rather on the large side, gyrating to 'Good Vibrations' has her in a fit of merriment.

Professor Van Straaten shows his impatience. 'So have you saved the best for last?' he asks Dr Foley.

'As a historian,' Dr Foley answers, 'it is my opinion that the most transforming event in cosmological science has been the unfolding set of revelations of Earth's — and man's — position in the cosmos. Of course I shall only be able to talk of western man and western cosmology; in earlier times, western cosmologists were blind to Muslim science and astronomy and therefore to the brilliance of their eastern elders.'

Dr Foley smiles at Miss O'Hara and proceeds with his thesis. 'In western history, there have been three major propositions on the Earth's position. The first geocentric model was originated by Thales of Miletus, the Greek mathematician, in 585 BC. However, it was Aristotle, in Athens during the fourth century BC, who became its primary proponent: his model placed the Earth at the centre of the universe and established the heavens as a realm of circular perfection. Thus the sun, moon and all the planets circled the Earth in orbits that were simple, crystalline, harmonious and musical, lacking beginning or end. In the second century AD, when Alexandria had replaced Athens as the intellectual capital of the world, the Egyptian mathematician Claudius Ptolemy further developed Aristotle's template. In his *Almagest*, the Earth was still at the centre, and the stars and planets whirled in circular orbits around it; but his model also included epicycles to take into account the orbital variations shown by Mars, Saturn and Jupiter. It looked like the insides of a clock and, indeed, comprised an incredibly complicated clockwork universe.'

'Yes,' Professor Van Straaten nods. 'Then came the rise of Christianity, when Rome displaced Athens and Alexandria as the world's intellectual capital. Unfortunately, there, the intellectual ideas were driven by religion, not science — and, in particular, by the idea that God had created the heavens and the Earth.' He casts an arrogant eye at Monsignor Frère, knowing that his remarks will ruffle his feathers. 'What the Roman Catholic Church did was to combine its own ideas of an omnipotent and omniscient god with Aristotle's and Ptolemy's thinking. Theologians came up with their template: God had created man to have dominion over all. Everything in the universe was meant to serve him. Man was the centre of the Christian universe, both literally and figuratively. The church even invented an Angel of God, which cranked a piece of machinery called the *primum mobile*, to explain why we had 12 hours of day and 12 hours of night. It was a beautiful model of the universe: God-driven, man-driven, ego-driven. Except that it was wrong.'

Mrs Cortland casts a quick glance at Captain Craig. When he doesn't intervene, she asks Dr Foley, 'You were saying that there were three major propositions on the Earth's position? What was the second?'

'The second, Mrs Cortland, came when cosmologists, around the fifteenth century, turned to the heliocentric model. It wasn't the Earth that was at the centre of the universe, but the sun.'

'And the Holy Mother church,' interrupts Professor Van Straaten, 'is still struggling to come to terms with that shift, isn't it, Monsignor? Cosmology had been captured by the theologians. When scientists stated that observation and calculation, rather than divine revelation, could reveal the workings of the heavens, they posed a direct threat to church writ and to the proposition that God made the world and the universe — especially that the universe was eternal and unchanging, just as God had made it on the first day. Any cosmologists who offered evidence that it might be otherwise were branded heretics. I wonder how many scientists were burnt at the stake, eh?'

Dr Foley hastens on. 'The Polish physician and clergyman, Nicolaus Copernicus, was the first to herald the shift. He thought the Ptolemaic system was a bit of a mess and spent much of his life trying to come up with a cleaner, simpler explanation of the motion of the planets. In 1514, he published his *Commentariolus*, putting the sun at the centre, and began what was tantamount to an astronomical mutiny. Indeed, the period from 1514 to 1690, from Copernicus through Brahe, Kepler, Galileo and Newton, has often been termed the Copernican Revolution. Galileo Galilei's appearance, of course, heralds the dawn of science. We have already heard from Professor Van Straaten at a previous dinner about that remarkable man, so I won't traverse the same ground here.'

'And the third shift?' Miss O'Hara asks.

'We have to fast-forward to 1923 for that,' Dr Foley says, 'to a certain young pioneering astronomer and scientist named Edwin Hubble.'

'Hubble bubble, toil and trouble,' the Professor quips.

'Hubble's observations through the Mount Wilson telescope in the San Gabriel mountains above Pasadena paved the way for man to make the leap from sun-centred universe to the revelation that, actually, the cosmos was bigger than man had thought it was. Previously, a Great Debate had raged in which most cosmologists believed in a single-galaxy universe. One of its proponents, Harlow Shapley, thought that every star they saw was inside the Milky Way. But with Hubble came the discovery that, for instance, what was then known as the Andromeda Nebula was, in fact, a galaxy that was outside the Milky Way. In 1924, when Hubble wrote to Shapley to tell him of his findings, Shapley said, "Here is the letter that has destroyed my universe." From that moment onward, the entire universe had to be remapped and everything in it reclassified. We weren't a one-galaxy cosmos. We were merely one luminous pinwheel among billions of similar whorls of stars. The universe was filled with countless Milky Ways, each as grand as our own galaxy.'

Dr Foley gives an enigmatic smile. 'My point is that at every revelation, ego-driven man had to redefine himself in relation to his universe. You see, within this vastness, we simply disappeared. The universe was infinite, or almost infinite, going on for ever and ever. This discovery has brought us face to face with the horrifying consideration of how very small and infinitesimal we were as a species. We weren't as big as we thought we were, after all. Not only that, but we had to redefine ourselves with each other. And in each case, every new position was accompanied by violence and murder, symbolised in that moment in *2001: A Space Odyssey* when the group of apes kills one of their own. A leader among the apes has used a jawbone as weapon in the murder. Triumphant, he throws the bloodied jawbone into the air, where it transforms itself into a spaceship — just like ours.'

> I, I love the colorful clothes she wears
> And the way the sunlight plays upon her hair
> I hear the sound of a gentle word
> On the wind that lifts her perfume through the air
> . . . Good good good good vibrations —

7

Captain Craig looks at Mrs Cortland and remembers the question she asked before dinner: 'We're almost there, aren't we?' Uncharacteristically, she had shivered.

She has regained her calm. But there was a time — oh how many billions of light-years ago was it now? — when the courage of all on board *Endeavour* had been tested to the limit.

That moment had come when *Endeavour* had reached its original destination: HUDF-JD2, the gigantic galaxy that lies within the Hubble Deep Field. Up to that point, all on board had thought they were simply on a voyage of discovery, a voyage which Mrs Cortland's late husband Peter had planned to lead.

'Our astronomers have detected something strange developing out there,' Peter Cortland had told Walter Craig. 'Although we suspect we know what it is or, more importantly, what it means, I'm building a ship to travel to HUDF-JD2 to take a look first-hand. Our projections suggest that the galaxy cluster which we see forming there billions of years ago is in a region of space so dense that there will by now be a supermassive black hole — HUDF-JD2-BH1 — of some hundred billions of solar masses. By comparison, the 3 million solar-mass black hole in our own galactic centre is a pipsqueak.'

Cortland's eyes had twinkled with amusement. 'I'm calling the ship the *Endeavour*. There's a good reason for the name — we expect not just one gigantic black hole, but two on an almost collision course. My people have nicknamed the smaller black hole Venus II.'

Captain Craig had smiled at the parallel with Captain Cook's mission to observe the transit of Venus.

'When Venus II transits in front of HUDF-JD2-BH1 at the closest point of its orbit, the production of gravitational waves will send out the largest seismic warping event in the space–time continuum since the Big Bang itself. The back-reaction on space–time will allow us to assess the anomaly in the background geometry of the universe. We've got to be there for the transit.'

Halfway through building the ship, however, Cortland, like many others on Earth, fell ill. 'Looks like it's up to you, old girl,' he had said to his wife. 'Complete the *Endeavour* and sail it for me.'

Then he summoned Captain Craig to his bedside and gave him his instructions.

'Observing the transit of Venus II is only the first part of your mission,' he said. 'Once you've done that, I have a second, secret set of instructions for you to open.'

Captain Craig had smiled. He thought of the boyish games he and Peter Cortland had played during their golden-weather New Zealand childhood. *A secret set of instructions*: Peter always had a way of talking that was talismanic, scattering his words like runes on glowing embers.

A peal of laughter interrupts Captain Craig's thoughts. He looks across the table and sees Miss O'Hara recovering from some joke that the Monsignor has told her. She turns to the waiter. 'My compliments to the chef,' she says. 'The Balinese salad was just yummy and the seven-spice Singapore duck simply delicious. Now I could dance all night! Come, partner me, Eliot.' She pulls the protesting Dr Foley to his feet, and spins him into a waltz.

Against the black velvet backdrop of the largest ballroom ever known, Captain Craig sees a sudden shimmer and scintillation through one of the starboard windows. It is Aunti-2, one of the three Advanced Unified Navigational Tracking Intelligence robotic probes that accompany the *Endeavour*, on its regular parabolic flight back to the ship. Aunti-2 is soon joined by Aunti-1 and Aunti-3, and Captain Craig hears them chattering away to Hemi.

'Is everything all right, Hemi?'

'Yes, sir,' Hemi sighs. 'Aunti-3 has complained that she stubbed her toe on a moon and Aunti-1 is cross at me for sending her too far forward to check ahead.'

'There could have been Injuns out there,' Aunti-1 says. 'I could have been scalped.'

Peter Cortland's scientists have given the probes the personalities of three grumpy old ladies who are constantly scolding Hemi as if he were their nephew. Aunti-3, in particular, has been programmed to sing mid twentieth-century pop songs in moments of stress.

'I'm glad you're safely back,' Captain Craig says. He knows that none of the human passengers would have survived the voyage had it not been for the aunties.

—

The Captain's thoughts return to that day when *Endeavour* had arrived at HUDF-JD2. Mrs Cortland still liked to keep calendar time and she'd marked the date in her diary: 13 April, 20 days before the transit.

HUDF-JD2-BH1 had lain before them, an ominous deep dark hole with a broad layered disk, like Saturn's rings, circling the central emptiness. Vivid, molten jets of X-rays, light, electrons and protons gushed out of the poles. As Venus II began to cut a dark shape across the path of one of the jets, the fabric of space started to convulse in shivers that grew steadily larger, rocking *Endeavour* in their wake.

Aunti-3 began to sing, 'I see the bad moon arising! I see trouble on the way!' She had hovered uncertainly while her braver sisters zipped closer to take a look.

'Peter was right,' Professor Van Straaten had said to Dr Foley. 'There's no doubt, from the way that the gravitational waves from Venus II are shaking us around, that what he suspected back on Earth was correct.'

'Let's wait to hear what the aunties have to say,' Captain Craig replied.

Very soon, Hemi had begun to relay their information. 'Captain Craig? The aunties report that the spectral analysis of the gravitational waves produced in that disturbance can be consistent only if the background curvature of the universe is positive. Furthermore, if we integrate the entire matter content of everything our sensors have encountered on the way here, it would appear that the density of clumped matter is above critical. The level of particle creation detected from the vacuum would also indicate that any dark energy has completely dissipated. Finally, measurements on the light of distant galaxies reveal that the expansion of space is slowing down and will ultimately reverse.'

'What does it mean?' Miss O'Hara had asked.

'Some time down the track, the red shift will turn to blue shift,' Dr Foley said.

'Blue shift? That sounds very, very bad.'

Dr Foley had smiled at her uneasily. 'What it signals is that our universe will not last for ever. While I was working for Peter Cortland we had our suspicions. When he was dying, I was the only one of his scientists he trusted to send out here to confirm them.' He turned to Captain Craig.

'Cortland told me that he had left you a further set of instructions, Captain. Perhaps it's time you opened them —'

And Captain Craig had opened the letter:

Walter, if you are reading this letter you must by now be aware that the universe is closed and sooner or later will start contracting. Sorry to do this to you, old friend, but you're humanity's only hope. Go forward to zero.

Accompanying the instructions was a codicil which was not to be opened until zero had been reached.

6

Dr Foley pulls a reluctant Miss O'Hara back to the dinner table.

Captain Craig turns to Professor Van Straaten. 'Professor, it's your turn to tell us what you consider to be one of the transforming moments in cosmology, is it not?'

> Spuntato ecco il di d'esultanza
> Onore ai piu grandi dei Regi!
> The happy day is filled with joy
> Honour to the mightiest of Kings!

The music the Professor has chosen to accompany his offering is grandiose, martial and triumphant. He has a self-satisfied expression on his face as he waits to see if any of his fellow guests can recognise it.

'I'm sure it's Giuseppe Verdi,' says Monsignor Frère. 'The triumphal scene from *Aïda*, perhaps?'

'Right composer,' Professor Van Straaten answers. 'But no, the opera is *Don Carlos*, which Verdi composed in 1884. It explores the private and political turmoil of France and Spain in 1559 after the treaty of Cateau-Cambrésis, when Philip II took the throne of Spain. The recording itself comes from 1966 and features the divine Renata Tebaldi with Carlo Bergonzi, Nicolai Ghiaurov, Dietrich Fischer-Dieskau and Grace Bumbry, all under the baton of Sir Georg Solti. Tebaldi was considered to have *un voce d'angelo.*'

'The opera and music are not familiar to me,' the Monsignor concedes.

'I will make you a copy for further reference,' the Professor says. 'You should enjoy it. The music graphically and dramatically encompasses a scene before Valladolid Cathedral. The king, queen, royal court and clergy assemble in front of a rejoicing populace. It is an auto-da-fé —'

Monsignor Frère hisses with indignation.

'— the public ceremony of the Spanish Inquisition where sentences are pronounced on the paraded heretics. At the end of the scene, the heretics are burnt at the stake. I am dedicating the music to you, Monsignor.'

The dedication is a slap in the face, but Monsignor Frère maintains his calm. By his demeanour, he shows that he will bide his time.

'Our dinner party dissertations have become more difficult as our trip has progressed,' the Professor continues, 'but like Dr Foley I have tried to keep the best till last. Indeed, Dr Foley, your thesis provides a good starting point for mine. This evening, ladies and gentlemen, I offer as my pièce de résistance the way in which the telescope transformed the sciences and, in particular, the cosmological sciences. At a previous dinner I talked about Galileo. Should not the maker of Galileo's telescope also be credited with Galileo's discoveries? With the telescope, Galileo was able to see more stars than had ever been seen before and to subvert church assumptions, for instance, about the moon — it was not perfectly circular, a mirror to the sun, but had a face covered with cavities and prominences. And the universe was not stationary. It was moving.'

'*Eppur si muove*,' Dr Foley recalls.

Professor Van Straaten gives a benign smile. 'But the biggest break-through, so far as the telescope was concerned, came when Hubble charted the recession of the galaxies. Dr Foley has already referred to this moment, on 6 October 1923, when Hubble, surveying the Andromeda nebula, found a Cepheid variable — a star so distant from our own galaxy that it proved mankind did not live in a cosy one-universe room. But Hubble also made a second discovery, so astounding that it caused yet another of those huge revolutions in our thinking about the universe. He saw what was known as the red shift effect — that the wavelength of the light of all the galaxies was stretched. And the farther away the galaxy was from our own, the more the light was stretched: the galaxies were moving away from us. In other words, the space in between the galaxies was expanding, like a balloon being inflated. This discovery of an expanding universe, at a rate that was named the Hubble Constant, led to enormous scientific curiosity about why our universe was behaving in this way. Ultimately, that led to the question of how.'

'The Big Bang,' Captain Craig murmurs. 'The very moment of creation.'

'The answer was not long in coming,' the Professor continues. 'In 1925, Georges Lemaître, a Belgian mathematician, hypothesised a time when the universe might have been as small as an atomic nucleus. He studied detailed mathematical models which built on solutions to Einstein's equations, that were first written down by a Russian, Alexander Friedmann, in 1922.

Lemaître proposed that the origin was 'a cosmic singularity, a day without a yesterday'. He also suggested that not only space began with the Big Bang; time did too. Thus the unfolding of the universe was also the unfolding of time and space — the space–time continuum.'

Professor Van Straaten takes a sip of his wine. 'But Lemaître's hypothesis flew in the face of the current scientific consensus, which was that the universe was infinite, eternal and static. Very soon, scientists began to take sides —'

'Big Bang versus Steady State,' Dr Foley remembers. 'It was a huge question, very controversial. Even Albert Einstein could not escape it. In 1917, before Hubble's discovery of the expanding universe, his theory of relativity naturally gave a universe in flux. He added a finely tuned cosmological constant to his equation, thereby hoping to stabilise his theory and continue its compatibility with the prevailing consensus of a changeless universe. But when Hubble's discovery was reported to him, Einstein realised that events had overtaken his views. He declared the cosmological constant to be his greatest mistake.'

The Professor nods. 'The irony is that scientists have subsequently argued over the cosmological constant! Mistake? Or yet another of Einstein's magnificent contributions? Dr Foley, you yourself discussed Einstein's great contributions to mankind at our first dinner.'

'$E = mc^2$,' Dr Foley says. 'Einstein was undoubtedly the greatest scientist of the twentieth century. From his Theory of Special Relativity in 1905 through his Theory of General Relativity in 1915, he changed the way we looked at time and space — and he was still working on his Theory of Everything on his deathbed. He was a paradigm of clarity, but he could be wrongheaded in endeavouring to maintain his own views.'

Professor Van Straaten agrees. 'His theories may have paved the way for quantum mechanics, statistical mechanics and cosmology, but when other scientists like Werner Heisenberg and Niels Bohr overtook his research by proposing uncertainty, unpredictability and probability into the equation — the possibility that in mathematics, at the subatomic level, behaviour could be bizarre and capricious — he kept to his own obstinate beliefs; he was wrong. However, he did support the idea of the expanding, evolving universe for most of his career. In contrast, Fred Hoyle was opposed to the idea and it was actually he who coined the derisory term 'Big Bang'. In 1948, Hoyle, along with Hermann Bondi and Thomas Gold, proposed a compromise which gave hope to those who still wanted an eternal universe. They theorised that the universe as a whole stayed the same, with new matter being continuously created at a slow rate, even as the individual galaxies moved away from one another and died. At the same time, proponents of the Big Bang such as Robert Dicke, George Gamow, Ralph Alpher and Robert Herman were busy calculating its consequences such as relic radiation — the cosmic microwave background — which would still fill the universe today.'

'The Big Bang won out,' Dr Foley says. 'The evidence was too overwhelming. No scientist today doubts that there was, billions of years ago, a flash of fire. A massive explosion. All the mass and energy in the universe was created in that core moment, as was the space–time continuum.'

'It must have been born out of spectacular and violent energies,' the Professor adds with awe. 'It must have inflated rapidly during the first 10 seconds. It then created a cataclysm of staggering dimension, a nuclear fusion event beyond any human imagining. And we know that its initial components — protons, neutrons and electrons — were first a primordial plasma, a fiery soup in which light was trapped. When the universe was 300,000 years old the soup cooled to the point that the first stable atoms formed, 75 percent hydrogen and 25 percent helium — and the light which scattered from the last free electrons was finally able to escape. It was 3000 degrees hot back then, and it has now cooled to form a microwave hiss that is the same from every part of the sky. Part of the hiss on a TV set, the static noise between channels, is the echo of the Big Bang, the microwaves that scattered from the last free electrons.'

The Professor turns to Mrs Cortland. 'The primordial plasma was very smooth at the time of the scattering. But small ripples — which were just one part in 100,000 more dense than the background — started to form clumps by gravitational attraction that eventually formed larger and larger clumps of gas. These systems of gas bonded and broke away from the expansion of the universe to form stars, star clusters and galaxies. Our own Milky Way formed in this way about 12 billion years ago. However, the heavier elements from which we are made did not form in the Big Bang; they were formed in the furnaces of short-lived massive stars which exploded as supernovae at the end of their lives, splitting their contents into the galactic disc. The shock waves from these supernovae also started the second and third generations of stars like our own, which formed about 5 billion years ago — well, 5 billion years before we left Earth, I mean! The second- and third-generation stars contain the heavier elements from which life is made. We are star stuff.'

'And over all these years since,' Dr Foley continues, 'the effect of the Big Bang has kept on creating all the galaxies and stars we both know about and don't know about and — until we saw the anomaly at HUDF-JD2 — it showed no signs of stopping. Now, we know that the expansion is not only slowing down but reversing and contracting, and soon we will actually make it to the end of the universe.'

'What will we find when we get there?' Mrs Cortland asks.

Captain Craig takes up the challenge of the question. 'The journalist and mathematician Charles Seife thought it might look like an enormous wall of radiation, a wall of fire still moving and not slowed down at all by gravity. Others have assumed a wall of ice, gradually slowing like the edge of a glacier —'

'Those views assume that there's a spatial edge to the Big Bang,' Professor Van Straaten cautions. 'There isn't an edge. As I just explained, the Big Bang was not an explosion in a pre-existing space. It happened everywhere at the same time, creating space with it. The wall of fire was the surface of last scattering: it is the most distant thing we can see, because light shows us the universe in our past, not the universe as it is now. When we reach the end of the universe, it will be a time rather than a place. And we may arrive for the Big Crunch.'

The Professor nods. 'Yes, and it will be spectacular. Everything will come rushing together, becoming more and more dense. The blue shifts will get larger and larger in the hottest bath of radiation imaginable. The echoes of the whole history of the universe — every movement ever made, every signal ever sent — will come crashing in as space smashes together under its own weight.'

'Some scientists,' Dr Foley agrees, 'speculate that the universe will process an almost infinite amount of information right at the end. In the initial stages of the Big Crunch it will not look quite like the beginning, since the matter will be in highly processed, clumped forms and there will be millions of black holes — quite different from the primordial soup from which it all formed. And yet, and yet . . . we just don't know what happens at such high densities.'

Professor Van Straaten smiles at Mrs Cortland. 'If the space–time continuum comes to an end and time as we know it stops, then perhaps the end is also the beginning. At that point, going forward may also be the same as going back in time.'

'Back?' Mrs Cortland asks. 'I don't understand.'

'Neither do any of us; we try to but there's a limit to physics,' the Professor sighs. 'In travelling to the end of the universe, we might also be travelling back to its beginning. We will soon find out.'

—

Could that also be happening? Could the *Endeavour*, in going forward to zero, also be going back to zero?

Surprised by Professor Van Straatan's conjecture, Captain Craig recalls the recurring dream he has been having in deep sleep.

A wild landscape in the country of his birth, New Zealand. A sudden mist descends and he is lost in it. Then he sees three elderly women from the village walking in front of him. Relieved, he runs after them. One of them turns and asks, 'Went the day well, sir?' He nods and asks directions. 'You are almost at your destination, lad. There it is.' They point to a faraway farmhouse on the other side of the valley. 'You had better make haste,' they say. 'Night is coming and, with it, a fierce storm.'

He walks to the farmhouse. As he approaches, Mrs Cortland opens the door. 'Thank goodness you were able to make it home before dark,' she says. 'Come in, come in.'

When he enters he sees that Monsignor Frère, Dr Foley, Miss O'Hara and Professor Van Straaten are having a cup of tea and chatting.

'Let Walter have a place by the fire,' Mrs Cortland scolds, and Monsignor Frère makes room for him. 'He'll catch his death. There's room for one more.'

The five people in the room smile at Captain Craig as if they have known him all their lives. He shifts on his feet nervously. Mrs Cortland brings him a cup of hot tea. 'This will bring you back to life,' she says.

'Do I know you?' he asks her. 'Do I know any of you?'

'Of course you do!' the Professor laughs. But he is uncertain, and his laughter fades away into bewilderment. 'Because if you don't, then who are we?'

The Monsignor winks at him. 'Interesting, isn't it?'

—

Professor Van Straaten leans forward, reflective.

'You know, it has always been my view that all of man's greatest achievements have been in the sciences. What achievements in the humanities can possibly compete with the great advances in medicine, health sciences, earth sciences, engineering, food sciences, biotechnology and information technology, to name just a few? Yes, literature has had its Prousts and Shakespeares, music its Bachs and Mozarts, and art its Rembrandts and Picassos, but they have provided only variations on the human artistic wish to represent cultural attainment from generation to generation, nothing more. My colleagues in the humanities have often disagreed with me, but I stand by my opinion that the sciences have been where the true advances are and that they have provided no equivalent achievements. Yet with all the scientific potential we had, what happened?'

'Indigenous people,' Captain Craig begins hesitantly, 'would tell you that the division of the sciences and the humanities into two separate disciplines was a grave mistake. How can the head function without the heart, the body without the spirit, the individual without understanding his role in the community?'

'Let's hope Peter Cortland was right,' the Professor says. 'He believed in the multiple Big Bang model, a universe that could recycle itself. He also believed in the universe as a 10-dimensional construct.'

Professor Van Straaten's voice cracks with despair. He gestures helplessly at the universe sparkling with the eyes of heaven.

'We had all this to play with, but we failed to heed the warnings of people like Jared Diamond, Ronald Wright and Martin Rees, among many others. Nor did we heed the warnings of history — the Te Rapanui experience, for example, when cutting down all the trees on Easter Island led to the destruction of that fragile environment. We couldn't even manage our possibilities, let alone our own planet.'

5

Was Peter Cortland right? Now that *Endeavour* had almost reached the end of the universe, would going forward to zero prove to be the right choice to have made?

Captain Craig recalls the arguments that raged among them after he had opened Peter Cortland's secret instructions. Stationary above Venus II, he and his passengers had tried to come to grips with the implications of a contracting universe, and with Cortland's belief in a universe as a 10-dimensional construct, let alone one that could recycle itself. Their courage — and their sanity — had indeed been tested to the limit.

Over the following three days they had continued arguing about what to do. One point became increasingly clear: returning to Earth was not an option. What was there to return for? Earth's sun would have expanded to a red giant long ago, engulfing the Earth tens of billions of years before. Still growing, the sun — if it had survived the collision between the Milky Way and Andromeda — would itself have died in a cataclysmic explosion that left nothing but a cold dense white dwarf.

But what did the final death of the Earth matter to humanity? On the point of *Endeavour*'s departure, the world's population was dead. Everyone. Gone. All condemned to death by ecological collapse or by the pandemics that ravaged the planet and lethally crossed the species barrier. Why should it have been such a surprise when the demise of the biosphere occurred? Mankind, with all the innocence of a child playing with ingenious toys, had caused it himself. How was anybody to know that the future would be so frail?

As had been predicted in the *Mahabharata*, the time of Kali had truly settled to Earth. Countries tried to stockpile resources on the one hand and to put up barriers to stop the viruses from spreading on the other. Behind national barricades, they tried to maintain law and order. When that failed, the survivors sought refuge from a poisoned planet by retreating to countries like New Zealand at the Earth's perimeters.

But all succumbed, all died. All life, not just humankind. Captain Craig's own wife and two infant children, once vital and full of life, gone, their beauty blighted by viral infection. Even Peter Cortland, while completing his ship within the shadow of Mount Hikurangi, the first place in the world to see the sun rise — gone. But not before he had given his childhood friend Captain Craig his enigmatic instructions — *Walter, go forward to zero* — and the codicil to be opened when zero had been reached.

There was no doubt that Cortland had planned for an ongoing voyage. Why else had he built *Endeavour* for time-dilation travel? Leveraging off his military contracts with the US government, he had secured antimatter supplies for his own nanotechnological corporation. Working with the most advanced technology available, his scientists had engineered the Cortland photon epsilon drive so that *Endeavour* could travel the staggering dimensions of the universe. It was his scientists who, working from the solution to Einstein's equations discovered by New Zealander Roy Kerr, perfected the techniques by which *Endeavour* was able to use black holes to slingshot its way across the space–time continuum. Only with such a drive could *Endeavour* make it to the end of the universe.

And why else, during the same time as the epsilon drive was being tested, had Cortland had another team of scientists working on a life-support system which could sustain human life over billions of years, in the intense radiation fields — and maybe, if Cortland's beliefs proved wrong, even in a Big Crunch? When *Endeavour* was not travelling at relativisitic speeds, all the passengers had to be stored for extended periods in suspended animation. Whether sleeping or awake, they also required oxygen supplies and artificial gravity, produced by rotation of the habitable spaceframe. Despite *Endeavour's* immense size, the vessel had been designed to take just seven people; Cortland himself had planned to be one of them. They were to be the only humans on board. The ship itself and all service crew were robotic, controlled and directed through Hemi's Artificial Intelligence matrix. The three aunties had been added to the design specifications just before Cortland died.

In the end, above Venus II, it came to a simple vote. Find a habitable planet and try to remake an Earth for all those sentimental reasons that afflict the human family? Or keep going to the end of the universe and hope that when you get there a solution will present itself?

Peter Cortland's vote was already clear. And so was that of Mrs Cortland. 'Let's go forward,' she had said. 'Even if Peter is wrong, we would still have a chance of making it through the Big Crunch, wouldn't we? If so, we could still find that habitable planet —'

Captain Craig looked at the other passengers. They had nodded in agreement. Whichever way you looked at it, any survival option was slim.

'In that case, Hemi,' Captain Craig instructed the avatar, 'full speed ahead.'

'As you wish,' Hemi had replied.

And he pointed *Endeavour* towards the monster black hole rotating at the centre of HUDF-JD2. Shepherded by the clucking, fretting aunties —

'Do we have to go there?' Aunti-2 complained. 'Cold, dark, windy'— they entered the swirling vortex.

The interaction of rotation and huge gravitational and magnetic fields did the rest. The ship was accelerated to huge speeds and deflected out rather than being sucked in. Before Captain Craig and the passengers knew it, *Endeavour* had been kicked forward and over the perimeter of the known universe.

Captain Craig remembers the silence that had suddenly descended. HUDF-JD2 had been the last tangible reminder of home. From now on they were travelling into the unknown, just like Cook had done those many centuries ago.

—

'Come now, Monsignor,' Dr Foley laughs. 'Don't let Professor Van Straaten put you off your stroke. Your turn now.'

With a start, Captain Craig comes back to the present.

'My learned friend,' Monsignor Frère begins, nodding at the Professor, 'has been at pains to underline the difference between theology and science, to theology's detriment. But the church acknowledged its mistakes and pardoned Galileo —'

'What a pity it took so long to do it,' the Professor says. 'His *Dialogue on the Two Chief Systems of the World*, of 1632, was placed on the Index Librorum Prohibitorum and stayed there for 200 years.'

'Please be generous, Professor,' the Monsignor responds. 'Doesn't science forgive itself for its mistakes? Allow yourself the generosity of also forgiving theologists. We may have been on different sides once, but no longer.'

'You still believe that God made the universe,' Professor Van Straaten exclaims. 'We are as irrevocably opposed as we ever were.'

'Even men of religion,' Monsignor Frère continues, 'interrogated the church's ideas on cosmology. Cardinal Nicholas of Cusa in fifteenth-century Germany was one such man. Not only did he dispute the concept of an Earth-centred universe, he also challenged church dogma by hypothesising the existence of other earths with other moons — and all inhabited by their own intelligent kind. This was a doctrinally dangerous position for any cleric, as it questioned the role of God, the Vatican as the One True Church and the entire purpose of the universe as having been made for the specific benefit of man.'

'You are painting your church in a benign light,' the Professor rejoins. 'The entire debate since the Middle Ages has been one of conflict between church and science. For instance, although Copernicus supported Cusa's doctrine he delayed publication of his own scientific findings — *On the Revolution of the Heavenly Spheres* — until 1543 and the very moment when he was beyond the reach of the church: on his deathbed.'

Monsignor Frère sticks to his guns. 'And to speak of the Galileo matter,' he continues, 'in 1992 Pope John Paul II spoke against the myth that had arisen from the church's treatment of Galileo and "the church's supposed rejection of scientific progress". It was not rejection but "tragic mutual incomprehension". Galileo himself would be pleased that, now, the Vatican Observatory embraces the scientific method. Just as scientists have learnt, we have learnt. The Bible has taught us how to go to Heaven, not how the heavens go.'

Turning to his fellow passengers, the Monsignor expands his appeal. 'Professor Van Straaten also conveniently forgets that in 1951 Pope Pius XII endorsed the Big Bang model. At the Pontifical Academy of Sciences that year he gave an address, "The Proofs for the Existence of God in the Light of Modern Natural Science", to wit: "Thus everything seems to indicate that the material universe had a mighty beginning in time, endowed as it was with vast reserves of energy, by virtue of which, at first rapidly and then ever more slowly, it evolved into its present state . . . In fact, it would seem that present-day science, with one sweeping step back across millions of centuries, has succeeded in bearing witness to that primordial fiat lux uttered at the moment when, along with matter, there burst forth from nothing a sea of light and radiation, while the particles of chemical elements split and formed into millions of galaxies . . . Therefore, there is a Creator. Therefore, God exists! Although it is neither explicit nor complete, this is the reply we were awaiting from science, and which the present human generation is awaiting from it."'

'We are not on the same side,' Professor Van Straaten mutters. 'The Pope's address was a thinly disguised attempt to align the Big Bang with the Book of Genesis. Your people manipulated scientific evidence for your own ends to persuade your flocks that there was no dichotomy between science and religion. Even your own scientist, Monsignor Georges Lemaître —'

'The inventor of the Big Bang model,' Monsignor Frère emphasises. 'A

Jesuit priest and previous head of the Pontifical Academy of Sciences — a point you conveniently glossed over when you were talking about him —'

'— firmly believed that science and theology should stand apart from each other.'

The Monsignor winces. 'Please do not quote one of my colleagues at me. I would remind you that Monsignor Lemaître made clear his position: "To search thoroughly for the truth involves a searching of souls as well as of spectra. Scientists would be wise to do both."'

'The church lost,' the Professor persists. 'Scientists know how the cosmos began, and God had nothing to do with it. Despite the persistence of ideas about an eternal, unchanging universe, the evidence that scientists have collected points to a cosmos that was born and that, at some point, will end — and God cannot change that. Nearly two millennia of philosophy and theology were replaced when science triumphed over religious superstition. Where, Monsignor, is the evidence that God himself actually exists? Wouldn't you have thought, with all of our scientific observations and calculations, that man would have seen him by now? Where is he hiding?'

'Gentlemen, please,' Mrs Cortland intervenes gently. 'Monsignor, what are you offering tonight as the most transforming event in the history of science and, in particular, the cosmological sciences?'

The Monsignor calms down. 'So far,' he begins, 'Dr Foley and Professor Van Straaten have told us how the universe was discovered and what lessons were learnt about the seen universe. I would like to posit that, from the 1990s onward, the most transforming event in the history of the cosmological sciences was the discovery of the unseen universe.'

Professor Van Straaten gives a small laugh of surprise. 'The time has come, the Walrus said, to speak of many things,' he sings, 'of baryons and gluons, and quarks and other things.' He nods grudgingly. 'Yes, yes, you surprise me, Monsignor. Well done.'

'If I may continue?' the Monsignor smiles. 'By the beginning of the millennium, apart from better telescopes, science had developed super-precise tools — cosmic microwaving, fibreoptics, interferometry, spectrometry, cosmic background imaging, super proton synchrotron, relativistic heavy-ion colliders, particle accelerators, charge-coupled devices, supersymmetry, microlensing and so on. Thus, cosmology entered an era of stunningly precise measurements. But that led to a startling discovery; when the cosmologists tallied up all the matter that they could see — everything in all the galaxies, stars and planets — there just didn't seem to be nearly enough stuff to make a universe! Not enough baryonic and leptonic matter — protons, leptons, neutrons, electrons, mesons, pions, muons, tau particles, antimatter, other antimatter twins, quarks and gluons —'

'Is the Monsignor being serious?' Miss O'Hara laughs. 'They sound like creatures in a fantastic zoo.'

'Indeed I am, young lady. But more surprises were to come, because when the scientists completed their tally of the stuff that was visible they had to face up to the fact that at least three quarters of the cosmos was composed of material that man could not see and had not directly measured, yet it must be there!'

'The Case of the Missing Matter,' Professor Van Straaten grunts. 'Yes, yes.'

The Monsignor is clearly enjoying himself. 'So how do you find this missing stuff if the world's most sophisticated telescopes can't even see it? Well, instead of looking for the missing matter directly, scientists began to look for it indirectly — not what it looked like, but what it did. Their best shot was to use the new super-precise measuring equipment to weigh the universe's mass and measure gravitational attraction — the mutual pull between two objects that have mass. Finally, they found what they were looking for.'

'They called it nonbaryonic matter,' Dr Foley explains to Miss O'Hara. 'Sometimes it was referred to as exotic matter, but most often it was termed dark matter. The suspicion was that this dark matter could be found in one of those zoo animals you referred to, darling — neutrinos, one of the most elusive particles known to science. The structure of the galaxy clusters, the motions and distributions of the galaxies, and the fine details of the cosmic background radiation all implied that the universe was filled with it.'

'But,' the Monsignor continues, looking out *Endeavour*'s windows, 'it appeared that there was something else out here —'

'Dark energy,' Dr Foley nods. 'A strange antigravity force that functioned ironically and suspiciously, very like the cosmological constant Einstein had self-discredited years before. It counteracted the effects of gravity by keeping up an outward pressure which for some billions of years had been strong enough to accelerate the expansion of the universe. But nobody could agree on what the dark energy was: whether it would stay constant and make the expansion of the universe accelerate for ever, or whether it would dissipate, allowing the universe maybe to contract. There were those who proposed a phantom energy which, while violating some basic physical principles, would make it possible for the universe to end suddenly in an unannounced Big Rip rather than a Big Crunch.'

'Yes,' Monsignor Frère nods. 'Whatever it is, this strange antigravity force has been the greatest mystery in our understanding of the universe for most of the twenty-first century.' He purses his lips. 'And if we were calculating its density against the total stuff — mass and energy — in the universe, back in the twenty-first century it would actually comprise by far the greater component.'

'Greater?' Mrs Cortland repeats, surprised.

'Which brings me to my point,' the Monsignor muses. He looks steadily at Professor Van Straaten. 'We now know since we passed HUDF-JD2 that the dark energy, if it was there, must have dissipated, making it a decaying quintessence field. But was the dark energy ever real, or were the cosmologists who suggested that we had misinterpreted distance measurements in a universe with large-scale lumpiness actually correct? Interpreting cosmological measurements is a complicated forensic science. It depends not only on what is actually measured, but also on the assumptions about the physical laws and the geometry of the universe, which are used for interpreting those measurements. One can never recreate the Big Bang in the lab and repeat the cosmic experiment. You know that, Professor, and I know that. And there are so many models — inhomogeneous universes as well as "quintessence" models. We didn't know everything when we left; do we finally know the model of the universe now?'

Monsignor Frère again expands his address to include the audience. 'I would have to say that, regardless of my colleague's protestations, the presence of the unseen affirms the continuing presence of God in the universe. I knew it when I was a boy staring at the night sky from my village in Nigeria, and I know it again tonight as we dine aboard the *Endeavour*. The universe is not a vacuum; it is, rather, a cosmological gene pool.' He begins to hum: 'All knowing, all loving, invisible God —'

'Oh no, you don't,' Professor Van Straaten interrupts. He knows exactly where all this is heading.

'Despite all the scientific advances in cosmology,' Monsignor Frère continues, 'humanity still believes in a higher purpose for itself and the universe it lives in. Professor, earlier you asked a question, "Where is God hiding?" He hasn't been hiding at all. Nor, so Albert Einstein believed, was He hiding anything from us; He was just asking us to search harder. Einstein thought of God as a gardener. Einstein was simply trying to catch Him at his work. So it's all a matter of where to look and how to look — not just with your head but also with your heart, not just with your instruments but with your intuition, not just with certainty but also with faith. This may be an enigma for you, Professor Van Straaten, but for people of faith, the answer is simple. If you wish to find God, eternal, unchanging, you need only seek Him in the invisible and the ways in which He continues to maintain the space–time continuum.'

'You're clutching at straws,' Professor Van Straaten mutters.

The Monsignor gives a sigh of regret. 'What a pity, Professor, that the relationship between scientists and the rest of us — mankind as a whole — has always been so . . . so adversarial.'

'You're as much to blame for that as we are,' the Professor answers. 'The church was the main agent in maintaining the deep conflict about the nature of knowledge and the rules which governed its use.'

'Yes, my friend,' Monsignor Frère says gently, 'perhaps. But I am honest enough to regret that we could not find a way of working together — you, me, leaders of governments, corporate leaders — before it was too late. We should have developed an international meritocracy to override the petty proliferation of national communities. All wanted their own nuclear bombs and their own research capabilities designed specifically to enhance their own financial, political and economic growth. The world grew out of kilter so quickly. It wasn't that we failed to heed the warnings, Professor. We just couldn't find the ways to deal with them as a planet. Man's own volatile nature sealed his destiny. Why did everything in the human world tend to disorder?'

> Fly toward the Lord
> Speed, oh, you poor souls
> Come to your salvation
> Kneel before the throne of God —

At that moment, the ship rocks.

Captain Craig hears Hemi give a surprised gasp. 'Yes, Hemi?'

'Captain, my fault entirely. Something extraordinary has occurred. It completely put me off my stroke. But I've restored the ship's trim. Aunti-3 has picked up some kind of transmission that can't be accounted for. Please convey my apologies to your dinner guests, but perhaps you and I could talk privately?'

'I'll come to the bridge,' Captain Craig answers.

'Impeccable timing,' Mrs Cortland whispers to him behind her hand as he stands and excuses himself. 'This will allow the table to be cleared for dessert, and for Miss O'Hara and me to repair to the powder room. Let's hope, by the time you get back, these silly men are over their irritation with one another.'

The *Endeavour* has three decks. Captain Craig makes his way to the bridge on the uppermost tower, where an array of monitors shows views fore and aft, and continuous computerised readouts from Hemi's mainframe.

He seats himself at the central console. 'So what is it, Hemi?'

'I have received a message for you.'

'A message? That's impossible. Everyone on Earth is dead.'

'The message does not come from behind us. It comes from in front.'

'Then put the message on the screen,' Captain Craig orders.

The screen shows a mathematical equation:

$$\sup\{|r(t) - r_\oplus|\} = |r(t) - r_\oplus|!$$

'Give me a translation, please, Hemi.'

STOP. COME NO FURTHER.

'What does it mean?'

'There are two possibilities,' the avatar says. 'It may be advice that we have reached our destination. Or, alternatively, it may be a warning to go back.'

The captain is thoughtful. The minutes tick by. 'Have we reached zero?' he asks.

'Not quite yet, Captain. We should do so within the hour.'

Captain Craig makes a decision. 'In that case, remain on course.'

4

'Moon river,' Aunti-3 sings, 'wider than a mile, I'm crossing you in style some day —'

The ship is like a silent celestial angel in solitary flight through a sea of stars. It cleaves through the blackness, serene and powerful, its light-wings at full extension, accelerating through the space–time continuum.

Once it had left HUDF-JD2, *Endeavour* had dropped off the map. An interesting conundrum given that, in fact, all the maps of the known universe were themselves wrong or, rather, obsolete, even before *Endeavour* left Earth. Dr Foley had explained it to Miss O'Hara in this way:

'Our maps of the universe really charted points of light which had taken years to reach our Earth. Thus Alpha Centauri was not as it was seen "now" but as it had been four years before. Similarly, as seen "today" the most distant galaxies appeared to us as they had been billions of years ago. Imagine Captain Cook setting off on his voyage to the South Pacific — the analogy would be giving him a map of Gondwanaland 350 million years ago to enable him to navigate his way.'

'So all along we've been navigating without a reliable map?'

'Yes,' Dr Foley had answered. 'Thank God for the aunties!'

—

Guided by the aunties, the *Endeavour* had maintained full speed through the uncharted waters of the cosmos. Half the volume of the universe was in deep voids, so her voyage was not too dissimilar from her namesake's, out of sight of land, week after week. Hemi would have preferred to point *Endeavour* at empty sky and avoid galaxies like the plague but, knowing that the humans on board craved light and 'landmarks' — and that the ship needed Kerr black holes to maintain its energy source — he and the three aunties inevitably plotted a course which was populous with galaxies and their separate discs of stars.

The trouble was that navigating this crowded route brought greater dangers. 'Better not go there,' the aunties would report to Hemi if violent quasars mushroomed ahead. 'The bogeyman may be waiting.' When intense bursts of star formation generated galaxy-wide superwinds, Aunti-3 was prone to sing 'Somewhere over the rainbow' and complain that if bluebirds could fly over rainbows, why couldn't they fly over superwinds?

Aunti-1 and Aunti-2 would just roll their eyes and advise Hemi, 'Batten down the hatches and reef those sails, boy, we're in for a big blow!'

Sometimes, when danger was unavoidable, as when two galaxies collided or massive stars collapsed in a shower of gamma rays, the aunties would simply order Hemi, 'Put on your skates, nephew, and let's get the hell out of here.' Their jocularity masked the sophistication of their measurements. They carried an array of optical, infrared, gamma-ray, spectrographic and other sensors so that Hemi could compute the dangers, raise or lower radiation shields, change course and continue to plough ahead through the reefs and island universes that dotted the celestial sea.

'What sights have the aunties seen,' Captain Craig has often wondered, 'while we were sleeping? What dangers have they ferried us through in this voyage to the end of the universe?'

He imagines that most of the time they would simply have got on with the collection of scientific data along the way. In this manner they were no different from Captain Cook and his crew on the original *Endeavour*'s voyage to Tahiti. They took soundings, photographed their discoveries, and mapped and catalogued their galactic findings. They scorned the lack of imagination shown by human starmakers who had attached cartographic numbers like NGC55, NGC253, M82, M81, M83, Centaurus A, M101 Pinwheel, M51 Whirlpool and M104 Sombrero. They preferred more exotic nomenclature like Hikurangi Gloriosa or Marama Sublima or Ariki Imperatrix; and on one occasion Aunti-3 suggested calling a particular chain of galaxies Vagina Splendida.

'You can't call it that,' Hemi said.

'Why not?' the aunties asked. 'Doesn't the galaxy look like that to you, nephew?' The aunties were, of course, teasing him. It was always a moment of triumph to them when they dropped their data into a small winking beacon, *We're still alive*, and set it adrift in their wake. They knew the gesture was futile; the beacon was like a message in a bottle that nobody would ever find.

During the early part of the voyage the universe was astoundingly beautiful. Proudly, the aunties had filtered through the dreams of the sleepers their marvellous discoveries. They showed them planets and satellite worlds of extraordinary magnificence, with interstellar rainbow clouds drifting between. There were worlds with fractured canyons of ice, thousands of miles deep, the shards refracting light as brilliant as the star of Bethlehem. Some of the worlds had nitrogen atmospheric conditions, emitting enshrouding mists that glowed with reflected light from their sun systems. Others were sulphur dominated, sending huge kaleidoscopic jets of violet and emerald gas into the stratosphere, like wings of angels a million miles wide. Many had ring systems of small moons captured by the planet's gravity, or countless mini moonlets, each a dazzling corona. There were stars — so many, many billions of stars — of all brilliances and kinds, binary, multiple, white dwarfs, neutron stars and pulsars. Spiral stellar arms wheeled like sparkling jewelled gateways to heaven.

All the while, Hemi and the three aunties kept the prime imperative. 'Oh, precious ones,' they whispered in soft, loving voices to the humans suspended at the brink of consciousness. 'It is our privilege and our honour to carry you.' The sleepers were like pharaonic passengers, embalmed aboard a glowing sunship. 'Royal ones, rest, be at peace, and know your journey is one that the stuff of dreams is made of.'

The aunties were careful, however, not to subject the sleepers to the moments of danger they had faced. The slightest emotional disturbance could upset the careful balance of the chemicals that flowed through their bodies as they slept. And so they were not told when solar flares emitted infrared radiation which threatened the ship's insulated hull cladding and protective aerogel layers. Hemi and the three aunties kept their own counsel when protostars collapsed, creating violent galactic cyclones; while the passengers slept on, the avatar desperately maintained the protective shields that kept all onboard life-support systems operational. When gaseous solar storms, heated to nearly 2 million kelvins, suddenly erupted into huge photospheric tsunami, Hemi and the aunties whispered soothing words of reassurance to the sleepers; engines already at overload, they desperately tried to override any malfunction. Sometimes there were asteroid belts, minefields a million miles wide, to avoid; any false move or collision could strand the ship for ever. At other times Hemi had to blast a way through with the light armaments carried for the purpose: the dorsal particle beam gun or the ventral weapons system.

Then there were the supernovae giving birth to Kerr black holes; as the giant stars' cores collapsed, the black holes would condense and begin to spin, sending out bursts of gamma rays in some of the most violent and energetic events in the universe. The explosions from a million suns in supernovae, like cosmological nuclear reactors, could incinerate the ship in a millisecond. So too the gravitational pull of black holes, planets, moons and stars constantly threatened to take her into a death spin. But *Endeavour* had prevailed.

When the dangers had been negotiated, Hemi anchored the ship in the lee of a benign star system. There, assisted by the three aunties and the robotic service crew, he patched the sails, repaired the shielding, and serviced and tested the photon epsilon drive. Once he was satisfied that all systems were go, he would hoist anchor again. The sails would unfurl, the *Endeavour* would quickly come to cruise speed and, far ahead, the three aunties would broadcast to the universe:

'Make way. Make way. Let us pass.'

Once the ship moved past the 700 billion light-years mark, the character of the universe changed. It had not yet begun to contract significantly, and the deep voids multiplied: in them were nothing but tenuous, low levels of hydrogen plasma. The voids were like huge crevasses — and *Endeavour* traversed them in absolute darkness.

Very soon, even the galaxies and stars seemed to wink out. Although one could never really ascribe human emotions to Hemi and the aunties, their behaviour betrayed an increasing nervousness. Ironically, it was they who now sought the light. They hated the total darkness of the deep voids but knew with utter and fatalistic certainty that they had to be negotiated. 'Will we ever see the light again?' they asked.

And all the voids seemed to be channelling the ship toward some wide primordial Night — Te Kore — of the deepest blackness. When they finally reached it, a chasm almost 72 billion light-years wide, Captain Craig remembered the Maori village of his birth. There, old women of the tribe had kept their oral traditions by chanting to him as he slept in their arms:

At the very beginning of Time was Te Kore, the Void. Then out of Te Kore came Te Po, the Night, the Long Night, the Dark Night, the Night All Powerful, the Night Without End, Te Po Nui, Te Po Roa, Te Po Tangotango, Te Po Kerekere, Te Po Tiwha, Te Po Te Kitea . . .

Even in Te Kore, Hemi and the aunties tried to keep everyone's spirits up. Aunti-3 took to singing a rousing Beatles song and Miss O'Hara would join her in the chorus:

So we sailed up to the sun
Till we found a sea of green . . .
We all live in a yellow submarine,
Yellow submarine, yellow submarine —

Sometimes Hemi would illuminate the ship. He could not do this often, however, as it meant draining *Endeavour* of its epsilon-drive antimatter resources. In fact, he miscalculated the distance to the exit, and the ship became completely becalmed. The only way to get out of the mess was for the aunties to roll up their sleeves and use their tractor beams to pull *Endeavour* through the never-ending blackness.

As if that was not enough, by the 760 billion light-years mark, the contracting universe began to create havoc within Te Kore. Gravitational wave shocks from colliding black holes stretched and compressed space.

'Better squee-eeze through, boy,' the aunties would say, 'and be quick about it.'

Hundreds of billions of light-years further, as the contractions of the universe quickened, the voids shrank more and more. The galaxies that clustered around them began to crash into each other, their light exhibiting all the ominous signs of blue shift. Hemi and the aunties gave them a wide berth, choosing the safe route through the shrinking voids. 'If it's blue it's dangerous stew,' they'd chorus. Sometimes, without warning, huge jagged warps would rend the fabric of the universe, tearing it to shreds.

The *Endeavour* was a valiant star waka, glorious to behold. It was like a small glowing seedpod, a dandelion, in that huge dark immensity. And Hemi and his three aunties were prepared to go down fighting to ensure that the precious ones within would be delivered to their rightful destiny.

Go forward to zero.

3

On his return to the dinner party Captain Craig is relieved to see that equanimity has been restored to the occasion. Indeed, Miss O'Hara is doing astrological readings.

'You're just in time for me to read your stars,' she tells him. 'You're an Aquarian, aren't you? In that case — aha, there appears to be a struggle for pole position taking place, and the sextile between the sun and powerful Pluto may be felt much earlier. Uranus, the planet of experimentation, is making waves, and risk is in the air. A calculated risk is a good thing, of course. But make sure you have a plan first.'

She turns to Dr Foley. 'Eliot? Would you like to be next? You're a Capricorn, yes? Your moon enters the indecisive sign of Pisces on Friday, and there may be a period when it's genuinely impossible to make up your mind about a certain individual whom you're emotionally attached to.' She says this with wide-eyed innocence. 'However, do not procrastinate, Eliot. Saturn will soon start its epic voyage through the sociable sign of Leo. This is the time for you to show your hand so that the person whom you admire, although remarkably different from you, may join you and you can advance together. Professor Van Straaten? Oh, you are going on a long trip.'

The others laugh.

'As a Cancerian,' she continues, 'planets pass through your travel zones. However, you are in for a bumpy ride. Blame it on the persistent presence of Sagittarius.'

Sagittarius happens to be Monsignor Frère's sign. He takes the dig in good grace but he can't help taking a poke back. 'My dear,' he says, 'give up astrology. We're already well across the universe and your star signs are all irrelevant history.'

'Yes,' Professor Van Straaten retorts. 'Just like God.'

—

As the guests are being seated for dessert, a beautiful, elegiac piece of music begins to play. It was Peter Cortland's favourite and Mrs Cortland has chosen it in his memory. But it also brings home to her the immense nature of the voyage:

> O, let me weep, for ever weep
> My eyes no more shall welcome sleep
> I'll hide me from the sight of day
> And sigh, and sigh my soul away
> They're gone, they are gone

The stars are everywhere and the darkness between is filled with a terrible and lonely beauty. Mrs Cortland begins to shiver. She remembers how, just before dinner, she had summoned up enough courage to finally ask Captain Craig: 'How long have we been travelling, Captain?'

He had given her a long look.

'Come on, Captain. I'm a big girl now. And I do own the *Endeavour*. How long has it taken us?'

Captain Craig had nodded. 'I'll ask Hemi to compute the time for you.'

The avatar had replied almost on the instant. 'Taking into account leap years, 1401 billion, 537 million, 656 thousand and 748 years, Mrs Cortland. But with time dilation and sightseeing stops, you have aged just 1 year, 5 months, 21 days and 3.8 hours — though, with the extended sleep times in between, elapsed ship time is greater. Still, even that is only 27 million, 543 thousand, 81 years, 6 months, 15 days and 23.7 hours.'

Only? Mrs Cortland had almost fainted. Oh, let's turn back. Oh please . . . turn . . . back. But there was no back. There was only forward.

'What beautiful music,' Monsignor Frère says now. 'So soothing after the Verdi.'

Mrs Cortland regains her demeanour. 'It's a baroque aria, "The Plaint", from Henry Purcell's *The Fairy Queen*. The opera is based on Shakespeare's *A Midsummer Night's Dream*, and was first performed in May 1692 at the Theatre Royal, London.'

'Who is the singer?' Miss O'Hara asks.

Mrs Cortland smiles. 'Her name is Margaret Ritchie, and she was an especially admired interpreter of Purcell. She made this recording in 1954. Her interpretation is moving, don't you think?'

'A sovereign voice,' Monsignor Frère concedes. 'A sovereign aria. So, what is your topic, Mrs Cortland?'

She suppresses a peal of laughter. 'I'm sure it will not surprise you but it is this: one would think, from looking at the history of the cosmological sciences, that it was a male history. And indeed, as in all the sciences, cosmology was the prerogative of men. But against all odds, women have also made their impact.'

'Oh no,' Professor Van Straaten groans.

'Oh yes, Professor,' Mrs Cortland answers. 'One of the first-known women mathematicians and astronomers was Hypatia, circa AD 375 to 415. Her father, Theon, was the last head of the museum at Alexandria, and Hypatia herself became one of the last guardians of the old Ptolemaic knowledge. She wrote a commentary on Ptolemy's work and invented astronomical navigation devices. Who knows what else she might have accomplished had she not been murdered by Christian monks during Alexandria's waning years? And all of you might extol Galileo, the revolutionary polymath-mathematician, physicist and astronomer, but never forget, gentlemen, that it was his daughter who was the most important person in his life. She was Sister Maria Celeste Galilei, and her relationship with her father was so close that his letters to her are sometimes marked in the margins with Galileo's notes, calculations and diagrams.'

Mrs Cortland looks at the other dinner guests. 'Often, where you found a man, you also found a woman — like Caroline Herschel, sister of Friedrich Wilhelm Herschel of Hanover. Her brother was the most famous astronomer of the eighteenth century, and Caroline helped in his discovery of Uranus. She also discovered eight comets during her own brilliant career, so let nobody think that she was simply her brother's assistant.'

Dr Foley nods his head. 'She snatched every leisure moment for resuming some work in progress. Often she was so intensely involved she didn't even take time to change her dress. Sometimes she put food into her brother's mouth as he was working.'

'So you've heard of Caroline Herschel?' Mrs Cortland asks. 'Do you also know the story of Edward Pickering and his women?'

'Pickering's harem,' Professor Van Straaten laughs. 'In 1877, Edward Pickering became director of the Harvard College Observatory. By that stage in the history of cosmology, photographing the stars had become as important as observing them, and Pickering was head of a large project of celestial photography and analysis. The thousands of stars had to be tabulated, their locations established and brightness classified. During Pickering's period, over half a million photographic plates were scrutinised by the observatory; it became the largest photographic library of the universe in existence. Who did the work? Universities in those days largely excluded women, so Pickering's staff were all young, bright, intelligent male computers. However, they were also inaccurate, careless, and often lacking in the concentration and meticulous attention to detail that was required. Pickering became so cross with them that one day, in a fit of exasperation, he sacked them all. Declaring that his Scottish maid, Williamina Fleming, could do better, he hired a team of women computers — and put Miss Fleming in charge.'

'Really?' Miss O'Hara gasps.

'Mind you,' Mrs Cortland cautions, 'Pickering paid them only 30 cents per hour, whereas he had been paying the men 50 cents. Nevertheless, this was probably the first example of the suffragette impulse in the sciences. The astonishing aspect of the story, though, is that after a while the women subverted the original brief. Not content just to harvest data, they began to analyse it and come to their own conclusions. One of the women, Annie Jump Cannon, took matters further. In 1911, realising she was cataloguing around 5000 stars per month, she decided to establish a better, more expansive and inclusive framework for classifying stars by their location, brightness and colour: O, B, A, F, G, K, M. Her system was universally adopted, and in 1925 she received an honorary doctorate from Oxford University, the first woman to be so honoured by that institution — and the first of many other honours for her, too.'

'Henrietta Leavitt was another of Pickering's team of women,' the Monsignor intervenes. 'Interestingly, both she and Miss Cannon were profoundly deaf.'

'She was probably more famous than Miss Cannon,' Mrs Cortland concedes. 'A graduate of Harvard University's Radcliffe College in 1892, she discovered more than 2400 variable stars during her career — a phenomenal accomplishment. Miss Leavitt was particularly fascinated by Cepheids and decided to focus all her concentration on a Cepheid-hunt within the Small Magellanic Cloud. She came up with 25 Cepheid variables, plotted a graph of the apparent brightness against the period of variation for the 25 stars — and, in 1912, revealed that the mathematical formulae she had used to measure the distances between the Cepheids could also be applied to measure the distances between any objects in the universe. It was a decisive discovery but Miss Leavitt did not receive recognition for it.'

Professor Van Straaten gives a little shameful cough. 'Professor Gosta Mittag-Leffler of the Swedish Academy of Sciences began the paperwork process for a Nobel Prize nomination. But he was too late. Leavitt had died of cancer three years earlier, when she was 53.'

'She wasn't the only one to be bypassed,' Mrs Cortland says. 'In 1967, Jocelyn Bell, a radio astronomy student at Cambridge University, detected regular pulses in radio transmissions that turned on and off rapidly, like a broadcast being made by some alien intelligence. She denoted it as an LGM, a Little Green Man. In fact, what she'd observed was a pulsar, a new type of pulsating star. It was her adviser, Anthony Hewish, however, who in 1974 was awarded the Nobel Prize for the discovery.'

'In New Zealand,' Captain Craig interrupts, 'we had young Beatrice Hill Tinsley, who did all her scientific research in the United States. In 1975 she postulated that galaxies change as they evolve, and she constructed computer models to explain the process. When she died of melanoma shortly after her fortieth birthday she was a professor at Yale and had made scientific advances worthy of a lifetime's effort.'

Dr Foley nods his head. 'For such a small country, yours has certainly given the world some great scientists — Ernest Rutherford, William Pickering, Maurice Wilkins, Ian Axford, Alan MacDiarmid and Roy Kerr among them. Karl Popper also? And then, of course, Peter Cortland —'

Mrs Cortland turns to Monsignor Frère. 'Monsignor, you have mentioned dark matter. Did you know that some of the most crucial discoveries about dark matter were made from the rotation rates of galaxies by Vera Rubin? Nor must we forget women like Wendy Freeman who, in 1999, led the scientific team which completed the Hubble Key Project.'

Mrs Cortland thinks of her poor, long-dead, diseased Earth and all of mankind, gone, gone, gone. 'I sometimes think how much better our future might have been if women had been allowed to take control of our destiny,' she says. 'I think we would have made a much better job of it. We certainly wouldn't have done any worse, don't you agree?'

2

And now it is Miss O'Hara's turn.

'This is so unfair,' she wails. 'You're all older than me and wiser, and I don't know anything about cosmology! Still, I'll try this my way. Roll cameras,' she instructs Hemi. 'Standby and action. Aunti-3? Take it away —'

'When you wish upon a star,' Aunti-3 sings in a lovely high soprano voice. 'Makes no difference who you are, anything your heart desires will come to you —'

'Maybe she'll crack on a high note,' Aunti-1 and Aunti-2 grumble hopefully. But Aunti-3 sings on, oblivious, and the interior of the dining room fills with three-dimensional hologrammatic images from Hollywood films. Monsignor Frère cries with delight as the spaceship from *E.T.*, like a sparkling, illuminated Christmas tree, comes sliding down from the ceiling and from it advance tiny, child-like aliens. Mrs Cortland laughs with joy when Han Solo comes sauntering into the dining room as if it were an otherworldly cantina. 'How are you, Gorgeous?' he says, and winks at her.

Finally, the starship from *Close Encounters of the Third Kind* comes rumbling in for a landing. But the laughter stops when the hatch of the starship opens and Rudi Giger's monster from the *Alien* series lurches out, a towering insectoid with a long tightly coiled tail. With a sudden pounce, it is on Professor Van Straaten, nuzzling him with its phallic head and inserting its inseminating organ into his stomach like a stinger. In a moment the Professor's stomach bursts open and from it comes a small, foetal alien which begins to devour him.

The holograms freeze and disappear. 'Quite a prelude,' the Professor tells Miss O'Hara as he mops his brow — and checks his stomach. 'It's completely put me off the rest of my dinner.'

Miss O'Hara laughs impishly. 'Now that I have your attention, let me focus on the large number of films and television series in the science fiction genre that came out of Hollywood at the turn of the millennium. In them we see our wonderment at the universe.'

'Is anybody out there?' Captain Craig muses.

'Space . . . the final frontier,' Dr Foley intones. 'These are the voyages of the Starship Enterprise, its five-year mission: to explore strange new worlds . . . to seek out new life and new civilisations . . . to boldly go where no man has gone before.' When everyone laughs, Dr Foley hugs Miss O'Hara. 'See, darling? No need to apologise for not being a scientist. You hold all of us in your thrall.'

'So much of our fascination with other intelligent life in the universe is in those films,' Miss O'Hara continues. 'At their most benevolent, the extra-terrestrials were like Superman, who came from the doomed planet of Krypton with superhuman powers that he put to use helping our own. They were wish-fulfilment films in which the aliens came to preach antiwar messages or brought gifts of extrasensory perception so that we could advance, emotionally and spiritually. Such films appealed to our own humanity, our yearning to become better people and to save our planet. When such aliens appeared on film they were often small, therefore not to be afraid of, or childlike and filled with light. They were like E.T. with that glowing finger of his, marooned on our planet —'

'E.T., phone home,' Monsignor Frère interpolates.

'The aliens were, in fact, not aliens at all but mirror-images of ourselves as we wanted to be. They were bipedal. They had faces and hands. They were, in all respects, just like us, but better.'

'They offered redemption,' Monsignor Frère says, his eyes lighting with pleasure. 'Often they featured a Messianistic hero like Paul Atreides in *Dune* or the rebel prisoner, Riddick, in *Pitch Black* and *The Chronicles of Riddick*. I have read a scientific paper that critiques *The Terminator* from a Christian perspective. The cyborg terminator in the first film becomes the John the Baptist figure in the second film; he saves Sarah Connor, the Mary figure, so she is able to give birth to her son, John Connor, the new Christ. And, of course, in *2001: A Space Odyssey*, man becomes a star child.'

'Don't get carried away,' Professor Van Straaten interrupts. 'Satan was also referenced in those films.'

'Behave, you two,' Mrs Cortland scolds them. 'Let Miss O'Hara continue with her dissertation. Go on, dear, and don't let those two men appropriate your thesis.'

'But Professor Van Straaten is right,' Miss O'Hara says. 'The interesting point about the films is that most of them favour a malignant vision of what intelligence is out there, and a more dystopian view of our future. For instance, there's the dark, apocalyptic world of *Blade Runner*, or of *A Clockwork Orange*, *Logan's Run*, *The Last Man on Earth*, *The Omega Man* and *Soylent Green*. All are built on intriguing premises, like *Planet of the Apes*, and most are filled with a paranoia, a fear that what is waiting in the universe is not angels but devils. They embody the fear of the unknown. Thus, the kind of aliens that were mainly portrayed were from the more fevered and nightmarish rooms of our imaginations. They were like *The Thing*, a real horror from beyond our solar system. The movie opens with the discovery of a flying saucer embedded in the ice at the Arctic Circle. Human rescuers recover the alien survivor and thaw it out but, like many of these aliens, this one then goes on a rampage, draining men of blood.'

'Yes,' the Monsignor agrees. 'Blood is sacramental in these movies.'

'Keep watching the skies,' Captain Craig nods. 'Those films fed western paranoia. They were really about America's fear of the Soviet Union and, later, about the wars in the Middle East or against global terrorism. Their American-centric vision affirmed America's divine right to intervene in any war on the planet. But not even America could save us in the end.'

'And what was the purpose of the aliens?' Miss O'Hara continues. 'In films like *Mars Attacks* and *Independence Day* they are intent on world domination. In some cases, like in *The Quartermass Experiment* and *War of the Worlds*, they have been waiting for just this moment to strike. In *The Terror from Beyond Space* and *Earth Versus the Flying Saucers*, humanity enters into an archetypal life-or-death struggle with the aliens, who are always inhumanly strong and virtually invulnerable to conventional means of attack. In other films like *Invaders from Mars*, *Invasion of the Body Snatchers*, *They Live*, *Supernova* and *The Puppetmasters*, they come to take over the intelligence of all humankind. They want us for their experiments, as in *The X-Files*, where they're supported by sinister government agencies, or they abduct us. In *Aliens* and *Predator* they are mindless creatures driven by the need to propagate for the survival of their own species.'

'In space nobody can hear you scream,' Professor Van Straaten remembers.

'Sometimes they are led by an alien queen,' Mrs Cortland contributes. 'I recall the chilling yet strangely erotic Borg queen in *Star Trek Insurrection*, committed to enslaving human minds to the Borg collective. But the most terrifying monster of all is the alien queen in *Aliens*. She's huge, monstrous, and when Ripley and her soldier forces blunder into her nest, she is hatching her eggs. As the eggs burst, the larvae feast on the succulent bodies of hapless human beings. The final confrontation between the alien queen and Ripley is really a working out of male fantasies of two women going head to head.'

'Nobody on Earth is safe from aliens,' Miss O'Hara continues, 'alive — or dead. There's a particularly sinister episode of *The Outer Limits*. It's called The Second Soul, and it's about a dying race which has come to Earth to save itself from extinction. They are a saprophytic species that can only survive on dead things, and governments therefore allow them to enter the corpses of the dead. Once this occurs, the corpses are reanimated. The episode ends with a child being born of the aliens and a dead corpse — a somewhat warped vision of the resurrection.'

Miss O'Hara tries to smile. 'Professor Van Straaten, nobody was safe from the scientists either! If you were not mad, as in *The Island of Dr Moreau*, you were psycho, as in *Doctor Strangelove*, or obsessed, as in *Demon*

Seed and *The Island*, or crazed, as in *Forbidden Planet* — or all of the above. In *Aliens* you stupidly wanted to save the alien for scientific research even at the risk of human extinction.'

She gets up from the table and goes to the windows to look out at the blackness beyond. 'Carl Sagan thought we lived in a huge demon-haunted world. Once it had been peopled by gargoyles and devils. Then it became populated by vampires, werewolves and zombies. And which side were the scientists on? Not ours, but theirs. With science fiction, our obsession with these dark visions strode out of the screens in new incarnations, with greater presence and invincibility. All those space monsters did indeed represent the Devil, Professor. And do you know what? They were really only nightmare abstractions of ourselves. Our dual nature is reflected in the character of Anakin Skywalker in *Star Wars: The Revenge of the Sith*. When Anakin turns his back on the Jedi, he turns from Christ to Devil as Darth Vader. By doing so, he enshrines the belief that just as man cannot save himself, neither can he find any deliverance from the universe.'

Mrs Cortland leans over to Dr Foley. 'Go to her, Eliot,' she says.

When he does so, Miss O'Hara leans gratefully into his arms. 'The fact is,' she says, 'you have to be careful what you wish for. All of us have looked up at the night, wished upon a falling star and hoped there was somebody else out there. We've dreamed of great alien civilisations that could give us the chance to transform into beings of greater compassion and wisdom and not be like the nightmarish demons that fill our imaginations. We have hoped that they might bring us perfection, innocence and all those qualities of humanity we have always aspired to. Even if they existed, humans are such a toxic species that any aliens would have been wise to stay well clear of us. As it happens, in all our voyages through space, we have not found any other life at all. There are no aliens out here, hostile, friendly or otherwise. There's been nothing.'

Miss O'Hara turns to the others. 'So, my contribution to tonight's debate? The most transforming event in cosmological science? It's this: the discovery that man is truly alone. It has always only and ever been in this huge immensity just — us. And if we couldn't find our salvation and transcendence within ourselves, what hope was there ever that we would find it out here?'

Tears of hopelessness twinkle on Miss O'Hara's cheek.

If your heart is in your dream
No request is too extreme
When you wish upon a star
Your dreams come true —

At that moment, Hemi interrupts the dinner.

'Captain, we are now in the final stages of our journey. The time has come to institute braking. May I begin inverse gravitational slingshot procedures?'

'Yes, of course, Hemi.'

Captain Craig and his dinner guests watch with excitement. What will the universe look like in the other extreme of Te Kore? As *Endeavour* slows, whirling around a giant black hole, a panorama of a jewel-box sky studded with glittering galaxies — wall after wall of them — is revealed.

The excitement turns to dread. 'Oh my Lord,' the Professor whispers.

The contracting universe has created chaos. On all of Hemi's screens flicker images of cosmic cataclysm. The walls of galaxies swell, collide, explode, shatter and compress together.

Miss O'Hara turns her head into Dr Foley's chest. 'Oh, hide me somewhere, Eliot!' But he knows there is no escape, nor anywhere to hide. The galactic collisions cascade and metamorphose from one level of destruction to the next. They overlap, combine and rip each other apart. Becoming superdense, they advance relentlessly on the ship.

Mrs Cortland begins to shiver, uncontrollably. 'Has it finally come to this? Just us? Are we the last to die?'

The others recognise the symptoms — they've all felt this way at one time or another. The only way to combat it is human touch — and Dr Foley puts his hand out to Mrs Cortland and grips hers. His warmth seeps into her.

'Peter would have been so proud of you,' he says to her.

Mrs Cortland gives a wry, sad nod. 'Yes,' she says. 'We've actually made it, haven't we —?'

At that moment, Captain Craig sees Aunti-3 whizzing off like Tinker-bell. 'Who's afraid of the big bad wolf' she sings, 'the big bad wolf, the big bad wolf? Who's afraid of the big bad wolf? Oh no, no, not I!'

Aunti-1 and Aunti-2 set off in hot pursuit. 'Wait up, girl, wait up!'

'Hemi, where are they going?' the Captain asks.

'We've received another communication, sir. The aunties have gone to investigate.'

Very soon, the aunties report back. They are chittering and chattering excitedly. 'Are you ready for an incoming message?' Aunti-1 asks. 'Coming ready or not.'

The screen flickers with a mathematical equation.

PROPOSITION:

Set

$$(1) \qquad |t = 0\rangle = \hat{a}^{\dagger}_{\alpha \wedge \Omega}|\mathrm{vac}\rangle = \int d\xi\, |\xi\rangle_{\oplus}|\xi\rangle_{\star}.$$

'Sir, do you recognise it?' Hemi asks.

Captain Craig begins to scan the equation:

BEGINNING CREATED HEAVEN

And the meaning dawns on him.

'I think so, Hemi,' he answers. 'It's the first verse from the Book of Genesis.'

1

'So this is how the universe ends,' Professor Van Straaten says.

'Or begins,' Monsignor Frère smiles.

The *Endeavour* is totally surrounded by gleaming walls of galaxies — millions and millions of them. It's a dizzying, disorienting sight as the walls continue their advance, towering around the ship. They are relentless and triumphant — and at their coming the voids are crushed from existence. Te Kore itself begins to collapse in the throes of death.

> Aue, e Te Kore e,
> Haere atu, haere, haere,
> Haere —

Captain Craig recalls Captain Cook's second voyage to the southern seas. On 12 December 1772, Cook had found himself at the edge of an endless pack of ice. On 17 January 1773, he had crossed the Antarctic Circle.

'Is my sense of wonderment,' Captain Craig muses, 'any different from Cook's when he reached the end of his world?'

He looks out the windows. Through the last remaining shards of Te Kore the ship sails, navigating the collapsing walls of the galaxies. *Endeavour*'s engines are whining at maximum capacity, trying to maintain stabilisation. The light-wings are reefed, minimising her profile so that the ship is not overturned by the cosmic winds buffeting from all around, and Hemi has dropped seven space-anchors to keep her from drifting. Everywhere, the robotic engineering and service drones are trying to keep the shields operational against the gigantic maelstrom outside. Galaxies, suns and black holes continue to smash together.

Suddenly, there is no blackness. Instead the view from the window flares with pure whiteness. The cosmic fluid is becoming so dense that sound waves start to propagate in it; they drown the roar of the ship's engines with the sounds of the entirety of creation.

> Aue e Te Ao Tawhito e,
> Haere atu, haere, haere,
> Haere —

The Artificial Intelligence is at full stretch. The power generators have moved into the red. The ship yaws, riding the currents of time as best it can.

'Nephew,' Aunti-2 scolds. 'Power down, man!'

'I'm sorry, Aunti-2,' Hemi answers, 'but I must maintain maximum stabilisation.' He has begun to use the light-wings in various configurations but they are whining with the stress load.

'Aunties,' Captain Craig asks, 'can you assist?'

'Sure thing, Captain. Why didn't you ask us earlier?'

They chatter to one another and then, agreed, whiz below *Endeavour*. They position themselves beneath the hull, cradling the vessel.

'Easy does it, old girl,' they say to the ship. 'Not long to wait now.'

The ship regains trim. The power generators move into green. The radiation shields hold. Even so, Captain Craig intercepts the fear on everyone's faces. Mrs Cortland stares at him. She holds Miss O'Hara in her arms. She lifts her face so that the light shines full upon it.

Captain Craig joins her. 'Do you know the story of Galileo Galilei's first appearance before the Florence Academy?' he asks.

Mrs Cortland shakes her head: 'No.' She looks taken aback.

Monsignor Frère overhears. 'If I may, Captain? Galileo was a young man at the time — was it 1607? — and barely into his twenties. But he already had a reputation as a man of science, so the Academy asked him if he could solve a problem which men of the arts, men of letters, had been debating for some years. The debate centred on Dante's *Inferno* and on the dimensions of Hell and of Satan.'

Mrs Cortland sees Dr Foley and Professor Van Straaten standing at a distance. 'Come, Eliot, join us,' she says. 'You too, Professor. After all, we've come all this way together.'

'I know the story, too,' the Professor says. 'It was one of the great debates between the sciences and the humanities. Galileo took up the challenge and, when he made his appearance before the Academy, he began by saying, "Dante's Hell is shaped like a cone one-twelfth the total mass of Earth. Its vortex is the home of Lucifer who stands locked in ice halfway up his gigantic chest. His bellybutton forms the very centre of the Earth. From Lucifer, sectoral lines extend to Jerusalem on the Earth's surface and east to some unknown point. Inferno itself is a vast amphitheatre divided into eight levels. In the fifth level are the swamp called Styx and the wicked City of Dis. Here, the heretics suffer in the presence of Lucifer himself." You can imagine,' Professor Van Straaten chuckles, 'the reaction of the Academy to Galileo's calculations!'

'But there was more to come,' Dr Foley adds, nodding his head. 'Galileo went on to say that there was a relation between the size of Dante the man and the size of the giant, Nimrod, in the pit of Hell and, in turn, between Nimrod and the arm of Lucifer. Therefore, if the academy knew Nimrod's size, it could deduce the size of Lucifer.'

'It was all there in *Inferno*,' the Monsignor continues. 'The divine Dante had himself written of Nimrod that his face was about as long and just as wide as St Peter's cone in Rome. "Thus," Galileo said, "his face will be five arm-lengths and a half and, since men are usually eight heads tall, the giant's face will be eight times as large. Therefore, Nimrod will be forty-four arm-lengths tall.'"

'I'm puzzled, Captain Craig,' Professor Van Straaten interrupts. 'Referencing Galileo at this juncture?'

'Oh, I know why he has done it,' the Monsignor smiles. 'Dante the man was to the giant as 3 is to 44. According to Galileo's calculations, "The relation of a giant to the arm of Lucifer is the same as the man is to the giant. The formula then must be 3 is to 44 as 44 is to X. Therefore the arm of Lucifer is 645 metres. Since the length of an arm is generally one-third the entire height, we can say that Lucifer's height will be some 2000 arm-lengths. This is the size of Lucifer."'

'The point of the story,' Captain Craig says, 'is that some historians say this was the inspiration for Galileo's further scientific investigations. If he could measure Hell and Satan, why not Heaven and God? And so he began his life-long assault on the stars. He thought Heaven had its own language. You had to understand its geometric figures before you could hear it talking. In particular, Heaven had a divine secret —'

'What was that?' Miss O'Hara asks.

'The language of God is mathematics.'

—

Again, Hemi interrupts the conversation.

'Sir,' he says to Captain Craig, 'we've almost reached zero.'

Already? Captain Craig has a sudden urge to put the clock back — oh, back 1401 billion light-years, back, back, all the way back. Back to a place called Earth, a valley that he came from, a people he belonged to, a wife and two beloved infant children whom he loved. He would travel all that way just for one second, one second only, to embrace them. Would it be worth it? Yes. Oh, yes.

'The interesting question is which zero?' Professor Van Straaten observes. 'Have we gone forward to a new beginning or back to the beginning —'

'Either way,' the Monsignor prays, 'let's hope that we do a better job of it this time.'

'Captain Craig,' Hemi interjects. 'I have intercepted a countdown. Would you like it displayed for everyone to read? Thank you, Captain.'

All the screens show the following:

PROPOSITION:

Set

(1) $$|t=0\rangle = \hat{a}^{\dagger}_{\alpha\wedge\Omega}|\text{vac}\rangle = \int d\xi\, |\xi\rangle_{\oplus}|\xi\rangle_{\star}.$$

With

(2a) $$\rho_{\oplus}(t) \equiv \text{tr}_{\star}(|t\rangle\langle t|)$$

undetermined; and

(2b) $$\hat{E}(r)|t=0\rangle = 0.$$

And evolution in time

(2c) $$|t\rangle = \hat{U}_{\alpha\wedge\Omega}(t,0)|t=0\rangle.$$

Let there be $t_l \in (0, t_1]$ such that

(3) $$\hat{E}(r)|t_l\rangle \neq 0.$$

And $\hat{P}_{\alpha\wedge\Omega}|t_l\rangle = |+\rangle\langle+|$:

and there is an ω such that

(4a) $$\hat{E}(0)|t\rangle \neq 0, \qquad\qquad 0 < [\omega t]_{2\pi} \leq \pi,$$

(4b) $$\hat{E}(0)|t\rangle = 0, \qquad\qquad \pi < [\omega t]_{2\pi} < 2\pi.$$

Define

(5a) $$D \equiv \{t|0 < [\omega t]_{2\pi} \leq \pi\},$$

(5b) $$N \equiv \{t|\pi < [\omega t]_{2\pi} \leq 2\pi\}.$$

And

(5c) $$\omega t_1 = 2\pi.$$

AND Let there be $t_H \in (t_1, t_2]$ and a partition $W_< \cup F \cup W_>$ of $\mathbb{R}_3$ such that

(6) $$\hat{N}_{\text{H}_2\text{O}}(x,y,z)|t_H\rangle = 0, \qquad (x,y,z) \in F.$$

and

(7) $$\int_F \hat{N}_{\text{H}_2\text{O}}(x,y,z)|t > t_H\rangle = 0.$$

Identify

(8a) $$\star \longleftrightarrow F.$$

And

(8b)
$$\omega t_2 = 4\pi.$$

AND Let

(9a)
$$W_< = W'_< \cup L,$$

with $W'_<$ connected, and let there be $t_E \in (t_2, t_3]$ such that

(9b)
$$\hat{N}_{H_2O}(x, y, z)|t > t_E\rangle = 0, \qquad (x, y, z) \in L.$$

Identify

(10a)
$$\oplus \longleftrightarrow L;$$

and define

(10b)
$$C \equiv W'_< :$$

And $\hat{P}_{\alpha \wedge \Omega}|t_E\rangle = |+\rangle\langle+|.$

And Let there be $t_p \in (t_E, t_3]$ such that

(11)
$$\oplus \Rightarrow \hat{N}_{S(A,G,C,T)}|t_p\rangle \neq 0, \qquad S(A, G, C, T) \in P_{LT},$$

And for $t > t_p$

(12)
$$\langle \hat{\dot{N}}_{S(A,G,C,T)} \rangle > 0.$$

And $\hat{P}_{\alpha \wedge \Omega}|t\rangle = |+\rangle\langle+|.$

And

(13)
$$\omega t_3 = 6\pi.$$

AND Let there be $t_L \in (t_3, t_4]$ such that

(14a)
$$\left. \begin{array}{ll} \exists \{r_D\} \subset F & \text{s.t.} \quad \hat{E}(r_D)|t > t_L\rangle \neq 0 \\ \exists \{r_N\} \subset F & \text{s.t.} \quad \hat{E}(r_N)|t > t_L\rangle \neq 0 \end{array} \right\} \longleftrightarrow D \cap N = \emptyset;$$

and let

(14b)
$$\{r_D\} \wedge \{r_N\} \Rightarrow \pm \wedge [\omega t]_{2\pi} \wedge [\omega t]_{182.5\pi} \wedge [\omega t]_{730\pi} :$$

And let

(15)
$$\{r_D\} \wedge \{r_N\} \subset F \longleftrightarrow \star \Rightarrow \hat{E}(r_\oplus)|t > t_L\rangle \neq 0.$$

And

(16a)
$$\hat{U}_{\alpha \wedge \Omega}(t > t_L, 0)|\text{vac}\rangle \text{ s.t. } \exists \odot \equiv \{r_D\} \wedge (\equiv \{r_N\}$$

with $\odot > ($ and

(16b) $\qquad \odot \Rightarrow \hat{E}(r_\oplus)|t > t_L\rangle \neq 0, \qquad 0 < [\omega t]_{2\pi} \leq \pi,$

(16c) $\qquad (\Rightarrow \hat{E}(r_\oplus)|t > t_L\rangle \neq 0, \qquad \pi < [\omega t]_{2\pi} < 2\pi.$

And

(17) $\qquad \odot \wedge (\in F \longleftrightarrow \star \text{ s.t. } \hat{E}(r_\oplus)|t > t_L\rangle \neq 0,$

and

(18) $\qquad \odot \wedge (/ D \wedge N \longleftrightarrow D \cap N = \emptyset :$

and $\hat{P}_{\alpha \wedge \Omega}|t\rangle = |+\rangle\langle+|.$

And

(19) $\qquad \omega t_4 = 8\pi.$

And Let there be $t_f \in (t_4, t_5]$ such that

(20a) $\qquad W'_< \Rightarrow \hat{N}_{S(A,G,C,T)}|t_f\rangle \neq 0, \qquad S(A, G, C, T) \in F_{SH},$

and

(20b) $\qquad W'_< \Rightarrow \hat{N}_{S(A,G,C,T)}|t_f\rangle \neq 0, \qquad S(A, G, C, T) \in F_{WL}.$

And for $t > t_f$

(21) $\qquad \langle \dot{\hat{N}}_{S(A,G,C,T)} \rangle > 0 :$

and $\hat{P}_{\alpha \wedge \Omega}|t\rangle = |+\rangle\langle+|.$

And let

(22) $\qquad F_{SH} \otimes \in W'_< \wedge F_{WL} \otimes \in \oplus.$

And

(23) $\qquad \omega t_5 = 10\pi.$

AND Let there be $t_b \in (t_5, t_6]$ such that

(24) $\qquad \oplus \Rightarrow \hat{N}_{S(A,G,C,T)}|t_p\rangle \neq 0, \qquad S(A, G, C, T) \in B_{ST},$

And for $t > t_b$

(25) $\qquad \langle \dot{\hat{N}}_{S(A,G,C,T)} \rangle > 0.$

and $\hat{P}_{\alpha \wedge \Omega}|t\rangle = |+\rangle\langle+|.$

AND Let there be $t_{\not\phi} \in (t_b, t_6]$ such that

(26a) $\exists \, \Phi(A,C,G,T) \text{ s.t. } \Phi(A,C,G,T) \models \alpha \wedge \Omega :$

and let

(26b) $\Phi(A,C,G,T) > S(A,C,G,T)$

$\forall \, S(A,C,G,T) \in F_{SH} \cup F_{WL} \cup B_{ST}.$

So

(27) $\hat{a}^{\dagger}_{\alpha \wedge \Omega}|\text{vac}\rangle \longrightarrow \Phi \equiv \acute{O} \cup \male \models \alpha \wedge \Omega.$

And let

(28) $\Phi \otimes \text{ s.t. } \Phi / \oplus \wedge \Phi > S \, \forall \, S \in F_{SH} \cup F_{WL} \cup B_{ST}.$

AND

(29) $\forall \, \acute{O} \vee \male \in \Phi \ \exists \, P_{LT} \text{ s.t. } \acute{O} \cup \male \Rightarrow \acute{O} \cup \male.$

And $\forall S(A,C,G,T) \in B_{ST} \cup F_{WL}$ there exists P_{LT} such that

(30) $\acute{O}_S \cup \male_S \Rightarrow \acute{O}_S \cup \male_S :$

Q.E.D..

And

(31a) $\hat{P}_{\alpha \wedge \Omega}|t\rangle = |++\rangle\langle++|.$

And

(31b) $\omega t_6 = 12\pi.$

The mathematical formulae stop.

Mrs Cortland presses Miss O'Hara's hands reassuringly. 'We'll be all right, my dear.'

The *Endeavour* rocks. The three aunties are like lifeboats beside it. They are chattering as if they know what is going on.

'Up, up and away, in my beautiful, my beautiful balloon!' Aunti-3 sings. Her voice is ecstatic. 'Yes,' Aunti-1 and Aunti-2 respond. 'We've done our job.'

'Captain,' Hemi says, 'I'm getting readings of huge energy forces coalescing all around us. Something is happening.'

The ship rocks, and rocks again. Then everything is happening at once. Echoes of the whole titanic history of the universe are crowding in, pushing and jostling with each other, fighting for the last sliver of space. Every movement ever made. Every word ever spoken. Every television show ever broadcast. Every ray of starlight ever shone. Space is collapsing under its own weight.

'It won't be long before the gravitational waves overwhelm us,' Captain Craig says. In his mind's eye he sees a trillion black holes colliding. Tears spring to his eyes at the thought of all that human history — despite the self-destructiveness, there had also been so much life, so much hope, so many dreams achieved and triumphs witnessed. As one of the last survivors, Captain Craig raises his voice in poroporoaki, in defiant tribute to the generations upon generations of men and women who had lived in this life and world:

> Tena koutou nga iwi katoa o te Ao,
> Te Huinga o te Kahurangi,
> Tena koutou —

Hemi's voice comes, soothing, to Captain Craig. 'Ten seconds to the first impact from the universe's shock waves. Nine, eight, seven . . . Sir, time to open the codicil to your secret instructions.'

'Open,' Captain Craig orders. On all screens there appears one word:

RESET.
'Four, three, two, one —'
'Do as ordered,' Captain Craig says.
'Zero.'

0

Time fades to nothing.
Real nothing. Not even space. Outside there is no outside.
Space is time and time is space. Space enough, perhaps?
Then:

$$H \,|\Psi> = 0$$

The ship is like a bloodied jawbone thrown through the air. The energy is more than 10 billion billion billion nuclear detonations. It roars over the *Endeavour*. In a trice, the ship is incinerated. Her avatar, Hemi, gives a huge, deep sigh. The glorious aunties are like angels on fire, fluttering into oblivion.

Captain Craig feels an intense pain. He looks at Mrs Cortland, Miss O'Hara, Monsignor Frère, Professor Van Straaten and Dr Foley, wanting to reassure them. But of what? Just before the endorphins kick in, he has a regretful thought:

'But we didn't have time to say goodbye to each other.'

—

And he is falling.

He feels a dizzying rush of acceleration, as if he is being sucked at headlong speed down a tunnel of dazzling light. Onward and onward he roars, and the sensation is so delirious that he wants to laugh and laugh.

All of a sudden he is through the tunnel and suspended above the blackness, watching the primordial fireball and the way its wave of light is moving so fast away from him. He becomes frightened and closes his eyes.

—

And he is falling.

When he opens his eyes he sees a wild landscape in the country of his birth, New Zealand. It is so familiar to him that he laughs with relief. A mist descends and he is lost in it.

This has happened before, he thinks. The mist opens and he sees three elderly women from the village walking in front of him. He runs after them. One of them turns and asks, 'Went the day well, sir?' The second says, 'Not you again.' And the third says, 'You're always losing directions. Well, you're almost at your destination, lad. There it is.' She points to a faraway farmhouse on the other side of the valley. 'You had better make haste,' the old women say. 'Night is coming and, with it, a fierce storm.'

He walks to the farmhouse. A light is coming from the window and, framed within the light, someone is watching him. As he approaches, the door opens. Mrs Cortland is there.

'Thank goodness you were able to make it home before dark,' she says. 'Come in, come in.'

He enters the house and sees Monsignor Frère, Dr Foley, Miss O'Hara and Professor Van Straaten having a cup of tea and chatting.

'Let the Captain have a place by the fire,' Mrs Cortland scolds. 'He'll catch his death. There's room for one more.'

The five people in the room smile at Captain Craig as if they have known him all their lives. Monsignor Frère comes to join him. 'Don't be afraid,' he says. 'There are some questions that science cannot answer. They may know what, how and when, but while faith and reason have co-existed in scientists as notable as Isaac Newton and Albert Einstein, only theologists know why.'

The Captain shifts on his feet nervously. Mrs Cortland brings him a cup of hot tea. 'This will bring you back to life,' she says.

A few moments later, Professor Van Straaten comes to talk to him. 'I wouldn't believe everything I see,' he says. 'At the end of the universe things still go bump in the night and every grave, opening wide, lets forth its sprites and demons. But Fate is always kind. It gives to those who love their secret longing.'

'Do I know you?' he asks the Professor. 'Do I know any of you?'

'Of course you do!' Professor Van Straaten laughs. But he is uncertain, and his laughter fades away into bewilderment. 'Because if you don't, then who are we?'

Monsignor Frère winks at him. 'Interesting, isn't it?'

Mrs Cortland claps her hands for attention. 'It's time to go,' she says. 'Dr Foley and Miss O'Hara, are you ready? The next great adventure is about to begin. As for the Captain, he has his own journey. Goodbye, my dear.'

—

And he is falling.

Suddenly Captain Craig finds himself in a small white room. He is alone. He is naked. How did he get here? Who is he? Why is he here? He begins to scream and pound on the walls. He falls to the floor in a foetal position, howling, hugging himself and weeping.

Time is limitless. How long has he been here? He does not know. He sleeps and 15 billion light-years go by. For one brief second he feels butterflies brushing his eyelids, and knows his wife and children have flitted by in his dreams. More light-years go by.

Finally, he awakes. He sees that there is a wardrobe in the room. In the wardrobe is a high-necked suit. With a sigh, he dresses in the suit.

A door appears in the room. Above the door is a clock. The time is just before midnight. Have they succeeded?

Captain Craig finishes dressing. He sees a mirror on the wall. He inspects his appearance. Combs his hair. Smooths out his trousers.

Takes a deep breath. Walks to the door.

Turns the doorknob.

Opens the door.

—

The table is set for six.

It is circular. Every guest, when seated, will be equidistant from the other. The host, Captain Walter Craig, has invited them for pre-dinner drinks at 7.30. Time, of course, has long lost all real meaning, but on board the ship a 24-hour day is still observed; it continues to locate, structure and define and, by setting a beginning for the journey, has enabled the Captain and crew to calculate the various coordinates they have reached as the journey has progressed.

The ship is an Artificial Intelligence called the *Endeavour*. Powered by its avatar, Hemi, it is a silent celestial angel in solitary flight through a sea of stars, cleaving through the blackness, serene and powerful, its light-wings at full extension, across the dead of night.

medicine woman

1

Another dawn, and she drags her old bones up from sleep.

Her name is Paraiti and when she is sleeping her bones are light and weightless. But as she wakes she is aware of all the stiffness, aches and numbness of a body that has aged. She opens her eyes, listening to her heart thumping away as it pushes the blood through thickened veins. She hears the usual wheeze and gurgle as her lungs force her breath in and out, and she feels a lump of phlegm in her throat. Creaking like an old door on worn-out hinges she heaves herself into a sitting position, opens the flap of the tent and spits into the cuspidor she keeps for holding her offensive body fluids.

Now that she is awake, Paraiti fumbles among her blankets for her Bible and hymnal and starts to chant a karakia. Old habits die hard, and she wouldn't dream of beginning a new day without himene and prayer. Her parents Te Teira and Hera, if they were alive, would roar with laughter to see her now; in the old days, when the Ringatu faithful were all at prayer in the smoky meeting house, she was the child always squirming and wriggling. 'Kaore e korikori koe,' Te Teira would reprimand her.

Although Paraiti went for a few years to a native school, she can't read very well; she trusts to her memory when quoting from the Old Testament or singing hymns. She raises a hand in the sign of the faithful.

'Kororia ki to ingoa tapu,' she begins. 'Glory be to your holy name.'

She lifts her eyes to the sky lightening above her, and gives thanks to God for having made the world. The huge forest canopy has been a protective umbrella for her sleep. Here, at the bend of a river, with giant ferns unfolding in the lower growth, she has had the perfect camping ground.

Karakia over, she whistles out to her stallion, Ataahua, and Kaihe, her mule. They whinny back — good, they have not foraged too far away in the night. Where's Tiaki, her pig dog? Aha, there he is, on the other side of the river.

She calls to him, 'Have you brought something for my breakfast or have you been selfish and wolfed it all down yourself?'

No, today Tiaki has been kind to his mistress. He jumps headlong into the water and swims across; he offers a fat woodpigeon, still alive and unmarked in his jaws.

'Homai te kereru,' Paraiti asks him. 'Give me the bird.' He sighs, knowing she will release it back into the woods. 'Ae, Tiaki, we let this one go. Give the first to Tane, Lord of the Forest.' She gives the pigeon its freedom and it creaks and whistles its way back into the trees. 'Now go, Tiaki, the second pigeon is for us.'

Right-oh, down to the edge of the river to wash herself, get the pikaro out of her eyes, and use a clean rag to wash her neck, armpits and nether parts. While she is at it, she sprinkles water over her head, and looks at her reflection, hoping to see some improvement. No such luck. Still the same old face, only getting older: big Maori nose, heavy upper lip, three chins, and lots of bushy hair. She fixes the hair by pinning it back with two large ivory combs but, aue, now she can see more of her face. Never mind: there's nobody else around to frighten.

Time for breakfast. Paraiti rekindles the fire and hangs a billy of water on an iron rod supported by two strong branches; she also puts a skillet among the hot embers.

Tiaki comes back with a second bird. Paraiti has a sneaking suspicion that he catches two birds at the same time and, somehow, has learnt the trick of pinning the second bird down with a stone, keeping it for later.

Now that he has served his mistress, Tiaki bounds off in search of his own breakfast.

Paraiti plucks the pigeon and puts it in the skillet; very soon it is sizzling in its own fat. From one of her saddlebags she takes some damper bread and honey. There's nothing like a fresh pigeon and damper bread running with honey to start the day. A cup of manuka tea made in the billy and, ka pai, she is in seventh heaven.

Once she's breakfasted, she's keen to get going. Quickly, she dismantles the tent and bedding and stows them in the saddlebag. She goes down to the river to rinse the breakfast implements, then douses the fire and cleans up around her. She buries the contents of the cuspidor in the ground. Nobody would ever know she'd been here.

At Paraiti's whistle, Ataahua and Kaihe come at the gallop. She loads Kaihe first, then she puts the bridle and saddle on Ataahua and taps him on the front knees. Once upon a time she could get on a horse without trouble, but these days it's too much for her old bones. Ataahua obliges, going down on his front legs. He waits for Paraiti to settle and then hoists himself up with a whinny of grumpiness; over the past few years his mistress has got not only older but heavier.

'Me haere tatou,' she tells Ataahua. 'Let us go.'

Pulling her mule after her, she fords the river and climbs the track on the other side. By the time she reaches the top of the ridge, Tiaki has joined her with a supercilious look on his face, as if he has given her only the second-best pigeon. The mist has lifted from the valleys and the air is clear. The forest is raucous with birdsong. Far away, Paraiti can see the smoke curling above the village of Ruatahuna, her destination.

2

Paraiti is not her real name, but the name people know her by. Mostly she is called Scarface — emblematic of the deep red welt that travels diagonally from her right temple across the bridge of her nose and, luckily missing her left eye, reappears to feather her left cheekbone. The scar was caused when Paraiti was a young girl, in 1880. Her family group was hiding deep within the Urewera country when they were set upon by constabulary forces who were hunting bigger game — the rebel prophet, Te Kooti. They restrained

Paraiti's parents with ropes while they ransacked the encampment. When they couldn't find Te Kooti, one of them took a burning stick from the cooking fire and slashed Paraiti with it. As her parents were led away to be imprisoned, her father Te Teira cried out, 'Daughter, quickly, go to the stream and lie down in the cold water.' Hera, Paraiti's mother, died while they were still incarcerated, and when Te Teira was released a year later, he went searching throughout Tuhoe and the King Country for his daughter. As soon as he saw the scarred little girl on the roadside at Te Kuiti, where she had been lovingly cared for, he knew it was her.

—

Today is the first day of June in this Year of Our Lord, nineteen hundred and twenty-nine. Paraiti is fifty-four years old now, and a traditional healer.

Maori people have not lost faith in their own healers. Indeed, although those who live in the cities and towns have access to the Pakeha doctors, those who still reside in tribal villages in the backblocks and remote coastal areas rely on travelling healers like Paraiti for medical help. Vilified by the government authorities for their work, the healers are still committed to the health and wellbeing of the morehu, the survivors of the land wars. Many of Paraiti's people of the Ringatu faith do not trust the authorities at all. And, of course, the Depression is beginning to bite. Who can Maori turn to, apart from their own healers, when they have no money to pay the Pakeha takuta?

Three weeks ago, Paraiti was still in her village of Waituhi, preparing for her travels. The autumn had been unseasonably cold, with southerlies driving into the foothills. Paraiti had huddled close to a warm fire in her old one-room kauta near the painted meeting house, Rongopai. Even so, she was determined to keep to her annual trip. She had become stir-crazy and wanted to be out on the road.

It was time for her to leave her hearth.

She carefully selected the medicines, unguents, potions, analgesics, antiseptics, styptics, philtres, emetics, blood purifiers and ointments that she needed. She took only kao, dried kumara, and water as provisions; food would be her payment from her patients and, should she require extra kai for herself and her animals, the Lord and the land provided. She knew all the traditional food-gathering areas — fern grounds, pa tuna, taro and kumara gardens and bird sanctuaries — and, as well, she had some special secret areas where she went to stock up on herbs and healing plants.

Paraiti took a small tent and a bedroll. For protection she put her rifle in a sling and a knife in her left boot. Although she might not be attractive, she was still a woman, and men were men.

She went to Rongopai, the great cathedral of her people, and in its stunning interior — verily a Garden of Eden — she prayed to God for safe passage. She filled five blue bottles with the healing waters that bubbled up from a deep underground spring behind the house, and sprinkled herself and her animals with the water. Then she strapped the saddlebags around Kaihe's girth, bridled and saddled Ataahua, tapped on his front knees and climbed aboard. Straightaway, she urged Ataahua up, 'Timata,' and headed into the foothills behind Waituhi.

A day's travel took her to the boundary between the lands of Te Whanau a Kai and Tuhoe, and there she sought Rua's Track, one of the great horse tracks joining the central North Island to the tribes of Poverty Bay in the east. She followed the track up the Wharekopae River, through Waimaha by way of the Hangaroa Valley to Maungapohatu. The only people who travelled the track were Maori like herself; sometimes they were families but most often they were foresters, labourers or pig hunters. On her third day, however, Paraiti joined a wagon-train of some forty members; they, too, were making for Ruatahuna. They knew who she was and were honoured to have her join them. And she, in turn, valued the opportunity to sharpen up her social skills, to share a billy of manuka tea and flat bread, to spend time playing cards and to korero with some of the old ones about the way the world was changing. But they made slow progress, so Paraiti took her leave of them and journeyed on alone.

And now, Ruatahuna lay ahead.

—

As she approaches Ruatahuna, Paraiti knows she will be late for the service. She can hear the bell ringing at the meeting house, Te Whai a Te Motu, calling the Ringatu faithful to gather together on this very special day. The First of June in the church calendar is the Sabbath of the Sabbath, as written in Leviticus 23:4: 'Ko nga hakari nunui enei a Ihowa, ko nga huihuinga tapu e karangatia e koutou i nga wa e rite ai.' It is also the beginning of the Maori New Year, with the pre-dawn heliacal rising of Matariki, the bright stars of fruitfulness. On this happy day, each person contributes seeds to the mara tapu, the sacred garden. This is part of the huamata ritual, for out of the old seed comes the new plant, symbolic of the renewal of God's promise to all his people.

Paraiti urges Ataahua quickly through the village. Some of the local dogs bark at them, and Paraiti gives Tiaki a warning glance, 'Don't bark back, it's Sunday.' He gives her a sniffy look and then growls menacingly at the dogs so that they whine and back away. Ahead, Paraiti sees her cousin Horiana's house. She knows Horiana won't mind if she ties the animals to her fence. 'Don't eat Horiana's roses,' she tells Kaihe. Even so, she is troubled to see that the roses are taking over the native vines in the garden.

Wrapping her scarf around her face, and taking with her a small sachet of seeds, Paraiti makes for the marae. Horses and buggies are tied to the fence outside and, hello, a few motoka as well. Inside, the meeting house is stacked to the gills; people are sitting up against the walls, prayer book in hand. Wirepa, the local poutikanga, pillar of authority, is leading the service.

'Kororia ki to ingoa tapu,' he intones. 'And verily, an angel appeared to the prophet Te Kooti, and the angel was clothed in garments as white as snow, his hair like stars, and he wore a crown and a girdle like unto the setting sun and the rising thereof, and the angel's fan was like the rainbow and his staff was a myriad hues. And the angel said to Te Kooti, "I will not forsake thee or my people either." And so we prevail to this very day, glory be to thy holy name. Amine.'

Paraiti sees Horiana beckoning and making a place beside her. Stooping, she makes her way over to her cousin.

'E noho, whanaunga,' Horiana welcomes her. They kiss and hug as if they haven't seen each other for a thousand years. 'We'll korero afterwards,' Horiana whispers, opening her prayer book.

Paraiti gives a sign of apology to Wirepa for interrupting the service. She hears a buzz as people realise she has arrived: 'Scarface' . . . 'Te Takuta' . . . 'Paraiti' . . . 'Scarface'. She smiles at familiar faces. She doesn't mind that people call her Scarface; they use the name as an identification, not to mock her. She lets herself be absorbed into the meeting house. It is such an honour to be sitting within Te Whai a Te Motu, with its figurative paintings and beautiful kowhaiwhai rafter patterns. Here, in the bosom of this holy place, Paraiti joins in praising and giving thanks to God.

The service adjourns to the mara tapu outside Te Whai a Te Motu. There, Paraiti and others offer their seeds for the sowing. Wirepa intones a final karakia. After the service there are people to be greeted and further korero to be had with the local elders.

After the midday meal, Paraiti sets up her tent in her usual place on the marae. Horiana, who acts as her assistant in Tuhoe, has been taking bookings. 'Lots of people want to see you,' she tells her. 'The usual problems. Nothing too difficult so far.' Always bossy, Horiana sits outside the tent deciding when clients should enter and depart. Inside, there are three chairs and a bed: a slab of wood covered with a fine woven flax mat. Stacked against one of the walls of the tent are the rongoa and the herbal pharmacy that Paraiti draws on for her work. Not all have been brought by her; some have been stockpiled by Horiana for her arrival. They include kumarahou for asthma; waoriki for arthritis; ake, kareao, miro or rimu gum for bleeding and haemorrhaging; hakekakeha or harakeke roots for blood cleansing and to promote regular blood functions; mingimingi, the mamaku pith and punga fern pith for scrofulous tumours, abscesses and boils; kawakawa for bronchitis and catarrh; weka oil, kowhai and bluegum juice for bruises, sprains and aching bones; harakeke and kauri gum to treat burns; puwha and mimiha gum for mouth and teeth ailments; harakeke for chilblains and bad circulation; houhere and tawa for colds; titoki for constipation; piupiu for cramp; wood charcoal for dandruff; koromiko buds for diarrhoea and dysentery; eel oil for earache; powdered moss for eczema and scabies; kaikaiatua as an emetic; pirita for epilepsy; seaweed for goitre; paewhenua for haemorrhoids; piripiri for urinary health; fernroot and convolvulus roots for lactation; flax leaf juice for sciatica; huainanga as an emetic to expel tapeworms and so on.

On a small table are the surgical implements of her trade. Unlike some of her brother and sister healers, Paraiti shuns Pakeha utensils and keeps to traditional ones: wooden sticks and scrapers, sharp-edged shells and obsidian flakes for cutting, thorns for opening up abscesses, stones to heat before placing on the body, lacy houhere bark and cobwebs as poultices and dressings, palm tree splints for broken bones; kahakaha fibre for bandaging, and various oils for massaging.

For any major bonesetting that requires steam treatment, Paraiti organises time at a makeshift spa. Her father gave her special knowledge of the various massages to heal and knit broken bones. He also taught her therapeutic massage for the elderly; he himself loved nothing better than to submit himself to Paraiti's strong kneading and stroking of his body to keep his circulation going. 'Daughter,' he would sigh, 'you have such goodness in your hands.'

The clinic opens, and the patients are of the usual kind. Some are easily treated — patients with coughs or colds and children with asthma or bronchitis. Boils are lanced and the ripe cores squeezed out before Paraiti returns the patient to Horiana to apply a poultice. Paraiti gives a short greeting to patients returning for a check-up, and notes whether a broken leg has set well, or a burn is in need of further bathing or lotions. Sprained joints, too, are treated with ease; with Horiana holding the patient, Paraiti pulls the joint back in place, then instructs Horiana how to bind it.

A young man with a deep cut on his forehead comes in. 'How did you come by this?' Paraiti asks.

'His wife threw a knife at him when he came home drunk from the hotel,' Horiana answers, rolling her eyes with contempt.

'You will need stitches,' Paraiti says. She makes a thread of muka and uses a wooden needle to sew the wound. As a dressing, she applies the ash from a burnt flax stalk. Throughout all this, the young man does not flinch. He's a cheeky one, though; just before he leaves he asks, 'Scarface, you couldn't throw in a love philtre with the treatment, could you? My wife's still angry with me and won't let me perform my customary and expert lovemaking duties.'

Paraiti's eyes twinkle. 'Oh really? But I have heard otherwise about your lovemaking. Do you think it might be the beer that is putting you off your stroke? No love philtre is required. Your wife will eventually forgive you and soon you will plough her in your usual diligent and boring manner, the poor woman. But if you must drink, chew puwha gum — it will mask your breath when you go home at night.'

Another young man comes in, but, as soon as he sees Paraiti, he changes his mind and goes out. He is embarrassed because he has a venereal disease. A male takuta is preferred to a woman healer.

A young woman with shell splinters in the heels of her feet requires a little more care; she carelessly ran across a reef while gathering pupu and mussels. 'I was being chased by a giant octopus,' she tells Paraiti.

Paraiti winks at Horiana. 'Oh yes, and what was his name?' She cuts around the wounds until the pieces of shell can be seen. Smiling at the young woman, Paraiti then lowers her head. 'Here is the kiss of Scarface,' she says. She bites on each piece of shell with her teeth and pulls them out. 'If your octopus really loves you and wants to ensnare you in his eight arms, and if that causes you to run over shells again, show him how to use his own teeth.'

The next patient causes some hilarity. He has constipation and hasn't had a good bowel movement for days. 'I have just the right potion,' Paraiti tells him. 'Crushed flax roots and, here, if you disrobe I will also blow some potion into your rectum so that the result comes quicker.' But the patient's wife is with him and she accosts Paraiti:

'Oh no, you don't! If anybody is to disrobe my husband and blow anything up his rectum, it will be me! Do I want the whole world to know how awful a sight his bum is? Best for him and me to keep that treasure a family secret.'

So it goes throughout the remainder of the day. Each patient pays Paraiti in coin or in food — a koha, no matter how small.

However, there are some who are sick without obvious symptoms and their treatment cannot be diagnosed with ease. With such patients Paraiti takes a history of their activities before they became ill and, if she suspects an answer, administers a likely remedy. If she is still unsure, she advises the patient to drink lots of clean water and gives them a potion against the pain or fever. 'Sometimes,' she tells them, 'the body has its own ways of making itself well again. Time will tell.'

There are other patients whom Paraiti will treat separately, away from the clinic at Horiana's house, because their conditions are more serious. One is a forester with a broken leg that will need to be broken again and reset; Paraiti believes his best recourse would be to go to the hospital at Rotorua but the forester refuses to let their doctors look at him — he is worried about the expense. Another is a young girl with an eye condition that bespeaks oncoming blindness. A third is an old koroua with a debilitating illness; nothing can cure old age but, as she often did with her father, Paraiti will give this old man a good massage and steam bath for temporary relief; as for the rest, he is already walking towards God.

The time comes to stop work for the day. 'Come back tomorrow,' Horiana tells the other people waiting in line. They are disappointed, but another day won't hurt them.

'But I will see the mother,' Paraiti says, pointing to a woman waiting with her daughter. She has noticed that the woman has constantly given up her place in the line to others.

'Thank you, takuta,' the mother says respectfully as she steps into the tent. She is trying to hide her distress. 'Actually, I do not come for my own sake but on behalf of my daughter, Florence. Do you have something that will enable her to keep her baby? She can never go to term and loses the baby always around the third month.'

Paraiti notes how small Florence is. She places her hands on the girl's stomach. E hika, this girl is very cold.

'How many times have you conceived?' Paraiti asks her.

'Three,' Florence replies, 'and three times my babies have died inside me. But I really want this child.'

Paraiti takes a look at the girl. She smells her breath; aue, she smokes the Pakeha cigarettes. She looks at her eyes; they are milky and clouded, and her fingernails and toenails are brittle and dry. Finally, Paraiti feels with her fingers around the girl's womb. Again, so cold. She speaks, not unkindly, to the girl.

'A baby in the womb is like a kumara being fed nutrients from the vine of your body. But your vine is not giving your baby the right foods. Your circulation is sluggish and, therefore, the nourishment is not getting to the child. Bad foods and bad vine are the reasons why, in the third month, your baby withers and dies. And then the garden in which your baby grows is not warm.'

Paraiti looks at Florence's mother. 'I will put your daughter on a diet which she must follow without straying,' she tells her. 'The diet is rich in nutrients. I will also put her on a regime of exercise which will improve her circulation. Florence must stop smoking Pakeha cigarettes immediately. Also, it is important that her blood temperature is increased. I will show you massage to make her body a whare tangata that is nice and cosy. Keep to the diet, the massages, and make sure she stays in the sunlight and eats vegetables and fruits and fish, especially shellfish. Try to make sure she is always warm.'

The mother holds Paraiti's hands and kisses them. 'Thank you, takuta.'

Paraiti sees them to the door of the tent. 'I will also give you some potions that will improve Florence's health while she is with child.'

'Will you attend the birth?' the mother asks.

'No,' Paraiti answers. 'The authorities will not allow it.' She turns to Florence. 'Go well, and be assured that if you follow my instructions, the birth should be normal and you will be delivered of a healthy child.' She kisses Florence on the forehead. 'What greater blessing can any woman have than to give birth to a son or daughter for the iwi? Will you let me know when the baby is born? Ma te Atua koe e manaaki.'

3

This is Paraiti's life and world. She is an agent of life, prolonging and optimising it. Paraiti's knowledge, therefore, is of the treatment of the body not the spirit, though sometimes these are intertwined.

But Paraiti does not live and practise at the higher level of a tohunga. She is not a mediator between the human world and the spiritual world. She does not heal mate atua, diseases of the gods; she has no competency in dealing with those sicknesses that are due to possession of the spirit. While she has known some very great priests — with skills in the spiritual, arcane and esoteric arts: prophecy, dream, sign, rehu, whakakitenga, makutu, moemoea and whiu — that is not her domain. Nor does she return spells onto those responsible for casting them.

Paraiti's father was such a priest, a man of immense wisdom, whom the iwi consulted on all matters of importance because of his powers of divination. Indeed, it was as a priest that Te Teira had served the great prophet Te Kooti, and remained loyal to him to the very end; this was why the people of Te Kuiti had looked after Paraiti, and had taken them both in after he was released from prison. Te Teira loved to talk about the early days of the prophet's victories. He used the language of the Old Testament, and likened Te Kooti's exploits to the great exodus and the flight of the Israelites from the lands of Egypt into Canaan. It was all metaphorical talk, but Paraiti was moved by its grandeur and imagery. 'In the end Te Kooti was pardoned,' Te Teira told Paraiti as they sat in front of the fire in their kauta. 'I will tell you how. The government wanted to run a railway line through the King Country, and issued a general amnesty to all criminals, no matter what they had done, to secure the land. The Prophet was saved by the iron horse!' he laughed.

'It was 1884 when that railway opened,' he went on. 'You and I were travelling to some hui or other, I can't remember which one, but you were my right-hand man, do you remember? We came across some Ringatu boys bending over the rails listening. We got off our horses too and bent down and listened. And your eyes went big and wide and you said to me, "Papa, the rails are singing a strange waiata!" Then suddenly, around the corner came that iron horse, a huge ngarara, a monster, belching smoke and roaring at us. Our horses started to buck and bolt but, resolute in the face of the ngarara, you raised your rifle and fired a shot at it.' Te Teira laughed. 'I suppose you were still trying to protect your papa, ne?'

Paraiti's shot did not bring the ngarara to the ground. But as it swayed and slithered past, she saw the many men and women who had been eaten by it, imprisoned in its intestines. She raised a tangi to them, a great lament. Of course, she had been mistaken. The passengers in the train were very much alive, dispersing into settlements — and the ngarara was just another monster eating up the land.

It was in Te Kuiti that Paraiti grew into womanhood. Although Te Teira would have wished for her to marry some kind farmer or fisherman of the tribe, raise children and live a happy life, those options were closed to her because of her kanohi wera, her burnt face. No matter that he was revered for his medical skills; even his great mana could not obtain a husband for her. She was twenty-four and already accustomed to rejection when, in a terrible moment of truth, she asked, 'Father, what man, in the moment of ecstasy, would look upon my face and not wish it was someone else's?' Te Teira himself acknowledged that his daughter was destined to become a spinster, with no provider once he was gone.

Paraiti's father had to go underground when the Tohunga Suppression Act was passed in 1908. The purpose of the Act was to replace tohunga, traditional Maori healers, with 'modern medicine'. The politicians made a lot of noise about 'charlatan' tohunga, but the Act was primarily directed at Rua Kenana who, some say, succeeded Te Kooti as prophet. 'As when the Pakeha pardoned Te Kooti,' Te Teira said, 'they brought in a law ostensibly for one thing when it was really for another.'

Te Teira had defied the Act by continuing to practise covertly. And he taught his daughter the arts of healing so that she could achieve economic independence as a functioning member of the iwi. In 1917, when Paraiti was forty-two, the Spanish influenza hit Maori settlements and the people were unable to get treatment from the Pakeha doctors. Paraiti joined her father in offering succour and support to the sick and dying in Te Kuiti. The irony was that the disease had been brought among the people by the Maori soldiers who had gone to fight in the Great War, on the other side of the world.

After the epidemic was over, Te Teira received a letter from a powerful kuia of Te Whanau a Kai on the East Coast, asking him to come and help her in improving the health of her people. Her name was Riripeti, and her persuasive powers were so great that, eventually, with the consent of the people of Te Kuiti, Te Teira accepted her offer. He migrated east with his daughter, and they ended up in Waituhi. There Te Teira finished instilling in Paraiti the safer knowledge — not the knowledge of the tohunga, but the knowledge of the healer. In particular, he bequeathed to her the rare skill of Maori massage, and the patience to massage deep beneath the skin and move muscles and bones and tissue to their proper places, should they be broken, torn or out of alignment.

And when he died in her arms of old age, four years ago, she was still massaging him and trying to keep his circulation going long after he became cold.

But Paraiti has a dilemma. As she closes her clinic in Ruatahuna for the day, her thoughts fly back to a request she received just before leaving Waituhi.

She was asked to take life, not to give it.

—

This is how it happened.

A week earlier, in the middle of packing for her annual trip, a thought popped into Paraiti's head: 'I think I'll ride into Gisborne and go to the pictures.' Just like that the thought came, and the more Paraiti pushed it away, the more it stuck in her mind. Truth to tell, she didn't need an excuse to go, so she made one up: she would buy some gifts for all the ladies who would be helping at her clinics on her travels. Horiana wasn't the only one, but for Horiana especially she would get her some of those Pakeha bloomers that would keep her nice and cool in the summer.

Paraiti got up at the crack of dawn, dressed in her town clothes, saddled Ataahua and set off for Gisborne. She stopped for a picnic lunch by the Taruheru River, then rode on to Gisborne and settled Ataahua in the municipal stables just across the Peel Street bridge. It was midday by the town clock when she joined the townsfolk on Gladstone Road.

Paraiti always came to Gisborne with some apprehension. Being among Pakeha was not natural for her; she felt she was crossing some great divide from one world to another. The slash of the scar across her face didn't help either; it marked her out in some sinister way. Even though these were modern times, and Pakeha liked to say that Maori and Pakeha were one people now, there were still signs of division: there were the Pakeha parts of Gisborne, particularly the palatial houses along Waterside Drive, and then there were the narrow shanty streets where the Maori lived.

Steadying her nerves, she made her way to the Regent to see what film was on. She was delighted to see that Charlie Chaplin's *The Gold Rush* was showing. She bought a ticket at the booth.

Humming to herself, Paraiti looked at the town clock again and saw that she had an hour to wait before the film began — time enough to go shopping. As she crossed Gladstone Road to Harrison Esq. Haberdashery, the latest model Packard went by with two women in it. One was a young Pakeha woman with auburn hair, of considerable beauty, and the other was a middle-aged Maori woman, probably her maid. When the Maori woman saw Paraiti, she pointed her out to her mistress.

Paraiti entered Harrison's and went over to look at the bolts of fabric. She felt she was in a magic land of laces, silks, wools, calicoes, twills and cottons. The colours were stunning — shimmering blues, glowing yellows and bright reds. A senior saleswoman appraised her as she came in and immediately approached her. 'May I help you?' she asked. There was no accompanying 'Madam' to her enquiry, but Paraiti's self-confidence had grown — and she had been to Harrison's before and she knew the kawa, the protocol:

1   Shop attendants were always supercilious but they were, sorry
      lady, only shop assistants, even if they were senior saleswomen.
2   She had as much right as anybody else to shop in Harrison's.
3   Her money was as good as anybody else's.

She unpinned her hat and placed it on the counter, claiming some territory. 'Why, thank you,' she said pleasantly, revealing her scar in order to intimidate the saleswoman. 'I'd like to see that bolt of cloth and that one and *that* one,' and she pointed to the ones that were highest in the stacks. Meantime, Paraiti rummaged through some of the other fashionable material and accessories that were on display. By the time the saleswoman returned, she had made her selection: a variety of attractive lengths of fabric, bold, with lots of flash. She also selected a couple of pairs of bloomers with very risqué ruffles on the legs. Pleased with her purchases, Paraiti waited at the doorway for the final piece of kawa to be observed:

4   When the paying customer is ready to depart, the door is always opened for her.

In a happy mood, humming to herself, Paraiti made her way back to the Regent, window shopping on the way, and took her seat in the theatre. Unnoticed, the Maori maid, who had been watching Paraiti in the haberdashery, and had followed her, took a seat a few rows back.

Paraiti loved nothing better than to sit in the dark where nobody could see her and get caught up in the fantasies on screen. She had seen Charlie Chaplin's previous movie, *The Kid,* and hoped that *The Gold Rush* would be just as good — and it was. The audience in the Regent couldn't stop laughing. Paraiti thought she would die — the tears were running down her face at the part where the starving man in the film kept looking at the little tramp and imagined seeing a nice juicy chicken. And she just about mimied herself when the little tramp was in the pivoting hut caught on the edge of a crevasse; the hut seesawed whenever Charlie walked from one side to the other. At the end she wanted to clap and clap: Charlie Chaplin was the greatest film clown in the world. She was so glad that she had come into town.

But when she came out of the theatre into the mid-afternoon sun and saw the Maori maid standing in the sunlight like a dark presence, she felt as if somebody had just walked over her grave.

'You are Paraiti?' the maid asked. She was subservient, eyes downcast, her years weighing her down — but her words were full of purpose. 'May I trouble you for your time? I have a mistress who needs a job done. If you accept the job, you will find the price to your liking.'

Although everything in her being shouted out, 'Don't do this, turn away,' Paraiti equivocated. She had always believed in fate, and it struck her that coming to Gisborne 'just like that' might not be coincidental. She found herself saying, 'Kei te pai, all right. Let me drop my parcels off at the municipal stables and then I will give your mistress an hour of my time.'

That task accomplished, the Maori servant introduced herself. 'My name is Maraea,' she said. 'My mistress is Mrs Rebecca Vickers. The Honourable Mr Vickers is currently in Europe on business. We are only recently arrived in Gisborne. Be good enough to follow me, but stay far enough back so that people do not know that we are together.'

Paraiti was immediately offended, but it was too late — she had already agreed to speak to Mrs Vickers. She followed Maraea into the Pakeha part of town. The houses on Waterside Drive, ranged along the river with willow trees greening along the bank, spoke of elegance and quality.

Maraea waved Paraiti to join her. 'The Vickers' residence is the fourth house along, the two-storeyed one with the rhododendron bushes and wrought-iron gate. When we arrive at the house I will go in and see if it is safe for my mistress to see you. Kindly do not approach until I signal to you with my handkerchief.'

'What have I got myself into?' Paraiti wondered. Increasingly irritated, she watched Maraea walk towards the house, disappear and, after a minute or so, return to the street and wave her handkerchief. Paraiti approached the house and was just about to enter through the gate when she heard Maraea whisper from the bushes: 'Do not come in through the front entrance, fool. Go around to the side gate, which is where folk such as you and I must enter. I will open the back door for you.'

Paraiti continued to the side gate. She opened it and walked along the gravelled pathway. A Maori gardener at work in the garden tipped his hat to her. Maraea stood at the doorway to the kitchen.

'Come in,' she urged Paraiti. 'Quickly now. And you,' she said to the gardener, 'Mrs Vickers is not pleased with the way you have trimmed the lawn. Do it again.'

Paraiti followed Maraea through a long corridor to the front of the house. The sun shone through the crystal glass of the front door. The entrance was panelled with polished wood and lined with red carpet. A tall clock ticked in an oak cabinet against one wall. A huge oval mirror hung on another wall. A small table with a visitor's book and a vase of lilies stood in the curve of the stairway to the first floor. Hanging from the ceiling was a crystal chandelier.

'Be kind enough to take off your hat,' Maraea said. She led Paraiti up the stairs and ushered her into a back sitting-room. 'Mrs Vickers will see you soon.'

—

'Come away from the window.'

Paraiti had been in the sitting room a good ten minutes before Mrs Vickers arrived. The room showed all the trappings and accoutrements of a prosperous Pakeha merchant. The green velvet curtains were tied back with gold tassels. Antique chairs fitted with gold damask cushions were arranged around small card tables; the room was no doubt used as an after-dinner smoking-room by the gentlemen, or a place where the ladies could congregate in the afternoons to chat over cards. To one side was a fireplace, with a beautiful chaise longue in front of it. The decorations had an oriental look — as if the Honourable and Mrs Vickers had spent some time in the East — and on the mantel above the fireplace was a photograph of a smiling couple, a young wife and her husband, standing with an Indian potentate. Electric lights in decorative glass lampshades were set into the walls, and everywhere there were mirrors. Paraiti had gravitated to the window, and was looking out at the garden below.

Turning, she immediately became disoriented; the hairs prickled on the back of her neck. In all the mirrors a young woman was reflected — in her mid twenties, with red hair, tall and slim, and wearing a beaded mauve dress. But which was the woman and which was her reflection? And how long had she been standing there?

On her guard, Paraiti watched as the woman approached her. She was pale, beautiful. Her hair had been tinted with henna and her skin was glazed to perfection; her eyes were green flecked with gold, the irises large, mesmerising and open. Paraiti resisted her hypnotic gaze, and immediately the woman's irises narrowed. Then she did something perfectly strange — seductive, almost. She cupped Paraiti's chin, lifted her face and clinically observed and then touched the scar.

The act took Paraiti's breath away. Nobody except Te Teira had ever been so intimate with her. 'I was told you were ugly,' the woman said in a clipped English accent, though not without sympathy. 'But really, you are only burnt and scarred.' She withdrew her hands, but the imprint of her fingers still scalded Paraiti's skin. Then she turned, wandering through the room. 'My name is Mrs Rebecca Vickers,' she said. 'Thank you for coming. And if you have stolen anything while you have been alone in the room, it would be wise of you to put it back where it belongs before you leave.'

Paraiti bit back a sharp retort. She recognised the battle of wills that was going on, and there was nothing to stop her from leaving, except that there was something about the situation, that sense of fate again that restrained her; she would bide her time. She tried to put a background to the woman: an English girl of good family and upper-class breeding, married to a man of wealth who travelled the world; she had brought with her to New Zealand her societal expectations, including the customary control of a household run by servants. She regarded Paraiti as being in a similar position to her maid. But there was also a sense of calculation, as if she was trying to manoeuvre Paraiti into a position of subservience, even of compliance.

'What might I help you with, Mrs Vickers?' Paraiti asked. She saw that Maraea had come into the sitting-room with a small bowl of water, a handcloth and a large towel.

'Thank you, Maraea,' Mrs Vickers said. Casually, with great self-possession, she began to unbutton her dress; it fell to the floor. Her skin was whiter than white, and without blemish. Aware of her beauty, Mrs Vickers stepped out of the dress, but kept on her high heels. Although she was wearing a silk slip, Paraiti immediately saw what her artful dress had been hiding: Mrs Vickers was pregnant.

'It's very simple,' Mrs Vickers said as she removed her underwear. 'I am carrying a child. I don't want it. I want you to get rid of it.'

Her directness stunned Paraiti. Mrs Vickers was clearly a woman accustomed to getting her way. Well, two could play at that game. She asked Mrs Vickers to lie on the chaise longue and began inspecting her. 'When did you last menstruate? How many weeks have passed since then?' she asked as she felt Mrs Vickers' whare tangata — her house of birth — to ascertain the placement of the baby and the point the pregnancy had reached. The uterus had already grown to the height of the belly-button, and the skin was beginning to stretch. Paraiti concluded her inspection. Mrs Vickers liked to be direct, did she? Time then to be direct and push *back*.

'You are a Pakeha,' she began. 'Why have you not gone to a doctor of your own kind?'

'Of course I have consulted European doctors,' Mrs Vickers answered, 'and much earlier than this, when I missed my period. Whatever they did to me did not work.'

'Then why have you not had further consultations with them?' Paraiti asked.

'Do not presume that I haven't done what you suggest,' Mrs Vickers responded, 'but even they failed again; they now tell me that I have gone beyond the point of no return. When Maraea saw you in the street today she thought you might offer me some hope. She told me that you Maori have ancient ways, and could get rid of it.'

'If your doctors can't perform your miracle for you,' Paraiti flared, 'don't expect me to be able to. Oh yes, I know of the herbal strategies that can lead to the termination of the pregnancy, but they work only in the first nine weeks. Some healers are able to induce the abortion by the steam bathing method and a concoction of flax and supplejack root juices. But your baby is at least twenty-four weeks grown — too late for the introduction of herbs that will make your uterus cramp and break down, so that the baby can be emptied and expelled from the womb.'

Angrily, Mrs Vickers put on her dress again. 'I knew this was a foolish notion, but Maraea told me you were renowned for your clever hands and that, by manipulation, you could secure the result I seek.'

'And you assumed I would do it just because you asked me?' Paraiti's voice overrode Mrs Vickers. 'Why are you so intent on ridding yourself of your baby? Most women would be overjoyed to be a mother. A baby is the crown of any woman's achievement.'

When she had been inspecting Mrs Vickers the baby had *moved*, cradling against Paraiti's palms. And oh, Paraiti's heart had gone out to it.

Mrs Vickers lost her temper. 'You stupid woman,' she raged. 'That is only the case if the husband is the father. How long do you think my husband will keep me when he discovers I am pregnant with another man's child?'

So that was it.

Mrs Vickers realised she had gone too far. She reached for a silver cigarette case, opened it and took out a cigarette. Maraea lit it for her. Then, coolly, 'Are you sure there is nothing you can do for me?' she asked, inhaling.

'You are already too far gone,' Paraiti answered. 'You will have to carry the child to term.'

Mrs Vickers exhaled. Then, 'Rip it from my womb,' she said in a voice that chilled.

'That would require you to be cut open,' Paraiti flared. 'It is too dangerous and you could die, along with the baby. Even if you survived you would be scarred and carry the evidence of the operation. Your husband would know that something had happened.'

'I will pay you handsomely for your work. And for your silence.'

'It is dirty, shameful work. No person would do it.'

'What you mean is that *you* will not do it,' Mrs Vickers said scornfully. 'Well, I will find somebody who is not as morally concerned as you are and, one way or another, I will be rid of this burden.' The smoke from her cigarette curled in the air. 'Maraea will pay you for your consultation. She will give you a cup of tea and cake before you leave.'

Maraea signed to Paraiti that the consultation was over. Just as Paraiti was leaving, she saw Mrs Vickers standing and tapping ash into an ashtray. Mrs Vickers' reflection locked eyes with Paraiti, and the room filled with eyes from all the mirrors.

'You doctors,' Mrs Vickers said. 'Pakeha or Maori, you're all the same, kei te mimi ahau ki runga ki a koutou.'

Paraiti gasped. She looked closely at Mrs Vickers' flawless skin and noted again the glaze so cleverly applied across her face. When she reached the kitchen she declined Maraea's offer of tea and cake. She wanted to get away.

'She will kill the baby,' Maraea told her, 'make no mistake about it. And if she kills her own self in doing it, well — if the baby is born, her life will be destroyed anyhow.'

You doctors, you're all the same, I urinate on all of you.

And Paraiti asked the question, even though she already knew the answer. 'He Maori ia?'

'Yes,' Maraea answered. 'She is Maori.'

4

It is another dawn and she drags her old bones up from sleep. She raises her hand in prayer, 'Kororia ki to ingoa tapu. Glory be to your holy name,' and praises God again for the gift of life and the joy of another day. What greater blessing could humankind receive than to be able to live and breathe, here, on the bright strand between earth and sky?

Five weeks have passed since Paraiti was at Ruatahuna. Horiana had just loved her bloomers; she half jested to Paraiti, 'They're so pretty, and it's such a shame to wear them under my dress; why don't I wear them on the outside?'

Pulling Kaihe after her and with Tiaki on guard, Paraiti had visited the sick, wounded and elderly of Ruatoki, Waimana and Murupara. Then, her heart lifting, she began a clinic for her patients at Te Kuiti.

It was so wonderful for Paraiti to be back among the people who had given sanctuary to her and Te Teira those many years ago. No sooner had she arrived than she was ordered by the great chief, Whaturangi, to pitch her tent close to Te Tokanganui a Noho meeting house, the great 'unification' marae, prototype for most of the later Ringatu meeting houses. 'Your dad would be cross with us if we didn't acknowledge you,' her cousin Peti growled, 'and there are enough angry ghosts floating around us as it is.' Indeed, in Paraiti's honour, a special remembrance service was held for Te Teira in the meeting house. Sitting there, within the latticed walls and with the beautiful painted kowhaiwhai rafters soaring above her, Paraiti again honoured the morehu, the loyal remnants of Te Kooti, survivors in a changing world.

Then it was down to business again. A stream of patients waited for a consultation, with Peti at the flap of the tent. A young man with a broken leg would now be able to walk, following Paraiti's skilful manipulation of his bones. An older forester, who had chopped off three fingers of his right hand, had the wounds cauterised. A child with chronic asthma would now breathe more easily if he followed the regime of herbal inhalants and exercises that Paraiti gave his anxious parents. A young girl was brought in covered in pustules; Paraiti looked after her during the night, using her poultices to draw out the pus and her soporifics to bring down the girl's fever. And if Paraiti was not able to cure all those who sought her help, at least she had tried to make them more comfortable.

From Te Kuiti, Paraiti cut across to the lands of Te Whanau a Apanui: Te Teko, Whakatane, Te Karaka and Ohiwa Harbour. More patients, more successful diagnoses and treatments, and always humour, as people laughed in the face of their illness or impending death. Like the old kuia, wasting away; when Paraiti inspected her, she was horrified, saying, 'E kui, you are all skin and bones.' To her, Paraiti had given a strong herbal painkiller, her skilful massaging hands, and the gift of a few more precious days to breathe and to praise the Lord.

Then, just after leaving her clinic at Ohiwa Harbour, Paraiti had a disturbing dream. The dream was a jumble of chaotic images. A face on fire — it was her face. A ngarara bearing down on her; she took up her rifle and shot at it. As the ngarara went by, Paraiti saw a woman with auburn hair coiled within the ngarara's slithering entrails. Then Charlie Chaplin appeared — how did he get into her dream? He was in a hut and it was seesawing on the edge of a cliff. But it wasn't Charlie Chaplin at all — it was Paraiti herself. Suddenly, as the hut slid over the cliff, Te Teira appeared, put out a hand and pulled her out of the hut. He cupped Paraiti's chin in his hands and wiped her face clear of the scar. He did this again and again.

Paraiti woke up puzzled and anxious. What did the dream mean?

The dream gnawed at Paraiti as she travelled around the coastline from Opotiki to Omarumutu, Torere and Maraenui. Wherever she went, she performed her healing duties. As for Tiaki, Ataahua and Kaihe, they loved swimming in the sea. Paraiti took Tiaki fishing with her in a favourite lagoon. She speared a fish and let the spear sink with the fish down to the bottom. 'Kia tere,' she commanded Tiaki. Immediately he dived after the speared fish, swimming down, down, down until he was able to grab the spear in his teeth and return to the surface.

Camping on the beach one evening, Paraiti saw an uncommonly bright star blazing across the sky. That night, she had the dream again. It had changed in two respects: the auburn-haired woman had now become the ngarara, and it was a child who was caught in its slithering shape.

—

This morning, Paraiti is waiting for Tiaki to bring her breakfast. Perhaps he has gone fishing without her and will bring her back a nice silver-finned kahawai. Of course she will have to throw it back into the sea — first fish to Tangaroa — but the thought of a fish for breakfast is enticing. She leaves her tent to get some driftwood together for a fire to boil water for her manuka tea. She puts the skillet on the fire so it will be ready for Tiaki's catch.

As she is ranging along the beach, with the surf rolling in, she sees an old koroua sitting on a log in the middle of a vast expanse of sand. He is smiling at her and waving to her as if he knows her.

As soon as she sees him, Paraiti's heart bursts with pain and love. She drops her driftwood and runs towards him like a young girl. When she gets nearer, he motions her to sit down next to him.

'Hello, daughter,' Te Teira says. 'Isn't it a lovely morning?'

Paraiti smiles at him. 'Yes, Dad.'

He closes his eyes and sniffs the sea air. 'Mmmn, kei te whiti te ra, such a day brings back so many memories, daughter.' Then he looks at Paraiti again, and she can feel herself drowning in his eyes, irradiated with his love. 'You always had good hands, daughter. They can save lives and they can heal people. You know what you have to do.' Then he is gone.

After breakfast, Paraiti talks to her animals. 'Well, Tiaki, Ataahua and Kaihe, I know you are expecting us to head southward to Ngati Porou, and I know you like to visit kin at Tikitiki, Tokomaru Bay, Tolaga Bay and Whangara, but we have to cancel our travels; maybe we'll go to Ngati Porou another day. Instead, we will go straight home.'

The animals simply look at her with a puzzled expression. 'So? What are we waiting for? Let's get going.'

Paraiti puts on her wide-brimmed hat. She packs the saddlebags, says a karakia on the beach and sprinkles sea water over her head and those of her animals. She taps Ataahua on his knees and mounts him.

It will be a long, hard ride. She wants to send a telegram from Opotiki and be at the Waioeka Gorge by nightfall, and reach Gisborne in two days' time, if all goes well.

Better get a move on. 'Me hoki matou ki te wa kainga,' she orders.

The waves thunder and spray around her as she heads inland.

5

Two days later, and Mrs Rebecca Vickers waits in the upstairs drawing-room of her home on Waterside Drive.

She is smouldering with irritation. Yesterday, Maraea had brought news that Scarface had telegraphed from Opotiki to say that she was returning to Gisborne, and had a matter of mutual benefit to discuss. An appointment has been arranged for this evening.

Mrs Vickers wears her auburn hair unpinned. She is dressed in a long crimson robe. Her full and generous pregnancy is clearly showing. Her backbone has curved to make space for the baby, and all the other organs have found their places around the whare tangata.

All her attempts to end her pregnancy have failed. The last butcher left her for dead on the bathroom floor. But the baby is still alive inside her.

Lighting a cigarette, she looks out the window. The day is already beginning to wane. She rings the bell for Maraea and tells her to bring the latest edition of *The Tatler* and switch on a reading lamp. The magazine has a full-page photograph of a young film actress, Merle Oberon: rich black hair, high noble forehead, exquisite cheekbones, the neck of a swan, and skin of unsurpassed whiteness. Regarded as the quintessential English rose, Merle Oberon is the woman of her generation — looks, style and manners — on whom Rebecca Vickers has modelled her own image. Opalescent eyes blazing, she throws the magazine to the floor. Waiting for Paraiti, she broods, eyes unblinking. If she doesn't play her cards right, everything will be over. Everything.

What is Mrs Vickers' secret? She has been passing for white since she was a young girl of twelve. Her father was English, her mother a Maori woman he met in Auckland and promised to marry, but didn't. Rather than return to her kainga, Mrs Vickers' mother instead fled to Christchurch, where her daughter was born out of wedlock. Mrs Vickers is therefore a halfcaste. In other countries where interracial relationships — or miscegenation — lead to children, those children are called, by blood quantum, halfbreed, Eurasian, mulatto or quadroon. But Mrs Vickers is more white than brown. Pigmentocracy has enabled her to blend in and thus assure for herself all the benefits of being Pakeha. So began, with her mother's connivance, her process of crossing over the colour bar.

No moral judgement should be assumed about her masquerade. Why not applaud a woman who has been able so successfully to move into the Pakeha part of town? And why not congratulate her for the huge accomplishment of catching the eye of the elderly Mr Vickers? As many other women have done before her, Mrs Vickers has parlayed her youthful sexuality to obtain matrimony and entry to high society, which she would not have obtained by pedigree. Aided by the application of an acidic nitrate, she has kept her skin glazed like porcelain; she knows full well that her white skin is her passport. She has perfected her masquerade with a long period spent in London, and an even longer period among the Raj in India, where her husband's wealth was at her disposal. She is not willing to lose everything for the sake of a moment of adulterous passion.

Mrs Vickers does not know it, but Merle Oberon is, ironically, her perfect exemplar. Born in Karachi, India, the English actress maintains her position as a famous film star only because people do not know she is Eurasian. Like Mrs Vickers, Merle Oberon, the famous English rose, also bears the taint of the tar.

Suddenly, she hears footsteps. It is Maraea. 'Scarface has arrived. She is waiting for you in the parlour.'

—

Paraiti is unprepared for Mrs Vickers' appearance. One month on, pregnancy has given her a transcendent, astonishing beauty. In her crimson robe, she looks like a gorgeous katipo spider.

'You said you had a matter of mutual benefit to discuss with me,' Mrs Vickers says angrily. 'If you've come to gloat, you can get out now.'

Paraiti is exhausted from her journey. She has not detoured to Waituhi — her animals are tied up three streets away. She takes the upper hand. 'You want something from me,' she says, 'and if you agree to my terms, I will do it. I will begin the induction of your baby, tonight if you wish, and you will abort it ahead of its time.'

Mrs Vickers' eyes dilate. She turns her back on Paraiti and looks into the mirror above the fireplace, trying to mask her elation. Her reflection blazes in all the other mirrors in the room. 'Tonight? What is the method?'

'You will begin a herbal abortion. I will give you a compound which you will drink at least three times a day for the next seven days. The compound has ingredients which will bring on contractions and cause your whare tangata to collapse. By the sixth day, the compounds will affect the pito, the cord that connects your baby to your womb, and it will begin to constrict. To assist the process I will come every second evening to massage the area of the whare tangata and manipulate the baby inside. The massage will be deep, forceful and extremely painful for you. But both the compound and the massage should have the desired effect. On the seventh day I will return to physically assist your baby's expulsion from your womb.'

'Seven days?' Mrs Vickers considers the proposal. She rings the bell for the servant Maraea. 'When does Mr Vickers' ship arrive in Auckland?'

'In six days, madam,' Maraea replies.

'He will be expecting me to be there . . .' Mrs Vickers turns to Paraiti. 'You must take less time.' It is not a request; it is a command.

Paraiti stays her ground. 'Less time means more risk to you,' she answers. 'I have already accelerated the normal dosage. When the cramps begin, your body may not be able to cope with the strain. Your heart could go into arrest.'

'Less time, I say,' Mrs Vickers lashes. 'You already know how strong I am. Just rid me of my burden.'

Paraiti's head is whirling: Yes, Mrs Vickers has the stamina. She must allow her to think that she has the victory. 'So be it,' she nods. 'I will deliver your baby on the sixth day.'

Mrs Vickers smiles with satisfaction. Then, 'I want to know if the baby will be born dead or alive,' she demands.

Paraiti realises she must be very careful about her reply. According to her calculations the pregnancy is under seven months, but the foetus should be fully viable. If so, the baby would have to survive the poisonous and dangerous ordeal as the whare tangata collapses. It could be dead before the contractions pushed it into the birth canal. Paraiti's voice quivers with emotion. 'There is every possibility that the baby will be stillborn,' she says.

Mrs Vickers looks at Maraea. 'Every possibility,' she echoes mockingly. Self-possessed, always aware, she turns to face Paraiti again.

'And why are you doing this, Scarface?' She moves with surprising swiftness, cupping Paraiti's chin with one hand and, with the other, stroking the scar that crosses her face. The touch of her hand stings.

'He Maori koe,' Paraiti answers, pulling back. 'You are a Maori.' But she can still feel Mrs Vickers probing her soul, and she warns her, 'Kia tupato, tuahine. Be careful. What I am proposing to do is against the law. You push me and I will change my mind.'

The threat of withdrawal has the desired effect. Mrs Vickers blinks and steps back. But she is soon on the offensive again. 'You mentioned your terms. What do you want, Scarface?'

It is now or never. 'I will not require payment for my services,' Paraiti says quickly. 'You will not understand this, Mrs Vickers, but my purpose is to save lives, not to take life away. Whether the baby is dead or alive, I will keep it.'

'What are you up to?' Mrs Vickers asks. 'Wait here while I consider.'

Paraiti watches as Mrs Vickers and Maraea leave the room. She hears them talking in low voices. When they return, Mrs Vickers mocks, 'I had not realised that your motives would be so humanitarian, but I agree to your request. What option do I have? You hold all the cards. I should have known you wouldn't want blood money to go with it. But I warn you, Paraiti, if the baby is alive, take it quickly for I would soon murder it. Now let us begin the treatment.'

Asking Maraea to bring up the saddlebag containing her medicines, Paraiti instructs both women on the dosage and its frequency. She measures out the first dose and administers it. Self-confident though she is, Mrs Vickers' eyes show alarm. Her face increases in pallor; after all, it is a poison that is being administered to her. Following the dose, Paraiti begins to massage Mrs Vickers. The massage is light at first and Mrs Vickers sighs and relaxes into it. 'This is not so difficult to cope with,' she laughs. But then Paraiti goes deeper, stronger, faster — above, around and upon the mound of the whare tangata. Soon, sweat starts to pop out on Mrs Vickers' forehead and she groans, 'No, please, enough, no.' For half an hour Paraiti keeps up the massage, her eyes dark and her face grim, until Mrs Vickers starts to scream with the pain.

Paraiti stops. Mrs Vickers moans; she can feel the after-effects of Paraiti's manipulations rippling within her womb.

But the massage isn't over.

Paraiti administers a hard, shocking series of chops with her hands on and around the baby within the whare tangata, then applies relentless pressure on the baby. *Please child, forgive me, but this is the only way.* She can sense the baby beneath her hands, fighting the unbearable pain — and Mrs Vickers screams and loses consciousness.

'Every second day, this?' Maraea asks, horrified.

'Yes,' Paraiti answers. 'Meantime, make sure your mistress drinks the compound. This regime is the only way to achieve the abortion on the sixth day. Under no circumstances can we slow or halt the procedure.'

It is time for Paraiti to leave. Just as she does so, Mrs Vickers revives and, exhausted, speaks to her. 'You and I, Scarface, we are not so dissimilar. You wear your scar where people can see it. I wear mine where they can't. Our lives have both been influenced by them. Me pera maua.'

Paraiti ponders her words, and then nods in reluctant agreement. 'I can find my own way out,' she says. She walks down the stairs, along the corridor to the side door. As she walks down the pathway and closes the gate behind her, she is aware that Mrs Vickers is watching her go. She continues along Waterside Drive and, when she is out of sight of the house, her legs fail her and she collapses into the shadows. 'Oh, child, forgive me for the pain I have done to you tonight.'

My purpose is to save lives, Mrs Vickers, not take them away.

She hears panting and sees that Tiaki has joined her; he licks her face. In the distance, tied to a fence, are Ataahua and Kaihe. Sighing to herself, Paraiti joins her animals. They could be home by dawn.

'I have gambled tonight,' she says to Tiaki as she mounts Ataahua. 'I have played a game of life and death. Let us pray that I will win.'

Together they fade in and out of the streetlights and, finally, into the comforting dark beyond the town.

6

Normally, Paraiti would have spent the rest of her haerenga on a circuit of the villages closest to Waituhi. The old woman with a dog, horse and mule are familiar sights among the Ringatu faithful in Turanga, which the Pakeha have renamed Poverty Bay.

Paraiti would have travelled throughout the lands of Te Whanau a Kai, Te Aitanga a Mahaki, Tai Manuhiri and Rongowhakaata. Wherever the Ringatu festivals take place, there you would have found her. Where the faithful gather to sing, pray and praise God, there she would be also: Waihirere, Puha, Mangatu, Rangatira, Waioeka, Awapuni, Muriwai and many other local marae. Still avoiding te rori Pakeha, the Pakeha road, she would instead have ridden the old trails along the foothills or rivers, the unseen roads that crisscross the plains like a spider's web.

But for six days, Paraiti remains in Waituhi, venturing only every second day to Gisborne, and returning at midnight. 'Where is Scarface?' her people ask, puzzled at this change in her routine. 'Is she ill? What will happen to us if she is unable to visit this year?' And some, worried, come to Waituhi to knock on the door of her kauta. 'Are you all right, takuta?'

When they are patiently told that everything is kei te pai and that she is only delayed, they leave.

Even so, Paraiti decides to make an appearance at a Ringatu hui at Takipu, the large meeting house at Te Karaka, so that the people will see she's still alive and kicking. Takipu is so beautiful that Paraiti cannot help but be grateful that her whakapapa connects her to such a glorious world.

The hui incorporates a kohatu ceremony, an unveiling of the headstone of a brother Ringatu healer, Paora, who died a year ago. The obelisk, the final token of aroha, is polished granite, gleaming in the sun. It is a sign of the love for a rangatira. As Paraiti joins the local iwi, weeping, around the obelisk, she reflects on the fragility of life. 'Not many of us morehu left,' she thinks to herself.

Afterwards, she spends some time talking to Paora's widow, Tereina. 'It was a beautiful unveiling for a beautiful man,' she says.

'Ae,' Tereina replies. 'A woman must have a good man at least once in her lifetime and I was lucky, he was the best.' Tereina smiles at the memory. 'The men may be the leaders, but when they die, it is the women who become the guardians of the land and the future.'

Returning to Waituhi, Paraiti cannot shake off Tereina's comment about having a man in her life. She has always been alone with her animals, unloved by any man except her beloved father. Would things have been different if she had not been scarred?

Her mood deepens as she thinks of all the changes she has observed in her travels. Since she and her father saw the ngarara, the marks of the new civilisation have proliferated across the land. New highways and roads. More sheep and cattle farms. Where once there was a swingbridge there is now a two-lane bridge across the river. And although the old Maori tracks are still there, many of them have barbed-wire fences across them, necessitating a detour until a gate is found. On the gate is always a padlock and a sign that says 'Private Land. Tresspassers will be prosecuted. Keep out.'

The changes are always noted by the travellers of the tracks and passed on to other travellers, 'Kia tupato, beware,' because, sometimes, horses or children can be ensnared in coils of barbed wire discarded in the bush after the fences have been laid. Paraiti has sewn up many wounds inflicted by barbed wire as pighunters and foresters have rushed after prey in the half light of darkness.

So the travellers keep themselves up to date with the death of Maori country. And Paraiti suddenly recalls Mrs Vickers' words. *You wear your scar where people can see it. I wear mine where they can't.*

Of all the changes wreaked by civilisation, it is the spiritual changes that are the worst. The ngarara is not only physical; it has already infiltrated and invaded the moral world that Paraiti has always tried to protect. She cannot but compare Mrs Vickers' situation to that of the young girl in Ruatahuna — what was her name again, Florence? — who had lost three babies while they were still in the womb. In one case, the baby is strongly desired; in the other, unwanted.

Perhaps the marks that really matter are, indeed, the ones that can't be seen.

—

How Paraiti manages to get through the next six days, she will never know. She prays constantly, morning, noon and night, her karakia unceasing and seamless. All that sustains her as she hastens to Waterside Drive and her rendezvous with Mrs Vickers is her immense faith, and the words of her father, 'You know what you have to do.'

But every second evening, when Maraea meets her at the side door, 'Come in, quickly, before you are seen,' Paraiti feels sick to her stomach that all her efforts might be for nought — that, instead of saving the baby, she will be complicit in its death. And every time she administers the herbal compound, following it up with forceful massaging and then the rapid blows to the womb, she realises that her anxiety must be as nothing when compared to that of the baby in the womb.

What must it be like to be in the house of birth, a whare meant to nurture and sustain, undergoing the trauma as its walls and roof are caving in? And in that environment, with stitched tukutuku ripping apart, kowhaiwhai panels cracking, and the destruction of all the whakapapa contained therein, what must it be like for the baby? Where can it go when the poutokomanawa begins to collapse and the poisons begin to flood through the placenta that feeds it? Even when fighting back, how can it know that even this is anticipated and is part of its brutal eviction?

'Forgive me, child, oh, forgive me,' Paraiti whispers as she maintains the treatment. Ironically, Mrs Vickers' own strength and stamina are working in the baby's favour.

And on the sixth evening, when Mrs Vickers, groaning in pain, cries out, 'Now, Scarface, do your work and rid me of this child,' Paraiti plays her trump.

She has been stalling for time. 'Your cervix has not dilated sufficiently,' she says to Mrs Vickers. 'The door of the whare tangata is not wide enough to enable the baby's delivery.' Paraiti has not increased the dosage, nor the massage therapy; every hour improves the baby's chance of survival. Turning a deaf ear to Mrs Vickers' torrent of curses, Paraiti tells her, 'I will do it tomorrow night.'

'Kororia ki to ingoa tapu,' she prays to the evening sky and all throughout the next day. Her animals, sensing her anxiety, honour her fervency with barks, whinnies and brays of their own; otherwise, they stand and wait in silence and on good behaviour.

—

'You planned this delay all along,' Mrs Vickers seethes. 'Well, two can play at that game, Scarface.'

The final treatment has forced her waters to break. The birth has begun. The contractions are coming strongly — and the baby has slipped from the whare tangata into the birth channel.

Paraiti ignores the accusation. 'Your trial will soon be over,' she answers, 'and it will be advisable for you to focus on the difficulties ahead. A normal birth is difficult enough. One that has been induced as forcefully as this, and before time, is more so.'

Yes, Mrs Vickers has stamina all right but, even so, she is being truly tested. She is dressed in a white slip, the cloth already stained at her thighs. Her skin shines with a film of sweat.

'How do you wish to give birth, Mrs Vickers?' Paraiti asks. 'The Maori way or the Pakeha way?' She knows the question has a hint of insolence about it but, after all, Mrs Vickers has Maori ancestry and it needs to be asked. Although the Pakeha position is prone, unnatural, Paraiti assumes that this is the way Mrs Vickers would wish the baby to be delivered. Her answer, however, surprises Paraiti.

'My mother has prepared a place so that I can deliver the Maori way,' she says. 'If it was good enough for her illegitimate child, it is good enough for mine.'

Her mother?

Paraiti realises that Mrs Vickers is talking about Maraea. 'Ki a koe?' she asks Maraea, and she looks at the older woman to affirm the relationship.

Maraea averts her eyes but nods her head briefly. 'Yes, I am Rebecca's mother. But I never thought the pathway would lead to this, Scarface, believe me.'

There is no resemblance at all. One is old, dark, indecisive; the other young, fair, purposeful. What kind of unholy relationship, what kind of charade is this between daughter and mother?

Leading the way, and supporting her daughter as she goes, Maraea beckons Paraiti down the circular stairs and then a further set of steps to a small cellar. She switches on a light and Paraiti sees that Maraea has done her work well. Two hand posts have been dug into the clay, and beneath the place where Mrs Vickers will squat are clean cotton blankets and a swaddling cloth to wrap the baby in.

With a cry of relief, Mrs Vickers shrugs off her slip and, naked, takes her place between the posts in a squatting position, thighs apart. Her pendulous breasts are already leaking with milk. 'No, I won't need those,' she says to Maraea, refusing the thongs that her mother wants to bind her hands with. 'Do your work, Scarface,' she pants, 'and make it quick.'

Maraea has already taken a position behind her, supporting her.

'Massage your daughter,' Paraiti commands. 'Press hard on her lower abdomen and whare tangata so that the baby is prompted to move further downward.'

The whare tangata is collapsing. But there is a heartbeat — faint, but a sign — to reveal that the baby still lives. 'I am here, child,' Paraiti whispers. 'Kia tere, come quickly now.' She takes her own position, facing Mrs Vickers, and presses her knees against her chest.

'You will pay for this,' Mrs Vickers says. And suddenly her face is in rictus. She takes a deep breath, her mouth opening in surprise, 'Oh.'

Paraiti places her hands on Mrs Vickers' swollen belly. She feels the baby beneath, as it pushes head first against the birth opening. Paraiti's manipulation is firm and vigorous as she presses and hastens the baby on its way. The contractions are rippling, stronger and stronger, and the first fluids stream from the vagina as the doorway proudly begins to open.

'Now, bear down,' Paraiti orders.

Mrs Vickers does not flail the air. Her face constricts and she arches her neck with a hiss. With a gush of blood, undulation after undulation, the baby slides out, head followed by shoulders, body and limbs, into the world. The baby is dark-skinned with wet matted red hair.

'A girl,' Paraiti whispers in awe. 'Haere mai, e hine, ki te Ao o Tane. Welcome, child, to the world of humankind.'

Quickly, she cradles her, clearing her face of mucus, ready to give her the first breath of life.

'No,' Mrs Vickers instructs. 'Let it die.'

Paraiti does not heed her. Maraea is weeping, restraining Mrs Vickers as Paraiti clears the baby's mouth and massages her chest. Immediately, she starts to wail. Her eyes open. They are green, shining, angry.

Mrs Vickers falls back, exhausted. She doesn't even look at her daughter.

Paraiti cuts the umbilical cord and ties it with flax. She places the child at Mrs Vickers' breast.

Mrs Vickers looks at Paraiti. 'You broke your agreement to deliver me in six days. I now break mine. This child has no future. Get out.'

—

'Have I failed?'

Paraiti's faith makes her keep watch by the sickle moon on the house of Mrs Vickers. Around two o'clock in the morning, she sees Mrs Vickers and Maraea getting into the Packard.

Earlier, when Maraea showed Paraiti to the door, she said, 'Rebecca will not kill the baby in this house. She wants to, but I have convinced her of the spiritual consequences of such an act — of having a child ghost destroy the calm of her life. But she will get rid of it. Keep watch and follow closely after us.'

'E Tiaki,' Paraiti tells her dog, 'kia tere. Follow.' Keeping to the shadows, Tiaki slinks silently in pursuit. Paraiti follows after on Ataahua.

The Packard is travelling fast. Ataahua is at the gallop. Even so, Paraiti has trouble keeping up and has to rely on Tiaki to run ahead, keep watch, return to show Ataahua the way, and run ahead again. Nevertheless, together they manage to hold on to the thin thread of pursuit, and when Paraiti reaches Roebuck Road, she sees the Packard parked on the bridge overlooking the river. On the other side of the bridge is a small Maori settlement.

Paraiti quickly dismounts and watches from the darkness.

Mrs Vickers gets out of the car and takes a sack from the back seat. She moves very slowly and painfully but with determination. Paraiti hears a thin wail from within the sack. Her eyes prick with tears. She cannot believe Mrs Vickers intends to throw the sack in the river.

But Maraea is objecting. She struggles with her daughter, saying, 'Kaore, daughter, no.' Mrs Vickers slaps her and she falls to the ground. Then, taking up the sack, she throws it over the bridge as cavalierly as if she is drowning kittens.

'Aue, e hine,' Paraiti cries.

She must wait until the car turns and makes its way back to Waterside Drive. Once it has gone past her hiding place she runs to the bridge to look over. The sack is floating away on the dark river; it won't be too long before it sinks. 'Haere atu,' she yells to Tiaki. She points at the sack in the river and he jumps off the bridge and splashes into the water.

Paraiti's heart is beating fast as she slips and slides down to the river's edge. She can hear the thin wail of the child again. 'Kia tere, kia tere!' she urges Tiaki. The sack is becoming waterlogged and it is sinking. 'Quick, Tiaki, quick!'

He is too late. The sack disappears under the water.

With a yelp, Tiaki dives after it — has not his mistress taught him at a favoured lagoon to bring back speared fish from the sea? The depths of the river are dark, so dark. But something flicks across his nose, a trailing piece of twine from the sack as it goes deeper, and he lunges —

Tiaki breaks out of the water. In his teeth, he has the sack. 'He kuri pai!' Paraiti calls to him, 'Good dog. Hoki mai ki ahau. Bring the baby to me.'

Her usually clever fingers are so clumsy! They take so long to untie the knot. 'Do your work quickly, fingers, quickly.'

And, oh, the baby is so still, with the tinge of blue on her skin. She already has the waxen sheen of death upon her. 'Move quickly, hands, you have always healed, always saved lives. Give warmth to the child, massage the small heart and body to beat again and to bring the water up from her lungs.

'Quickly, hands, quickly. And now —'

Paraiti holds the baby by the ankles and, praying again, gives the child a mighty slap on her tiny bottom.

The heart begins to pump, the lungs expel the water and the baby yells, spraying the water out of her mouth. She tries to draw breath but starts to cough; that's good, as she will get rid of all the water from her lungs. Very soon she is breathing and crying, and Paraiti continues to rub her down, increasing her body warmth. Tiaki noses in to see what she is doing. He whimpers with love and licks her.

'Oh, pae kare,' Paraiti says to herself. 'Oh, thank God.' She takes a moment to calm down. Then she addresses the baby, 'I will call you Waiputa,' she says, 'Born of water.' She sprinkles her head with water to bless her.

Waiputa is already nuzzling Paraiti's breasts. 'You're not going to have any luck with those old dugs,' Paraiti tells her. 'I better find you a wet nurse.' She looks across the river at the Maori settlement; there's bound to be some younger woman there, breastfeeding her own child, who owes Paraiti a favour and won't mind suckling another child.

As for the future? Paraiti smiles to herself. 'What a menagerie we will make, Waiputa! A scar-faced woman, two old nags, a pig dog and you.'

Others had begun their lives with less.

7

Seven years later.

Time has been kind to Paraiti. Although her eyesight has dimmed a little, her memory is as sharp as ever, her medical skills intact, and her hands still do their blessed work. Tiaki has grown a bit greyer and is not as formidable a hunter in the forest as he used to be; instead of hunting a second pigeon he sometimes nips the first one on a wing so that it can't fly too far and, when Paraiti releases it, sneakily, that is the same one he brings back. Both Ataahua and Kaihe are casting a keen eye on the pasture across the road where they can be retired to live out the rest of their years. Time for some other young colt and mule to take over.

This morning Paraiti woke as usual at dawn, said her karakia, performed her ablutions, packed the saddlebags and set off down the road. She still makes her annual haerenga and, in the year 1936, she is on her way to a hui at Te Mana o Turanga, Whakato marae, Manutuke, the birthplace of the prophet Te Kooti. Oh, how she loves that meeting house! So full of carvings and stories of the people. Whenever she visits, it is like the past comes to life before her.

And she is so looking forward to the hui, too. There are two major thanksgiving festivals in the annual Ringatu calendar: one is held on 1 June, coinciding with the beginning of the Maori New Year, when the mara tapu is planted to commemorate God's promise of salvation to all humankind; the other is held on 1 November, the celebration of the Passover, established by the prophet Te Kooti according to Exodus 40:2: 'Hei te ra tuatahi o te marama tuatahi koe, whakaara ai i te tapenakara o te teneti o te whakaminenga.'

The tapu is lifted from the sacred garden and what has been planted on 1 June is harvested — symbolic of the resurrection of Christ. In this ceremony of 'the Lifting of the First Fruits', the people make a commitment for the next six months to walk in righteousness.

Paraiti usually travels by the side of the Pakeha roads now. Many of the great Maori tracks are fenced off, and the last time she travelled on Rua's Track, she had trouble hanging on when she was negotiating the steepest part. But she still grumbles about the ways that civilisation is advancing through the world, and she is always pointing out more of its marks.

She comes to the fork of the road where roadmen have been constructing a combined road and rail bridge. She's never seen one quite like it. The road has been made of a black and sticky material. Tiaki sniffs at it and growls. Ataahua and Kaihe stand patiently waiting for the order to move across.

'It might be like the Red Sea,' Paraiti mutters. 'We could be halfway and next minute, aue, the waves will come over us.'

'No it won't, Nan,' a young voice says. 'It's called tarseal. Come on, there's no traffic. Let's cross now.'

Riding Kaihe is a pretty young girl, dark, with auburn hair. Paraiti has an assistant now, a whangai daughter, Waiputa. Waiputa now fills her waning years. She is someone to love; the new seed for the future, blossoming from Paraiti's old life. In turn, Waiputa is someone who loves her Matua. They make a good team, the scarred one and the unscarred one.

'Tarseal, eh?' Paraiti answers. 'You're learning lots of big words at that school of yours.'

She pulls Kaihe across the black river. Aue, motorised traffic is faster than a horse and an old mule. It can come out of nowhere and is onto you before you know it. Roaring across the bridge like a ngarara comes a huge sheep truck and trailer.

'Quickly, Nan,' Waiputa says. 'We have to get to the other side of the road.'

But Paraiti knows how fast she can go. Quick? She is already at quick. There's nothing to do except face the ngarara. 'E tu,' she says to Ataahua and Kaihe. Together, they turn to the oncoming monster. Paraiti reaches for her rifle.

The truck driver signals to her, 'Get off the road,' and then slams on the brakes. The truck squeals to a halt, its trailer rattling, wheezing, collapsing before the old woman and her whangai daughter. The driver swears and starts to open the door. But when he sees the old, greying dog snarling and the little red-haired girl baring her teeth, he shuts it again, quick and lively. 'Stupid old woman,' he yells at Paraiti as he drives his truck around them.

Paraiti gets to the other side of the road. Waiputa looks at her and wags a finger. 'Bad girl, Nan. We could have been killed.'

'I know,' Paraiti answers. 'And I realise it was just a truck. But you know, in the old days, I would have shot it.'

Paraiti peers at the sun and begins to laugh and laugh. Then, looking at the road ahead she pulls down her sunhat and says to Waiputa, Tiaki, Ataahua and Kaihe:

'Looks like we're just going to have to last forever.'

meeting elizabeth costello

It is his friend, the Nigerian novelist Emmanuel Egedu, who writes to tell him about the fifteen-day voyage from Christchurch to the Ross Ice Shelf aboard the *Northern Lights*, a cruise ship operated by the Scandia Line. 'I thought of you immediately,' Emmanuel says in his letter, 'and was quite shocked that although Scandia had invited writers from around the world to join the staff, they had not invited the famous Maori novelist, somebody representative of the very region the ship is travelling through.'

Emmanuel has underlined the word 'staff'. In his letter he explains that Scandia like to provide the paying guests with an onboard programme of education and entertainment. They offer berths to scientists, writers, artists, filmmakers and a faded Hollywood movie star in exchange for the occasional lecture or two.

'To be frank, Wicked,' Emmanuel continues, using the nickname his close colleagues have given him, 'it's been too long since that joyful time we spent together beside the pool at that dreadful literary conference in Djakarta and, should the ship get into trouble with icebergs, I am counting on you to clear the way by doing a Maori war dance. When the invitation comes, do accept it, won't you? Apart from which, you might enjoy meeting our dear Australian colleague, Elizabeth Costello.'

The proposal interests him and, when the offer comes, he does not refuse. On the morning of 10 December he joins the ship in Lyttelton harbour. There is a note waiting for him from Emmanuel: *Welcome aboard, Wicked. Do join me for a drink at the bar before dinner this evening.*

There is a scene involving his cabin, which is smaller than those assigned to Egedu and Costello, mainly an argument with the young, blond Swedish coordinator named Mikael, which we will skip. We resume at the bar where Emmanuel, wearing a vivid green dashiki and suave Italian shoes, welcomes him with a broad smile and firm handshake. After exchanging the usual pleasantries about how well the other is looking, Emmanuel notices the look of wariness as Mikael hoves into view.

'Making enemies already?' Emmanuel laughs. 'This will be like old times!' Emmanuel is referring to the scandal that erupted at Djakarta when Wicked gave an address accusing the white academics of maintaining the English canon out of fear of the black and indigenous peoples. The professors were the usual passive, boring Oxford lot who used university subsidies to have an exotic experience, but they were the majority of participants at the conference. He was stupid enough also to ostracise the black academics, whom he accused of conniving with the white academics, so he took to sunbathing by the pool, which was where Emmanuel had discovered and joined him. 'Secretly, my dear friend,' Emmanuel continues, 'the company tried to interest Keri Hulme, not you, in coming. What will you have? A martini on the rocks? Let's get you a drink, then come along and meet dear Elizabeth.'

He meets Elizabeth Costello at a cocktail party in an adjoining room. She is in her mid seventies, tall, somewhat dowdy and mannish, and when he introduces himself it is clear that she has never heard of him. She looks at him without any interest and he thinks she has already dismissed him as some bantam boxer punching outside his weight; the thought amuses rather than angers him.

'A Maori novelist?' she asks. 'Is there such a thing?'

'As much as there is an Australian novelist,' he answers. 'If there wasn't, you wouldn't exist, would you?'

'Neither would I,' Emmanuel intervenes, trying to keep the peace, 'as an African novelist.' Emmanuel effectively deflects her interest and, for a moment, they banter in an angry yet somehow complicit way about the questions of nationality and race and whether or not they should define the novelist.

He watches them both arguing, and he realises that Elizabeth Costello likes to control. He also suspects, from the way she and Emmanuel bait each other, that they have some intimate history. Later in the evening he quizzes Emmanuel.

'You do know, don't you, that although Elizabeth claims to be Australian, she was actually born in Africa? And although she has been married, her son is adopted? I met her when she was already a writer and I was just a young African country boy. She seduced me, but our sex was rather strange — isn't that always the way with white people?' Emmanuel gives an unsettling, disturbing wink. 'There's more to our Elizabeth than meets the eye.'

We skip to the next morning, when Elizabeth Costello is due to talk on 'The Future of the Novel'. Mikael does the introductions and recalls her curriculum vitae. He calls her 'the famous Australian writer', which she winces at, and refers to her fourth novel, *The House on Eccles Street* (1969), the work that made her name. The main character of the novel is Marion Bloom, wife of Leopold Bloom, principal character of *Ulysses* (1922) by James Joyce. In the past decade there has grown up around her a small critical industry; there is even an Elizabeth Costello Society based in Albuquerque, New Mexico.

When she stands to speak, it is clear that 'The Future of the Novel' is a talk Elizabeth Costello has given before, one that expands and contracts depending on the occasion. Given the small audience and the disdainful look she gives them, it appears today's will be the contracted version.

'The future of the novel is not a subject I am much interested in,' she begins.

The shock of this disclosure, coming as it does from a novelist who has made her life and reputation from writing, is such that it brings gasps of surprise from the audience, which it is clearly designed to do.

Unfortunately, Wicked goes further.

He laughs.

It is the manner of the laughter that offends. It is uncontrolled, loud, and when he looks into Elizabeth Costello's eyes, he knows that she will make him pay for it.

The rest of her talk is gestural. It is the kind of cynical, world-weary, analytical approach to writing, characterised by irony and self-hatred, which has made her the darling of the literary critics of the *Observer* and the *Times Literary Supplement*. It is all very dreary — a portrait of the artist as suspicious interrogator of any large purpose for the novel, the novel as non-novel, the writer as non-believer in any belief whatsoever, and the applause at the end lacks enthusiasm.

Elizabeth Costello takes it out on him. 'It was impertinent of you to laugh,' she says when the crowd has drifted away.

'I wasn't laughing at you,' he answers. 'I was laughing *with* you. You see, I happen to agree with you. The future of the novel, at least the traditional English novel, is a subject that I also am not interested in.'

Elizabeth Costello is not a person who likes to be agreed with. 'You use the conditional "at least",' she says, not about to give in quite yet. 'Define the traditional English novel.'

'It is the novel you write,' he answers. 'The novel that comes from the English tradition and which you practise in Australia.'

'Nonsense,' Elizabeth Costello replies. 'Kindly do not associate the Australian novel with the English tradition. It is totally different.'

'Is it?' he probes gently. 'I would suggest that the Australian novel is simply a version of the English novel. And, in your case, Ms Costello, it has reached the point of exhaustion. There is nothing at all Australian in your own work. *The House on Eccles Street*, for instance, is cannibalised from *Ulysses*, is it not? I'm not interested in the novel as a form that feeds upon itself.'

'And I presume that the *Maori* novel,' Elizabeth Costello replies, 'does not feed on the traditional English novel either? Presumably you have a way out to offer us?'

The battle lines are drawn.

'A way out?' he answers. 'It's not for me to offer you a way out, Ms Costello. I want the traditional English novel that you stand for dead and buried. Come to my session tomorrow, where I shall be conducting the funeral service.'

It is bold, foolish talk and he realises that his passion has got the better of him. He had, in fact, planned to give an address of another kind altogether: something about the lyricism and life-affirming literature of his own people as practised by Hone Tuwhare, Patricia Grace and new kids on the block, Hone Kouka, Briar Grace-Smith, James George, Kelly Ana Morey and Paula Morris. He has even brought along clips from the film *Whale Rider*, always something to please the audience and make them go 'Aaaah' at the image of an Arcadian paradisiacal world, a Maori Eden that exists somewhere beyond the jaded, recycled, western aesthetic which, not having any new directions to pursue, maintains itself by continuous plastic surgery. Instead, that afternoon, he crafts a new address: 'The Indigenous Novel in Antarctica'.

But Emmanuel Egedu is next on the bill. This we will skip, except to note that his address is called 'The Novel in Africa', and that again Emmanuel has got himself in the line of fire between his friend Wicked and Elizabeth Costello. Still steaming from her encounter the day before, Elizabeth Costello takes offence at Emmanuel's references to the orality of the African novel, his exoticisation of himself as an African novelist, and his talk of an 'essential' African writer. 'Why are there so many African novelists around,' Elizabeth Costello asks, 'and yet no African novel worth speaking of?'

Wicked thinks to himself, 'Obviously, Elizabeth Costello, you have never heard of *Things Fall Apart* by Nobel prizewinner Chinua Achebe,' but he lets it pass. Nevertheless, forewarned is forearmed, and the next morning, when he takes the podium for his own speech and sees Elizabeth Costello sitting in the front, he knows that she is gunning for him. Before he begins, he introduces a piece of exoticism and essentialism which is sure to get her back up: he utters a karakia, a Maori prayer, calling on the gods of the Maori to aid him in his speech. The prayer is in Maori and performative and there are sighs of pleasure from the audience. They have suffered through two impossible authors, neither of whom had once mentioned the kind of writers they love to read for a few minutes before turning out the light, but at least the third looks as if he will offer some entertainment. Emmanuel, sitting with a very nervous Mikael, knows better. 'As American columnist Ann Landers once said,' he whispers to Mikael, 'things are always darkest before they become totally black.'

He begins. 'When I came yesterday morning to listen to Ms Costello I was pleased to hear her say that the future of the novel is not a subject she is much interested in. She was talking about the traditional novel, of course, which I take to mean the novel as it has developed primarily through the western tradition she writes in. Perhaps if more people believed as Ms Costello does, we could all contribute to its death because, as far as indigenous writers are concerned, we owe absolutely no allegiance to the western tradition — and no favours.'

Around him he can see the poor audience looking at each other glumly: oh no, not another of these arrogant literary buggers.

'Let me try to substantiate my statement,' he continues. 'You see, the western novel is the ultimate achievement of a narrative tradition that has privileged the western way of seeing things, doing things and valuing what is good and what is bad according to western thinking — and indigenous people have been trapped in this western way since they were children. For instance, when I was a child, this narrative tradition was enshrined in nursery rhymes like Jack and Jill and Little Miss Muffet. You all know Jack and Jill, don't you? Why not recite it along with me?'

Ah, this is better. A few hearty souls begin to recite the nursery rhyme, no doubt remembering school days when life was lovely and people played cricket on the green. The human condition is ever hopeful. Time to open their eyes.

'Yes, well, just imagine a young Maori child trying to come to grips with what that nursery rhyme is saying. Who are Jack and Jill? Why is Jack wearing a crown? It's his own fault if he breaks it when he falls down. And why is he going up a hill to fetch water? What a silly place to put a well! We might laugh about his predicament, but the indigenous child has begun the terrible involvement in an upside-down world where nothing makes sense and people build wells on tops of hills. Little Miss Muffet reinforces his indoctrination. Recite this one with me, and then I will ask you the same questions I asked about Jack and Jill. Who is Little Miss Muffet? She, and Jack and Jill, have become the main characters in life's drama, and they are white characters; the Maori characters, by not being there, have been invisibilised and sidelined. They do not belong in the traditional narrative text. What's a tuffet? Cultural symbols and messages are being created, and a new language to replace the old. What are curds and whey? And why should Miss Muffet be afraid of a spider? My grandmother would say, "What a silly girl! Why doesn't she say hello to it, kia ora!" Because, you see, in our valley we talk to spiders. And this is the most damaging message of all: Miss Muffet is frightened of the spider. If she didn't run away from it she would probably have killed it. And by killing the spider, Miss Muffet would be telling all of us this should be our natural response. But for Maori it isn't. Your nice Little Miss Muffet with her golden curls and innocence would be nothing more than a murderer and she would be telling young Maori children that it is okay to murder. Her way of looking at the world is totally anathematic to ours.'

In the audience he hears a deep, tragic sigh. They are all thinking, 'Oh, but he looked so lovely in his photograph.' He presses on.

'You see, this is my business,' he continues. 'To critique history from an indigenous perspective and to evaluate and interrogate the processes by which indigenous peoples have been colonised, historicised and marginalised. And after all, would you expect otherwise? I am a Maori writer and therefore a member of the international indigenous literary tradition, those populations who are the original inhabitants of the land and who have been, in most cases, displaced. The populations I talk about have suffered the trauma, the psychic, physical and cultural disruption caused by the intervention of western practice and the imposition of its political, cultural, social and economic systems. From the very beginning of my writing career, therefore, I have tried to escape it and, ultimately, to oppose it.

'I made my first attack on the western form when I wrote my very first short story at the age of eleven. It goes like this: Once upon a time there was a princess locked in a tower guarded by a fierce dragon. Every day she would see a different handsome prince riding by on his white horse, and she would run to the window and yell, "Help me, help me, save me from this dragon!" But because she was so ugly, the princes on their white horses would keep on riding by to rescue a more beautiful princess further down the road. Day after day this would happen. Yet another handsome prince on yet another white horse until, one day, the princess got so sick and tired of waiting that she went out and married the dragon.'

There is laughter. Uneasy laughter, but laughter nonetheless. Mikael is looking very sick.

'Well, ladies and gentlemen, some people would say that my fiction has not improved. But do take note of what is happening. Although the story begins within the accustomed tradition of the fairytale, it soon begins to escape the frame. For instance, the princess is not pretty. The princes are not chivalrous. When the princess finally comes to her senses, she takes her future into her own hands. She leaves the land of safety and, by marrying the dragon, enters the land of danger. And the story does not end happily ever after — it goes somewhere else.

'All indigenous writers have had to do just this. Escape the frame. Subvert the main discourse. Take the future into their own hands. In our case, what we have tried to do is to find an escape route from the primary text, that alien construct you call the western novel, which enshrines what is known as the canon. The idea of a canon for literature appeared in the fourth century AD when a list of texts, primarily books of the Bible, were deemed worthier of preservation than others. Their truths were privileged over others. Their perceptions, world views, ethics and moral values were privileged over others. They distinguished the orthodox from the heretical. The canon had the effect of maintaining the status quo of the dominant culture: privileging the Bible, the works of William Shakespeare, so-called classics like *Heidi, Swiss Family Robinson, Oliver Twist, Jane Eyre, Robinson Crusoe, Wuthering Heights, Treasure Island, The Last of the Mohicans* — you get the picture. Critics of canon-formation, and I am one of them, have noted, however, a disturbing and indisputable fact about the canon: very few of its representatives have been non-Christian, non-white, women or lower class. So if you're looking for the Koran or the sayings of Buddha, forget it. If you're looking for a black author, they are not there, although perhaps Chinua Achebe and Toni Morrison may by now have made the list. Women and lower-class authors are probably also recent additions because the canon, by privileging men of the upper classes, excluded women and the lower classes from the practice of writing.'

He pauses to take a sip of water.

'Let us take the case of William Shakespeare,' he resumes. 'I must admit that I love Shakespeare's works but my love for them must be balanced with my understanding of their early role as colonising texts because they were used to reinforce and legitimise the arguments that Europeans made to substantiate the civilising ethos and the displacement of indigenous cultures in our own lands. They also helped establish the primacy of the canonic story with its own canonic heroes and heroines, and a way of writing a story that has been difficult to escape. The imposition of

Shakespeare's works as literary classics has been so successful that there are now many indigenous professors and students who study and keep the Shakespeare industry going in their own countries. They have indeed been well and truly colonised. However, there is one character in Shakespeare who, ironically, invokes for us the dilemma of the indigene. His name is Caliban and he appears in *The Tempest*. This is his cry, the voice of the "savage and deformed slave" against the rule of his master, Prospero, who has taken control of his island:

> This island's mine, by Sycorax my mother,
> Which thou tak'st from me. When thou cam'st first,
> Thou strok'st me and made much of me, would'st give me
> Water with berries in't, and teach me how
> To name the bigger light, and how the less,
> That burn by day and night; and then I lov'd thee,
> And show'd thee all the qualities o' th' isle,
> The fresh springs, brine-pits, barren place and fertile.
> Curs'd be that I did so! All the charms
> Of Sycorax, toads, beetles, bats, light on you!
> For I am all the subjects that you have,
> Which first was mine own king; and here you sty me
> In this hard rock, whiles you do keep from me
> The rest o' th' island —

The anger, the invective, is showing in his delivery. He can sense that feathers are ruffling in the audience.

'Caliban, of course, in the Shakespeare play does not triumph. After all, *The Tempest* is not his story and he is not the main character.

'Neither is Man Friday in Daniel Defoe's *Life and Death of Robinson Crusoe*. This novel, written in 1719, can of course be read in many different ways, but what strikes you, from an indigenous perspective, is its function as a Christian allegory and its explicit approval of the hierarchies structuring colonialism and race. Crusoe is the imperialist conqueror. When he is shipwrecked, he tries to maintain the hierarchies of superiority not only as a Christian but also as economic man, by domesticating the Amerindian Man Friday.

'These hierarchies — Prospero/Caliban or Crusoe/Man Friday — are maintained and privileged in just about any novel or work of art perpetrated by western writers and artists in which indigenous characters occur. You can see them at work in James Fenimore Cooper's *The Last of the Mohicans*, published in 1826. Regarded as a landmark of American fiction, from an indigenous perspective the novel raises a number of concerns. First it established as an accepted literary convention the division of Native Americans into two groups: those like Chingachgook, the Mohican of the title, were good because they sided with the settlers. Those like Magua, chief of the Mingos, who did not side with the settlers, were bad. Incidentally, the character of Magua could well have been modelled, not on an Indian chief at all, but rather on a Maori chief named Te Puhi who led the *Boyd* massacre of 1809, widely publicised in the United States, in which sixty-six people were killed. Actually, in the novel, both Chingachgook and Magua die because there was, in the white American settler mind of the times, no place for the Indian, good or bad. It was, after all, this book and the subsequent novels in the Leatherstocking saga that white men were reading in Kentucky when all Native Americans in that state were banished to the plains by President Andrew Jackson and given blankets infected with smallpox to accompany them on their journey; it was these books that the pioneers had read or were reading when they pushed forth to those very plains and set about duplicating in the west what had already been accomplished in the east: making the Native American vanish.

'And if you couldn't kill off indigenous characters, you appropriated them. Consider Herman Melville's *Typee*. Melville was the esteemed writer of *Moby Dick* but *Typee* was not his finest hour. In the book there appears a character by the name of Fayeaway, who is supposed to be a native Melanesian girl from a cannibal valley, except that she is very fair and has blue eyes. She is the prototype for all those 1950s Hollywood movies where the indigenous heroine was played by Rhonda Fleming, Debra Paget, Joan Taylor, Cyd Charisse, Gene Tierney or anyone remotely exotic-looking. She is really the European playing dress-ups and masquerading in indigenous drag. The white writer likes to mimic, to steal, to play in various guises.

'The African writer, Nobel prizewinner Chinua Achebe, commenting on these outside perspectives, said at the beginning of his career, "It dawned on me that although fiction was undoubtedly fictitious, it could also either be true or false" — and he was right. And it was for this reason that I began my own career as a Maori novelist and an indigenous writer. So, ladies and gentlemen, we're almost at the end of my address —'

The audience are looking at one another, glad that they will soon have the chance to escape the session and go to the bar for a stiff gin and tonic.

'To reiterate, I am pleased that Elizabeth Costello has said she is not interested in the future of the traditional novel. I repeat, neither am I. If I had my way I would throw Eng Lit out of the syllabus. When will we stop being seduced by American and British literature and disconnect the white umbilical we have all been feeding from all these years? When will we give primacy to our own indigenous Shakespeares, Goethes and Prousts? When will European countries stop exporting to the colonies all those books called classics by dead white guys? When will we stop exhibiting all the classic symptoms of the Divided Self? Only when we stop feeding off the white breast.'

There is a gasp of outrage from the audience.

'In my own career, I have tried not to participate in the maintenance of the western tradition and its culturally based outcomes. I have tried to escape the western canon and, if I haven't always been successful, I have at least subverted it or bent it out of shape at times. And I have tried to write in opposition to it, by creating the Alternative Text to the Primary Text. How? By writing the Indigenous Story. The story of Caliban. The story of Man Friday. The story of Magua. By saving that spider from a little blonde-headed, sweet, innocent-yet-murderous girl called Little Miss Muffet. Thank you.'

There is a stampede for the doors. Mikael is trying to soothe the passengers. His job is on the line. Elizabeth Costello waits until the bitter end.

'It was most impertinent of you,' she begins, 'to use my speech as the starting point for what can only be called a rant.' Then she slaps him. 'You know you deserve that,' she says.

Elizabeth Costello has always presumed to have the upper hand, but she is totally unprepared for what happens next.

He slaps her back.

'You are not excused,' he says, 'simply because you are an old white woman, from the perpetuation of the tropes of white power.'

He is pleased to see the fear in her eyes.

Later that evening, there is a knock on the door. It is Emmanuel, shaking his head mournfully and clucking. 'I understand, my dear Wicked,' he says, 'that you are to be put off on the next iceberg sailing north.'

The cruise continues. The frozen continent is beautiful, the ice scintillating with indescribable colours. The southern sea has the cool opaque sheen of inscrutable dreams.

A week later, the SS *Northern Lights* returns to Christchurch. There is a scene with Mikael regarding his payment, which we will skip.

When the ship puts in to the harbour, Wicked goes down to Emmanuel's cabin to say goodbye.

'You're not leaving us, are you?' Emmanuel teases. He has found sexual entertainment in the form of a beautiful Russian singer. 'But no doubt we'll meet again. Perhaps in California? I have been offered a position as a research fellow at the University of California campus at Irvine. I am genuinely fond of you, my Maori brother.'

He walks down the passageway. He decides, what the hell, to say goodbye to Elizabeth Costello. The door is not fastened properly and when he raps on it, it swings slightly open.

He looks through the door and sees a mirror. The mirror is angled in such a way that it shows the interior of the cabin: a small bedroom and a bathroom. The door is open to the bathroom, and he sees another mirror. In the mirror is reflected the image of somebody who appears to be Elizabeth Costello. But is it?

Whoever it is, is putting a wig on their head and slipping into female drag. *There's more to our Elizabeth than meets the eye.*

At that moment, the whole history of western literature suddenly clicks into place. Why had he never seen it before?

Appalling and chilling though it is, it all starts to make sense to him.

author notes

i've been thinking about you, sister

In March 2006, Brian Bargh emailed me to ask if I would contribute a story to an anthology of Maori writing that Huia Publishers was jointly publishing with Welsh language publisher, Parthian. We discussed the proposal over the telephone — but there was a catch: could I write a story of the kind I had published in *Pounamu Pounamu*, my first book, in 1972? I explained to Brian that thirty-four years is a very long time for a writer and I had moved on from that kind of natural, lyrical story. I recommended that he look at 'Going to the Heights of Abraham', which I published in 2000 and was probably the last best example of what he was looking for.

'What about that story you read at the Auckland Writers' Festival last year?' he asked. I was taken aback. I had been a guest in two sessions — 'The Nature of Blood' with James George and my old friend Caryl Churchill and 'Maori Battalion March to Victory' with James George, Patricia Grace and Mick Brown.

I realised that what Brian was referring to was one of the anecdotes I had mentioned in the latter session, but which one? I'd talked about the seventy-fifth anniversary of Gallipoli, fiftieth anniversary of the end of World War II, the attempts by family and friends of Private Manahi to get his bravery recognised by the awarding of the Victoria Cross, and my honour at being best man at the wedding of my ninety-year-old father-in-law, Tony Cleghorn — Tony had been in Intelligence during World

War II and served with Dan Davin and Paddy Costello. I'd gone on to refer to a visit I had made to the Vietnam Memorial in Washington DC — a stunning black wall on which are listed all the soldiers who fought in Vietnam — and then discovering, in a small glade not far from the memorial, a smaller one commemorating the women who had fought in Vietnam, but there was no similar memorial to gay men and women. When I came to write *The Uncle's Story* (2002), I was inspired to honour gay men in a war where they were not supposed to be, to help ensure that the processes of history are inclusive of all men, women, children, victors and victims, the dead and the living.

I concluded by telling about my parents' visit in 1989 to the war grave of my mother's brother in Tunisia. 'I've Been Thinking About You, Sister' is a fictionalised and expanded version of that anecdote; family has always been central to my work. Along the way I explain why I couldn't write it the way I might have done thirty-four years ago.

ask the posts of the house

There are some events in boyhood which become crucial in the formation of your sense of morality, ethics, justice, and which draw the line for what you will and will not accept when it comes to moral behaviour. One of those events occurred in 1959 when I was fifteen, and I first broached it in my novel, *The Matriarch*, in 1986. Since then, I have periodically tried to write the story, originally called 'Happy Families', but always discontinued it. When my publisher at Reed, Peter Dowling, asked me to consider publishing this collection, the first of my unfinished stories to come out of my desk was 'Happy Families'. I wondered whether or not, this time, I could complete it.

The writing of the story was done in November 2006 when I was hard at my job as a professor at the University of Auckland, marking exams and creative writing portfolios. I try to teach my students to write through life but, in the case of this story, ten minutes here, half an hour there, on planes to Wellington for board meetings and other engagements, was really pushing it and not good for cohesion or consistency; but the salmon were running.

I wonder why my earlier attempts to write this story failed? I take solace from a recollection made by my friend and colleague, Christine Cole

Catley, who was a good friend of Frank Sargeson, one of New Zealand's greatest writers. Christine had sent him a manuscript to look at, 'a first novel by a member of one of my writers' workshops. I must make sure, he said, to tell writers to get well away from any autobiographical framework. This novel, he said, was surely too close to the writer's life. "Yes, yes, I can see why you like it, quite so, but tell her to make the imaginative leap!"'

By the way, I have three Rs which I apply to my writing process: research, (w)riting and revision. Each is given equal weight, and I wouldn't dream of letting my work go to print without putting it through the rigorous process entailed. Although research doesn't always appear as obviously in this story, it is the two thirds of the iceberg that you don't see. It is the unseen or psychic text that supports the written text.

in the year of prince harry

The title of this story is all that remains of the novel which I had planned to write in 1996 when I turned fifty-two. However, the year previously I had published *Nights in the Gardens of Spain* (1995), and because the two books would have been similar — though one was a tragedy and *Prince Harry* would have been a madcap comedy or farce — I put it aside and instead finally completed *The Dream Swimmer* (1997), which had been knocking at my door since 1987. Apart from anything else, I didn't think I could make the transition so quickly from the dramatic nature of *Nights* to the lighter touch of 'In the Year of Prince Harry'.

Originally I had planned the novel to take place over the entire year of a gay man's life as he approaches fifty. I had been at a party of mainly younger and desperate gay men who thought that life was over at forty. I wanted to write the novel to celebrate the fifty-year-old gay man and to affirm his existence and place in a world that emphasises youth. I have learnt to laugh along with life and to be always grateful that life keeps on coming at you, whether you want it to or not.

Most novelists will agree, I think, that writing madcap comedy or farce is extremely difficult. Changing a novel to a short story format is also difficult. If you compress too much, the short story becomes a digest version. Here the compression has been achieved by removing two storylines. Had I written 'Prince Harry' as a novel, the three sons would have been two daughters and the book would have been a sequel to *Nights*.

'Prince Harry' exemplifies how music has greatly influenced the way I think about the construction of the long short story and novel. If I hadn't become a writer I would have loved to further my studies in music and become a composer. The closest I have come to music composition has been as a librettist working with New Zealand composers Ross Harris (*Waituhi: Life of the Village* and *Tanz der Schwäne*), Dorothy Buchanan (*The Clio Legacy*), Peter Scholes (*Symphonic Legends*), Rod Biss (*Waiata Aroha*), John Rimmer (*Galileo*), Edwin Carr (*Ariki*; unperformed) and Gareth Farr (*The Wedding*); other music projects with composers Jenny McLeod, William Southgate, Jack Body, David Hamilton, Paul Grabowski, Marian Mane and Matthew Suttor either never got off the ground or were discontinued. Another somewhat epic project to write a four-opera *Ring* cycle, based on Maori myth, waits in the wings.

I can remember first thinking about the similarity of music composition with narrative composition when I heard a stunning lecture given by Anthony Burgess, the author of *A Clockwork Orange*, when I was a student at Victoria University of Wellington in the mid 1960s; he said that the condition of literature was most akin to music involving poetry, aesthetics, rhetoric, philosophy and what the Romans call *politior humanitas*. In my writing, I consider the key the work should be written in and I often construct the work in movements or acts, with due regard to statement, variation, harmony, recapitulation and resolution. The orchestration of the work matters immensely to me, and I have found that the advice of teachers such as Virginia Zeani to singers applies also to writing: 'Float the words on the breath! Make the sound round! Sing in the middle of the note! Bring out the colours! Sustain! Sustain!'

'Prince Harry' was completed just after watching fireworks over Piha beach when the year turned over from 2006 to 2007.

ihipi

In 2002 I was invited by Ray and Di Henwood to submit a proposal for a play to Circa Theatre, Wellington, for its twenty-first centennial celebration. My play, *Woman Far Walking*, had just been successfully staged by the International Festival of the Arts (2000) and was on its second tour of the country, and the proposal to write another play interested me. I knew that fine young Maori playwrights like Hone Kouka, Albert Belz and Briar Grace-Smith were writing wonderful plays set in contemporary New Zealand. What could I do that was different? I decided to propose a play set in mythological times. Its major point of difference would be that it was written entirely in Maori.

During the early 1980s, I had had a long and interesting conversation with Professor John Roberts about the idea of writing a dramatic piece in te reo Maori that would have about it the resonance of Maori myth. Neither of us was actually talking about the possibility that I could do such a thing — we were thinking of Hone Tuwhare, Katerina Mataira, Rore Hapipi or Arapera Blank — and, anyway, I had no competency whatsoever in te reo, and I was still in the ten-year embargo I had placed on my writing career in 1976. But the prospect had always intrigued me. In 2002, with the Circa proposal in mind, I thought of resurrecting it.

The dilemma was, which Maori myth? And would I be able to bring something fresh and original to it? Deciding that I couldn't, I turned my attention to creating a new Maori myth. 'Ihipi' was the result: a fusion of Egyptian and Greek myth, Kabuki theatre, and including personal homages to the Japanese writer Ryunosuke Akutugawa and filmmaker Akira Kurosawa. At the time I was hoping to achieve a drama of obsessional and sacrificial love, which could be performed in an abstract heightened manner invoking ancient classical theatre traditions from throughout the world. My notes indicate that the play was going to be divided into the classical Summer, Autumn, Winter, Spring, to correspond with the cycle of birth, life, death and renewal.

When I wrote to Ray and Di I warned them that they would either love or hate this. In the event, Circa decided to pass on the play and it was never written. But I have used my notes for it to write a short story version.

dead of night

'Dead of Night' first appeared in *Are Angels OK?*, an anthology edited by Bill Manhire and Paul Callaghan and published by Victoria University Press in 2006. The entire project, which was to explore the parallel universes of New Zealand writers and scientists and publish the resultant work, was sponsored by the Royal Society of New Zealand, the MacDiarmid Institute for Advanced Materials and Nanotechnology and the International

Institute of Modern Letters. As part of the project, I was honoured to join Paul Callaghan, Jo Randerson, Margaret Austin, Glenda Lewis, Kim Hill and Eva Radich in a trip to the United Kingdom to speak about 'Dead of Night', and what it was like to work with scientists, in a presentation to the Cheltenham Science Festival, Cambridge University and the Royal Society in London.

'Dead of Night' is one of the most vexatious literary challenges I have faced in my career. It took over five months and more than twenty drafts to write. It started off as one story and ended up as another. It took me out of the worlds I normally write in and into the worlds of science and mathematics, the whole history of the cosmological sciences and, well, the history of everything, really. And to write it, I relied tremendously on the collaboration with five scientists: Howard Carmichael, whose main field is quantum optics, David Wiltshire, whose research interests are in black holes, quantum gravity and theoretical cosmology, and Michael Walker, Rob Ballagh and Matt Visser. Any validity that 'Dead of Night' has in scientific terms is entirely due to them and, as you will note, I have credited Howard and David as co-writers of the story. My son-in-law, übergeek Stephen Pritchard, contributed the design specifications for *Endeavour*.

I like to think of 'Dead of Night' as a dissertation on the life and death of the space–time continuum. Like all my work, it is embedded with a Maori kaupapa and my constant environmental concerns. In my opinion it is not enough just to save the planet; we've got to give ourselves the chance to get off it so that future generations can fulfil their destiny and truly achieve the inheritance that belongs to them.

One of the major discussions that takes place in the story is whether or not God had a part in the creation of the universe and of our world. Because this is contestable to many scientists, and because I had to honour my scientist collaborators, I devised a particular schema which I borrowed from the 1940s classic film, 'Dead of Night'. In the film an architect by the name of Walter Craig stops at a house where there are five other people and tells them that he has seen them all before. So my story could, for instance, 1) similarly be about a man, lost in a mist, who comes across five people he has seen before in a dream, and his dream is about being on a spaceship called the *Endeavour* journeying to the end of time and space, or 2) really be, as it is written, a story about six people travelling to the end of the universe. Then, again, it could 3) be a story evolving out of a man's brain at the moment of death.

Whatever the reading, I did in fact write two endings for the story. The one that is printed is the original circular ending. For those who are interested, the following is the interventionist, 'second chance' ending published in *Are Angels OK?*. Further adjustments made to the story include the restructuring of the narrative as a countdown from 10 to zero.

'dead of night' alternative ending

The mathematical formulae stop.

Mrs Cortland presses Miss O'Hara's hands reassuringly. 'We'll be all right, my dear.'

The *Endeavour* rocks. The three aunties are like lifeboats beside it. They are chattering as if they know what is going on.

'Here we go, girls,' Aunti-1 says.

'Captain,' Hemi says, 'I'm getting readings of huge energy forces coalescing all around us. Something is happening.'

The ship rocks, and rocks again. Then everything is happening at once. Echoes of the whole titanic history of the universe are crowding in, pushing and jostling with each other, fighting for the last sliver of space. Every movement ever made. Every word ever spoken. Every television show ever broadcast. Every ray of starlight ever shone. Space is collapsing under its own weight.

'It won't be long before the gravitational waves overwhelm us,' Captain Craig says. In his mind's eye he sees a trillion black holes in collision. Tears spring to his eyes at the thought of all that human history — despite the self-destructiveness, there had also been so much life, so much hope, so many dreams achieved and triumphs witnessed. As one of the last survivors, Captain Craig raises his voice in poroporoaki, in defiant tribute to the generations upon generations of men and women who had lived in this life and world:

> Tena koutou nga iwi katoa o te Ao,
> Te Huinga o te Kahurangi,
> Tena koutou —

'Look!' Professor Van Straaten says.

His voice is hushed, tinged with awe. The universe may be in its death throes, but a countervailing option is making itself apparent on all Hemi's screens. It's an image that is so familiar, oh so familiar.

'The double helix,' Dr Foley whispers.

He rushes to the window to look out, closely followed by the others. The double helix is a million miles high. It is also the koru pattern, twisting and turning — a dazzling signal in the flaring, blossoming light. The spiralling helices flow around the *Endeavour*, enclosing it, locking it into the world of now. The world of us.

'What is happening?' Mrs Cortland asks.

'We're getting a second chance,' Dr Foley says.

There is a moment's silence. Then Hemi's computers go haywire. Huge twisting ribbons of energy, of heating and expansion and contraction, come pouring around *Endeavour*. The ship becomes the binding central nucleus, sealed into the double helix. Captain Craig looks at Professor Van Straaten and nods to him:

'You are right, Professor. The end of the universe is not a place. It is a time. It's alpha and omega, the beginning and the end.'

Turbulent and ten-dimensional, time begins to vibrate in different modes, splitting, rejoining and moving fluidly backwards and forwards — and *Endeavour* rides on time's waves through an everchanging, swirling continuum.

Hemi's voice comes, soothing, to Captain Craig. 'Ten seconds to the first impact from the universe's shock waves. Nine, eight, seven . . . Sir, time to open the codicil to your secret instructions.'

'Open,' Captain Craig orders. On all screens there appears one word:

RESET.

'Four, three, two, one —'
'Do as ordered,' Captain Craig says.
'Zero.'

0

Time fades to nothing.

Real nothing. Not even space. Outside? Outside there is no outside.

Space is time and time is space. Space enough, perhaps?

All there is is the double helix, floating within an immense womb of blackness. At its centre, *Endeavour*, cradled by the three aunties.

'Up, up and away, in my beautiful, my beautiful balloon!' Aunti-3 sings. Her voice is ecstatic.

'Yes,' Aunti-1 and Aunti-2 respond. 'We've done our job.'

Vibrating, singing, pulsing, the double helix splits, streaks, fragments, rejoins, coalesces, mottles, blossoms and flares. At each transformation, it refracts and flashes like a scintillating crystal ribbon, repeating itself over and over, twisting and turning, binding together futures without end:

Now is everything and everything is now.

Breathtakingly beautiful, the complex helices twist into the primeval Word:

The Greek letter Ψ.

The wave function of the universe, the Word reveals all the infinite, heart-aching wonder of all our possibilities.

Then:

$$H\,|\Psi> = 0$$

The ship is like a bloodied jawbone thrown through the air. Time begins again. The energy is more than 10 billion billion billion nuclear detonations. It roars over the *Endeavour*. In a trice, the ship is incinerated. Her avatar, Hemi, gives a huge, deep sigh. The glorious aunties are like angels on fire, fluttering into oblivion.

Captain Craig feels an intense pain. He looks at Mrs Cortland, Miss O'Hara, Monsignor Frère, Professor Van Straaten and Dr Foley, wanting to reassure them. But of what? Just before the endorphins kick in, he has a regretful thought:

'But we didn't have time to say goodbye to each other.'

—

And he is falling.

He feels a dizzying rush of acceleration, as if he is being sucked at headlong speed down a tunnel of dazzling light. Onward and onward he roars, and the sensation is so delirious that he wants to laugh and laugh:

Tuia i runga, tuia i raro,

Tuia i roto, tuia i waho,

Tuia! Tuia! Tuia —

All of a sudden he is through the tunnel and suspended above the blackness, watching the primordial fireball and the way its wave of light is moving so fast, creating a new cosmos. He becomes frightened and closes his eyes.

—

And he is falling.

When he opens his eyes he sees a wild landscape in the country of his birth, New Zealand. It is so familiar to him that he laughs with relief. A mist descends and he is lost in it.

This has happened before, he thinks. The mist opens and he sees three elderly women from the village walking in front of him. He runs after them. One of them turns and asks, 'Went the day well, sir?' The second says, 'Not you again.' And the third says, 'You're always losing directions. Well, you're almost at your destination, lad. There it is.' She points to a faraway farmhouse on the other side of the valley. 'You had better make haste,' the old women say. 'Night is coming and, with it, a fierce storm.'

He walks to the farmhouse. A light is coming from the window and, framed within the light, someone is watching him. As he approaches, the door opens. Mrs Cortland is there.

'Thank goodness you were able to make it home before dark,' she says. 'Come in, come in.'

He enters the house and sees Monsignor Frère, Dr Foley, Miss O'Hara and Professor Van Straaten are having a cup of tea and chatting.

'Let the Captain have a place by the fire,' Mrs Cortland scolds. 'He'll catch his death. There's room for one more.'

The five people in the room smile at Captain Craig as if they have known him all their lives. Monsignor Frère comes to join him. 'Don't be afraid,' he says. 'There are some questions that science cannot answer. They may know what, how and when, but while faith and reason have coexisted in scientists as notable as Isaac Newton and Albert Einstein, only theologists know why.'

The Captain shifts on his feet nervously. Mrs Cortland brings him a cup of hot tea. 'This will bring you back to life,' she says.

A few moments later, Professor Van Straaten comes to talk to him. 'I wouldn't believe everything I see,' he says. 'At the end of the universe things still go bump in the night and every grave, opening wide, lets forth its sprites and demons. But Fate is always kind. She gives to those who love their secret longing.'

'Do I know you?' he asks the Professor. 'Do I know any of you?'

'Of course you do!' Professor Van Straaten laughs. But he is uncertain, and his laughter fades away into bewilderment. 'Because if you don't, then who are we?'

Monsignor Frère winks at him. 'Interesting, isn't it?'

Mrs Cortland claps her hands for attention. 'It's time to go,' she says. 'Dr Foley and Miss O'Hara, are you ready? The next great adventure is about to begin. As for the Captain, he has his own journey. Goodbye, my dear.'

—

And he is falling.

Captain Craig finds himself in a small white room. He is alone. He is naked. How did he get here? Who is he? Why is he here? He begins to scream and pound on the walls. He falls to the floor in a foetal position, howling, hugging himself and weeping.

Time is limitless. How long has he been here? He does not know. He sleeps, and time continues to go by. Suddenly he hears a voice: *Open your eyes*. Perhaps it is his own voice; he doesn't know.

When he does wake up, he sees that there is a wardrobe. In the wardrobe is a white suit. His heart is beating loudly. He dresses in the suit.

A door appears in the room. Above the door is a clock. The time is just before midnight.

He finishes dressing. He sees a mirror on the wall. He inspects his appearance. Combs his hair. Smooths out his trousers.

Takes a deep breath. Walks to the door.

Turns the doorknob.

Opens the door.

medicine woman

'Medicine Woman' comes from 1990 when I briefly flirted with writing for television. In that year I resigned from a sixteen-year career as a diplomat. On my return I was asked by Ripeka Evans to put together script proposals for a government-sponsored Maori television production company. That venture never got off the ground and subsequent political rethinking coalesced instead around the establishment of a separate Maori television channel. The story of the eventual setting up of the channel is surrounded by scandal and controversy, but in 2007 it has stabilised and it continues to increase its viewing public and ratings.

My notes of the period tell me that I worked up a number of pilot proposals including *Hana's Daughters* and *Red Hot Mamas* (two situation comedies, the first about three Maori sisters in Auckland and the second set in a bar on K Road, Auckland), *God's Own Country* (a soap opera involving Maori characters, set on a high-country sheep station), *The Maori Princess* (a children's historical drama in three one-hour episodes, about a young Maori girl who goes to England to take up her titled father's estate), and *Winnie* and *The Matua* (a two-part adult mini-series).

Of the proposals, Ripeka was most interested in *Red Hot Mamas*, which I began to script with Ginette McDonald and Mika, and *Winnie* which, if it had proceeded, would have inaugurated the Maori production company. Sixteen years later, I have drawn on my notes for the first hour-long script of *Winnie* and redesigned it as a short story, 'Medicine Woman'. The character of Paraiti is based on a travelling Maori doctor my parents took me to when Pakeha doctors could not solve my chronic breathing problems; she hooked her finger into my throat and pulled out threads of phlegm. If I was to develop 'Medicine Woman' as a mini-series today, the second part would follow the story of Waiputa, the whangai daughter of Paraiti, who joins the Pakeha medical profession. Estranged from Paraiti, Waiputa goes in search of Rebecca Vickers, who lies to Waiputa, telling her she was stolen by Paraiti. There is a trial scene, but eventually Waiputa is reconciled with Paraiti and decides to work as a rural Maori doctor. In a tender final scene, she massages Paraiti in the same way the old woman had massaged her father, Te Teira, in his old age.

The following texts were consulted in the writing of the story: Judith Binney, *Redemption Songs* (Auckland University Press, 1995); Murdoch

Riley and Brian Enting's indispensable *Maori Healing and Herbal Medicines* (Viking Sevenseas, 1994); and Roger Neich, *Painted Histories* (AUP, 1993). Any errors of fact should not be attributed to the above-named texts. I am not an expert on the Ringatu or, particularly, on traditional Maori healing and medicine, and I apologise for any inaccuracies.

meeting elizabeth costello

When friend and editor Fiona Kidman emailed me in 2004 to ask if I would submit a short story to *The Best New Zealand Fiction* (2005), I immediately said yes. Fiona and I go a long way back, to the 1960s when we were at the very beginning of our literary careers, and we still seem to publish books at almost the same time. To this day, we celebrate each other's achievements by sending the same message, 'Still hitched to the same star'.

The story I submitted to Fiona was 'Meeting Elizabeth Costello'. I had read the novel, *Elizabeth Costello*, by J M Coetzee, which introduces a rather remarkable character, an Australian novelist by the name of Elizabeth Costello who is given to making astonishing speeches on all kinds of subjects.

Most of the novel is given over to these speeches verbatim. In one section, Ms Costello is invited to lecture on a cruise ship leaving Christchurch and sailing to the Ross Ice Shelf; her speech is entitled 'The Future of the Novel'. An African writer, Emmanuel Egedu, is also on board; his speech is on 'The Novel in Africa'. I decided to interpolate into the action a third writer, a certain Wicked Ihimaera, to give a speech on 'The Indigenous Novel in Antarctica'.

'Meeting Elizabeth Costello' stands on its own, but I hope you will read Coetzee's novel — it's one of those books you can really have a good argument with and, on my part, I am indebted to Coetzee for providing me with the opportunity to put down my thoughts on the issues involving indigenous writing, and on being a Maori writer.

Auckland, 2007

acknowledgements

COVER ILLUSTRATION
The background cover illustration is reproduced by kind permission of
Hone Te Ihi o Te Rangi Ngata (Ngati Porou, Ngati Ranginui, Ngaiterangi).
Hone has been drawing, painting, carving and exhibiting all his life, and
has won awards for his illustrations. His first exhibition was in 1984, aged
11, at Nga Puna Waihanga's first gathering in Gisborne. Hone graduated
from Waiariki Polytechnic with a diploma in craft design Maori. He has
worked at the Rotorua Bathhouse, as collections curator for Tauranga
Museum, and as anthropology intern at Field Museum in Chicago, US.
Also known as the hiphop master DJ Poroufessor, Hone now lives in
Auckland, inspiring rangatahi to develop their art and music skills, and
illustrating his own range of children's books.

MUSIC CREDITS
'Bad Moon Rising': Words and music by John Fogerty
© Jondora-Music
For Australia and New Zealand:
Alfred Publishing (Australia) Pty Ltd (ABN 15 003 954 247)
PO Box 2355 Taren Point, NSW 2229
International copyright secured. All rights reserved. Unauthorised
reproduction is illegal.

'Copacabana' by Barry Manilow. Reprinted by kind permission of BMG Music Publishing Australia.

'Good Vibrations': B. Wilson/M/ Love, © 1966. Printed with permission
of J. Albert & Son Pty Ltd.

'Moon River', music by Henry Mancini, lyrics by Johnny Mercer.
Reprinted by kind permission of BMG Music Publishing Australia.

'Up Up and Away', music and lyrics by Jimmy Webb. © 1967 Jonathan Three Music Company,
USA./Sony/ATV./Music Publishing (UK) Ltd (46.25%)./EMI Music Publishing Australia Pty Ltd.
International copyrights secured. All rights reserved. Used by permission.

'Vaya con Dios': Larry Russell, Inez James and Buddy Pepper, 1953. Universal Music Publishing/
Warner Chappell.

'When You Wish Upon a Star', music by Leigh Harline, lyrics by Ned
Washington. Reprinted by kind permission of EMI Music Publishing Australia Pty Ltd.

'Yellow Submarine' The Beatles, Paul McCartney/John Lennon, © 1966 Northern Songs. Used by
permission of Music Sales Ltd./Sony/ATV./EMI Music Publishing Australia Pty Ltd. International
Copyright secured. All rights reserved.